The First Question

By James Arendorf

Inspired by true events and real people

We succeed, when we have lost everything.

We succeed, when we have no choice.

Contents

Chapter 1

The Will

Sunday, June 15ᵗʰ, 1890.

The city of Georgetown, in the continent of the United States of America, was covered by the soft heat of the summer month. It was a beautiful and peaceful afternoon. The enormous doors of the Long Memorial Lancaster Cathedral were grandly opened. Sloan Wilfrid stopped outside for a minute, admiring the splendor of the impressive Cathedral.

In his early thirties, Sloan Wilfrid was a tall svelte man. His brown hair was in perfectly ordered waves. His small round glasses reflected his shinny gray eyes. His dark suit with a white shirt was buttoned up to the neck by a black tie, and it made him look elegant.

A peaceful silence reigned inside the Long Memorial Lancaster Cathedral. The place was empty. All the wood benches were empty, the corridors were empty, and the balconies were empty. There was nobody inside. At the other end of the Cathedral, a closed coffin was placed. A few bouquets of white roses with a delicate perfume surrounded the coffin.

Sloan Wilfrid walked toward the Chapel, and he placed a small bouquet of white flowers, that he had brought with him. He searched on his right and left, for a human presence, but no one appeared. He then turned around to sit in the front row, right in front of the coffin.

Although he had known the deceased man only recently, Sloan Wilfrid was sad for this loss. He turned his head twice to seek for any other visitor, but nobody came to this funeral. Sloan Wilfrid was alone. His heart was heavy, not only for the death of this man, but also because of the loneliness of the deceased in his last hours. Sloan Wilfrid expected to meet many people, but he was the only one to pay a last tribute to the man.

This place of prayer and appeal imposed serenity and an absolute quiet. Sloan Wilfrid admired the architecture of the magnificent Long Memorial Lancaster Cathedral; the enormous windows looked like paintings of colored glass, the sky light lit up the place with a soft and peaceful glow, the walls were decorated with graceful sculptures.

A few minutes later, the presence of an old man interrupted Sloan Wilfrid in his thoughts. The man walked slowly toward the coffin, and he placed one white rose on top of it. The old man looked poor; a faded jacket, dusty shoes, stitched pants in several places. Sloan Wilfrid wondered who could this old man be; he had never seen him before. The man turned around toward Sloan Wilfrid, and he greeted him with a sympathetic smile:

- Good evening.

Sloan Wilfrid returned the courtesy and he greeted him back. The old man sat on a bench, a few steps away from Sloan Wilfrid, who couldn't stop staring, curious about the identity of the unknown old man.

A moment later, a woman and a child stepped inside the Cathedral. The woman was wearing a long dress in a pale green, an old shawl over her shoulders and a white cover on her head. The child was about 10 years old, he firmly held the woman's hand, he wore a white old shirt, and short pants. Undoubtedly, the woman and the boy were poor people too. Something unusual caught the attention of Sloan Wilfrid; the two new visitors were both holding one white rose in their hands. They walked timidly toward the coffin; they placed the roses on it, they turned around and took a seat one rank behind the old poor man. Sloan Wilfrid kept watching these three people, wondering:

- But ... who are they? ... How did they know the deceased man? ... Is it possible that these people could be in the wrong funeral? ... I don't understand how the deceased man could have known them ...

At one moment, Sloan Wilfrid felt a strange presence behind him. He turned his head toward the entrance of the Cathedral, to discover a line of dozen individuals, walking one after another, holding one white rose in their hands, moving toward the coffin. All the individuals were doing exactly the same move; with their heads down, they bowed before the coffin, they gently placed the white rose on top of it, and they returned to sit on the wood benches, in front of the Chapel. Ordered movements, in an absolute calm. The benches of the Long Memorial Lancaster Cathedral were filled with hundreds of individuals in only a few minutes. Old men, women, children, young and mature individuals, they all looked humble and poor. Quickly, the coffin of the deceased man was covered by a cloud of magnificent white roses.

Sloan Wilfrid was confused and amazed at what was happening in front of him. He didn't understand neither the presence nor the relationship that all these modest individuals could have had with the deceased man. After few moments, Sloan Wilfrid decided to leave the place. He got up and walked toward the exit, observing all these unknown visitors, seeking in vain to recognize even only one of them.

Near the Cathedral's door, the priest was standing; he welcomed the visitors with a generous smile. In his sixties, the priest was wearing a long black outfit, and a long red scarf around the waist. Sloan Wilfrid saluted the priest, in a respectful way:

- It's a sad day, Reverend.

The priest replied in a compassionate voice:

- Indeed, my son. May God bless you for coming today.
- He was a great man. It's the least we can do for him. Sighed Sloan Wilfrid.
- I believe he is now in good hands, my son. The priest said with a confident voice.

Sloan Wilfrid greeted the Priest and he turned around to leave the Cathedral. He barely took two steps outside; when Sloan Wilfrid discovered an amazing scene. A crowd of visitors in a long line, outside the Cathedral. There were at least thousand individuals, all walking slowly one after another in a quiet order, and they all carried a white flower each. The Priest noticed Sloan Wilfrid's confusion, he came close to him:

- Is something in your mind, my son?

Sloan Wilfrid asked with a hesitant voice:

- Reverend...who are all these visitors? I don't recognize any friend or family of the deceased.

The Priest observed the long line of individuals who walked slowly toward the coffin, and he replied in a reassured tone:

- God didn't want this man to leave our world, all alone. They came to pay a last tribute to the deceased.

This answer didn't satisfy the curiosity of Sloan Wilfrid, he insisted in a confused voice:

- Yes, I understand ... but these men and women ... who are they? ... I have never met them before ...

The Long Memorial Lancaster Cathedral gladly received on its benches, hundreds of men and women. And the immense Cathedral was ready to welcome with open arms the next thousand visitors to come. A respectful silence was imposed in this place. A wonderful smell of freshness and human kindness hovered in the air. The Priest looked at Sloan Wilfrid, and he smiled:

- These men and women ... They are the People!

Monday, June 16th, 1890.

The sun illuminated, with its last day lights, the Grand Mansion located on the West side of Georgetown City. The Mansion was enormous, built in gray bricks, with black roofs, and hundreds of rectangular windows. In the inside, the lobby of the Grand Mansion was vast. Brown wood furniture was shining. At the entrance of the house, you would immediately notice beautiful bouquets of white flowers, arranged in all corners, in large porcelain vases. A pleasant smell swung in the air, fresh jasmine. An imposing staircase stood right in the front of the hall, taking you left and right of the upper floors. The large and transparent windows welcomed the sun light, and the magnificent chandelier in the center of the hall, shined with a thousand golden lights.

But the thing that would hold the most your attention was the floor. It was made of thousand small arabesques mosaics, of all colors and geometric shapes. The floor was a large beautiful Masterpiece.

It was the first time ever in her life that the little 12 years old girl accompanying her father, entered inside such a beautiful place. A majestic Mansion.

On the right of the hall, there was a large living room, its door was wide open, and around 20 people could be seen inside. Women were in long black silk dresses and embroidered satin, luxurious jewelry embellished their necks and their hands. Men wore black and white suits. Everyone was whispering, talking and laughing. Some were sitting on chairs; others were standing next to the fireplace or near the large windows.

While she was observing the scene, the little girl wondered if this gathering was a party, and if she and her father were in the wrong place.

The little girl was wearing blue worn overall, a white boy yellowed shirt with sleeves lifted up, small old shoes and a big black cap covering her hair. Her father was wearing a large leather timeworn jacket, wrinkled pants, big shoes printed with mud, and an old hat. The father and daughter felt like outsiders, in this luxurious place.

As soon as the little girl and her father appeared in the entrance of the living room, many eyes turned on their way, scrutinizing them from head to toe with a scornful stare. A man at the entrance blocked their way. The man was short and overweight; he was bald and had a sharp nose. He was wearing the same outfit as the other men inside the living room; a black and white suit, a black tie, all spotlessly clean, smooth and elegant. The little girl's father smiled nervously and he greeted him with a lower tone:

- Hello Si...

The short and fat man interrupted him, in an arrogant voice:

- The entry of domestic workers is through the other door.

The father tried to say a word:

- It's because we were asked to com...

But the short and fat man at the entrance of the living room, seemed to lose patience, he interrupted the father for the second time, he stared at him and his daughter with disgusted eyes:

- Make a u-turn and enter through the door of the left corri...

Except that this time, before the father could explain their presence in this place, the short arrogant man was interrupted by a calm and confident voice behind the father and his daughter:

- Thank you for your guidance, Mr. Kinsley. But Mademoiselle and her father will attend the reading of The Will.

The little girl turned around to find a man she had already met before, a few months ago. The man had brilliant gray eyes, behind small round eyeglasses. A natural smile was printed on his lips. He wore a refined suit, identical to all the men inside the living room. Mr. Kinsley answered, curious:

- And why so?

Mr. Sloan Wilfrid replied spontaneously:

- Their names appear on the list of people called for today.

Mr. Kinsley let out a mean laugh:

- But ... why? It's useless for this kind of people to attend such an important meeting!

Mr. Wilfrid surpassed the father and his daughter, and he walked a few steps toward Mr. Kinsley, until being right in front of him. And with a calm but authoritative voice, Mr. Wilfrid answered, without losing his natural smile:

- Orders from the Late Mr. Governor, himself.

In an instant, Mr. Kinsley's mean laugh turned into an offended face expression. In an obligatory move, Mr. Kinsley was forced to immediately get out of the way and let pass Mr. Sloan Wilfrid, who indicated to the father and his daughter to follow him inside the living room.

The little girl was amazed by the splendor of inside the place; she walked with astonished eyes and silent exclamations. The walls were in finely drawn wallpaper. Several portraits of landscapes were hung in golden frames. Twenty chairs and comfortable divans were placed in a parallel order. The fresh and captivating smell of jasmine flowers covered everything it touched. And thanks to the last lights of the day, the large windows of the living room unveiled the splendid greenery of the grand Mansion's garden.

The little girl and her father chose to stand at the far end corner of the living room, away from the intimidating distinguished people. Mr. Sloan Wilfrid joined several men at the other side of the living room.

Moments later, a man made quite an entrance in the place. He walked slowly, leaning with a sovereign move on his shiny wooden cane. He was tall and very big. He was in his mid-fifties, a white skin, and his light brown hair with white highlights made him look almost bald, he wore a long cape embroidered with silver touch, on top of his luxurious black and white suit.

As soon as this man took his first steps in the living room, many people surrounded him. Some shacked his hands, others presented their condolences:

- We are sincerely saddened by your loss ...
- Our condolences Mr. Ferdinand Edelmen ...
- Your uncle was a great man ... May he rest in peace ...
- This is an unfortunate event Mr. Ferdinand Edelmen ...

The man replied in a calm voice:

- Thank you ... thank you ...

Other people bowed in a formal way:

- We came especially today, to present our esteem ...
- Accept our respects, Mr. Ferdinand Edelmen...
- We are at your service, Mr. Ferdinand Edelmen...

The man answered:

- I have no doubt about that ... thank you ... thank you ...

And some people even congratulated him:

- Our congratulations for this succession ...
- You deserve this responsibility ... you will be more than qualified ...
- Our city will now benefit from your wisdom, Mr. Ferdinand Edelmen ...

Mr. Ferdinand Edelmen greeted all the people on his way, with a proud and victorious smile. He settled on a large divan next to a woman, and was instantly surrounded by dozen men. He must be someone very important, the little girl thought.

Conversations and laughs resumed. Servers walked between people to serve drinks and pastries on silver platters. The little girl and her father remained immobile, watching this luxurious event.

After a short time, a second man entered the living room. His cold and haughty eyes scanned the place, in an instant. He was tall and very thin, with marble skin. He wasn't smiling, and had such an arrogant look, that his chin was up abnormally. He had white hair drawn on both sides of his forehead. He had a cold and unsociable appearance.

The man walked toward Mr. Edelmen, and he greeted him with a serious tone:

- Please accept my sincere condolences, Mr. Ferdinand Edelmen.

Mr. Edelmen replied:

- Thank you, my dear Ernest Laszlo. It is an unfortunate event for us all.

His last sentence didn't match his face expression. Mr. Ferdinand Edelmen didn't seem sad or unhappy to receive condolences. In fact, he struggled to hide his happiness and to hold back his smile. Mr. Ferdinand Edelmen bent and he whispered to the man in front of him:

- Finally! It was about time, Ernest!! I was starting to lose hope...

Mr. Ernest Laszlo answered in a discreet voice:

- I applaud your patience, Mr. Ferdinand Edelmen. Today's meeting is only a formality. I expect you in my office tomorrow morning, to sign the last papers, in order to legalize them.

Mr. Ferdinand Edelmen patted him on the shoulder, muttering:

- You have done a good job, my dear Ernest Laszlo! A very good job!!

The man of marble skin and cold appearance almost smiled. He answered, bowing his head respectfully:

- It is only but your right, Mr. Ferdinand Edelmen.

Mr. Ernest Laszlo walked toward the center of the room, he stood behind the only office that was in the living room, and he put down a large folder that he was holding firmly in his hands. Then, he announced in a strong voice:

- Ladies and gentlemen, May I have your attention!

Instantly, everyone went quiet and sat down on the many chairs and divans available, all eyes were focused toward the man behind the big desk. The little girl and her father also sat on chairs at the end corner of the living room. The man continued with a serious and formal voice:

- Ladies and gentlemen, good evening. I am Ernest Laszlo, Main lawyer and in charge of the Affairs of Late Mr. Governor. I thank you all, for being here today and for answering the invitation.
  It is regrettable to all of us on this day, to be attending and reading the Will of a man who forever will leave his mark in the history of our State, if not our entire country. The Late Governor of the State of Washington, Mr. Iskander Balthazar was an exceptional man whose qualities are confirmed by all the people he has worked with and have known him. His wisdom and strength have marked and touched all of us. At this moment, May he rest in peace.

The living room plunged in a minute of silence. Mr. Ernest Laszlo went on with his speech, but this time, with a slightly more relaxed voice:

- Now, ladies and gentlemen, we will proceed reading the Will of Late Mr. Iskander Balthazar.

He took out of his folder a large envelope sealed with a red stamp; he opened it with a paper knife, and took a few papers out. He read aloud:

"I, Iskander Balthazar, in my complete physical and mental health, and of my own independent will, I hand down all the rights of my BalthEnterprise company, all my real-estates, as well as all my assets in the Bank, to one and only single Heir. This cannot be opposed by judicial means or by use of any other instance."

The Lawyer, Mr. Ernest Laszlo threw a complicit glance at Mr. Ferdinand Edelmen, who seemed very calm, displaying his victorious smile. Mr. Ernest Laszlo continued:

"I, Iskander Balthazar, have decided that My BalthEnterprise Company will be led by the current Board of Directors, under the tutelage of the lawyer that I have chosen, and who will be the legal guardian and representative of all my properties and assets, until the final handover.

The Heir I designate, will be represented, protected, advised and supported by the lawyer that I chose, as it is the duty giving to him by the laws of the United States of America."

A few whispers in the living room were heard. The Lawyer, Mr. Ernest Laszlo read over a sentence for a second time, doubting that he misunderstood its meaning:

"... The lawyer I have chosen, and who will be the legal guardian and representative of all my properties and assets ... until the final handover ..."

Nothing disturbed the victorious smile of Mr. Ferdinand Edelmen. He drank his tea, paying absolutely no attention to the reading of the Will. The Lawyer, Mr. Ernest Laszlo continued to read:

"The Heir I designate will be represented, protected, advised and supported by the lawyer that I chose, as it is the duty giving to him by the laws of the United States of America.

I therefore appointed as lawyer and my business manager Mr. ..."

The Lawyer, Mr. Ernest Laszlo stopped reading and he froze. He looked intensely at the paper in his hands. For the first time since his presence in the living room of the Grand Mansion; Mr. Ernest Laszlo lost his arrogant look and he appeared disoriented. He didn't expect to see a familiar name in this Will. He continued in a confused voice, hardly hiding his surprise:

"I therefore appointed as lawyer and my business manager Mr. . Mr. Lyor Kaplan Laszlo."

The little girl, sitting at the end corner of the living room, recognized this name. She remembered meeting Mr. Lyor Laszlo, a few weeks before. She leaned from her seat to catch a better glance at him. The young man was sitting in the front rows between several gentlemen. He appeared pale and shocked. He was stunned to hear his name in this Will, and he was very surprised to know that he was ... The Guardian of the entire fortune of Late Mr. Governor Iskander Balthazar!

Mr. Lyor Laszlo was not the only one surprised. Most of the present people in the living room could not hold their exclamations and confused whispers. No one understood why the name of the young Lyor Laszlo, the son of Mr. Ernest Laszlo, was pronounced.

Mr. Ferdinand Edelmen put down his tea cup and he straightened up on his chair. The appointment of the young Lyor Laszlo attracted the attention of Mr. Ferdinand Edelmen and it erased his smile. The woman sitting next to him, asked in a confused voice:

- But ... Why is there a legal guardian? Why was he appointed for? I don't understand why we need one ... What does that mean?

And just like everyone in this living room, Lyor's father, Mr. Ernest Laszlo couldn't explain or think of a proper answer to this question. He continued reading the document in a tone much less comfortable than before:

"The Heir I designate shall dispose of all the content of the coffret at the Bank, under the number: 7047-73. My Heir will be the one and only owner of the content of that coffret.

My condition to the inheritance is: only after the success of all challenges, that my Heir will own immediately and unquestionably ... my entire fortune."

A few voices exclaimed, all confused and puzzled:

- What challenges? What is this?
- What is he talking about?
- Get it over with! The only Heir is well known. It's a waste of time!
- But it's not normal ... there should be no conditions!
- Is this a joke?

Mr. Ernest Laszlo interrupted the voices that began to rise slowly in the living room:

- Ladies and gentlemen!! Ladies and gentlemen!! I ask for your silence so that I can complete the reading of Mr. Iskander Balthazar's Will!

"All the challenges will be held in public sessions on the appropriate date.

If and only if the Heir I appointed, fails the challenges, I give power of attorney to Mr. Lyor Kaplan Laszlo to divide my entire fortune, according to the law, on all living and active members of my family; meaning my nephew, my niece and their descendants ..."

Instantly, a massive wave of protests arose in the living room of the Grand Mansion:

- That's not possible!! That's ridiculous!!
- But my father is the only Heir to his uncle and no one else!!
- It's absurd!! What is this masquerade of challenges???
- Is it really my uncle's Will?? Or has he been disabled when writing it??
- It is not credible at all!!
- It's a fraud!!! It's not right!! Your Law firm will be held responsible for this!

The little girl and her father stared at this scene, surprised by what was happening. The little girl whispered:

- What is it father? What's going on?

Her father replied:

- I have no clue. I don't even know why we have been called up here.

The nephew of the deceased, Mr. Ferdinand Edelmen had lost his proud and arrogant smile with which he greeted people at his arrival earlier. He seemed confused, struggling to understand and to assimilate what was actually happening in front of him.

The lawyer, Mr. Ernest Laszlo seemed bewildered by the turn of things. It was not what he had expected to read in this Will. He firmly held the paper in his hands, rereading the text for the 4th time in silence, without being distracted by the voices around him. After a brief moment, Mr. Ernest Laszlo was forced to raise his voice to calm everyone in the living room:

- Ladies and gentlemen!! Silence please!!

He continued out loud, clearly upset:

"The Heir I appoint to succeed me, is ..."

Mr. Ernest Laszlo froze for a moment, hesitant. You could clearly notice the sweat on his forehead. At this moment, he even doubted his ability to read correctly. After an eternal and tense moment of silence, Mr. Ernest Laszlo announced with a trembling voice:

"The Heir I appoint to succeed me, is ... Mademoiselle Dalya Kartal Bouvard".

Whispers and confusion rise up gradually in the living room:

- But who is it? Who is she?
- We have never heard of this person before ... is it a distant family?
- Have we ever met her?

Mr. Sloan Wilfrid could not restrain his surprised smile, while hearing this name. Mr. Ernest Laszlo was shocked; he read the Will in his hands for the 10th time. The nephew of the deceased, Mr. Ferdinand Edelmen became all red, he lost his voice and his ability to move. The nephew seemed to have trouble breathing normally.

And although he tried to hide his surprise as much as he could, the young Lyor Laszlo sitting in the front rows, couldn't help but turn around and look toward the end of the living room with a confused stare. He was the only one to turn around to observe ... The Future Heiress of the Governor Iskander Balthazar's fortune!

Little by little, all the eyes followed the stares of the young Lyor Laszlo. All the heads turned around, all the bodies turned around, all the exclamations and surprises turned around ... toward the end corner of the living room.

Everyone stared at a 12 years old little girl, sitting on a chair, at the end corner of the living room.

Everyone stared at ... Dalya Kartal Bouvard.

Chapter 2

A clam chowder soup

Saturday, March 01st, 1890. 3 months and 2 weeks before.

The cold winter was still ruling at every corner of Georgetown city. The weather was chilly, few rays of sun hardly made it out of the gray clouds, the trees were unfilled of any color; the ground was hardened by the snow and by the cold winter.

At 01:00 PM. The Toscana restaurant was working in full action. In the kitchen, the Chef was giving orders incessantly to his aides. All the ovens were turned on. Dishes disappeared rapidly from the counter. The servers walked quickly, judiciously avoiding the spikes of tables and stepping on their colleagues.

The Toscana restaurant was the most refined and popular place to be, in all Georgetown city. The best Italian specialties were served. The interior decoration and the furniture was the most luxurious. Beautiful chandeliers adorned the ceiling and illuminated the entire place. The tables were decorated with white tablecloths, finely ironed and clean. The silverware was as shiny as the refined plates. The most delicious dishes were presented by servers impeccably dressed and agile. Large comfy chairs were placed in perfect symmetry, allowing each guest discretion and an enjoyable time.

At 01:30 PM, a luxurious black car stopped in front of the restaurant. The 2 doormen who were whispering while waiting for new customers, they straightened up in a second, they opened the door of the arriving car and they draw up a red carpet in front of the door.

A man slowly made his way out of the car. He leaned on his cane and walked toward the restaurant. His walk was slow but firm. He was a tall man, strong and vigorous, despite his advanced age.

Immediately, a strange animal came out of the luxurious black car. The animal was the size of a tiger; his fur was tattooed of black spots on a light shining gray color, it had piercing sapphire blue eyes, a long tail floating gracefully in the air. The animal was an intimidating beauty. It followed the footsteps of the great man toward the inside of the restaurant.

The headwaiter interrupted his conversation with a woman and he hurried toward the new client. He bent to greet the new visitor:

- Welcome Mr. Governor. Your table is ready.

When crossing the Toscana restaurant, servers stopped, all the customer's conversations stopped, all the movements and noises stopped at once. All eyes were motionless and focused on the great man and the animal following him.

When he arrived at his usual table, the great man took off his gray coat, gloves and hat. A server rushed to take them. Without his hat, you could notice the great man's white hair. A little smooth white beard covered his chin. His light pink skin revealed wrinkles on his face and his neck. He was wearing a gray suit perfectly custom-made. At nearly 70 years old, the great man looked imposing.

The animal appeared to be acquainted to the Toscana restaurant. While his Master was settling, the animal sneaked between the multiple chairs, laid down on the edge of a large window, in front of the great mans' table. Movements and voices in the restaurant revived slowly, but lower than before the entrance of the prestigious customer.

The headwaiter asked in a respectful voice:

- What does the Governor wishes to order today?

Mr. Balthazar replied in a calm and melancholic voice:

- The same thing I ordered every Saturday, for the past 40 years.

The headwaiter withdrew:

- As you wish, Mr. Governor.

Before leaving, Mr. Balthazar remembered something:

- Someone called … Mr. Ernest Laszlo will join me, before lunch today. Let him in.
- Understood, Mr. Governor.

Mr. Balthazar's lunch table was placed in front of the enormous transparent windows of the Toscana restaurant. He observed what was going on outside for few minutes, while his animal was taking a nap in front of him. A short moment later, the headwaiter interrupted the great man is his thoughts, to announce the arrival of his host. Mr. Ernest Laszlo greeted Mr. Balthazar in a formal move, waving his hat in a respectful way:

- Mr. Governor!
- Mr. Ernest Laszlo. I thank you for coming so rapidly. Replied Mr. Balthazar, welcoming him with a head sign.
- The request of the Washington State Governor is a priority for my office! Said Mr. Ernest in a proud voice, before he continued:
- May I present to you Master Sloan Wilfrid, my assistant and right hand lawyer. And this is Lyor Laszlo.

Two men behind Mr. Ernest Laszlo raised their hats and they greeted Mr. Balthazar. A man with little round eyeglasses, and a younger man. Mr. Balthazar waved at them to sit and join him. The 3 men handed their hats and coats to the waiters and they all sat down. Mr. Ernest noticed the presence of the animal lying down on the edge of the window in front of their table. And despite his joyful smile, it was clear that Mr. Ernest wasn't fond of this animal:

- I see that your ... friend is still in a good shape.

Mr. Balthazar replied politely:

- Séraphine is much more than a friend.

The animal stood up gently, joined her Master and sat on the floor leaning on her Master's chair. Straightway, Mr. Balthazar addressed the 3 men:

- I asked for your presence today ... because you are considered the best Law firm of all Washington State. Understand, Gentlemen, that I request total and complete discretion of this meeting. I wish to deal with this matter peacefully and without creating any controversy.
- Your wishes are commands, Mr. Governor! Replied Mr. Ernest in a serious and firm tone. And I can assure you, that our profession is bounded by confidentiality rules. Your request will be handled discreetly.
- May I know how would you like to proceed? Asked Mr. Balthazar in a serene tone.

Mr. Ernest Laszlo looked at his assistant, Mr. Wilfrid, who straightened up and answered Mr. Balthazar in a very respectful voice:

- The first step will be to determine your entire fortune and organize all the titles and paper properties. This includes all real-estates, documents of the company, Bank accounts, lands and capitals. Then, on the second step, we will estimate the value of all your properties on the current market. Our goal will be to define your entire fortune on paper...

Mr. Ernest Laszlo turned to Mr. Balthazar, with assurance:

- And of course, the last step will be to prescribe your nephew, Mr. Ferdinand Edelmen as legitimate Heir of your fortune. He has all the qualities required to succeed you in the manag...

Mr. Balthazar spontaneously interrupted him:

- I understand that my niece has fairly the right to inherit too?

Mr. Ernest didn't lose his confidence and he replied with a wild smile:

- Yes, definitely ... but from my experience in these matters, a woman would be unable to manage this entire fortune by herself. And your niece, Mrs. Honoré Edelmen does not have the qualifications to lead BalthEnterprise Company. It would be a far too difficult and stressful task for her. This is why Mr. Ferdinand Edelmen, your nephew, he would be perfect for this tas...

Mr. Balthazar declared with a natural voice tone:

- We'll see about that later ...

The Lawyer, Mr. Ernest Laszlo completely ignored the Governor's answer. He insisted with his usual confident air:

- Anyway, the Heirs of your fortune are very clear. You have one nephew and one niece. And in my opinion, the best and only person able to manage the entire heritage, is your nephew, Ferdinand Edelmen. He is willing to take over and continue your work all ov...

This time, the Governor interrupted Mr. Ernest Laszlo with a voice slightly more acute than before:

- Mr. Ernest Laszlo. I thank you for your unrequested point of view on that matter. But I call upon your services only to prepare the documents required for the succession. As I know, the choice of my Heir belongs only to me.

The animal sitting down, near the chair of her Master, let out a growl and stared at Mr. Ernest Laszlo with a threatening look. One would have thought that the animal felt her Master's irritation. Mr. Balthazar caressed the animal's head, whispering in a soft voice:

- Calm down, sweetheart ... calm down.

Mr. Ernest Laszlo hid as best as he could, his uncomfortable state; he realized that he committed a slip-up, according to the cold attitude that Mr. Balthazar displayed. He replied in a tone much less haughty than since his arrival:

- But of course, Mr. Governor ... that's obvious ... you have every right to choose your successor ...

Mr. Balthazar asked directly Mr. Wilfrid:

- How much time will require the preparation of this case?
- It's a work of about twenty days, Mr. Governor. We will try to finish it as soon as possible. We will need to meet with the accountant of your company, in order to collect informations about the shares and capitals of ...

Mr. Balthazar listened carefully to all Mr. Wilfrid's explanations. He inclined his head as a confirmation, from time to time. Mr. Ernest Laszlo placed a few words, while keeping his distance from offending the Governor for the second time. Only the young Lyor Laszlo remained silent in front of the 3 men who were talking. Mr. Balthazar asked in a calm voice:

- When can you start?

Mr. Ernest Laszlo was quick to answer:

- Tomorrow morning, Mr. Governor. Master Wilfrid will be in charge of collecting the titles of all the properties, lands and real-estates. He will also arrange the transfer of your stock papers. Lyor Laszlo will be in charge of preparing the documents for the heritage and the transfer of properties.

Mr. Balthazar observed the young man sitting in front of him, who has been silent since the beginning of this meeting. The young Lyor Laszlo didn't look like his father, Mr. Ernest. The young man was about 21 years old. He was of medium height, strong and well built. He had inherited dark brown wavy hair, a tanned skin, honey color eyes, and a large well designed nose. With his ancient features, Lyor Laszlo looked like a Greek statue. He was wearing a very elegant dark blue suit.

After a brief moment, Mr. Balthazar asked, all curious:

- Lyor Laszlo ... is he your son?
- Yes ... and he wants to specialize in business law, said Mr. Ernest in an amused laugh, before continuing:
- But, in my opinion, he doesn't have enough of what it takes to be a lawyer. It's way too big for him. I advised him to be an accountant or a business man ...

Mr. Balthazar observed the young man for a while, before Mr. Ernest Laszlo interrupted him:

- If you will excuse us, Mr. Governor. We should withdraw and let you enjoy your lunch. If there is anything I can do ... I am at your service.
- Thank you, Mr. Ernest Laszlo. But I do not wish to bother you unnecessarily. I would like to be informed regularly of the progress of this case.
- Of course, Mr. Governor. I can assure you that I will personally keep an eye on this case. And I place Master Wilfrid and Lyor Laszlo at your service. On their next visit, they will keep you up-to-date.

When Mr. Ernest Laszlo stood up, his two aides followed him. They greeted Mr. Iskander Balthazar, and they left the Toscana restaurant. The headwaiter immediately served lunch to the Governor, left alone in his usual table, with his strange animal.

Next Saturday. March 08th, 1890. At 01:30 PM. At the Toscana restaurant.

Mr. Iskander Balthazar was watching the activity on the street, through the large windows of the Toscana restaurant. He was lost in his thoughts. And as usual, his animal was lying down on the edge of the window in front of him. When the headwaiter announced the arrival of two men, Mr. Iskander Balthazar turned to welcomed them. Mr. Sloan Wilfrid was visibly impressed at the presence of the great man. He bent respectfully and smiled:

- Good afternoon, Mr. Governor.

Mr. Iskander Balthazar smiled back at him. Meanwhile, young Lyor was very calm and composed. He greeted the Governor, with a head bow. The two men settled on the chairs next to Mr. Iskander Balthazar. Instantly, Mr. Wilfrid put on his little round glasses, he took out a folder from his bag and placed it in front of the Governor:

- As you have requested, Mr. Governor, here is the list of all your properties. This week, we extracted from the Interior Ministry, the land papers of your Baltimore property in ...

Mr. Balthazar examined the documents, while listening to Mr. Wilfrid:

- Next week, we will travel Lyor and I, to Cape Cod, in order to get your home's papers ...
- You must not forget my 2 lands around Hyannis. Although their acquisition is recent, you need to speed up the process of the property papers legalization.
- Yes, Governor. They are on my list ...

After 15 minutes, Mr. Wilfrid had explained the work progress to Mr. Balthazar and answered all his questions and noted his remarks about the upcoming work. When suddenly, without taking his eyes off the documents in his hands, Mr. Balthazar asked in a more joyful voice:

- And how are you doing today, Mr. Lyor Laszlo?

The young Lyor was taken short by this question. He answered a bit hesitant:

- Very well ... Mr. Governor. Thank you.

Mr. Balthazar continued:

- Health is the most precious treasure in the world. It's an invaluable thing.

The great man looked at the two men in front of him, before continuing without losing his smile:

- I guess, you are both wondering ... just like everyone else ... how much time left, do I still have?

Mr. Sloan Wilfrid froze in his chair; his smile disappeared. The young Lyor was also surprised by the very direct question of Mr. Balthazar. Lyor Laszlo met the Governor before but only distantly, in occasions and parties. However, this was the first time the young Lyor was having a direct conversation with the great man.

After a few seconds of hesitation, Mr. Wilfrid had the courage to answer in a polite and compassionate voice:

- Mr. Governor is a man admired and respected by everyone. We wish you all, a good health and a good recovery.

Mr. Iskander Balthazar let go of a slightly sad laugh:

- Gentlemen ... gentlemen ... all three of us, we know perfectly well that many people don't wish me a good health and a good recovery.

After a long sigh, the great man carried on, this time in a hopeless voice:

- My nephew ... my family ... my friends ... Right now, they all look like vultures flying over on top of me ... they are eager to bury me alive and finally inherit the fortune that they have desired for so long. For so many years, I've built an empire. Perhaps I should have spent more time to build a family. Everyone is impatient for my death ...

Mr. Wilfrid dared to interrupt the great man:

- With all due respect, Mr. Governor ... by everyone, I meant the People. You did so many things for this city and this country. All the laws that you have supported, all the institutions you have funded ... it is all natural and normal that the People of this country pray for your recovery.

Mr. Iskander Balthazar replied with a convinced voice:

- The People deserve all the sacrifices made, Mr. Wilfrid. I did what I could, to help.

After a brief moment of silence, Mr. Balthazar addressed the young man:

- Mr. Lyor Laszlo ... is it true that you wish to follow your father's path, by studying the business law?

Lyor straightened up on his chair, and said with a confident tone:

- Yes, Mr. Governor.

The great man was curious:

- I thought I heard that you were in your first year of Law school?

Lyor explained:

- Yes, Mr. Governor ... I passed the admission test to legal studies in September, and I am currently studying my first year in Georgetown Law University.
- And what is it that you do in your father's office?
- In parallel to my studies, I am following a practical training in his cabinet, to gain experience. Mr. Sloan Wilfrid is my mentor.

Mr. Sloan Wilfrid proudly continued:

- Lyor Laszlo assists me in preparing the documents and legal proceedings. It's his first case.

Mr. Iskander Balthazar observed the new apprentice lawyer for a minute. Although young, Lyor Laszlo had a calm and poised attitude, cold and steady facial features. The opposite of his father, the young Lyor was silent still and almost invisible; he never gets involved in conversations.

The Governor made a sign to the headwaiter. Shortly after, three large bowls of soup were served to the three gentlemen. Clam chowder soup, it was Mr. Balthazar's favorite; clams, potatoes and carrots cut into small cubes, milk and cream, herbs, corn and fresh mushrooms.

After his 3rd spoon of soup, Lyor Laszlo noticed that Mr. Iskander Balthazar couldn't even taste his first spoon without it being emptied of its contents. The Governor's right hand was shaking continuously. He tried 4 times to finally enjoy half a spoon of soup. Sloan Wilfrid and Lyor Laszlo exchanged uncomfortable stares. They both pretended to look elsewhere, as to not embarrass Mr. Iskander Balthazar.

After his 10th attempt, the great man had failed to taste 2 full spoons of soup. This movement seemed so difficult for him. The Governor gently put his spoon down, muttering in a miserable tone:

- I can't help myself and enjoy a simple bowl of soup, which I have enjoyed for 40 years.

Lyor and Wilfrid remained immobile; they didn't know what to do and what to say in front of this scene. Mr. Balthazar laid back on his chair and he stared for a long moment at his bowl of clam chowder soup, still all full. The Governor thought aloud with a desperate voice:

- All my efforts ... all my work ... all the things that I've accomplished ... everything will disappear the minute after my death. The person to whom I am about to leave my fortune, have the least concern and care about the People of this country ... no sense of duty or responsibility at all.

Mr. Balthazar let out a long sigh. The animal lying down on the edge of the window, stood up, walked around the table, then approached her Master, put her head on the knees of the great man and she looked at him with sad eyes. Mr. Balthazar caressed the animal's little head, and he smiled:

- I can't do anything to help myself. And I can't do anything to help the People.

Mr. Wilfrid and Lyor Laszlo couldn't find any words to relieve Mr. Balthazar; they shared a compassionate smile and they simultaneously put down their spoons, without daring to finish their soups. The three men watched silently the activity on the other side of the street, through the large windows of the Toscana restaurant.

Chapter 3

The little Bouvard family

Saturday, March 22nd, 1890. 7:30 in the morning.

Every Saturday, about thirty men would gather their carriages in an empty lot, on the street in front of the Toscana restaurant. They install their small wooden kiosks, they attach on top some protective fabric from sun and rain, and they unpack their products and arrange them on their kiosks. Within minutes, the market in front of the Toscana restaurant is ready to greet the visitors who appear within the first lights of the day.

Antman Bouvard had emigrated very young from a North Country to Georgetown city, with his own parents. And for the past 35 years, he has sold vegetables and fruits on a carriage, with his own father, before taking over.

During week days, Antman Bouvard wandered through several farms around the city for supplies of vegetables and fruits, which he sold on his carriage walking through the different streets of Georgetown. Saturday was his only stable income day, where Antman installs his kiosk in the market, in front of the Toscana restaurant and where his revenue was more guaranteed than the other days of the week.

Antman Bouvard carried his merchandise on a two-wheeled cart; he pulled it from behind with a belt attached to his back and holding 2 long wood boards in each hand. In his early forties, Antman Bouvard was a tall strong man, with a tanned skin because of long days of work.

Since a few years now, his daughter joined him for work. Since her birth, Dalya Bouvard had always been strangely different from the other children. She was a little girl, mostly quiet and very special. Small, thin but active and energetic, a light pink skin, a few foxing spots on the nose and cheeks, she had beautiful Sapphire blue eyes that she inherited from her paternal grandfather, Idriss Bouvard, and her light brown hair was almost always tied in a badly arranged bun and hidden by a cap. She always wore denim overall, a white shirt with sleeves lifted up and small black shoes.

Dalya Bouvard was a hard-working little girl, she assisted her father each day, helping him the best she could. During the week days, Dalya lend a hand to her father, pushing their cart all around Georgetown streets. And on Saturday, the market day, while her father sells vegetables in the kiosk, Dalya would sell small bags that she manufactured herself. The little girl got the fabric from potato bags abandoned by farmers; she cleaned the fabric, then cut it into small squares and sewed the edges with a large needle and fiber, therefore to create usable shopping bags.

On that day, Antman Bouvard had already installed his kiosk in the middle of the other ones, and he was placing beets and cabbages on the counter. Dalya sat on an empty box and she was arranging her hand-made bags before the clients' arrival. When suddenly, a little boy appeared in front of their kiosk:

- Good morning Mr. Antman! Good morning Dalya!

Alfie jaq was the same height as Dalya, but he was chubby, white skin tone, filled and pink cheeks, brown eyes, dark brown hair. He was wearing an oversized man's jacket; a scarlet red tie made him look like a businessman, a beige shirt, short pants, long socks, small shoes and a big fishing hat covering his head. He carried a big backpack filled with a stack of newspapers. Despite his small size, his chubby form and his full bag, Alfie jaq's steps were light and bright.

- Good morning, Alfie! How is our city doing today? Asked Dalya's father, while moving a large container filled with tomatoes.
- Full of news Mr. Antman! And fortunately! Thanks to that, my job is alive! Replied Alfie, while putting a newspaper folded in half on a container.

Dalya greeted him with a smile. A second boy stopped right in front of their kiosk.

- I have been waiting for you for nearly half an hour! Why are you so late? Asked Alfie with a furious tone.
- My father needed me to fill the new spices in jars. Replied Maurice Gus, breathless.

Maurice Gus, the Hindu son of the spice merchant in the 4th street of Georgetown, was almost the same age as Dalya and Alfie. Only Maurice Gus was the exact opposite of Alfie jaq. From his Hindu origins, Maurice had inherited a much tanned skin, very soft dark hair and big clear walnut eyes. He was small and very thin. He was wearing a large mint green cap, much larger than his head. And being always chilly, he wore an old shawl around the neck, a large old winter sweater, and green short pants. He was holding a wooden box in his hand and a small bag on his shoulder.

- We will not succeed in business at this rate! How do you expect us to gather money and open our grocery store next year? Exclaimed Alfie, impatient.
- We are 11 years old ... we cannot open our grocery store next year. Replied Maurice, with a different accent and a calm tone.

Since long ago, Alfie and Maurice have always managed to work together. Maurice offered to polish passerby shoes, while Alfie sold newspapers to them, while their shoes got cleaned. Being both very poor, Alfie and Maurice had one and only dream; to open their own store one day and become very rich. These two boys had the business flair in their blood; they never lacked ideas to earn money. Alfie and Maurice always helped their poor families first, sharing half their mediocre gains of the day, and they reserved the other half of money for their dream ... as far as it may seem.

Maurice took out a small box from his pocket and he handed it to Dalya:

- Good morning Dalya. I got you what you asked for, the other day. But be careful, this box should be opened very gently and slowly. This powder spreads everywhere in seconds. Use only a little bit of it, on a piece of fabric and you can turn old shoes, into new ones.

Dalya thanked Maurice, and she gave both him and Alfie, two small baskets filled with some fruits and vegetables of the day.

- Good day to you, Mr. Antman! Good day to you, Dalya! Said Alfie and Maurice simultaneously, before disappearing in a corner of the street.

Ready to start her busy day of work, Dalya stood up and she displayed her handmade bags to passersby, while repeating in a small voice:

- Good morning, Mam. Would you like to buy a shopping bag for your groceries!
- It's 1 cent for these solid and useful bags, Sir!
- Do you need a bag for your purchases, Mam?

After a long and busy morning of hard work, Dalya was able to sell few bags and help her father serve some customers. While Dalya was putting in her pocket one cent of a client who just bought one of her bags, she took a glance toward the Toscana restaurant, at the street in front. Dalya noticed a tall silhouette getting out of a luxurious black car. The same silhouette that the little girl was watching every Saturday at 1:30 PM, since the day she began working with her father. Dalya followed the silhouette of the great man, until he went inside the restaurant and he sat, just like every Saturday, on the same table in front of the large windows.

Dalya was mostly curious about the mysterious animal that followed the great man. While visiting some country farms with her father, Dalya was familiar with most of the animals in ranches. She even knew a few types of cats and dogs, by watching the passersby in gardens and streets. Except that Dalya had never seen an animal like this one before, anywhere else. A great allure, a black and white tattooed fur, large legs, a long tail and a royal walk ... the animal was fascinating!

- It's a Snow Panther. That's what I've been told by a server of the Toscana restaurant. Alfie informed Dalya, one day. Apparently, it's a female, a pretty rare and unique specie ... she doesn't leave the old man's side for a second. She is calm and docile, but ... with a strong character. She allows nobody to touch her!

A few minutes later, Dalya noticed two men settling at the lunch table near the great man. The two men presented documents and papers to the great man, which he read immediately. The scene caught all Dalya's attention, while her father was serving vegetables to a woman.

After a while, Dalya watched the headwaiter place bowls of soup in front of the three gentlemen. Dalya observed the two men easily using their spoons; she counted up to 4 times until the great man could drink one full spoon of soup, without dropping its contents.

When her father asked her to bring him another basket out of the cart to serve a 3rd client, Dalya obeyed. Then, she returned in front of the kiosk, and tried to sell more of her small bags, while taking every second, a little glance toward the great man, who was sitting in the Toscana restaurant. Antman noticed his daughter's eyes focused on the restaurant.

- He still can't drink his soup, can't he? …a very rich man, and yet he cannot drink a simple bowl of soup!! He thought he could buy everything with his money?! Arrogant rich people!! They think they can have it all!! Well done to him! Dalya's father said with a mocking tone.

After selling her 5th bag, Dalya paused for a moment to observe the three men head out of the Toscana restaurant. The great man and his animal settled inside the black luxurious car. The other two men continued on their way, and disappeared in the middle of the crowd.

While Dalya was watching the three men, her father asked her in a curiously sweet tone:

- How many unsold bags do you still have there?

Dalya jumped, her heart raced very quickly. She feared what would happen in the next few minutes. Dalya ignored her father; she turned around her head and pretended to arrange her bags. When suddenly, and before she could even act, Dalya felt a quick and rough hand grab her small purse. Her father was standing right behind her. He was holding her small purse in his hands, and he emptied it of its content, under the scandalized looks of his daughter:

- But … It's … why …
- You've sold very well your bags today! Her father let out a happy and proud laugh, while counting the coins.
- But … It's my money! Dalya exclaimed with an imploring voice.
- Oh … oh … oh! It's not your money, silly twit! Everything you win belongs to me! Dalya's father replied, in a mocking tone.
- But … I worked really hard to get that money! It takes me days and nights to make and sew these bags, so I can sell them here …
- Yes … Yes … for sure. But you don't need this money anyway! … You're housed and fed. Isn't it enough for you, eh? Antman Bouvard hid the coins in his pocket.
- But… I need the money … We need to buy milk for my siste...
- Yes … Yes … of course … I'll pay you back next Saturday, when we sell the rest of the merchandise. Replied her father, with a neglecting voice, before throwing at her face the small empty purse.

Dalya was out of words, she felt her throat tight and had tears in her eyes:

- But … my money …

Her father returned to his place behind the merchandise kiosk. He seemed happy to have his pocket full of extra money. He ordered to his daughter, with an encouraging tone:

- Hurry up and sell the bags that you still have! Come on! Go ahead!

Dalya worked very hard to save some money; she often stayed awake entire nights to clean and sew her potato fabric bags, so she can sell them on the market. Every Saturday, she would stand long hours, trying to convince passersby and customers to buy her little bags. And every Saturday, Dalya succeeded in selling most of her handmade bags. But despite all her efforts to hide her profits, her father would always take all the money that she earned. And he always said the same arguments that Dalya always struggled to understand:

- The money that you earn by selling your bags, isn't yours.
- Everything you win is mine.
- You're already housed and fed, you don't need the money.
- I'll pay you back next Saturday.

Dalya always felt crushed and hurt when her father would take the money of her hard work, never paying her back, always leaving her ... without a penny!

The rest of the day ended like the previous ones. Dalya managed to sell only one more bag. And despite her crushed motivation, Dalya helped her father to serve clients, and arrange their kiosk of vegetables and fruits.

When the lights in the Toscana restaurant went on, it announced the end of the day for the merchants in the market, in the front street. The merchants put back the unsold merchandise in their carriages, uninstall their kiosk, and greet each other before leaving, each on their way.

When he opened the door house, Dalya's father yelled as usual, with a cheerful voice:

- Good evening family!

A woman replied in a strict and a cold way:

- How much money you have got today?

It was the first question that Dalya's mother, Mrs. Augustine Bouvard asked, whenever they returned back home. Dalya and her father were so used by it, that the question wasn't offensive and crushing anymore. Antman replied in a happy and amused tone:

- We have gained enough money to be well fed, well covered and well happy!

A silhouette of a woman came out of a room. She was small, very thin, blond dull hair, small dark black eyes, a pale white skin, a very thin pink mouth ... Dalya's mother looked as a severe and a cruel woman. She insisted:

- How much exactly?

Antman Bouvard walked into the kitchen; he put his big bag on the table in the middle of the room. And he declared in a proud voice:

- 20 cents!

Augustine Bouvard screamed immediately, outraged:

- That's all?? But it is not enough! We must pay the milk for the little ones, and we have to reimburse the grocery store, and pay covers, and buy the...

This exact scene happened every night in the Bouvard house. The second Dalya and her father would cross the house door, Mrs. Augustine would confront them with questions about their profits of the day; she reminded them of their debts to pay, and their failure to meet the needs of the family. Dalya and her father got used to this home welcoming since always. Although often, it was the last thing that they wanted and needed to hear, after a long busy day of hard work.

Antman Bouvard wasn't someone educated or born into a rich family. He had only his cart on which he carried his merchandise. He had to work hard every day to ensure a decent life for his family. Mrs. Augustine on the other hand, had never worked a day in her life, and she was not an educated woman either. For as long as Dalya can remember, her mother was always pessimistic, negative and aggressive.

Mrs. Augustine spent all of her days cleaning the small tiny house where they lived. Dalya could never understand what her mother was cleaning all day long; they lived in a very small 2 rooms house. The first room was the kitchen; it included an old kitchen lever, a small stove and an ancient cook, an old wood table and 5 chairs around it in the middle of the room. In a corner of the kitchen, under a small window, there was a little place hidden by a sewn curtain, a scrunched coverage was lying down on the ground, some tinkering was on a shelf fixed to the wall, it was the place where Dalya would sleep. And the second room of the house was an even smaller bedroom for her parents.

All of a sudden, two little creatures came out of the bedroom, moving quickly on two hands and two feet. They wore the same pink washed out onesies. They were Dalya's little twin sisters; both had light brown eyes, little blond curls flying in the air to the rhythm of their movements. They crawled and pronounced their 1st words since a few months now. Although small and chubby, they were very lively and active. They were called katalina and katiana. But since their birth, about 15 months ago, everyone called them Ari and Adi.

Antman Bouvard lifted the twins in the air, they giggled joyfully.

- My little Ari and my little Adi are in good shape!
- Ant! Ant! Ant! They happily and simultaneously yelled.

Despite all the efforts of their parents to correct them, the little Ari and Adi insisted to call their father Ant instead of Daddy.

Dalya's mother, Mrs. Augustine realized that nobody was listening to her daily criticisms; she went silent and got busy by warming up dinner for the family. Dalya helped her mother placing the old dishes and cutlery on the dining table, while her father was busy playing with the little twins. When dinner was ready, they all took their usual places around the table. Dalya and her father served themselves some potato soup and bread. Ari and Adi were served by their mother on their own bowls of soup. They were all very hungry after a long busy hard working day.

26

Chapter 4

A wake-up call

When dinner was over, Dalya washed the dishes as usual, while her mother was giving a bath to the twins, before putting them to bed. As for her father, he quietly eclipsed outside by the front door. Since few months now, Dalya was curious to know where her father would disappear each night. He only came back until very late at night.

But something else bothered Dalya since a long time too. She questioned the exact amount of their sales. Dalya was convinced that the amount of earnings on that day was 35 cents, without including the 5 cents of her handmade bags that her father took away from her. This makes a total of 40 cents. So why did her father reveal only 20 cents to her mother? How could it be only 20 cents?

In recent months, Dalya tried as hard as she could to add sales, subtract purchases ... but she could never understand the amounts reported by her father, his amounts were always well below Dalya's calculations. She could never understand her own calculation error. And yet, she never dared to ask her father.

The Bouvard family was very poor; very often they had to settle only for bread and water as a meal. The week sales on the carriage through the streets, and the Saturday market sales, were not always sufficient to meet the needs of the little family. Dalya was hoping to raise some more money to cover at least some of her family's expenses. But despite the meager profits she made with her handmade bags, Dalya's father would always take her money.

Dalya looked astray and lost in her thoughts, while washing the dishes and looking through the small kitchen window. When suddenly, Dalya felt a painful pinch on her cheek. Her mother's voice pierced her little ear:

- YOU DIDN'T WASH THE COFFEE POT THIS MORNING!! WHY DO I HAVE A STUPID GIRL LIKE YOU!! EVERY DAY YOU BECOME EVEN MORE STUPID!! WHEN ARE YOU EVER GONNA LEARN! REWASH THE COFFEE POT IMMEDIATELY!!

When Mrs. Augustine dropped her daughter's cheek with a brutal move, Dalya nearly lost balance and almost fell to the ground. Her cheeks were red and painful. With tight throat and tears in her eyes, Dalya took the small coffee pot, to clean it for the second time. She could never understand why her mother was hard and cruel with her, always abusive and aggressive.

With her small trembling and damaged reddened hands, Dalya cleaned the small coffee pot; she turned it around in all sides so she won't miss any spot, she rinsed it, and then she scrub it again and turned it around ...

When all of a sudden, Dalya froze in her move, looking at the small coffee pot in her hands.

At this moment, despite her painful red cheeks, despite the yelling of her cruel mother who still resounded in her ears, and against all odds ... Dalya's face lit up. And she smiled.

The next morning, Dalya woke up on the first sun rays passing through the small kitchen window. When she pulled the curtains of her little corner, Dalya noticed that her father was already outside to arrange the cart. Her mother had already prepared breakfast and was busy washing a stain on her husband's shirt. Suddenly, the twins Ari and Adi came out of the bedroom, with hurried steps, they were both screaming:

- Dindin! Dindin! Dindin!

Dalya stood up from the floor; she took her sisters into her arms, she placed them on their chairs and she gave each one of them a bottle of warm milk. Dalya turned around and said:

- Good morning mother.

Mrs. Augustine was always in a bad mood in the mornings. And the nights too. In fact, Dalya was never sure when her mother was in a good mood. Mrs. Augustine replied in a crushing voice, with her usual threatening look:

- I hope that you will get enough money today! We have to pay for the milk, and the covers and the ...

Dalya sat down at the table, silent, not daring to say one more word. Morning and night, Mrs. Augustine would repeat the same speech:

- Bring money!
- Pay debts!
- You are incapable to cover the family's expenses!

Those were the sentences that Mrs. Augustine kept saying to her husband and her daughter, every single day. And no matter how much money Dalya and her father brought back home, it was never enough for Mrs. Augustine. She always asked for more.

Since a long time now, Dalya learned to ignore her mother. Dalya quickly ate a piece of bread and some milk, and then she decided to join her father outside, before her mother would grind more negativity toward her.

- Dalya, hurry up! We have to go see your uncle Giorgi, about this wheel! Yelled Dalya's father, while he was arranging the last container of vegetables on his cart.

After a long walk and few farms on the way, Dalya and her father stopped in front of a funny and strange house. The workshop looked like a big mess. All kinds of items and gadgets were crammed, hung, suspended, or placed. Disorder overcame the entire place. One could hardly notice the entrance door and the windows of this house. The only person who could manage himself in this disorder was Giorgi Bouvard, Dalya's paternal uncle.

When the cart stopped, a middle-aged man, barely a few years older than Dalya's father, very tall and very thin, came out quickly to meet his new visitors. His peppery curly hair was in the same disorder as his workshop. He was wearing a long apron with multiple pockets, full of items and tools. A big coal color moustache filled his slim face. On top of his head, he was wearing large round glasses with an amplifying effect. He had a friendly, welcoming, and especially energetic appearance. Dalya's uncle, Giorgi Bouvard had a passion for crafts; he was gifted in fixing, creating, and finding solutions to almost anything.

- Good morning, Antman! Good morning, Biggo! What challenge did you bring me today? He said with a bright joyful voice.

Uncle Giorgi always called Dalya Biggo; he always believed that his niece was much grown up than her appearance and her age.

- Good morning, Giorgi. Replied Dalya's father. Well ... the wheel is getting weak, and we need the carriage to go to work. I tried to fix it with a rope, but it's still fragile.
- Hold on one minute! I have just what you need! Said uncle Giorgi, proud to have quickly found a solution to the broken wheel.

Uncle Giorgi returned to his workshop. But just before getting inside to look for a tool, Dalya followed him. An idea spun in Dalya's head during the previous night. And she couldn't stop thinking about it. Dalya said:

- Uncle Giorgi ... may I ask for something, please?
- But of course, Biggo. Anything you need!
- Do you have a small coffee pot to lend me?

He seemed a bit surprised by his niece's request:

- Coffee pot?! I should have one ... in this corner ... hold on one second!

He disappeared in his workshop, and returned after a few minutes and a few noises. Uncle Giorgi handed Dalya a small object, with a big smile:

- Here you go, Biggo. This small coffee pot is as old as me, but it's still useful! It's yours if you want it.

Uncle Giorgi continued on his way to explain to his brother Antman, how he can readjust the wheel without damaging the carriage. Dalya took the small coffee pot, she inspected it for some long minutes, she moved it in all angles, she examined it carefully, and she waved it in all directions. Dalya made the same moves she has done the day before, while washing the dishes. Little by little, Dalya's discovery was confirmed. While observing this little item in her hands, her eyes lightened up, her heart beat fast, her breath froze and ... Dalya smiled, for the second time!

Chapter 5

An insignificant item

Saturday, April 05th, 1890.

Spring officially moved into the city of Georgetown. Trees were becoming greener and more alive, flowers bejeweled the ends of the branches, birds appeared more often, the sun looked bigger and wilder, the sky was a clear blue painting, and the air was fresh and sweet. The sprint season was wonderful.

Saturday morning. The market day in front of the Toscana restaurant. Dalya was eager to see the luxurious black car arrive. She kept checking the restaurant's door every minute, at the slightest movement; while she helped her father set up their kiosk and serve the customers.

At 01:30 PM. As expected. A luxurious black car stopped in front of the restaurant's door. And the same tall silhouette stepped slowly outside, leaning on a cane. The strange animal followed him immediately.

When Dalya's father finished serving a customer, he noticed that his daughter was distracted by something else.

- And here again ... the rich old man ... unable to drink his soup! Why does he even bother to come to that restaurant if he can't even eat?! He laughed.

But Dalya didn't listen to any of her father's words. She was entirely focused on what was going on at the front street, in the Toscana restaurant. Because on that day, Dalya was willing to act!

While her father was cleaning a few empty boxes, Dalya crossed the street and she headed toward the restaurant. The great man was accompanied by two men, a man with round glasses and a younger man; the three gentlemen were all standing a few meters away from the entrance door of the Toscana restaurant. When she got close enough to them, Dalya addressed the great man, in a nervous voice:

- Good morning, Sir ... I'd like to show you an ite...

Mr. Iskander Balthazar looked at Dalya in a quick glance, and then he whispered something to one of the two men. Then, the great man entered the restaurant, followed by his animal. Immediately, the younger of the two men, placed 2 cents in Dalya's hand, before he disappeared inside the restaurant, followed by the man with round glasses. Dalya remained motionless and speechless:

- But ... this isn't what I've asked for ...

30

Dalya didn't think that her plan would be so difficult to execute. She returned to her kiosk and watched the three gentlemen removing hats and coats, and settling on the same usual dining table. Immediately, one of the men pulled some papers out from his folder and handed them to the great man, who plunged into reading the documents just like the previous times. Dalya whispered:

- I have to try again!

Her father, Antman Bouvard was busy moving a case of carrots and he didn't care to know what his daughter was up to. Dalya pulled out of her bag an item wrapped in a rag. Then, she quietly vanished and walked toward the Toscana restaurant entrance door, for the 2nd time. Dalya spoke to one of the two doormen, with a hesitant but a polite voice:

- Hello ... I would like to talk to the old man ... the one sitting on that table, please.

The two doormen stared at Dalya from head to toe, in a mocking glance. One of the two doormen asked her:

- Who is it you want to talk to?

Dalya pointed her finger toward the great man who was busy reading some documents. Immediately, the two doormen burst out laughing:

- All the people of Washington State want to talk to this gentleman!
- He has no time for a little girl like you. Go play somewhere else!

Dalya insisted:

- It's important! It's because for a long time he was unable to e...

One of the doormen interrupted her with a brusque movement:

- Go play somewhere else! You're blocking the way for our customers!

Dalya didn't have any time to explain, the other doorman pushed her toward the street. Dalya underestimated her idea to approach the great man. But she wasn't willing to abandon so easily!

While standing near her dad's kiosk, Dalya observed the great man reading and chatting with the two men next to him. When she thought very hard for a moment, Dalya had a 3rd idea to approach the great man and talk to him. She removed the fabric surrounding the small item that she was holding, and for the 3rd time, she crossed the street, heading toward the Toscana restaurant. Except that this time, Dalya walked directly toward the enormous windows of the restaurant. When she got right in front of the great man's lunch table, Dalya waved at him so that she could be noticed.

The Snow Panther lying down on the edge of the large window, was observing the street in a careless and sleepy gaze, listening to her Master and one of the two men discussing. When suddenly, the animal noticed the little girl waving outside the restaurant's window. The Snow Panther stood up quickly; Mr. Balthazar immediately noticed the fast reaction of his animal. When the great man inclined his head, curious to see what caught the attention of his animal so suddenly, Mr. Balthazar noticed a little girl waving at him. Mr. Wilfrid stopped his explanations; he and Lyor Laszlo turned around their heard too, toward the large windows. This time, Dalya got the attention she was seeking since this morning. And in front of the three men, Dalya moved the item she had in her hands with a repetitive movement. Mr. Balthazar was confused:

- But ... what is this? ... what is she doing?

Mr. Balthazar barely finished his question, that the two doormen outside the restaurant, they realized that Dalya was making signs in front of the Governor's window. They screamed simultaneously, trying to chase her:

- HEY!! YOU!! GET AWAY FROM THE WINDOW!! IMMEDIATELY!!
- STOP DISTURBING OUR CUSTOMERS!! GO PLAY SOMEWHERE ELSE!!

Dalya escaped before they could catch her. Mr. Wilfrid said before continuing to explain his work to the Governor:

- She's just a kid playing some games ... so I was saying, the Stock papers are ready for y...

Dalya returned to her father's kiosk, who was unaware of what his daughter was doing, he was busy removing containers of potatoes and displaying them on the front. Disappointed to have failed, Dalya sat on an empty box, holding firmly her item, and observing the Toscana restaurant.

- If only I could have a chance to talk to him! She thought.

The Snow Panther sat back in its usual place, without losing its awakening. The animal froze in front of the restaurant's large windows, with its sapphire blue eyes focused on the little girl at the other side of the street.

After some few minutes, the headwaiter served 3 bowls of soup to the gentlemen. Dalya straightened up and she followed the great man's movements. His hand was trembling; all the content of the spoon was quickly emptied, before he was able to taste anything. In front of this scene that she watched a hundred times, Dalya decided to act ... for the 4th time, no matter what the cost!

Dalya stood up, she looked around on her right and left, she searched for a clue to pass her idea on to the great man. She fumbled in her father's carriage, looking for anything that could help her. Dalya found some work tools, old newspapers, vegetables boxes, gloves, an old hat, a bowl, a large pair of scissors, a bag of straw, an iron pipe, long strings ... Suddenly, she froze. When Dalya noticed a bowl, her face lightened up, in an instant!

Dalya hurried toward the Toscana restaurant. And this time, she hid in the corner of the street. She waited until the moment the doormen were busy helping a fat and a rich woman getting out of her car. Dalya stepped out of her hiding place, and then she walked straight to the restaurant's window. Mr. Balthazar was still struggling to drink his soup with his trembling hands. While Lyor Laszlo and Mr. Wilfrid were making very slow moves with their spoons, looking at him with a pity glance.

Dalya stopped in front of the large windows, right before the three gentlemen. She waved with her hands. When the animal noticed the little girl, it stood up rapidly, for the 2nd time. The animal started banging smoothly on the window with its right paw, over and over again, its tail was moving actively up in the air. Mr. Wilfrid was the first to see Dalya this time, exclaiming:

- Again? … Really?

Mr. Balthazar looked for the second time at the little girl. And this time, Dalya had only few seconds to execute her plan. She took her bowl, she poured a small amount of water from a bottle, then she took her item, and she imitated the great man, by shaking her hand and trying to drink. She repeated this move 3 times in front of the three gentlemen. Mr. Balthazar exclaimed in a shocked tone:

- But … what is going on? Why do we keep bothering us? Who is this girl? How dare she imitate me … how dare she plays like this??

Mr. Balthazar couldn't understand the unusual reaction of his animal:

- Séraphine! Calm down!! What is wrong with you? Stop knocking on the window!

Exasperated by the offensive imitations of the little girl in front of him, Mr. Balthazar was about to call the headwaiter to make the little girl step away.

Usually, the young Lyor Laszlo was always silent and quiet during their business lunches. He spoke very rarely. Except on that day, Mr. Balthazar was interrupted by the calm and distracted voice of the young Lyor Laszlo, who was staring at the repetitive movements of this little girl:

- She drinks water … she drinks water from the bowl … she drinks water from the bowl with her trembling hand … she can drink water from the bowl with her trembling hand … but … how?

Mr. Wilfrid rearranged his glasses and he tried to get back Lyor and the Governor's attention:

- Gentlemen … she is just a little girl having fun. We'd better finish this meal, so we can continue our work. We have several papers to rev…

But, the young Lyor Laszlo seemed focused and unfazed in his thoughts:

- She drinks water from the bowl … Her hand is trembling … it doesn't overflow …

- What are you talking about? What do you mean? Mr. Balthazar grew impatient.

Lyor Laszlo ignored both men and he continued to whisper without losing sight of the little girl, who repeated precise movements for the 10th time:

- She can drink water from the bowl with her trembling hand ... The item that she is using ... it does not overflow the water she drinks ... even when her hand trembles!

At this precise moment, Mr. Balthazar looked back at the little girl in front of him ... and this time, in a much more different stare than before. The young Lyor turned around to Mr. Wilfrid and the Governor, who were both confused. Lyor announced in a convinced and confident voice:

- Mr. Governor, I believe this little girl has a tool to help you drink your soup!

Mr. Balthazar seemed shocked, yet somewhat doubtful of the young Lyor's discovery. But a spark of curiosity settled in his mind, he made a sign to the headwaiter:

- Call this little girl! Bring her to me, immediately!

The two doormen realized Dalya's trick. But before any of them could chase her away, the headwaiter advanced the doormen and he called Dalya, before she would escape:

- Little girl! Hold on a minute!! Someone would like to meet you!

For a long time, Dalya dreamed to step inside the Toscana restaurant. She has always been fascinated and curious to see the inside of this luxurious place. Within her first steps, the smell floating in the air was so delicious that Dalya's empty stomach was full. The enormous chandeliers spread glowing and warm lights. The tables were all occupied and garnished with exquisite food on shiny cutlery. The guests were all elegant and looked distinguished. The servers were impeccably dressed in well ironed white outfits. Everything was ordered and refined.

Dalya followed the headwaiter toward Mr. Balthazar's table. She felt the stares of most of the customers and even the servers. Although she was shaking and stressed, Dalya walked forward anyway.

Dalya noticed the presence of a young waitress, among all the men servers in the Toscana restaurant. She was a young girl of about 20 years, almond eyes drawn in Asian shape, small, slim, straight hair and a pretty pink skin tone, in a white uniform just like the other male servers. The girl was wearing a pretty little cherry flower pin in her hair. Everyone in the Toscana restaurant called her Tudi. And as soon as Dalya got close to her, the young waitress moved from her path and she inclined her head in front of the little girl.

The headwaiter and the little girl were few steps close from the great man's table. When all of a sudden, the animal stepped down from the edge of the window, into a quick jump and walked toward the little girl. Dalya stopped and she took one step backward, all frightened to see the animal approaching her. The little girl was paralyzed by the sapphire blue eyes of the animal. Dalya realized she was barely taller than this creature. When the Snow Panther paused in front of Dalya, the animal stared at her for a moment, and then she turned 2 times around the little girl.

- What is … what is your animal doing? Asked Mr. Wilfrid.
- I don't have any slight idea … She has never acted like this before. Mr. Balthazar was confused, observing his Panther's moves.

Everyone watched silently what was going on between the animal and the little girl. Mr. Iskander Balthazar, the 2 men sitting on his table, the headwaiter, the Asian waitress with the cherry flower pin in her hair, the other servers, the customers … all the activity in the Toscana restaurant froze on that moment. The scene was unusual. Having been always passive and reckless, the animal never showed any interest in whosoever.

After completing 4 tours around the little girl, and having stared at her from all angles, the animal stopped again in front of Dalya, and its sapphire blue eyes observed intensely the little girl. And then, the animal made a strange and an unpredictable move.

- What … is it really doing a … am I seeing it correctly? Mr. Sloan Wilfrid exclaimed.
- Yes, I think so. Young Lyor Laszlo was as surprised as everyone else from the strange reaction of the animal toward the little girl.

In front of all the people present in the Toscana restaurant, in front of all their surprise and confusion … the Snow Panther folded its front legs, lowered her head down, and bowed in front of the unknown little girl, who was still standing motionless.

Mr. Balthazar straightened up on his chair, and he had some hard time to believe what he was watching:

- But … it's impossible … it's the same gesture Irea had received … How did she know? … It's impossible!

After a long silent moment, the Snow Panther stood up, and then she stepped away allowing the little girl to join the table of the three men. Dalya walked in hesitant steps, shocked and intimidated by the behavior of the strange animal. The Snow Panther returned calmly to sit by her Master, without taking her eyes off the little girl.

Mr. Balthazar received the little girl, with a curious and puzzled stare. Séraphine was peaceful as a pet, but not sociable with people, nobody ever dared to approach her or touch her, other than her Master, she never showed any interest in anyone. And even more, bowing to … an unknown little girl!

Being close to him for the first time, Dalya noticed that Mr. Balthazar had beautiful clear purple eyes, giving his face an imposing look. He addressed Dalya in a calm and welcoming voice:

- Good afternoon, Mademoiselle.

The two men next to Mr. Balthazar turned toward her. Dalya was so intimidated by the luxurious restaurant, by the three men sitting in front of her and the behavior of the Snow Panther. Dalya was overwhelmed; she blushed and looked down to her feet. Mr. Balthazar ordered the headwaiter for a chair. When Dalya sat down, Mr. Balthazar asked:

- Do you know who I am?

Dalya moved her head for a no. Dalya had never tried to find out who was the great man she has been watching for a long time now. She was only interested in helping him drink his soup more easily. Mr. Balthazar was not offended that the little girl didn't know who he was. He was not expecting a poor little girl to recognize him. He presented himself in a kind voice:

- I'm the Governor of the Washington State, my name is Iskander Balthazar. And here is Mr. Sloan Wilfrid and Mr. Lyor Laszlo, my lawyers. May I know your name?

She whispered timidly:

- Dalya ... Bouvard.

Mr. Balthazar smiled:

- Dalya ... well, that's a pretty name.

The great man stared at this unknown little girl for a brief moment, before adding:

- My Panther, Séraphine seems to ... like you.

Dalya noticed that the animal sitting on the floor near her Master, looked at her with a peaceful look. No one could explain the behavior of the Snow Panther a minute earlier, not even her own Master.

- We were curious to know what you were doing in front of the window, couple of minutes ago. Asked Mr. Balthazar.

Dalya pulled out of her pocket the small item, and she handed it to the great man. Mr. Wilfrid and Lyor Laszlo straightened up on their chairs, curious about this strange object. Mr. Balthazar took the tool in his hands, not knowing exactly what it was. Dalya gathered her courage and she explained in a slightly trembling voice:

- It's a ... special spoon, Sir. I made it for you. It will allow you to drink the soup without dropping ... a drop.

Mr. Balthazar appeared confused, he hesitated for a moment:

- A special spoon ... really? ... Without dropping a drop?

Dalya replied in a confident voice:

- Yes, Sir.

Mr. Balthazar stared one time at the strange spoon in his hands, and one time at the unknown little girl sitting next to him. After a brief moment of hesitation, the great old man decided to dip the spoon in his soup. With his trembling hand, he raised the special spoon to his mouth, and he drank.

The great man repeated his move a few times. At the end of his 5th attempt, Mr. Balthazar was astonished and couldn't believe what had just happened. Mr. Wilfrid, young Lyor Laszlo, and Dalya, they all held their breaths, waiting for any drop that will overflow. After a silent moment, Mr. Balthazar whispered:

- For the last 5 years that I have been trying ... It's unbelievable!

Lyor Laszlo was so proud to have guessed right and understood Dalya's movements through the window of the Toscana restaurant. Mr. Sloan Wilfrid could not help but ask the little girl, in a curious tone:

- May we know ... Mademoiselle ... How did you made this spoon?

Dalya explained with a proud and confident voice:

- It's a small coffee pot, Sir. I removed the iron handle, and I replaced it with a wooden one, so as not to use a pad on the handle when it is hot. I also adjusted the wood handle, to make it longer and more convenient to use. Then, I fixed it with two nails on the coffee pot. I warmed up the pot on the stove fire for two hours, and then I reduced its size by tapping it with my father's hammer. I tightened the beak of the small pot to avoid dropping over any soup or liquid drop.

When Dalya finished her explanation, the three men observed her with astonished eyes. Mr. Balthazar examined the strange spoon in his hand and he asked:

- And so ... if I have got it correctly ... I am drinking the soup with a refabricated ... small coffee pot?

Mr. Wilfrid, who understood all Dalya's work to get this special spoon, exclaimed in an amused tone:

- That's quite clever!

Mr. Balthazar observed the spoon in his hand for a few minutes. He repeated, in a lost confused voice:

- A small coffee pot to drink the soup ... a small coffee pot to drink the soup ... a small coffee pot ...

It was as if Mr. Balthazar couldn't believe that an insignificant item could solve his problem and help him enjoy one of his last pleasures of life; the clam chowder soup.

All of a sudden and unexpectedly, Mr. Iskander Balthazar laughed. A laugh that nobody had heard since a very long time. He laughed full heart, until tears filled his eyes.

Mr. Sloan Wilfrid and the young Lyor Laszlo smiled together, in front of this unpredictable scene. The headwaiter and the servers stopped to observe the Governor's table. All the customers of the restaurant turned around toward the table of the three gentlemen; they all wondered what on earth might have incited their unusual laugh!

Dalya remained immobile and quiet on her chair. In front of the three men who laughed, she smiled. The Snow Panther, who has been the first one to notice the little girl, stared at Dalya Bouvard, in a strange serene gaze.

Sometimes ... one insignificant incident ... one insignificant item ... one insignificant deed ... can change the path of your life ... Forever!

Chapter 6

The poor who helps feed the rich

Saturday, April 26th, 1890.

The climate changed dramatically. The Sun remained a little longer during the day. The heat became increasingly heavy. The greenery was getting comfortable everywhere. A few warm air breezes passed from time to time. But the climate was not the only change, in these last days of April spring...

The Toscana restaurant lived the same scene, like the previous Saturdays. A luxurious black car stopped in front of the restaurant door, at exactly 1:30 PM. A tall silhouette came out of it, followed by a Panther, and two other men.

And just like the previous Saturdays, the three men settled into their usual table in front of the big restaurant windows. The Snow Panther took her usual place on the edge of the window.

And just like the previous Saturdays, the younger men withdrew their documents, they presented them to the great man and they explained the content. The great man read, corrected, consulted a few pages and asked questions.

And just like the previous Saturdays, after about 30 minutes of work, the great man made a sign to the headwaiter to serve them lunch.

And just like the previous Saturdays, the same clam chowder soup bowl was presented to the great man and his guests.

Except that this time ... unlike the previous Saturdays, Mr. Balthazar took out a special item from his pocket, he took a dip in the soup bowl, and then with his trembling hand ... he drank the entire full spoon in a single move, with eyes closed, and an innocent smile on his lips.

As futile as this moment may seem to most people, Mr. Iskander Balthazar enjoyed this true moment of happiness. When he had finished his first sip, he raised his eyes toward the street in front of him, through the large windows of the Toscana restaurant, and he noticed a little girl, standing in the middle of the market, holding a stack of small handmade bags; she was watching him too, with a little smile on her lips.

- What ... He seriously managed to drink his soup this time? Dalya's father was disappointed of what he had just seen.
- Yes ... He finally made it. Replied Dalya, all proud.
- Well well ... who would have ever thought it will happen?! I wonder how he did it? Antman Bouvard moved some empty cases to the carriage, unaware that his own daughter, Dalya had something to do with it.

Usually, Dalya was the one watching what was happening at the Toscana restaurant. But since few Saturdays now, it was Mr. Balthazar who was curious, following the activities of the little girl at the market on the other side of the street. Mr. Sloan Wilfrid and the young Lyor Laszlo, didn't hesitate anymore to eat their soups this time, without worrying to be rude toward Mr. Balthazar. The great man couldn't get the little girl out of his mind, he kept thinking about their conversation, a few weeks before.

- How much is this ... spoon? Mr. Balthazar asked, not quite sure how he should name this strange item he was holding in his hands.

Dalya didn't know what to answer; she stared down at her small shoes. In front of the girl's silence, Mr. Balthazar pulled out a cent from his pocket and he handed it to Dalya. Before she could even know how much money there was in the great man's hand, and with a rapid move, Dalya closed Mr. Balthazar's big hand with her little fingers, murmuring in a calm voice:

- It's free, Sir.

In all his life, never someone has dared to do such a gesture toward Mr. Iskander Balthazar. Dalya took out of her pocket the 2 cents that Lyor Laszlo had given her earlier, before the men entered the restaurant. Dalya placed the money on the lunch table, in front of the young man, and she said in a polite tone:

- Thank you.

Lyor Laszlo was always silent and calm during these lunch meetings. But this time, he asked all confused:

- Why don't you accept this money?

Dalya replied spontaneously:

- Why should I?

Lyor was astonished by the little girl answer:

- But ... you're poor.

Dalya was also amazed by the young man's answer:

- And ... is it a reason enough to accept whatever money we are given?

Lyor replied:

- Well ... Yes! It seems the fairer thing to do!

Dalya seemed confused by the young man's logic:

- Why does accepting money from a stranger, should be the right thing to do?

Lyor insisted:

- But ... you interrupted us earlier, at the entrance of the restaurant.

Dalya enlightened him:

- And ... have I asked for this money?

Mr. Wilfrid intervened in a small voice:

- It is true that Mademoiselle has not made this request when we ent...

Lyor ignored Mr. Wilfrid, and he affirmed in a convinced tone:

- Well then, you want something else other than money!

Dalya also, affirmed in a confident tone:

- No.

Lyor stared at the little girl:

- So then ... you just have fun making tools and offering them to people ... without compensation?

Dalya replied naturally:

- Yes.

Mr. Wilfrid smiled and exclaimed:

- It is smart an...

Lyor interrupted him, bewildered and eager to understand:

- It is illogical ... Why are you doing this?

Dalya answered immediately, in a curious voice:

- Why not?

Lyor Laszlo lost his calm:

- But ... Nobody asked you to make this tool!

Dalya replied:

- I did not expect a request either!

Lyor was struck by this answer:

- But then ... why have you insisted to help Mr. Governor?

Dalya asked, very curious:

\- Do you need a reason to help someone?

Mr. Wilfrid attempted to intervene to calm the tone that was heating up between the two young people:

\- One must admit, that it's very nice of you to help Mr...

Lyor Laszlo interrupted him, and he exclaimed in an exasperated tone:

\- Don't you have any appropriate answers to my questions?

Dalya Bouvard replied in a spontaneous voice:

\- Don't you have less idiot questions?

Mr. Iskander Balthazar followed with great attention the conversation between the two young people, and the attempts of Mr. Wilfrid to calm them down. Lyor Laszlo and Dalya Bouvard seemed to have two very different visions of things.

Yet, while observing these two people ... at this precise moment ... a strange idea ... an impossible idea ... came across the Governor's mind.

And one must admit that Lyor Laszlo wasn't the only one confused by the answers and gestures of this unknown little girl, Mr. Balthazar and Mr. Wilfrid were surprised and confused too as well. She wore her hair in a large cap, small overall sewed in several places, an old yellowed shirt underneath with sleeves lifted up, black old shoes. It was clear enough that the little girl was poor, and turning down money seemed something equally unusual and ironic.

Mr. Wilfrid took off his small round glasses and he addressed the little girl in a much calmer and nicer tone than Lyor's:

\- Mademoiselle ... Mr. Governor would like to thank you for your gesture. We urge you to accept his money.

Dalya replied very politely:

\- Thank you, Sir ... But I work to deserve the money. Helping someone feel better, I do this for free.

Mr. Balthazar, thunderstruck by this answer, he lost his voice and his words. The Governor was ashamed to have pushed away the little girl the first time she tried to talk to him when he was stepping out of his car, thinking that she was a beggar. Mr. Lyor Laszlo observed the little girl; he was still in chock for being called an idiot.

Despite all her explanations, the spontaneous and honest answers, none of the three men could understand the gesture of this poor stranger. Mr. Balthazar decided to try one last time, he asked the little girl with a kind voice:

- Forgive our curiosity and our confusion. But I insist to know why ... why did you made this spoon especially for me? And why did you insist to offer it to me?

Dalya paused for a moment, not knowing what to answer. But in front of the three curious men who were eager to hear a reply, Dalya finally said in a natural voice, and with a nice smile:

- Because if I have an idea in my mind and if I don't use it ... it itches, Sir.

Lyor Laszlo thought he misheard Dalya's last words, he exclaimed, barely hiding his astonishment:

- It ... what?

The young Lyor, Mr. Balthazar and Mr. Wilfrid, none of them ever expected to meet this special stranger. Although they all knew many different kinds of people, they have never met a person like this little girl. They were ashamed of calling her a beggar at their first meeting. Although she was too young and poor, Dalya never ceased to surprise.

When Dalya stood up to greet Mr. Iskander Balthazar, he replied with a confused smile and upside down mind. For the first time in his life, words were missing from the Governor; he watched the little girl on her way out of the Toscana restaurant and returning to her father's kiosk, at the street in front.

Mr. Wilfrid interrupted Mr. Balthazar in his thoughts:

- Is everything alright, Mr. Governor?

Mr. Balthazar replied yes with a bewildered face, while his eyes focused on the other side of the street. Wilfrid and Lyor knew very well that Mr. Balthazar was watching the little girl who captivated all his attention, especially since their last meeting.

Dalya helped her father serve the last customer, before returning to sit on an empty case and clean her handmade bags.

Mr. Iskander Balthazar called the headwaiter, who rapidly came close to him:

- What do you know about the little girl sitting in the market, at the street in front?
- Not much, Mr. Governor. She comes with her father every Saturday, the market day, to set up their kiosk and sell vegetables and fruits.
- I wish to learn a little more about her.
- Understood, Mr. Governor.

Chapter 7

Some good nectarines

Saturday, May 10th, 1890. 6:30 in the morning.

Dalya woke up before the first sun rays appeared. Since long time ago, she got used to the hard kitchen floor where she sleeps, in her little corner. Dalya arranged her old cover, and she opened the curtains of her small corner. Her mother, Mrs. Augustine was cleaning the kitchen floor with a sponge and a container filled with water near her, with an aggressive move. Why was her mother cleaning the kitchen floor so brutally and so early in the morning? Dalya couldn't answer this question, but she could clearly hear her mother whispering:

- How should we live now? What will become of us? We will all die of hunger! We'll be all thrown out in the street!

Suddenly, Dalya's mother took the water container with a brusque move and she crushed it to the ground. The water quickly spread all over the kitchen. Mrs. Augustine repeated the same sentences:

- We will all die of hunger! We'll be all thrown out in the street! He is an incapable who will leave us with nothing!

Mrs. Augustine stood up rapidly, and then walked toward the kitchen lever. In a violent move, she dropped into the lever all the dishes already clean; plates, containers, forks, glasses. She began to clean them once again, placing back the wet dishes with an ear-piercing move. Mrs. Augustine made such a violent noise that the walls trembled. Dalya was used to her mother's aggressive scenes and bad temper, every morning and every night.

Dalya didn't wish to stay in her own house any longer, she walked up to the door to get out, when her mother's shouting stopped her:

- WHERE DO YOU THINK YOU ARE GOING?

Dalya turned toward her mother:

- Today is the Saturday market. I will wor...

Mrs. Augustine displayed her devilish black look and yelled with all her might:

- BUT HOW CAN YOU WORK? HOW ARE YOU GOING TO DO SO? YOU THINK YOU ARE AS SMART AS YOUR FATHER? YOU THINK YOU'RE GOING TO SUCCEED? YOU ARE A POOR LITTLE IDIOT! YOU'RE A FAILURE! AND YOU'LL

ALWAYS BE A FAILURE! WE'LL ALL DIE OF HUNGER! WE'LL ALL BE THROWN OUT IN THE STRE...

Dalya made a sharp U-turn and she got out of the house, closing gently the door. Dalya didn't share the same pessimistic, negative and aggressive character of her mother. Dalya didn't believe that staying home, doing nothing else than cleaning the floor and dishes for the 15th time, could do any good. Mrs. Augustine liked to stay focused on the problem. Dalya preferred to focus on the solution.

The first lights of the day finally appeared. Dalya arranged the cart and she began her day. Her father was a strong man. He easily raised the cart; he fixed the belt on his back, and then pulled the cart forward. Dalya did the same thing. Despite her small size and the heavy load of the cart, Dalya walked small steps from her house toward the usual farms, to collect fruits and vegetables, and then she headed to the market place. It was a long way, she probably wasn't going to arrive early as usual, but Dalya was determined to go all the way and work on that day.

Small slow steps. But small determined steps, for sure.

Dalya managed to pull the cart, all well. As soon as she reached the marketplace in front of the Toscana restaurant, two neighboring merchants hurried up to help the little girl, install her cart and her kiosk, before she could even ask them for help.

It was 01:55 PM; Mr. Iskander Balthazar anxiously waited for the arrival of Dalya and her father, he was wondering what could have held them and slowed them down. When suddenly, the Snow Panther straightened up. Mr. Balthazar inclined his head curious of what was going on, and he noticed two merchants helping Dalya set up her kiosk. The little girl took the cases one by one and she arranged the fruits and vegetables she had been able to carry, in front of her kiosk. When she finished, Dalya made a little place on the kiosk for her small handmade bags. Dalya stood behind and she exclaimed to passersby with an enthusiastic tone:

- Today we have good carrots to garnish your dinner!
- Buy a kilo of peppers and we offer you a free bag!
- Good nectarines will be ideal for a pie!

After a while, 2 usual clients brought vegetables and fruits from Dalya. Although little and small, Dalya was dynamic. She served the customers rapidly and with a nice smile. Some time after, when Dalya was busy arranging empty cases in her carriage, a stranger stopped in front of her kiosk. Elegantly dressed, he asked in an arrogant tone:

- I would like one kilo of these potatoes.
- Right away, Sir! Said Dalya with a dynamic voice.

Dalya immediately began to choose the best potatoes for the customer. When suddenly, the stranger interrupted her in a voice so grave and loud, that she bounced:

- No no no!!!

The merchants in the neighboring kiosks turned around their heads. Dalya froze behind her kiosk, and she asked:

- Would you like something else... other than potatoes, Sir?
- Who else can serve me here? The customer seemed upset.
- Me ... Sir. Dalya replied spontaneously.
- No no no! Not you!! Someone else!! He shouted loudly.

Dalya didn't understand the new client's reaction, nor what he was asking for. She tried with all her might to guess what he wanted:

- Forgive me ... Sir ... but I don't know what you mean.
- I wish to be served by someone else! He replied in a haughty voice.

Dalya murmured hesitantly:

- Someone else? ... I don't understand Sir ...

The man explained in a mocking tone:

- I will not buy merchandise from a little girl! That's ridiculous!! Call someone big so that he may serve me! I prefer to deal with a man!

Dalya was in shock for a moment, not knowing what to do or what to answer. She was the only one working in the kiosk and she desperately needed to sell her merchandise and earn money that day!

When suddenly, an idea popped in Dalya's head. She returned to her cart, she took out two big empty vegetable cases, and a small container that her friend Maurice Gus had brought her, a few weeks ago. Dalya placed the vegetable cases one on top of the other, behind the kiosk. The client watched and wondered what the little girl was up to. Dalya opened the small coal container; she spread out with her two tiny fingers some black powder under her little nose. Then, she climbed up on the two big empty cases, and with her most beautiful smile below her coal moustache, Dalya announced to the customer:

- As you have requested Sir, you are now in front of a big man. Is it decent and alright for you now, Sir? Shall we get down to business today?

The other merchants in the neighboring kiosk, who were following the scene since the beginning, burst out laughing. The customer had become all red, he was so upset and humiliated, he left the market so mad without buying anything else.

Although she was a quiet and mostly a shy little girl, Dalya Bouvard had an extraordinary imagination. She had a bigger mind than her age, and she was more aware and responsible than the other children of her same age.

While reading the documents handed over by Mr. Wilfrid, Mr. Balthazar wrote some notes to add, some sentences to correct, while frequently observing the events, at the street in front. The little girl worked very hard to serve all customers and make money.

- Hello Dalya. Alfie interrupted her, by placing a newspaper folded in half on her kiosk.
- Are you working all alone today? Asked Maurice, while he handed her a basket that was too far from her.
- Yes ... and I hope this day will end up well! Dalya replied breathless.
- That is if the day starts well already, said Alfie, looking a little stressed while adjusting his large red tie.
- Why are you late today? Asked Dalya, filling two small bags of vegetables and fruits of the day.
- We have been retained by these police officers! They are not in a good mood today. Replied Maurice, disappointed, his large mint green cap was barely holding on his head.
- And as usual, they stopped us to read the papers, and got them all scrunched up, without paying anything! These police officers! Alfie said, outraged.
- At least, you didn't clean up three pairs of shoes! I had to shine up 2 times the Chief police shoes! Maurice was breathless.

Dalya handed them two small bags filled with fruits and vegetables, with an encouraging smile:

- Come on guys!! The day is not over yet!
- Thanks. Said Maurice, while taking the two little filled bags from her.
- Always the right words!! Replied Alfie, who seemed to have regained some cheerful spirit.

Alfie and Maurice greeted her and they disappeared at the corner of a street. Dalya got busy cleaning some fruits before the arrival of her next clients. When suddenly, a strong and arrogant voice stood out from the crowd. Dalya closed her eyes for a second, and she murmured:

- Please not them! Not today!! Please not them!

Opening her eyes, what Dalya has feared was confirmed; the police Chief accompanied by his 2 aide officers, were in front of the kiosks of the market. The police Chief was a very small man, about 50 years old, with a big belly, and cruel black eyes. He wore a tight black suit, and at each of his movements, his jacket buttons were about to burst. His two aides were very long and very thin. They foolishly smiled all the time, following their leader all day. The 3 men in their black suits looked like crows.

Whenever they were on patrol, near the market in front of the Toscana restaurant, the three crows did their grocery shopping from almost all the kiosks in the market, and they went without paying anything. None of the poor merchants ever dared to stop them. He who defied the crows, could be sure to spend many nights in jail. Alfie and Maurice were not the only ones to hate these officers.

- It is the only goods that I have, to sell today ... Sir! Exclaimed the fisherman in a pleading tone.
- On this sunny day, it will deteriorate if it stays too long in your kiosk! replied the police Chief, while ordering his two helpers to take the best fish, before continuing with an amused laugh :
- And besides ... it will be delicious in my soup tonight!
- But ... I've got rent to pay, Sir. The fisherman seemed lost and devastated, while observing his kiosk being emptied by the two police aides, and the poor man was unable to stop them.
- Don't worry ... don't worry ... Tomorrow, you will have all new merchandise to sell! Replied the police Chief in a careless tone, while staring at the other kiosks full of goods.

When the police aides moved to a second kiosk, the poor fisherman looked miserable, he sat alone on a container and watched his empty kiosk.

- The lettuce you gave me last time, was not very good! Exclaimed the police Chief toward a woman who was selling all kinds of lettuce and green salad.
- It's that ... the season is a little harsh for the salad leaves ... Sir. Replied the woman in a trembling voice.
- So, what?! Am I to starve?!
- No ... no Sir ... that is not what I meant. The woman trembled.
- What am I supposed to eat? Asked the police Chief in an upset tone.

The police Chief pointed his finger toward the endives and the green salads. His aides officers executed immediately, and they filled their bags of lettuce, right in front of the shocked eyes and repressed voice of the poor woman.

- I beg you ... Sir ... please. The poor woman muttered, before being interrupted by the evil police Chief with his threatening look.

The lettuce and salad kiosk was emptied in a few minutes. The aide officers displayed a victorious smile; the poor woman had tears in her eyes. The other merchants couldn't do anything against the crows. Whenever these police officers showed up at the market, the merchants were ruined.

- So, as I heard ... There are some good potatoes today!! Exclaimed the police Chief, staring at Dalya with a scornful look.

Dalya remained silent, fearing what will happen in the next few minutes. In a vivid move, the police Chief used one of her empty handmade bags, and he began to fill it with potatoes at his ease. Having completed the first bag, the police Chief handed it to one of his aides behind him, and he said in an amazed voice:

- And well ... well ... There are some pretty pears too!

With a terrified look and a repressed defense, Dalya observed the man while he emptied all her merchandise in the bag, under the malicious laughs of the two aides behind him. At this rate, Dalya won't have anything to sell. And she needed money so much, on that day!

The police Chief handed to his aides, the second bag packed with all the pears of the kiosk.

- But ... These are good carrots that I see here! I have always loved carrots ... they're my favorites ... especially in salads!

Dalya's heart raced, she barely held her tears. Most of her merchandise was stripped today; most of her income was lost today. The police officer robbed almost everything.

Under the forced silence of Dalya, the police Chief finished filling his third bag and he handed it to his aides. Then, the police Chief took a carrot, he cut it with his knife and he chewed it in 2 bites. He picked up a 2nd carrot without even looking at it, he cut it in half and he swallowed it immediately. He took a 3rd carrot; he turned around his eyes to observe the other kiosks, wondering what he could rob them too, while he chewed a 4th carrot ... a 5th carrot...

If there is one thing that no one can tolerate in this world ... it is injustice!

Suddenly, Dalya had an idea. And as terrible as the idea may sound, it was the only way to stop the repression of these three crows.

Dalya observed the police Chief for few moments, he was chewing the carrots quickly, one after the other, while observing the other kiosks all around. Dalya waited for the exact perfect second, and then she gave a quick help tap to a tiny red hot pepper ... that quickly swung down from the upper side of the kiosk ... the tiny red hot pepper swung so fast, and landed right on the very spot Dalya hoped for. The police Chief was observing with satisfaction his aides who were robbing other merchants; he didn't see what his hands were grabbing from Dalya's kiosk. The police Chief cut the vegetable in two, and then he swallowed it in one go!

The show after that moment, was memorable and unforgettable!

In a second, the police Chief became all red. His mouth was wide open, but he has lost his voice and his breath. His eyes were in tears and wide open. His waistcoat buttons detached brutally because of his sudden movements. His hair straightened up. His legs betrayed him, and he crashed to the ground. The other 2 Police aides rushed to rescue their leader, without understanding what could have possibly happened to him. They tried to help their leader to at least stand up, but he was moaning and struggling on the ground.

Dalya hardly retained her laugh, and she forced herself to keep a sorry face, even if she was not really that sorry. All the neighboring merchants didn't understand what was happening to the police Chief, but their hate was common toward the three crows. None of the merchants could hold back their laughs in front of this scene.

Oh, because sometimes ... We don't need to be big and strong to face injustice.

In the street in front of the Toscana restaurant, the great man followed the scene; he was very curious and he wondered why the red face police officer was groaning on the ground. Mr. Wilfrid and Lyor realized that Mr. Balthazar was not listening to their explanations, as it was the case in all the previous Saturdays. The girl in the front street, caught most of Mr. Balthazar's and his Panther's attention. Neither Mr. Wilfrid nor Lyor dared to ask him why so much interest for this unknown little poor girl. They could hardly get 10 minutes of Mr. Balthazar's full attention, without the great man starring toward the other side of the sidewalk.

After about an hour of work, Dalya had already served a few customers. She sold the rest of the vegetables and fruits that the crows forgot to rob. At the Toscana restaurant, the 3 gentlemen had finished their lunch and their work too. Mr. Balthazar, Mr. Wilfrid and the young Lyor, they stood up and wore on their hats and coats.

Mr. Iskander Balthazar was the first to walk out of the restaurant; he paused for a moment in front of his car, doorman who was already holding the car door opened for him, just like every previous Saturday.

Except this time, Mr. Balthazar stood still for a long moment before getting inside his luxurious car. Suddenly, and without caring about the people behind him, Mr. Balthazar bypassed his car, leaving the doorman holding the car door, and he walked straight ahead, with his Snow Panther following him like a shadow.

Mr. Balthazar did something he had never done before, in the past 40 years he visited the Toscana restaurant: he crossed the street. Mr. Wilfrid and Lyor exchanged surprised looks and they seemed confused for a moment, they didn't understand what Mr. Balthazar was doing, and where was he heading. They followed him rapidly, trying to stop all the cars that were about to crush the Governor.

Dalya was cleaning some potatoes that she didn't have time to dust off this morning. When suddenly, she felt a presence in front of her kiosk. She raised up her head to find a familiar face: Mr. Iskander Balthazar, himself!! Standing and smiling in front of her kiosk!! And he wasn't alone. The young man was on his right; the man with the little round glasses was on his left. The Snow Panther stood up on two legs and put her two front legs on the kiosk. Her little head was barely over the counter.

- Good afternoon, Mademoiselle. Said Mr. Balthazar in a friendly voice.
- Good ... afternoon ... Sir. Dalya replied a little embarrassed.

She wondered what Mr. Balthazar could be doing in front of her kiosk. In fact, Mr. Balthazar himself was surprised at what he had done; he didn't quite surely know why he walked to this place. The great man just suddenly felt the strange and unusual desire to be in front of this kiosk. Mr. Wilfrid and Lyor behind him were standing still, they were also curious to understand what has taken the Governor to walk toward the market.

Dalya looked at Mr. Balthazar for a moment, impatient to know what he wanted. But, after a few minutes of silence, and noticing the hesitation of the great man, Dalya dared to say, displaying her prettiest smile:

- We have good potatoes today, Sir ... They will be perfect for your soup ... If you want any?
- Yes ... Yes ... I would like to have a few, please. Mr. Balthazar quickly answered in a happy voice.

Nobody had ever proposed to Mr. Balthazar to buy potatoes, he had never done grocery shopping in all his life, and even less buy from a poor little girl's kiosk. Dalya took a little basket; she filled it with the best potatoes, under Mr. Balthazar's amazed watch and the surprised faces of Mr. Wilfrid and the young Lyor Laszlo. They have never thought to attend grocery shopping with the Governor!

- Would you like me to add you some nectarines, Sir? They come from the best farm in the city. They are very juicy and sweet this summer! Dalya asked the great man, in a cheerful voice.

Mr. Balthazar stared at the poor little girl, all amazed; he let out a little giggle just like a happy child. As if nectarines were the greatest gift anyone could have given him. Dalya addressed the great man in a spontaneous tone:

- Would you like one of my shopping bags, Sir? It's a strong bag, reusable and big enough for all your groceries. I made it myself, Sir.

Mr. Balthazar looked at the pile of the small bags placed on the side of the kiosk. And always as curious as he is, he examined one. It wasn't a refined bag, but robust enough, finely cleaned and sewed. Dalya was proud of her handmade bags. Mr. Balthazar was short of words, just amazed by the many abilities of the poor little girl.

Dalya didn't wait for an answer to her question, she chose the best nectarines, big and beautiful, and she stuffed them in the handmade bag with the potatoes. She handed the full bag to Mr. Wilfrid, who took it immediately. Dalya didn't want to force the Governor to use his shaking hands and carry a heavy bag. And then, Dalya gave two beautiful nectarines to Mr. Balthazar, with a nice smile:

- Offered by the house, Sir!

The great man took the fruits from the hands of the little seller, and he gave one of the nectarines to his Snow Panther, who was still standing on two legs, her head barely above the kiosk. Mr. Balthazar was touched by the caring and considerate gestures of the poor little girl. He took 3 coins from his pocket and he handed them to Dalya, with his trembling hand. This time, Dalya took the money, she looked and counted; she put two pieces in a little pouch next to her and she held out her hand toward the great man. Mr. Balthazar didn't understand what the little girl was returning to him, until he noticed 1 cent back in his hand.

- Potatoes and nectarines are 1 cent, and the bag is 1 cent ... It's just 2 cents for your purchases, Sir ... you gave me 3 cents. Explained Dalya, in front of the confused face of Mr. Balthazar.

Lyor Laszlo, on the right of Mr. Balthazar, let out an annoyed whisper:

- She never stops!

For the first time in his life, someone returned the extra-money to Mr. Balthazar. Dalya could have kept the change, but she didn't. Mr. Balthazar was simply astonished and fascinated by the little girl's behavior and manners. The great man observed her for a moment, and then asked:

- I haven't seen your father today. Where is he?

Dalya went silent in a second, her joyful face and smile disappeared suddenly. Dalya became pale and she lowered her eyes, looking down at her shoes. Mr. Balthazar immediately regretted asking this question, he realized right away that he had just made a mistake. Dalya replied in an embarrassed voice:

- He ... has been sick ... since few days now, Sir. He couldn't get out of bed, today.

Mr. Balthazar understood Dalya's reaction. He couldn't keep himself from being curious:

- And even so ... you came alone today? ... To work, instead of your father?
- Yes, Sir ... someone has to work to buy medicines. It is important for us to continue to work ... in sunny days, but also in rainy ones. Dalya replied, naturally and with an undefeated determination.

Mr. Balthazar smiled with an admiring stare, and then he greeted her:

- Good day to you, Mademoiselle.

She replied back with a smile:

- To you too, Sir...

Dalya watched the great man head back to his luxurious black car, always accompanied by Mr. Wilfrid, Lyor and the Snow Panther. Settling inside his car, the Snow Panther took the seat close to Mr. Balthazar and the two gentlemen sat in front of him. Mr. Balthazar called out the headwaiter before the doorman closed the car's door:

- Where does this little girl's family live?
- In an old house, of two small rooms, in the East side of Georgetown city, Mr. Governor.

The car door closed. During the entire trip, Mr. Balthazar was silent, focused in his thoughts, observing the beautiful big nectarine in his hand. Mr. Wilfrid and Lyor Laszlo couldn't dare to interrupt him.

After a long silent moment, and his eyes still focused on the nectarine in his hand, Mr. Balthazar ordered, in a calm but confident tone:

- Mr. Wilfrid ... do whatever it takes.

Sloan Wilfrid observed the beautiful nectarine in the great man's hand. And as smart as he is, without any more words needed, Mr. Wilfrid guessed exactly what the Governor wanted him to do. He replied:

- Understood, Mr. Governor. Right away.

Suddenly, Mr. Balthazar let out a strange giggle, he murmured in an amused tone:

- Well seen, young Lyor Laszlo ... very well seen ... very well seen ...

Mr. Wilfrid and Lyor Laszlo exchanged a curious look, they were both confused about what the Governor meant by these words. Lyor dared to ask:

- Forgive me ... Mr. Governor. I didn't understand your comment ... What did I see well?

Mr. Balthazar simply looked at the young Lyor Laszlo and he smile at him. The young man was not reassured by the mysterious words and strange smiles of the Governor.

Without losing his smile, Mr. Iskander Balthazar offered the last nectarine to his Snow Panther. He caressed her little head in a caring way and he addressed her in a kind loving voice:

- It will be my last act, Séraphine ... that is all that I can do ... one last act.

The animal looked at her Master. The animal's sapphire blue eyes were as powerful as a thousand storms to come. The Snow Panther seemed to be the only one to have understood what was going on in the head of her Master ... the great Governor Iskander Balthazar.

Chapter 8

Rain drops from the ceiling

Tuesday, June 17th, 1890.

Dalya's father, Antman Bouvard didn't know the identity of the man who dropped the medicine at his home, one month ago, when he fall seriously ill. Antman didn't know why he was requested to attend the Will reading with his daughter, and why his daughter's name was pronounced that day, and who was the deceased man, and why he was requested later to be present at the grand Mansion. So many questions were in his mind, and Antman was eager to find their answers. He was confused about all what was going on around him lately.

Dalya and her father headed toward the grand Mansion, the day after the Will reading. An employee of the grand Mansion, a man of about 50 years old, impeccably dressed in a black white suit and gloves, opened the door. Dalya's father introduced himself:

- Good evening Sir. We are here to see Mr. Ernest Laszlo, he asked us to come here ...

The employee allowed them inside the grand Mansion, immediately. He walked them to the living room, where the Will was read the previous day. But before entering the living room, Dalya felt something following them from behind. She slightly turned around to see the Snow Panther following them a few steps away, walking slowly and calmly.

- Mr. Ernest Laszlo, the man and his daughter have arrived.
- Let them in, Benjamin.

There were not as many chairs this time, in the living room. But always the same luxurious leather divans, colorful carpets, paintings and portraits on the walls.

Dalya and her father met six men sitting in the living room, not including Lyor Laszlo, Mr. Sloan Wilfrid, and Mr. Ernest Laszlo who read the Will the day before. Dalya recognized one man. Mr. Ferdinand Edelmen, the man who walked with a cane, and people congratulated him before the Will reading. He was strangely upset that day, sitting on one of the big chairs in the living room, his hands firmly holding his cane.

Dalya couldn't help but notice a woman's presence. She was the only woman in the living room, and she was a remarkable beauty. She was wearing a long golden silk dress that reflected her long wheat color hair. She was tall and thin. Her skin was smooth and pink. She wore purple diamond earrings which accentuated her beautiful purple eyes, the same ones Mr. Balthazar had. In her mid-forties, and despite her age, her beauty was even more dazzling.

Mr. Sloan Wilfrid, the man with the little round glasses, was the only one to greet Dalya and her father, he asked them to sit down. All the other men sitting in the living room, stared at

54

the little girl and her father, and they examined them from head to toe. Dalya had the strange feeling that she and her father were not welcomed, but she couldn't know why. She felt tension and an intense silence, invading the living room. The Snow Panther had sneaked between the divans, under the silent stare of all the present people and she chose to lay down on a large couch, in the far end of the living room.

Mr. Ernest Laszlo addressed Dalya and her father in an arrogant tone:

- I guess you must be wondering the reason why you have been asked to come here?

Dalya and her father remained silent, facing the men who stared at them in a very curious way. After a long silent moment, Mr. Wilfrid was the first to speak, he explained to Dalya and to her father, in a calm but serious and grave tone:

- The Washington State Governor, Mr. Iskander Balthazar passed away on the night of Saturday, June 14th, after a long and courageous battle against a disease that he contracted, 6 months ago. Despite all the best doctors' interventions, the disease was incurable.

Dalya was unaware that the great man was ill. The last time Dalya met Mr. Balthazar in the Toscana restaurant, he was accompanied by Mr. Wilfrid and the young Lyor. Dalya felt a heartache; she liked the presence of the great man in the restaurant every Saturday. Although she didn't know him very well, and from the few times they spoke, Mr. Balthazar was always respectful and nice to her. Mr. Wilfrid adjusted his glasses, and he continued:

- Last night, on Monday, June 16th, and under the instruction of late Mr. Balthazar, you have attended his Will reading in public. Mr. Balthazar was one of this country's wealthiest men. His fortune was appointed to a sole Heir ... with some very specific conditions.

Looking at Dalya, Mr. Wilfrid seemed a bit hesitant to speak his next words:

- It appeared that ... the Washington State Governor, Mr. Iskander Balthazar ... has named you as ... as His Heiress.

Dalya and her father listened to Mr. Wilfrid's explanations. He spoke slowly and clearly. But despite their following, the little girl and her father couldn't understand the meaning of his words. Dalya's father asked again in a confused voice:

- I ... I don't understand. My daughter is ... Heiress?

Mr. Wilfrid couldn't add a word; he restrained to confirm the evident answer. When suddenly, the Lawyer Mr. Ernest Laszlo straightened up from his chair, he put down his cup of coffee in a brusque move and he spoke in an accusatory tone to his employee:

- Sloan Wilfrid! Can you bother to explain what went wrong? It had to be a normal transfer of fortune! You have treated thousands of same cases!

Mr. Wilfrid replied in a calm and a respectful voice:

- Mr. Ernest ... we have prepared very well all the documents for the transfer of the late Governor's fortune. He asked for a model to write his Will, and we have provided him one. Everything was in perfect norms, and impeccably prepared ...

Mr. Ernest Laszlo was upset not only by the turn of events, but also by the calm of his employee:

- Well then ... where does this girl come from? Why does her name appear in this Will?

Mr. Wilfrid continued in an unfazed and serene tone:

- I don't have any idea about the reason for this decision, Mr. Ernest. But I understand that Mr. Balthazar was free to choose his Hei...

Suddenly, Mr. Ferdinand Edelmen stood up and he yelled with all his strength:

- FREE TO CHOOSE?? FREE TO CHOOSE?? ... MY UNCLE HAD NO RIGHT TO CHOOSE ANYONE EXCEPT ME!!! MY NAME WAS SUPPOSED TO BE IN THIS WILL!!! I AM THE ONLY HEIR!!

The only woman who was in the living room, sitting on a big divan, said in a soft and calm voice:

- I'm not a ghost yet, Ferdinand.

Mr. Edelmen turned toward his sister, Mrs. Honoré Edelmen; he forced himself to lower the tone of his voice:

- Of course, my dear sister ... but that is not the problem.

The woman picked up her cup of tea, while answering him with a beautiful smile:

- Oh but, that's where you have been wrong dear brother. Maybe if you were not so greedy, our dear Uncle would have left you the biggest part of his fortune. But ... wishing to eliminate me from the heritage, and choosing to have everything for yourself ... you have lost everything.

Mrs. Honoré ended her sentence with a giggle, which reinforced her brother's anger, he screamed:

- ERNEST LASZLO! I HOLD YOU RESPONSIBLE FOR THIS! SOLVE THIS RIDICULOUS MATTER IMMEDIATELY!!!

Mr. Ferdinand Edelmen sat down on his divan, exhausted and breathless. But the woman didn't hold herself from sticking the knife even deeper:

- Instead of uniting with your sister, to have this fortune ... you send your straw man ... your distinguished lawyer and friend, to ensure your heritage ... and also our ruin.

A 2nd man spoke in the same sarcastic tone as the woman:

- Mr. Ernest Laszlo, you were supposed to personally work on this case. We had confidence in your professionalism and your experience. But I guess with age, your skills are perhaps fad...

Mr. Ernest Laszlo stood up rapidly, and he interrupted him in an aggressive tone:

- Sir!! I ask you to carefully consider your upcoming words before pronouncing them! I wouldn't accept anyone to doubt my expertise! I have personally met Mr. Balthazar before the formalities of his Will, and it was agreed that Mr. Ferdinand Edelmen will be his Heir...

The woman gave an icy glance at Mr. Ernest Laszlo, the Lawyer changed his words immediately:

- ... With of course, a joint management of the assets and properties with Mrs. Honoré...

The 2nd man asked with a smile:

- Well then ... How do you explain the appearance of this little girl's name instead of Mr. Ferdinand Edelmen?

Mr. Ernest suddenly found himself short of words. Neither he, nor Mr. Wilfrid, nor any of the other men in the living room, had an answer to this question. The 2nd man wasted no time to drive the debate. He seemed to enjoy belittling the lawyer, holding him responsible for this case:

- And Mr. Ernest ... I'm also curious to know why your son's name, and not yours is in this Will? Is it serious to empower a young apprentice lawyer of such a large fortune? Isn't it a risky decision to load a young 21 years old student in his first year of law, of ... BalthEnterprise? ... How did you managed to miss one of the biggest transfers of wealth in this country?

The last sentence of the 2nd man was so humiliating and crushing, Mr. Ernest Laszlo went all red and was about to explode in a second. Mr. Wilfrid felt that Mr. Ernest Laszlo would lose his temper, and knowing his employer's character, better than anyone else, Sloan Wilfrid decided to intervene in a strong and brave tone:

- Gentlemen, allow me to clarify something important. Our work as lawyers and in charge of the heritage of the late Governor's fortune, has been well done and made according to the legal procedures in norm. We have met and evaluated Mr. Iskander Balthazar's entire fortune, we have prepared all the necessary documents and we have followed all the formalities. Now ... when it comes to his successor or the lawyer in charge of his fortune, this choice is up to only Mr. Iskander Balthazar. We are really as surprised as you are, of the way things evolved!
- It's ridiculous! The largest fortune of the United States, is in the hands of a little unknown 12 years old poor girl, with no social-rank, no nobility, no education ... and in the hands of a 21 years old Law student!! There must be a mistake somewhere! Exclaimed a 3rd man in an outraged tone.

- I'm afraid that there are no errors, Sir. We checked the Will at least a hundred times. It is clearly written, without any flaws. Replied Mr. Wilfrid.

A 4th man asked in a curious voice:

- And how can we be sure that the Governor was in a perfect state of mind when he wrote his Will? How can we be reassured that this Will is not an ambush or a forgery?

Dalya and her father remained silent, watching the scene that was unfolding before their eyes and ears, they couldn't dare to interrupt the conversation of these distinguished men and they couldn't ask for more explanations on what was going on. The young Lyor Laszlo remained mute, he was still shocked by his nomination, he didn't move from his chair. Only Mr. Wilfrid ventured to answer the questions of the angry men sitting in the living room.

This time, Mr. Ernest Laszlo recovered his authoritarian and imposing voice, to respond to this attack:

- Gentlemen!! This is the Will written by the late Governor Iskander Balthazar himself, in full physical and mental capacity. We were all witnesses on his last days. He was perfectly lucid and aware of his actions. His signature has been legalized within the authorities. The envelope has been placed in a safe deposit coffret at the Bank with 5 people as witnesses, including myself. This Will was opened in public by the Law that grants me this privilege. For the 2nd and the last time, I forbid you to doubt the credibility of my office!!

After his threatening tone, none of the men dared to doubt Mr. Ernest Laszlo again. A brief moment of silence followed, the 4th man asked:

- In the Will ... There is a reference to some challenges, before having full access to this fortune ... What are these challenges? Why did he require them? How are we supposed to even recognize them?

Mr. Wilfrid replied immediately:

- Mr. Balthazar talked in his Will, about a safe deposit coffret at the Bank, for Mademoiselle Dalya Bouvard. We believe that it contains more clarifications about these challenges ...
- But ... why her? Why did he choose her? Among his family, his friends, all the people he knew ... Why did he choose this unknown little poor girl? Said the 3rd man, who was lost and confused as much as everyone else, by this decision.

Everyone stared at the little girl with a curious look. When finally, the 5th man stood up, he approached Dalya's father, and he addressed him in a nice tone:

- Sir, you do understand that it is a rather unusual situation. Your daughter will inherit a fortune, if she succeeds at the challenges set by Mr. Balthazar. And as you must know, he was a highly educated and wise man, I don't think that these tests will be easy for a poor little 12 years old girl, who have never received any education ... We would like to offer you 1 000 dollars, provided you give up now. It's better than to lose everything, and the fortune of Mr. Balthazar will be spread according to the Law to his real succ...

- But that's illegal! You cannot do that!! You cannot arrange things to suit your way!! Mr. Wilfrid yelled and rapidly stood between the 5th man and Dalya's father.
- Would you like to see Mr. Balthazar's fortune with these strangers? The 5th man lost his kindness and his calm in an instant.

Mr. Wilfrid pulled out his glasses with a quick move, his eyes were shining brightly and audaciously, and the tone of his voice arose for the first time since the beginning of this meeting:

- If these are the wishes of Mr. Iskander Balthazar, then yes! He wrote the Will and he was very clear in it. This girl must pass these challenges, whatever they are, and succeed! And if she fails, only then the fortune will be spread to the members of Mr. Balthazar's family!
- But why are you defending this little unknown girl? Asked the 5th man.

Mr. Wilfrid answered in a strong and determined voice:

- I'm not defending this little girl, I am defending the law! And if these are the last orders of late Mr. Iskander Balthazar, then we are required to obey his wishes!
- This is a unique and complex case ... can't you get around the law? Or find a way to regain control of this fortune? Asked the 2nd man.

Mr. Ernest Laszlo retorted:

- Sir!! If we do not follow the instructions of this Will, the credibility of my office may be put into sake and I don't w...

Mr. Balthazar's nephew, Mr. Ferdinand Edelmen, interrupted him suddenly in an aggressive tone:

- ERNEST LASZLO!! NOBODY CARES ABOUT YOUR OFFICE!! ALL I CARE ABOUT NOW, IS THIS FORTUNE SLIPPING AWAY FROM ME BECAUSE OF A 12 YEARS OLD GIRL!

The woman finished drinking her cup of tea, and she let out a chuckle, all amused:

- A small unknown child shakes the most powerful and important men of the city ... never in my life I thought I'd see my dear brother beaten by a 12 years old girl ...

This time, Mr. Ferdinand Edelmen seemed to lose all control over his nerves. Before anyone could stop him, Mr. Balthazar's nephew rushed straight toward Dalya, his hands clenched and threatening, his evil eyes were darker, he yelled with all his might:

- YOU LITTLE JUNK! I'LL MAKE YOU REGRET THE DAY YOU WERE BOR...

In front of the angry man walking toward her, Dalya jumped from her chair, she wanted to escape from Mr. Edelmen's hands, but she fell immediately to the floor. At this precise moment, Dalya felt a shadow appear so suddenly out of nowhere in front of her and she heard a deafening roar. When she opened her eyes, still shaking and trembling, Dalya was surprised by what she discovered.

The Snow Panther, who was lying down on a divan in the other side of the living room, she flew in a speed of light; she advanced Mr. Ferdinand Edelmen, and she served as a shield to Dalya, who was paralyzed on the floor. When the Snow Panther roared, everyone in the living room was shaken and they all stood up in one move. Mr. Ferdinand Edelmen froze without daring to approach a step further. Even Mrs. Honoré who was calm and joyful since the beginning of the meeting, her sarcastic smile disappeared and she let out a scream of fear. Dalya's father stepped away from the animal that surrounded his daughter. Lyor Laszlo and Mr. Sloan Wilfrid exchanged a puzzled and shocked look. Mr. Ernest Laszlo nearly fall to the ground when the Snow Panther passed a few centimeters by him.

Everyone went silent. Everyone stared at the Snow Panther who protected the poor little girl, fallen to the ground. Never had the animal appeared as aggressive and angry. The Snow Panther launched fierce looks toward everyone, defying anyone to move. Her great allure was hiding almost Dalya's entire body. Her legs were tense, with enormous sharp claws were very well visible. Her mouth wide open showed her shining white and frightening canines. Her hair straightened up; making her tattooed light magnificent gray fur, appear intimidating and terrifying. The Snow Panther was in a defensive position.

No one dared to move or say a word. Everyone in the living room wondered the reasons for the very unlikely and strange behavior of the animal toward this unknown girl. And although Dalya herself didn't understand the reaction of the Snow Panther, she was grateful for her protection from Mr. Ferdinand Edelmen raging anger. Dalya dared to get up slowly from the ground. When she stood up, Dalya realized all the shocked eyes looking toward her. Séraphine didn't withdraw and certainly didn't give up her threatening and defying stare.

After a long tense and silent moment, a 6th man, who was all quiet since the beginning of the meeting, he dared to move. He was the oldest of them all. He spoke in a calm but cold voice:

- Gentlemen ... Gentlemen ... This is only an animal with maternal instinct ... We must admit that we have all been taken by strike in this case. Every move ... every slightest misstep could endanger our credibility of us all. The only thing we can do, for now ... is to wait for this Will to be clarified, and for this little girl to open the deposit coffret at the Bank. A couple weeks more or less, don't really matter. The fortune of Mr. Iskander Balthazar will be indisputably bequeathed to his nephew, Mr. Ferdinand Edelmen and his niece Mrs. Honoré Edelmen. After all ... a poor little 12 years old girl, misplaced only by chance, cannot change the natural course of things.

The come back home was silent. Dalya and her father didn't exchange a word throughout their walk. Each of them needed some time to assimilate what had happened in the grand Mansion. Each of them was trying to convince himself that no, it wasn't a dream, but a reality that they lived. Their lives would change forever.

Entering home, Dalya's father immediately sat on the dining table that was barely holding on its 4 legs. Dalya sat down on the floor, on her rumpled old cover, in her little corner at the kitchen. They both were silent, still in shock. Dalya's mother came out of the bedroom. She had just finished giving a bath to her twins and put them to bed. Realizing that her husband and Dalya were silent, she asked:

- What's going on?

Her husband answered in an evasive voice:

- Our girl ... is rich.

Realizing that his wife didn't understand his words, Antman Bouvard continued:

- Dalya ... is the Heiress of a ... fortune.
- But what are you talking about? What fortune? Dalya's mother grew impatient.

Dalya's father seemed to gradually get back to his senses; his voice brightened up and became more lucid:

- A rich old man died, and ... he left his entire fortune to our daughter Dalya!

Dalya's mother still couldn't understand what was going on, she asked again:

- But how? What for? Why?
- I have no idea. Someone called Sloan Wilfrid said that Dalya must pass ... challenges. If she succeeds, we will have all the money ...

Before she could even understand what it was all about, Dalya's mother brutally grabbed her daughter who was sitting on the floor in her corner, she pinched her daughter's cheeks so hard and screamed at her:

- WHAT DID YOU DO YOU FILTHY IDIOT?? WHAT HAVE YOU BEEN UP TO? HOW DO YOU KNOW THIS OLD RICH MAN? WHY DOES A STRANGER LEAVE YOU HIS ENTIRE FORTUNE?

Dalya answered in a trembling voice, tears in her eyes, standing on her knees while her mother pinched her cheeks even stronger and stared at her with her evil black eyes:

- I ... I didn't do anyth ... I ... I don't know!

Antman didn't care about his wife torturing his daughter, he kept thinking aloud, in a confused voice:

- This old rich man always had lunch at the Toscana restaurant in front of the market ... every Saturday. He couldn't drink his soup ... that's all we know ...

Dalya was unable to defend herself against her mother. She wished the Snow Panther was present at that moment, to protect her from her mother's cruelty.

When Mrs. Augustine finally let go of her daughter's cheek in a brusque move, Dalya fell back on the ground, tears in her eyes, with reddened and burning cheeks. And despite that, Dalya couldn't confess to her parents that she offered the great man a special spoon to help him drink his soup. Dalya herself didn't understand why the great man named her as Heiress. She gave him only a spoon...

- And you think she'll succeed? She's an idiot! She will never be anything more in her life! Mrs. Augustine let out a cruel and piercing laugh before returning to dry a few dishes on the kitchen lever, while saying:
- This isn't even worth a try; she is a good for nothing! And you seriously think, that as incapable and idiot as she is, she can really succeed??

Mr. Antman interrupted his wife:

- But it's an incredible opportunity! If you think I'll let this fortune escape from me, you are a fool!
- I know her, she's my daughter, and I tell you she's an idiot! Augustine yelled, exasperated to see her husband so sure of himself.

Dalya had never heard an encouraging word from her own mother. As weird as it sounds coming from a parent, Mrs. Augustine Bouvard repeatedly said to her daughter that she will forever be a maid to serve her family; she will sell vegetables and fruits on the cart, clean the dishes and do the housework at home, day and night, for the rest of her life. Dalya could never remember any nice, cheering, or attentive gesture from her own mother. Mrs. Augustine never made her daughter Dalya, feel loved and encouraged.

During her parents' conversation, Dalya remained silent in her small corner, hearing her mother saying she was an incapable and watching her father happy to have a fortune in his sight. Mrs. Augustine got irritated of her husband's optimism; she left the kitchen, muttering aloud, without being concerned to hurt anyone:

- She is a less than nothing! She will never succeed! She is a nobody!

Dalya dared to say with a hesitant voice:

- I don't think I can do it ...

Antman Bouvard turned toward his daughter. He interrupted her with an aggressive and menacing voice:

- Oh but of course you're going to succeed! It doesn't matter how hard it is! You have to do it! It's a fortune; I will be rich for life! This money is very important! There is no way I let this fortune get away from me! Is that clear enough, you silly twit??

Dalya didn't understand her father's reaction. It was clear that the Bouvard family was very poor, and this fortune would change their lives forever. But Dalya's father was blinded by this heritage; he became more aggressive and very determined to get it, at all costs. He didn't even know what these challenges were about, and if his daughter was even able to succeed or not. Since the announcement of the Will, Antman Bouvard decided this fortune as a goal ... no matter what the sacrifice may be.

Although June season was hot and the air was very heavy, sudden rain hit Georgetown city, that night. Dalya's father stepped out, just like all previous nights, to an unknown destination, and he wasn't to come back home until very late at night.

Dalya didn't move away from her little corner on the kitchen floor. She hid in her place, she pulled the curtains, and she lay down on the skinny rumpled old cover that she arranged on the hard ground. Dalya observed the rainy sky from the little square kitchen window. The little girl thought about the Snow Panther who protected her, her nomination during the Will reading, the evil look on her mother's eyes when she heard the news, her father's aggressive and fortune goal behavior ... Dalya had many things in her mind, that night.

Dalya's family was so poor, that they lived under a leaky roof. During every storm, drops of rain overwhelmed the two tiny rooms of the Bouvard house. Ten small containers were placed a bit everywhere in the kitchen, to catch the rain emerging from the leaky ceiling.

Some of us would hear the monotonous sound of raindrops on the containers; others will hear the pleasant melody produced by these same raindrops. Some of us will see a cruel poverty; others will see an invincible positivity. What we choose to hear and see, define our lives.

The sound of water drops composed a soft music that Dalya liked whenever it rained. And as uncommon as it can be to see rain in the middle of summer season, life do have fun sometimes sending us some beautifully inexplicable events ... flipping our destiny.

Chapter 9

Everything in an instant

Thursday, June 19th, 1890. 11:00 in the morning.

A black car stopped in front of Georgetown city Bank. Sloan Wilfrid was the first one to step out of the car, he looked cheerful and calm. It was clear that he had a very good night sleep and nothing in the world could upset him. It was a beautiful summer morning, with clear sky and a fresh air.

The young Lyor Laszlo was the second to come out of the car. He had a pale face, dark black circles under his eyes, clearly indicating that he had not slept since many nights now. Lyor joined Mr. Wilfrid, who was admiring the large Bank entrance, with a happy smile displayed on his lips. The young Lyor whispered in a stressed and a nervous voice:

- I'm not qualified for this! I don't have enough experience for this matter!

Mr. Wilfrid replied without losing his smile and his stare at the large Bank entrance:

- Think again Lyor ... you are.
- How can you be so sure? Asked Lyor curious.

Mr. Wilfrid explained in a serene voice:

- Because he nominated you, and only you. And it wasn't someone impulsive, he was well aware of what he was doing.
- He was talking to his Panther, Wilfrid!!
- So, what?? I sing with my parrot, and yet I am a lawyer.
- He named a stranger as Heiress! She was selling vegetables and fruits at the market! He doesn't even know her!
- It was perfectly his right, Lyor. Our job is to only advise the clients, we provide them with all possible options, but we can never force them or influence their decisions.

After a few silent minutes, Lyor asked, with a hesitant voice:

- Do you think that he chose this little girl because of ... because of the Panther's gesture toward her, at the Toscana restaurant? ... That would be insane!

Mr. Wilfrid let out a chuckle:

- This mighty Snow Panther! I like her ... She is incredibly smart!

As much as this situation frustrated and stressed young Lyor Laszlo, Mr. Sloan Wilfrid could not help but be amazed, thinking about their scenes in the Toscana restaurant:

- And I must admit that the little girl is quite unique of her kind. Mr. Iskander Balthazar seemed to enjoy her presence and he liked her.

The young Lyor retorted immediately:

- This is all ridiculous! I don't want to be the guardian of a little 12 years old girl! I have better things to do with my time! I have my Law studies, my lawyer's license to get, the work at my father's office ...

Mr. Wilfrid smiled:

- This little girl seems calm and a bit shy. I don't think she's going to cause us any worry.

Yet, the young Lyor was not reassured:

- But this is insane! It puts me in a difficult situation with my father. I already have trouble enough to work with him in his cabinet ... I don't have enough experience and I don't have my degree yet, I can't afford to upset my father and have him on my back! This little girl puts me in a difficult position ... I can't accept it!
- Oh but I'm afraid that this is no longer your decision, Mr. Lyor Laszlo ... You have been chosen. And it's decided!
- But ... Why me? He was supposed to nominate my father to manage his fortune and not me! Why did he pick me?? He knew very well that I'm an apprentice lawyer; I am only in my 1st year of Law studies!! And he makes me in charge of all his business!! I have the responsibility of BalthEnterprise!! Do you realize what's happening to me? It's more than I can handle! That's impossible!!

The young Lyor Laszlo was confused and concerned about his nomination in Mr. Balthazar's Will. For several days, he couldn't sleep, eat or work correctly, without wondering why Mr. Balthazar appointed him for this responsibility. His father, Mr. Ernest Laszlo, was also shocked and even more upset than his son, because of the Governor's decision. Mr. Ernest was very embarrassed by the turn of events against his friend, Mr. Balthazar's nephew.

When suddenly, Lyor Laszlo declared in a strong voice:

- I refuse this nomination! The legitimate lawyer must be my father! The rightful Heir must be Mr. Ferdinand Edelmen!

Mr. Sloan Wilfrid, who since their arrival, was admiring the enormous Bank entrance, he finally turned around to face Lyor Laszlo. His smile evaporated in an instant, displaying a more serious and somber look:

- Do you think that your nomination was an impulsive decision, Lyor?

Lyor didn't understand Mr. Wilfrid's point. The man continued in the same serious tone:

- It is not an accidental matter or a hazard game. It is one of the biggest fortunes in the United States. This is Mr. Iskander Balthazar, the most famous and the most popular

Governor in this country. He was perfectly lucid and aware of any decision he took. You think you have a choice, but you are wrong. Whether this decision pleases you or not, no matter how many people can't understand this choice, regardless of whether your father and Mr. Ferdinand Edelmen accept it or not ... Mr. Iskander Balthazar has decided to appoint you, and only you as the legal guardian and this little girl as the future Heiress. Period!

Lyor didn't seem very convinced by Mr. Wilfrid's arguments. But he agreed on one point, he had no other choice, no other alternative but to take on this responsibility.

Mr. Wilfrid was the first to see Mr. Ernest Laszlo's car appear at a corner of the street. He turned around toward Lyor before the black car arrived in front of the Bank, and he said in a protective tone:

- You won't be alone, Lyor. I'll be by your side.

The young Lyor was somehow reassured to hear these words. He never considered Mr. Wilfrid as an employee in his father's office, but much more than that. Mr. Sloan Wilfrid was a friend, a counselor and a mentor to the young apprentice.

When the black car finally stopped in front of the Bank, the door opened and Mr. Ernest Laszlo came out. And at first glance, he wasn't in a very good mood. He didn't even greet his son Lyor or Mr. Wilfrid. He asked with an angry voice:

- Where are they?

Mr. Wilfrid replied cheerfully:

- Mademoiselle and her father should be here in fe...

Mr. Ernest didn't wait for the end of this answer. He was already few steps ahead near the Bank entrance, leaving his son and Mr. Wilfrid behind and still.

- I will speak with the Bank Director before their arrival. From now on, I will be personally in charge of this affair. Your incompetence cost us too much, Wilfrid!!
- As you wish, Mr. Ernest. Mr. Wilfrid replied without losing his smile or his politeness.

The Bank entrance was so enormous that Dalya felt so tiny. She paused for a moment to observe the large windows and the great walls of this building.

Although the street was submerged by the summer heat of June month, the inside of the Bank was cooler and chilly. Everything inside was in brown luxurious wood, the shiny parquet floor, the impeccably neat offices, the walls were in polished and carved wood, beautiful giant chandeliers hung from the ceiling in parallel lines. The place smelled brand new wood. Dalya and her father walked in slow steps, preceded by Mr. Sloan Wilfrid and Lyor Laszlo.

At the end of the immense Bank hall, Mr. Ernest Laszlo was talking with some men. When he noticed Dalya and her father, Mr. Ernest stared at them from head to toe in a disgusting gaze. One of the men whispered something to an employee sitting in his office at the reception. The Bank employee stood up, and he asked everyone to follow him through some big stairs leading to the upper floor.

After a hundred steps, they reached the 3rd floor of the Bank. They walked through a long corridor, the ground was in bright gray marble and almost slippery, the walls were painted white; the doors of the offices were all closed in sparkling silver handles. Dalya and her father followed the Bank employee, and the three lawyers.

When the Bank employee stopped in front of a wire gate door separating a corridor, Mr. Ernest Laszlo turned toward Dalya's father, and he explained with an arrogant tone:

- In his Will, the Governor had mentioned placing a safe coffret for this little girl ... Now that my son is her legal representative in this matter, only Lyor should accompany her in the safe room to attest of the opening of the coffret. We'll wait outside.

Dalya continued her way with only the Bank employee and the young Lyor Laszlo. When the three of them arrived in front of a small door, the employee led them inside the room. It was a big room, with an empty desk and 2 chairs in the middle. The walls were filled with thousands of drawers up to the ceiling. Each coffret was labeled in a number and had a small opening to unlock. The Bank employee opened a drawer with a key he already had, he took out a medium coffret. Then, he gently put it on the table. Dalya noticed an inscription on the coffret; it was the same number she heard when the Will was read: 7047-73.

Before leaving the room to let Dalya and Mr. Lyor alone, the Bank employee explained to Dalya:

- Mademoiselle, all the content of that coffret is your property. You may dispose with it at your ease.

Instantly, Dalya sat down on one of the chairs. She carefully opened the coffret and she pulled out of it a small size box in a shiny metal, and 3 envelopes. She put all of the content on the table. Lyor sat down too on the chair in front of her and he watched her, silent and curious.

Dalya took the small box, and she examined it from all sides. It was the first time that she discovered such a strange box. It was a small square in smooth gray metal, without any opening. Not knowing how to open it, or what it was, Dalya put it aside. And she continued to discover the content of the Bank coffret. Dalya read the titles of the 3 envelopes. The first one was in her name, the second one was addressed to Mr. Lyor Kaplan Laszlo, and the third one was written to Mr. Ernest Laszlo. When Dalya handed the last 2 letters to the young man sitting in front of her, he seemed surprised to see those letters in his and his father's name.

Dalya immediately opened the letter and she read the content of a lovely handwriting:

The Sun brightens and softens everything it touches.

And while it offers its light abundantly, it will never cease to shine.

At the right time, and in the right place, you will find, all by yourself,
the answers to all your questions.

Miss Dalya Kartal Bouvard, it was a real pleasure and an honor to
have met you.

Iskander Balthazar

Dalya was short out of words. Although she didn't understand what Mr. Balthazar meant by his first two sentences, Dalya was touched by the joy the great man expressed by knowing and meeting her. She looked at the young man sitting in front of her; Lyor had already opened his own letter and read its content. He seemed as much lost by his letter as Dalya was of hers. Dalya and Lyor were hoping to find answers to their questions:

- Why did the Governor chose Dalya and Lyor among many other people? Why did he select them although he barely knew them?
- Why did he make them both in charge of this enormous responsibility?
- When and where will Dalya know the answers to her questions?

Not only Mr. Iskander Balthazar left no clue to their many questions in his last letters, but his sentences were much more of a puzzle for the little girl and the young man.

Dalya took her letter and the box, and she followed Lyor outside the room. In the Hall, Mr. Ernest, Mr. Wilfrid and Dalya's father were waiting for them, all eager to know the content of that Bank coffret. Mr. Ernest Laszlo asked in a hurried and authoritarian tone:

- Well? Is it done? What was in it?

Antman Bouvard, Dalya's father couldn't help himself from asking his daughter with an enthusiastic air:

- How much money was there in that Bank coffret? How much exactly?

Dalya replied in a small intimidated voice:

- I found only a box and 3 letters.

Lyor Laszlo explained:

- Mr. Balthazar left 3 letters. One for her. One for me. And another one ... for you, Sir.

Mr. Ernest Laszlo took the letter his son handed him, and he opened it in a vivid move. He could barely hide his confusion when he read his letter. In an instant, Mr. Ernest Laszlo became pale, and was clearly shocked. He read the letter several times to make sure he has well understood it. Mr. Wilfrid standing near Mr. Ernest, was also curious about the content of this letter. Sloan Wilfrid came closer to his employer, he readjusted his round glasses, he took a glance at the content of this letter, and he said in a natural voice:

- It seems to be the instructions of Mr. Balthazar for ... for ...

Mr. Wilfrid paused a moment, he looked at Dalya with a surprised air, without being able to hold his laugh:

- Well ... at least that thing is clear enough!

Mr. Ernest gave a cold and upset stare toward Mr. Wilfrid. Dalya and her father couldn't figure out what Mr. Ernest's letter contained. But the Lawyer quickly pulled himself together and he addressed Antman Bouvard in his usual authoritative voice:

- Now that we have consulted the Bank coffret, I request your presence tomorrow morning at 10:00 in the grand Mansion of late Mr. Governor. And ... bring the rest of your family.

Dalya and her father couldn't dare to ask the reason why Mr. Ernest Laszlo ordered them to be present, the next day, at the grand Mansion. They left the Bank, just as confused and curious as before they came in.

That night, Dalya barely slept. In her little corner, lying down on her crumpled cover on the kitchen floor, Dalya examined a thousand times the strange box she had received, trying to guess how the box opens, how it works, if there is something inside, and how it would be used. Dalya also wondered what were these challenges, how is she going to achieve them, and above all how will she recognize them. Dalya read over Mr. Balthazar's letter at least a hundred times, looking for any clue to her questions. Hours of reflection, but without any proper answer.

Friday, June 20th, 1890. The day after the Bank visit.

Mr. Antman Bouvard held his little twins in his arms, walking in front of Dalya and his wife. The little twins wore small caps to protect them from the Sun. They were crazy happy getting out of the house for once and they enjoyed their long walk. They pointed their little fingers at each bird, animal, house or flowers on their way. While Mrs. Augustine Bouvard didn't stop moaning and complaining the entire road to the grand Mansion:

- But why should we come here? What possibly could we be doing here? What does this Mr. Balthazar want from us anyway? Why do we have to walk up till here?

Neither Dalya nor her father could answer these questions, as they themselves didn't have any clear answers.

When they all arrived at the grand Mansion's door, they were received by the same employee as the previous times. Dalya wondered if the Snow Panther will be present this time. But the animal appeared nowhere. The grand Mansion employee made them all enter in the same living room. Mr. Wilfrid and young Lyor Laszlo were sitting on a large divan. Mr. Ernest was standing in front of an enormous window. As soon as he noticed Dalya and her family enter, he stared at them with an arrogant look, and without even greeting them, he ordered with an upset tone:

- Let's get moving!!

Young Lyor Laszlo immediately stood up, and he followed his father. Mr. Wilfrid asked the Bouvard family to follow them. They walked all through a second door on the other side of the living room.

And immediately, they all stepped into an immense beautiful green garden. Mr. Ernest didn't turn back to check whether or not they followed him, he walked toward a specific direction with hurried footsteps. They marched for a few minutes, before arriving in front of a small abandoned house, in the middle of some great and tall oak trees. All the windows were broken, the door was moving forward and backward, the paint had come off, the stairs lacked several steps. It was very clear that this house was inhabited for some long time.

Mr. Ernest Laszlo opened the small house door. The floor was dusty, the furniture was covered in white fabric, and the wallpaper was colorless. It was a pathetic mess. A strong moldy smell emerged from everywhere.

All gathered at the entrance to this small house, Mr. Ernest announced, in a disgusted tone:

- Mr. Governor ... has left instructions in his letter. This House will be allowed for you to stay in, you and your family, until the end of the challenges ... Or more certainly just for the next few weeks, until we figure out a clear explanation to Mr. Iskander Balthazar's Will ...

Dalya's father asked in a joyful and surprised voice, not believing what the grand lawyer meant:

- We can live ... here? In this house?
- 3 bedrooms, a kitchen, a living room. Mr. Balthazar insisted that your daughter should have her own bedroom. Replied Mr. Ernest, with a forced and annoyed tone.
- Thank you, Sir!! Thank you so much!! Dalya's father said, all enthusiastic and excited by this offer.
- It is not me you should thank ... it is only because of the charitable soul of late Mr. Governor. Replied Mr. Ernest in a haughty tone.
- Thank you, Sir!! Thank you very much, Sir!! Dalya's father repeated.
- I remind you that this is all just temporary. Only for the next few weeks!
- Yes Sir!! Thank you very much, Sir! Thank you very much, Sir!

When suddenly, a voice asked:

- But ... why?

Everyone turned around toward Mrs. Augustine Bouvard who spoke for the first time since her arrival in the grand Mansion. The four men were surprised by the woman's question.

- Why are we allowed to live in this house? Why is this man letting us live here? Mrs. Augustine seemed very confused and struggling to understand what was going on.
- It's temporary, only until our daughter passes the challenges. Antman rushed to explain.
- But ... why? Dalya's mother got more upset. Why does he let us live here for free?
- The gentleman has been generous to give us a house to live in. Dalya's father gave a threatening look to his wife, in an attempt to keep her quiet.
- Let's go home!! Right now!! Mrs. Augustine raised her tone.
- We will have a safe roof for the next few weeks. It cannot be refused! Such an opportunity will not be repeated! Dalya's father exclaimed.
- BUT WHY? I WANT TO UNDERSTAND WHY! Ordered Dalya's mother in an exasperated voice.

This time, Mr. Ernest Laszlo took a step toward Mrs. Augustine Bouvard and he yelled:

- BECAUSE GOVERNOR ISKANDER BALTHAZAR DECIDED SO! HIS WISHES ARE ORDERS WHETHER YOU LIKE THEM OR NOT. HIS INSTRUCTIONS ARE CLEAR TO US; THIS HOUSE IS AVAILABLE TO THIS LITTLE GIRL'S FAMILY. IF YOU DON'T LIKE THE HOUSE, WOMAN, YOU CAN RETURN TO YOUR PREVIOUS RAT HOLE!

Mr. Ernest Laszlo replied in a tone so brutal that Dalya's mother didn't dare to say another word. And without giving the family a second to think, Mr. Ernest turned toward the exit door, in furious steps:

- The house will require renovations' work. I don't care about it, handle it yourself!!
- Yes, Sir!! I will do it myself, Sir! Thank you, Sir!! Thank you so much!! Dalya's father followed him.
- So, it's done! The house is yours as from today. Wilfrid, give him the damn keys!! We will meet in a week!!

Mr. Ernest Laszlo headed toward the grand Mansion, followed by his two men. Dalya couldn't believe what had just happened. She and her family would live in a house ... a real house! She will have her own bedroom! She won't sleep anymore on the hard kitchen floor, on her rumpled cover ... but in her own bedroom!

Dalya had thousands of questions in her head:

- Why Mr. Balthazar offered this home to her family?
- Why a house near the grand Mansion?
- What does Mr. Balthazar want from her?
- How did he know that her family was poor and needed a home?

Her little twin sisters, Ari and Adi ran everywhere in the garden. They had already adopted this house. In their previous poor home of two rooms, Ari and Adi lacked space to play. Now, the twins were living a pure moment of happiness, the front garden was a real magnificent paradise for them.

Dalya's father already began planning aloud the renovations in his mind. Dalya's mother didn't seem quite convinced of this generous offer, but she began to clean and remove sheets out of the furniture. She, who loved cleaning, was served and about to be busy for some time.

Before joining her parents inside the new house, Dalya noticed a small white ball lying down in the garden of the grand Mansion. Dalya recognized her even from a long distance: The Snow Panther. The animal watched the new residents of the annex house, in a curious stare.

Dalya's new house was so much larger than their old house of two rooms. Dalya placed the strange box and Mr. Balthazar's letter on her desk. Her bedroom had a comfortable bed, a small desk with an oil lamp, a large closet for clothes, although Dalya had almost none, large windows with breathtaking views on the immense garden. The room required some cleaning and renovations. But despite the dirty windows, the dusty furniture, the almost extinct wallpaper, the wet ceiling ... only one idea occupied Dalya's mind. She didn't fully understand what was going on, but she still couldn't believe that from now on, she had a room all to herself! She won't sleep anymore on the hard kitchen floor, and her rumpled cover ... She will sleep on a bed! ... A real bed!

Saturday, June 28th, 1890. In the annex house of the grand Mansion.

While Dalya and her father were preparing the cart to go out for their usual work at the market in front of the Toscana restaurant, Mr. Sloan Wilfrid's silhouette appeared through the forest. Dalya's father rushed to greet him, in a very enthusiastic voice:

- Good morning, Sir!!

Mr. Wilfrid's eyes were held by the transformation of the annex house of the grand Mansion:

- Good morn... you have done all this work? In one week?
- Yes, Sir!! Replied Dalya's father, proud and happy.

The annex house transformed into a habitable house, within a few days, and thanks to the considerable effort and nonstop hard work. To the delight of Antman Bouvard, he worked all by himself to repair windows and doors, to renovate and repaint the furniture. He added steps on the main staircase, he scratched and put a coat of paint on the damaged areas, he repaired and fixed all the windows and doors of the house. There were basic furniture; beds, dressers, chairs, tables, divan ... and although these new home furniture were worn and old, Dalya's father managed to polish them, clean them up and readjust them, to make them look new and usable.

Dalya's mother complained less and less, the tidying and cleaning of the new house took on her usual negativity. Dalya helped her parents, as best as she could, to bring the few mediocre supplies they owned from their previous home, she also did some renovations' work on their new home. The little twins Ari and Adi were the only ones who didn't care about the renovations, they spent all their time outside in the garden, picking flowers, running and playing.

Mr. Wilfrid could not hide his surprise while discovering the new face of the annex house. He turned toward Dalya and her father:

- Mr. Ernest Laszlo ... requests your presence at the grand Mansion. He is waiting for you. He wishes to discuss with you something important, this morning.

Dalya and her father followed him to the grand Mansion. When they stepped inside the living room, the young Lyor and Mr. Ernest Laszlo were sitting on a big divan. The Snow Panther was lying down comfortably on the best divan in the living room, and no one dared to stop her. The young Lyor was still quiet and almost invisible. While his father, Mr. Ernest looked upset, he seemed angry about this situation that was escaping his control. Mr. Ernest immediately addressed Dalya's father:

- Mr. Governor gave me clear instructions. Among these, a house was allowed to you and your family.
- Yes, Sir. That's very generous from Mr... Dalya's father said before being interrupted by Mr. Ernest:
- Understand that this house is temporary! In a couple of weeks, you will return to your old house! Is that clear enough for you?
- Yes, Sir!! Dalya's father replied.

Speaking to Dalya, Mr. Ernest Laszlo said in a threatening tone:

- I am warning you, little beggar! You are not allowed any whatsoever access to the grand Mansion! I shouldn't find you walking or wandering around in the Governor's residence! I won't accept that a veggy seller ste...

Mr. Ernest Laszlo was interrupted by the Snow Panther, who uttered a grunt. And though the noise was in a low tone, the Lawyer Mr. Ernest jumped in a sudden move. When he turned his head around, the Snow Panther was staring at him with a serene but aggressive gaze. After the previous scene in the living room against the nephew Mr. Ferdinand Edelmen, the Snow Panther terrorized everyone.

Dalya's father asked with a hesitant voice:

- Will this ... animal ... will it remain in the grand Mansion?

Mr. Sloan Wilfrid enjoyed seeing his employer, Mr. Ernest Laszlo, in the collimator of a ferocious Panther. He replied with a large smile:

- Yes. Mr. Governor also left us instructions about his Panther, Séraphine. She will remain at the grand Mansion until the final nomination of the Heir. The grand Mansion employees take care of her.
- Is there a ... risk for us ... to live close to this animal? Asked Dalya's father.

- The Snow Panther is mostly docile and calm. As long as she is not provoked. Mr. Wilfrid was amused to see Mr. Ernest startle at the slightest spontaneous movement of the animal.

Mr. Ernest turned toward Dalya's father:

- And ... Mr. Governor has ordered some other instructions, too. Mr. Iskander Balthazar has charged my son Lyor of this little girl's training and education.

Dalya and her father didn't understand what Mr. Ernest meant by that. The lawyer continued:

- According to the informations gathered about your family, your daughter is an ignorant; she has never been in a school before. Is that right?

Dalya's father was ashamed; he lowered down his eyes, not knowing what to say or what to answer. He had never been able to offer his daughter a school education. He could barely bring his family food and covers.

- Although I see it as useless and a waste of time for this little girl ... the Governor wanted her to have an education at the Royal Georgetown College. I've sent a letter to the school Headmaster to inform him of that.

Mr. Ernest examined Dalya from head to toe, with a disgusted and mocking glance:

- I guess, for the next weeks, this little illiterate and ignorant girl, can occupy her time and learn at least to read and write! Lyor and Wilfrid will take her to school Monday morning at 8:00.

Lyor said:

- I have the Ohand case to prepare before the hearing. I can't take this girl to scho...

Mr. Ernest turned toward his son and he interrupted him with a cold stare and authoritarian voice:

- This is not a request, Lyor! You got yourself into this mess; you will do exactly what I tell you to do! Don't worry about the work, I will ask a more competent person than you are; to handle the Ohand case! You won't be a lawyer any sooner anyway; you are still far away from being one!

After being repressed by his father, the young Lyor didn't dare to add one more word. He replied in a demeaned and humiliated voice:

- As you wish, Sir.
- You will take this girl to school, you and Wilfrid, Monday morning at 8:00! Reaffirmed Mr. Ernest Laszlo in a strong tone.

Dalya was shocked; she couldn't believe what was happening. She had always wanted to attend school like all the other children. Often, Dalya wondered what they could possibly learn in this place, she wondered what it was like inside. She had never dared to ask her father to attend school. Despite her young age, she was well aware that her family was too poor to afford the cost of her education.

Antman Bouvard was happy for all the chances that came to him these last days:

- Thank you for the opportunities you offered to my fam...
- Mr. Governor had a very kind soul ... If it was me, you wouldn't have anything! This is a waste of time for people of your kind! Replied Mr. Ernest, angry and arrogant.

The Lawyer Mr. Ernest continued:

- There is one last thing to deal with. Mr. Governor was well aware of your financial situation, he ordered us to arrange a more stable job for you, in order to meet the needs of your family and ensure a steady income. The Toscana restaurant needs a delivery man, for products and goods, someone who can transports merchandise from the city port into their place. Your salary will be 26 dollars per month.
- Thank you, Sir!!! Thank you, Sir!!! Dalya's father screamed overjoyed.
- It is the Governor you should thank for this. Stick it very well in your head; all of this is just temporary!! Said Mr. Ernest.
- Yes Sir! Thank you, Sir!! Dalya's father replied without being able to contain his joy, before continuing:
- And for the challenges that my daughter has to achieve to have the fortune ...

Mr. Wilfrid explained in a tone much calmer and nicer tone than his employer's:

- Up to this moment, we have no other information about these challenges. Mr. Governor hasn't left us any instructions on this subject. But it is assumed that each thing will come out in its time.

Mr. Ernest Laszlo stood up rapidly:

- I need to go back to much more important business. I've lost enough time with your kind. Now that you are informed of all Mr. Governor's orders, Lyor and Wilfrid will expect this little girl ... on Monday morning at 08:00.

The Lawyer, Mr. Ernest Laszlo stepped out of the living room without greeting anyone, like all the previous times, followed by his son and his employee. Dalya and her father returned to their new annex house, and they picked up their cart. They were speechless and happy of what has just happened. Dalya and her father left the grand Mansion, and they headed to Georgetown city ... for their last day of work in the market, in front of the Toscana restaurant.

In only few days, Dalya's life was completely altered. In only few days, Dalya was nominated in a Will to inherit a fortune, she was given a big house for her and her family to live in, she got a bedroom to herself and a bed to sleep on, her father was given a job and a stable income, and today she had an admission into a school!

Dalya Bouvard received more than what she had ever dreamed of ... everything in an instant!

Chapter 10

An ignorant

Monday, June 30th, 1890.

Dalya was in the kitchen at 7:30 in the morning. She has barely slept the night before, stressing at the idea of attending school for the first time in her life. The day before, Dalya cleaned her best clothes; a white boy shirt and blue denim overall. She tied her hair in her large cap. And she waxed her black shoes to make them look shiny.

Dalya's father was sitting at the kitchen table and her mother was preparing breakfast. When Dalya said good morning, her mother replied in a mocking voice:

- Don't dream too much of staying in this school! They'll throw you out very soon!

Her father didn't hold his laugh while serving himself some more milk.

Dalya never dared to answer her mother's criticism and attacks; she was bullied and terrorized by her mother who took away all confidence from her. Often, Dalya couldn't understand why her mother didn't like her. Dalya was so used to her mother's criticism; not a day passed without her share of offensive remarks from her own mother.

Dalya sat down on the chair by the kitchen table, and she ate silently her breakfast; buttered bread and warm milk. At 7:45 AM, she left the annex house.

In the living room of the grand Mansion, Mr. Sloan Wilfrid was enjoying a cup of coffee and the young Lyor Laszlo was watching the garden through the big windows. When Dalya entered, Mr. Wilfrid put down his cup, and he greeted her with his usual and cheerful smile:

- Good morning to you, Mademoiselle Dalya Bouvard. Are you ready for today?
- Yes, Sir. Replied Dalya in a shy voice.

Lyor Laszlo turned around to stare at Dalya for a moment, and then without a word, he stepped outside the living room. Mr. Wilfrid and Dalya followed him.

Before getting in the car with the two men, Dalya was surprised to find the Snow Panther in front of the grand Mansion's exit door. The animal was sitting motionless, watching the little girl, with a peaceful look. It is only when the car went further and out of sight, that the Snow Panther moved and went back inside the grand Mansion.

All the way in the car, Lyor Laszlo observed the landscape outside, and he didn't address a single word to Dalya sitting in front of him. While Mr. Wilfrid finished reading his newspaper quietly.

A few minutes later, and after a trip that seemed forever to Dalya, they arrived at destination. Dalya stepped out of the car after the two men, to be in front of a building of a Royal splendor. A large red brick building stood in front of them. Hundreds of large square windows. The main gate in black wrought iron was huge. Trees planted around the building stood up majestically. The school was beautiful and intimidating.

Mr. Wilfrid and Lyor Laszlo headed toward the main entrance of the school. On the left corridor wall, many students' portraits were hanged up, with their names underneath. When Mr. Wilfrid stopped in front of a small office, he asked the woman to meet the Headmaster, Mr. Sylvere Darkfett.

She was a big woman about 40 years old, strong and chubby. She had beautiful caramel skin tone, her long light brown hair was wavy and falling on her large shoulders, and her eyes were in a sweet almond color. She was wearing a long green dress. Her office was impeccably well arranged. All the papers and office equipment were very well classified and neatly organized. A small white sign on the front of the office indicated a name, in a nice writing:

Miss Uplerine Amana
Executive Secretary
Royal Georgetown College

The woman led them immediately into the next room. A large desk was placed in the center, the big windows along the wall let on a soft light, several paintings were hung up, and black wooden chairs were placed in front of the large desk.

When Dalya entered behind Mr. Wilfrid and Lyor, she noticed a small man's silhouette behind the big office. He was a small sized man. His shining white hair was irreproachably arranged. A pink skin tone pointed out his wrinkles and his little black eyes. He wore a very refined dark suit. He raised his head from his files as soon as the two men and the little girl entered his office. It was Mr. Sylvere Darkfett.

- Mr. Lyor ... Mr. Wilfrid ... It is a great pleasure to see you!

Despite his smile, Mr. Darkfett didn't inspire any kindness or sympathy.

- Thank you for meeting us Headmaster. Replied Mr. Wilfrid.
- Well then ... It's her ... isn't she? The new ... little ... Heiress? Said Mr. Darkfett all curious, while examining Dalya from head to toe.

Mr. Wilfrid asked him:

- Have you received Mr. Ernest Laszlo's letter, about Mademoiselle Dalya Bouvard?
- Yes ... of course. But I must admit that this situation is quite special.

Director Sylvere Darkfett addressed the two gentlemen sitting in front of him, in a serious tone:

- I'm afraid, gentlemen, that it is not going to be possible.
- How is that? Mr. Wilfrid asked.
- Well ... Mr. Ernest Laszlo, with all due respect and admiration that I have for him ... his request cannot be done. We don't accept temporary students, for only a couple of weeks ...

Mr. Wilfrid replied:

- We still haven't figure out the exact meaning of the Governor's Will. She must pass some challenges, but we have no idea about when or how or what these challenges are. It may take weeks or even months.

Director Darkfett was pleased to add:

- Well ... that is not the only issue, here. All the admissions in this school start at the age of 6 years old, and not after. I am afraid it is way too late to accept a 12 years old girl.
- We have just received this request, only few days ago. Mr. Wilfrid explained.
- Yes, I'm well aware of the facts. Said the Director in a polite tone. But despite this, we cannot admit this girl in our school. Understand, gentlemen, that we have no specific program for ... illiterate people.
- Isn't it a learning school? Aren't you supposed to teach young people to read and write? Asked Mr. Wilfrid, confused by the Director's words.
- Well, yes ... certainly. But in this school, all education levels are organized according to the ages of the students. A 12 years old illiterate girl has no place in our class of 6 years old students! It would be completely inappropriate. The Director let out an amused laugh.
- Can there be an exception or arrangement of any way? Mr. Lyor said with an impatient tone.

In fact, Lyor just wanted to settle this matter as quickly as possible, in order to get out of this school and get back to his work in his father's office. Director Darkfett relaxed on his chair and he announced with a proud voice:

- Since the time that I've became Headmaster of this school, there was never any exception, whatsoever. Understand gentlemen, that this school is the best one in the American East Coast. And by being rigid and inflexible on the terms and conditions of admissions, the Royal Georgetown College was able to maintain its reputation and its high education level. Now, if we start accepting anyone ...

Director Darkfett examined Dalya with a cold stare. Mr. Sloan Wilfrid asked:

- The back to school is in 2 months from now ... September 1st, isn't it?

Director Darkfett understood immediately what was in Mr. Wilfrid's mind, before he could even speak of it. The school Headmaster answered the question, and also the idea behind the lawyer's mind:

- Yes, that's right. But we cannot keep her in our school until then! ... There is no free teacher to be in charge of her. And after all ... what can we possibly teach her?

- It seems to me that it is the only appropriate solution. Mr. Wilfrid defended his idea with an authoritarian tone, before he continued:
- I understand that the first thing you need to do is to make Mademoiselle Dalya pass an admission test, in order to determine her level. And then, you can decide how to improve her weaknesses.
- Her weaknesses?! Director Darkfett exclaimed with an astonished laugh. What weaknesses? We are talking about an illiterate and ignorant little girl! It won't require only some lessons to catch up on her flaws, but she needs an entire education since the beginning! This little girl will have a better place in another school, I'm sure ...

Mr. Wilfrid lost his patience, but not his calm. He took off his little round glasses and he spoke to the Director in a firm and strong voice:

- Director Darkfett ... These are the instructions of late Mr. Governor, Iskander Balthazar. And as his Law firm in charge of his Will, his wishes are orders. Whether you like it or not, Mademoiselle Dalya Bouvard will be admitted into your school!

Director Darkfett seemed forced to act politely toward the two lawyers:

- Well ... we will see what we can do ...
- Mr. Lyor and I have some work to attend to, this morning. I am aware that her admission tests will take some time. We will come back to pick her up at ... say 4 p.m.?
- Yes ... Of course, gentlemen.

Mr. Wilfrid and Lyor left the office, leaving Dalya alone with the school Headmaster. He observed Dalya some long minutes, which seemed an eternity for her, before saying:

- A little illiterate and ignorant girl ... who dares to claim the fortune of Mr. Governor ... in my school ...

Dalya was intimidated and uncomfortable. She couldn't dare to look up at the Director, who was staring at her in a contemptuous and disgusted look.

- I guess that this situation is paradoxical and quite unusual for a little veggy seller girl.

Dalya couldn't answer. The Director continued, always in a cold voice:

- I must inform you that only the children of noble blood, the Heirs and the sons of diplomats are permitted an education in this school, so they can manage their fortunes and matters of this country. People like you ... people of your kind should just work. They don't need to read or write ... or even attend schools.

In front of Dalya's silence, the Headmaster sighed:

- But ... given Mr. Governor's generosity toward a poor little girl ... we are asked to momentarily allow you to be in this school. Now, we will make you pass a first level test, of alphabets and numbers, it will help us determine how to rebuild your education. Follow me.

Dalya's stress and nervousness increased as they roamed the long empty corridors of the school. Director Darkfett's welcome was not kind at all. Dalya feared what was about to follow.

After a short walk in the empty school hallways, Director Darkfett took Dalya into a classroom. There were many chairs and small tables arranged in a symmetrical way. A big desk was placed in front of dozens of chairs. The chalk board was so huge; it was hanged across the room. Inside the classroom, a man waiting for them, was sitting in front of the big desk.

- Professor, here's the new ... girl, I told you about.

The awaiting man was the complete opposite of the school Headmaster. He was tall and slim. A middle-aged man. He had brown bright hair, a light tanned skin tone, a big smile that unveiled his perfect white teeth, enthusiastic and joyful brown eyes. He was wearing a blue checked suit and a nice bow tie.

- She will not be a student in this school. But we have to make her pass an admission test. I will let you be in charge of it. I will be in my office. As soon as you're done, let me know immediately!
- Yes, Director. The Professor said with an active voice.

Director Darkfett observed Dalya one last time, before leaving the classroom and letting her alone with the teacher.

- Good morning, I'm Jullien Canfield. But you can call me Professor Canfield. I'm very pleased to meet you, Mademoiselle. The Professor said, in a cheerful tone.

She smiled and replied timidly:

- Good morning Professor, I'm Dalya.
- Oh, I know who you are! Everyone knows who you are! He exclaimed with an amused tone, before adding:
- Now, we have many tests to do. It looks like a busy day ahead of us. Shall we start?

The Professor picked up some papers from his office and he nicely asked Dalya to take a seat in front of a small desk. He placed in front of her some papers and a pencil:

- Let's start with the alphabets. Here is a blank paper; I would like you to write the alphabets that you know. I would also like to hear you say them, so I can know your pronunciation level. Even if you skip some, don't worry. Just write everything you know.

The Professor sat on a chair near Dalya, to catch a better sound of her voice, without losing his friendly smile. Dalya hesitated a few seconds, then she took the pencil and she wrote on the white paper, pronouncing timidly:

- $\mathcal{A} \mathcal{B} \mathcal{C} \mathcal{D} \mathcal{E} \mathcal{F}$...

All of a sudden, Professor Canfield lost his smile and he interrupted her:

-   Hold on a minute! How ... but ... how many alphabets do know you, Mademoiselle?

Spontaneously, in a timid voice, Dalya replied:

-   All, Professor.
-   But it's not what I have been told ... are you familiar with numbers, as well?
-   Yes ... Professor.
-   Can you count? Subtract? Multiply?
-   I think so ... Professor.

Professor Canfield repeated his question to make sure he didn't misunderstand:

-   But ... so ... can you read, write and count?

Dalya inclined her head to confirm. Professor Canfield regained not only his big smile, but also a shocked face expression:

-   But ... The Director ... he told me that you can't read, or write. Why didn't you tell him that you did?
-   He didn't ask me ... Professor. Dalya answered.

Professor Canfield laughed. Dalya couldn't guess why. The Professor stood up and left the classroom, to come back a few minutes later, with a pile of papers in his hands, and in a cheerful tone, he said:

-   Mademoiselle ... given that you can already read, write and count, I would like to test your knowledge then! I will make you pass some tests of the same age as yours, 12 years old students.

Professor Canfield placed on Dalya's small desk a paper:

-   We will start with the 1st test: Literature. Here is a 10 questions quiz, on the knowledge that students of your age have already mastered. You have 30 minutes to answer. Read the questions many times and write down everything you know about the subject.

Dalya took the paper in front of her and she read the questions one by one:

Question 1: what is the stories series for which Mr. Thomas Malory is most well-known?

Question 2: what is a sonnet in Literature? And who introduced it at the beginning of the 16th century?

Question 3: who is the author of the book called Utopia? When was it is published?

Question 4: the Farie Queen Poem, who does it refer to? Who is the author? When was it published?

Dalya didn't finish her reading until the 10th question, she had no idea what it was talking about, nor who was Mr. Thomas Malory, she never heard of Utopia or the Farie Queen Poem. Dalya froze in front of the quiz paper. After 5 silent and immobile minutes, Dalya raised her head toward the teacher sitting in front of her, in his big office. Professor Canfield looked at her with an encouraging smile; he understood the little girl's motionless. The Professor stood up, he took the old quiz paper, and he placed a new one in front of Dalya, while addressing her in a kind voice:

- The Literature is somehow a difficult class. We'll try again with a 2nd easier course: Arts. You also have 30 minutes to give your answers. Just do the best you can.

Dalya read the 2nd quiz paper:

Question 1: who is the artist of the painting called: the disheveled girl?

Question 2: identify the 3 types of prints reproduction?

Question 3: explain in more details the watercolor paper making?

Question 4: in what kind of painting the artist Jan Van Dael is specialized in?

This time again, Dalya didn't know what it was all about. She had never heard of the disheveled girl or Jan van Dael ... Dalya froze, not knowing what to say or what to do. Because of her silence, the Professor guessed that Dalya had no knowledge of Arts either. To help her de-stress, Professor Canfield said in an amused tone:

- You know ... There is one advice that I always say to my students ... Whatever the questions in front of you, never return an exam paper without writing a word in it.

Professor Canfield stood up, and he continued:

- For example ... If you are asked to describe the ear, and unfortunately you know only the eye's description. Then you can write: the ear is not the eye, because the eye is a vision organ that allows us to capture the light and images of our environment ... even though it may seem off topic, the more important thing is to try and do your best.

Professor Canfield displayed a cheerful smile:

- And you never know, maybe the person who will correct your test paper, might like the eye's description better than the ear one!!

Dalya smiled. Professor Canfield approached her, he took the 2nd quiz paper and he handed her a 3rd one:

- Here is the 3rd test in History. There are 20 questions. Take all the time you need.

Dalya examined the paper:

Question 1: who is the 1st President of United States of America? In which year was he elected?

Question 2: what were the 3 powers cited in the United States of America constitution in 1789?

Question 3: explain in more details the independence war of the United States of America.

After few seconds of hesitation, Dalya took the pencil and she wrote on the paper. It was the first move that Dalya made since the beginning of her test. Professor Canfield sat on the desk in front of her, pleased that he encouraged the little girl to do her best.

Dalya remained focused on the paper for a few minutes. Professor Canfield quietly watched the little girl work in front of him. When Dalya put her pencil down, Professor Canfield realized that she had completed her quiz; he stood up, he took Dalya's quiz, and he read her answers, immediately and curiously. In an instant, Professor Canfield's happy face vanished and became a puzzled look. His friendly smile instantly disappeared, and he observed the little girl, in a confused serious stare.

After seconds of silence, Professor Canfield pulled himself together; he placed a new paper on Dalya's desk, and he said in an oddly serious tone:

- Here is the ... 4ᵗʰ test: Mathematics. You have 35 questions.

The Professor sat back on his chair, without taking his eyes off Dalya. She read the paper:

Equation 1: 7047 / 73

Equation 2: 284 * 97

Equation 3: 101-2017

Equation 4: 408 + 2016

Dalya took her pencil, and she wrote down her answers in a slow movement. After a couple of minutes, Dalya put down her pencil, and she looked at the Professor. The man hesitated for a moment, not understanding what was going on, when he finally asked the little girl:

- Is everything alright, Mademoiselle?
- Yes, Professor ... I finished. Dalya replied in a shy voice.
- You finished ... the Mathematics' quiz?
- I think so ... Professor.

Professor Canfield stood up, he took the paper, and he quickly read the content. Dalya still couldn't understand the confused expression on the man's face. Professor Canfield put in front of her, another quiz:

- Here is the 5ᵗʰ subject: Physics.

For all the evaluations, Dalya wrote down the answers she knew. She was somehow sure of her answers; she did her best and wrote everything she knew about the questions. Dalya didn't exceed 10 to 15 minutes to complete and give back her papers. And during all the evaluations, Professor Canfield had the same confused expression on his face. The smile he displayed when he first met Dalya, didn't appear anymore. Professor Canfield looked serious and puzzled.

After about an hour in the classroom, Professor Canfield sat back on his desk, he reviewed all Dalya's answers a 2nd and a 3rd time. He observed the little girl with a curious look, for several minutes. Dalya didn't understand Professor Canfield's attitude. When finally he stood up and he addressed Dalya, in a hesitant voice:

- Mademoiselle ... I'll ask you to please wait here, for a minute.

Professor Canfield left the classroom, leaving Dalya sitting alone. She had never been in a school before. Dalya had done her best and wrote all she knew. But several questions tormented her:

- Isn't it what Professor Canfield advised her to do? To write everything she knew?
- Then why the Professor's face and attitude changed when he read her answers?
- Was she really ignorant like everyone thought? Were her answers all false and ridiculous?
- Her mother who has always told her that she was an idiot and a failure, was she right? Was Dalya that incapable?

Professor Canfield came back into the classroom, holding a stack of papers. He put them down on his desk, and then he spoke to Dalya, in a nice tone and with a nervous strange smile:

- Mademoiselle Dalya ... I would like you to pass some more tests, if you don't mind.
- Yes, Professor ... Dalya replied in a small voice.

Professor Canfield gave Dalya many quiz in the same subjects as the previous test. Dalya answered as best as she could the courses of History, Mathematics and Physics. And Dalya was unable to write a single word on the courses of Literature, and Arts. During this entire 2nd evaluation, Professor Canfield observed Dalya with his complete attention. He remained silent, eyes focused on the little girl who was answering the tests.

When Dalya finished writing her answers of the last Physics question, Professor Canfield came near her, and he read Dalya's paper. And just like all previous times, Professor Canfield re-read Dalya's notes 2 to 3 times, looking at her with confused glances. Dalya watched the teacher's odd behavior; she gathered some courage and said in a shy voice:

- I have ... never attended school, Professor. Director Darkfett is well aware of that ... I wrote everything I knew, Professor ... my answers may not be corr...

But Professor Canfield didn't listen to any word that the little girl was saying, he seemed disoriented. The teacher replied, in a serious voice:

- I will be back in a minute. Please don't move from here!

Professor Canfield came back minutes later, accompanied by Director Darkfett himself. The teacher gave all Dalya's quiz papers to the Headmaster. Director Darkfett briefly read all the answers, and then after several seconds of silence, he looked at Dalya and exclaimed:

- But ... this is impossible!

Dalya couldn't understand Professor Canfield's nor Director Darkfett's reaction. She remained still and silent, in front of the two men who strangely stared at her. The Professor looked amazed and surprised; the Headmaster was clearly upset and angry. Without lowering his cold stare off Dalya, the Director yelled all furious:

- HOW COULD SHE HAVE CHEATED?!

The Professor answered instantly:

- Director! I was here in front of her during all the tests, it is impossible that she could have cheated in any probable way...
- BUT IT'S IMPOSSIBLE!! DON'T YOU UNDERSTAND?? IT'S IMPOSSIBLE!!

Professor Canfield gave the Director all the other quiz papers:

- Yes, Director ... I understand that it is impossible. And yet, these answers ...

Director Darkfett couldn't hold back his anger:

- She cheated! She surely played a trick on you! She will pass a 3rd test. Bring over another evaluation, immediately! This time, I'll be sitting here and I'll watch her myself!

Professor Canfield was disappointed of Director Darkfett's reaction. He was quite sure that Dalya didn't cheat. Director Darkfett sat down on a chair right in front of Dalya; he stared at her in a cold and menacing way. The 3rd evaluation included exactly the same subjects as the 2 previous tests. And Dalya answered the same previous subjects, and she couldn't answer the same subjects as before.

Director Darkfett was silent and angry during the entire 3rd evaluation, while Dalya answered the questions and Professor Canfield put on her desk, one quiz after another. This time, the Director himself corrected all Dalya's test papers. And after a long silent moment, he ordered to Professor Canfield with a furious voice:

- Send a messenger to request the presence of Mr. Lyor and Mr. Wilfrid! It's urgent!!

Dalya was sitting on a bench in the school main hall, in front of the Secretary's office, Miss Uplerine Amana. The woman was observing the little girl, with frequent discreet glances, while placing papers in a large folder. Dalya couldn't understand everyone's reaction; previously, Dalya was almost invisible. And right after her name was mentioned in the Will, everyone kept staring at her in a strange way.

After some long waiting minutes, the young Lyor Laszlo and Mr. Wilfrid appeared in the entrance of the school. Lyor looked very upset. He ignored Dalya sitting in the lobby, and he quickly entered the Director's office, followed by Mr. Wilfrid. A few seconds later, Dalya heard her name called from the next office. When she entered, Lyor Laszlo, Mr. Wilfrid and Professor Canfield were all sitting on chairs in front of the big desk; Director Darkfett was motionless in his seat.

- I hope it's worth interrupting us in the middle of a business meeting. What is it now? Said Lyor with an impatient tone.
- We thought that Mademoiselle Dalya's test would last at least all day. Asked Mr. Wilfrid.
- I'm sorry to inform you, gentlemen, that we have a problem, the Director said in an annoyed tone.
- Mademoiselle Dalya Bouvard's test is completed. Said Professor Canfield, with a large enthusiastic smile.
- Already? Lyor said. I'm assuming that it's a hopeless case ...
- Oh ... but it is not quite what we have expected it to be. The Director handed Dalya's evaluation papers to the two gentlemen.

Mr. Wilfrid and Lyor Laszlo took the quiz papers, without guessing the reason behind neither Professor Canfield wild smile nor Director Darkfett pale face. While reading Dalya's answers, Lyor's anger and Mr. Wilfrid's calm vanished, and was replaced by a state of shock. Mr. Wilfrid and Lyor exchanged a disoriented and confused look. After a silent moment, Mr. Wilfrid asked the Director:

- All these answers were provided by ... Mademoiselle Dalya Bouvard?

All four men already knew the answer to this obvious question, but they struggled to accept it. Director Darkfett was forced to reply and confirm:

- Yes.

Professor Canfield was very pleased to add:

- These evaluations normally take 5 to 6 hours. Mademoiselle Dalya provided answers in the subjects of History, Mathematics, and Physics. The only 2 subjects she didn't answer to are Literature and Arts. Mademoiselle Dalya passed the tests 3 times ... and the last evaluation was in the presence of Director Darkfett himself.
- How is this even possible! According to our informations, this girl has never been in a school before, in her entire life. Both her parents are illiterate. It is ... impossible! Repeated Mr. Lyor after reading the quiz papers for the 4th time.
- And you made her pass the tests ... 3 times? Asked Mr. Wilfrid.

Professor Canfield displayed his most joyful smile, with which he greeted Dalya the first time they met. Professor Canfield explained proudly:

- Yes, Mademoiselle went through 3 evaluations. The first quiz was a test of the same age class, 12 years old. The second and third quizzes were tests of an advanced class, of 15 years old students.

Lyor Laszlo asked Dalya, in a surprised tone:

- How did you manage to answer all these questions?

Mr. Wilfrid let out a giggle:

- She knows the different legal powers mentioned in the constitution!! I wasn't aware of them before my first year of Law studies!!

Dalya looked down at her feet; she didn't know what to say. She was intimidated by the 4 men, and even more by the situation. She didn't understand what she had done wrong, and why these men were surprised by her answers. Noticing her shyness, Professor Canfield approached her. He asked in a nice voice:

- Mademoiselle Dalya Bouvard. We would like to understand how a little girl like you, answered all these questions. Is it true that you have never been to school before?

Dalya answered no by a head sign. Professor Canfield continued:

- Alright. Has someone ever helped you follow a training program? Do you have a teacher in your family? Apart from your parents … a friend or an uncle or a cousin?

She answered no by a head sign. Professor Canfield went on in a friendly tone:

- Then ... Let's start from the beginning. Who taught you to read and write?

Dalya said timidly:

- My paternal Grandfather ... Idriss Bouvard.
- Did he teach you History, Physics, and Mathematics?
- No, Sir ... He passed away when I was 7 years old. He taught me only letters and numbers.
- I'm sorry for your loss. Said Professor Canfield in a sympathetic tone. So then, your paternal Grandfather taught you the alphabet and numbers. But then how did you accumulate all this knowledge? Where did you learn all of this from?

After some hesitation, Dalya finally said:

- I don't know, Sir ... You told me to write down everything that I knew ... and that's exactly what I did ...

Professor Canfield explained with an amused tone:

- Mademoiselle Dalya Bouvard ... you probably don't realize what is happening here, but you have passed tests of an advanced level than your age. All the answers that you have written are perfectly correct. And if you have answered right in all these tests, that makes you a very smart little girl ... and it is a quite special gift ... do you understand what it means, Mademoiselle?

Dalya had never thought to be a smart person. No one has ever told her that she was smart. It was the first time in her life that she heard this remark. Her mother always told her that she was an idiot. Her father cared more about money than his daughter's intelligence or education. Dalya looked at Professor Canfield, and she replied in a hesitant voice:

- I like to read.
- Ah!! ... But that is amazing! And what kind of books do you like to read? Where do you have access to books? Asked Professor Canfield.
- Oh no ... we don't have enough money to buy books, Sir ... There is Alfie jaq, a friend of mine, who delivers me the daily morning newspapers, and in return, I prepare him a fruits and vegetables' basket.
- You read newspapers? Mr. Wilfrid amazed, let out this question, while readjusting his round glasses and looking more closely at the little girl.

The four men watched Dalya, trying to understand this strange little girl. Professor Canfield continued in an uncertain tone:

- So then ... If I understand correctly, you read the newspapers every day?
- Yes, Sir ... That's all what I can afford. They talk about a lot of things.

Professor Canfield guessed little by little Dalya's knowledge source:

- Yes ... you are very right ... There's an extraordinary amount of information in the press articles ... and how did you know the answer to question 2 of History, for example?

Dalya's voice seemed more confident:

- It was in the newspaper a few weeks ago. An article talked about the 3 powers of the constitution, defining the power of the new president after his election ...

Dalya explained and spoke with much more confidence and ease. The four men sat still, with a stunned and shocked gaze. Never in their lives, they thought they would meet such a phenomenon. When Dalya went silent, Professor Canfield exclaimed:

- It's fascinating! ... Simply fascinating! ... The press allowed you to have knowledge in History. And then, how could you solve Mathematics equations so quickly and faultlessly?

Dalya thought for a minute, and then she replied:

- I work with my father; we sell fruits and vegetables on a cart, all around the streets of Georgetown city. And once a week, on Saturday, we set a kiosk in the market in front of the Toscana restaurant. It's our only day of stable income. During that day, we must serve the customers very fast to make the most sales possible ...
- ... And so, you have to quickly calculate the sales' amounts. And that's how you acquired a great knowledge in Mathematics!!

Professor Canfield completed Dalya's sentence, with a surprised and amazement expression on his face, he was happy to have been the first to discover how smart this little girl was!! Mr. Wilfrid too seemed to understand a little more the particularity of Dalya. He asked in a friendly tone:

- And for Physics? Where have you learned ... quantum force, for example?
- I love spending time in my uncle Giorgi's place. Nobody understands his language and his words, he sounds and looks weird, but he is nice. I deliver him a vegetables and fruits basket, every week at his workshop. He creates many gadgets, useful and practical ones. He teaches me how it works and he shows me many things whenever I visit him ...

The four men looked even more stunned than before. They never met a person of this intelligence, without previous education. Director Darkfett finally said after a long silence:

- The Literature and Arts aren't her strong points ...

Professor Canfield interrupted him quickly:

- Because we teach these subjects only in schools and academies. Yet, this little girl excels in the most difficult subjects. Even our best students can't reach her results in a record time. With her intelligence and her great ability to assimilate all the information she receives, Mademoiselle Dalya Bouvard can learn the entire program of Literature and Arts in only few months!
- And therefore ... in what class can you place her for the upcoming school year, in September? Asked Mr. Wilfrid.
- I'm afraid that this is where the problem occurs!! Replied Director Darkfett.
- May I suggest placing her in the 1st graduate class, with 15 years old students? Professor Canfield replied excitedly.
- But it's impossible! Director Darkfett nearly jumped out of his chair. She is barely 12 years old. If she is placed in this level, it would be a risk to our own students. That's absurd!! And then, what's next?! Tomorrow she'll come back to teach us what the GDP of a country means ... This is ridiculous!!

A little shy voice pronounced three simple words:

- Gross Domestic Product.

The four men turned around their heads toward the little 12 years old girl. She spoke with a shy little voice:

- For ... the measure of the monetary value of all finished goods and services produced in a country ... I think. It was explained in the newspaper a month ago ...

Professor Canfield was fascinated and over the moon. Director Darkfett was furious and pale. Mr. Wilfrid took off his round glasses and he couldn't hold his laugh at this unexpected situation. The young Lyor Laszlo was confused and upset.

On their way back to the grand Mansion, in the car, Lyor Laszlo observed Dalya for the first time since they have met. Sitting in front of him, Dalya felt the stares of the young man on her. Dalya avoided his eyes by looking at the gardens and houses on their way back to the grand Mansion. No word was pronounced. Upon their arrival, Dalya came out of the car. Mr. Sloan Wilfrid leaned toward the door and he said in an amused voice:

- Your classes will start tomorrow morning, Mademoiselle. You must be at school at 8:00.

Mr. Sloan Wilfrid smiled at her and closed the car's door. Dalya observed the car on its way back to the city, and then she turned around toward the annex house.

Passing through the grand Mansion, Dalya didn't have to look too far to find the Snow Panther. The animal was standing inside one of the living rooms in the grand Mansion; Séraphine was watching every movements of the little girl through the large windows. Dalya wondered why the animal always stared at her? Does this animal follows everyone else, or is it just Dalya? Séraphine was a very strange creature.

Dalya's mother, Mrs. Augustine was busy hanging long white sheets on the freshly installed wires. Dalya's little sisters were playing at chasing a ball outside in the garden, and as soon as they noticed Dalya approaching, they ran toward her, screaming happily like they always used to do:

- Dindin!! Dindin!! Dindin!!
- You are home so early! Did they throw you out already? I bet they realized you're an idiot fast enough!! Her mother laughed with an amused tone, while continuing to hang the laundry.

Dalya couldn't say a word to her mother about the evaluations and tests that Professor Canfield and Director Darkfett made her pass. Dalya sat on the grass in the small garden and she watched her little twin sisters racing after the ball, laughing full hearts.

Something strange was on Dalya's mind, since she left the school minutes ago. Professor Canfield told her that she was smart. But ... her own parents had repeatedly told her that she was an idiot and a good for nothing, for as long as she can remember. That's what Dalya always believed about herself. She was convinced that she was an ignorant. Dalya was confused; who should she believe? Who was right and who was wrong? Her own parents or a teacher she has just barely met?

That day, for the first time in her life, the little 12 years old girl doubted herself; was she as smart as Professor Canfield said ... or idiot as her own parents made her believe?

Chapter 11

The first day of school

Tuesday July 1st, 1890.

At 7:15 AM, Dalya crossed the immense garden of the grand Mansion. And just like the previous times, the Snow Panther was waiting for her at the main door entrance of the Mansion. Séraphine was early up, sitting on a wall. Dalya went on her way, occasionally turning back her head to check if the Snow Panther was still staring at her. Séraphine didn't move, she watched the little girl walking along the road until she disappeared.

8:00 AM precisely, Dalya was sitting on a bench, in front of the Secretary's office. The school was empty because of the summer holidays. The Secretary, Miss Uplerine Amana, was watching in discreet and curious glances the little girl, while writing on a large registry. After few minutes, Director Darkfett rang and Miss Uplerine Amana spoke to the little girl in a nice voice:

- Mademoiselle Dalya Bouvard. The Headmaster is waiting for you.

Director Darkfett was sitting behind his big desk. He raised his head toward Dalya and greeted her with an arrogant tone:

- I had one last hope of not seeing you here, this morning!

He stood up and came in front of Dalya, to better examine her, with a menacing stare:

- I would like to make it very clear for you! This prestigious college is reserved only to the nobility, and not to people like you. We never allow in ignorant and veggy sellers, like your kind. Your yesterday's evaluation was pure luck. I will not let an illiterate and an ignorant little girl like you, smearing the reputation of this prestigious academy. Do not enjoy yourself too much here ... for I will not allow you to stay for long!!

Director Darkfett took a paper from his desk and he handed it to Dalya, in a forced and arrogant way:

- This is the special program of private courses you're going to take with Professor Canfield. I will never consent to allow you in class with other distinguished students! You are attending this school, only for a couple of weeks. After all, it would be indecent to let the noble students of this school be joined by a veggy seller ...

Dalya had never expected a welcome, but she didn't expect all this aggressiveness either. She couldn't understand why Director Darkfett was very hard and cruel with her. She could only stay silent and lower her eyes. When Director Darkfett asked her to return back to the classroom where she passed her tests the day before, Dalya obeyed immediately. When she was in the hall, Dalya felt relieved to be away from the school Headmaster. Professor Canfield was already waiting for her in the classroom. And just like the previous day, he greeted her with his joyful smile:

- Good morning Mademoiselle Dalya Bouvard! I am delighted to see you here among us!

Dalya sat on the chair in front of him. Professor Canfield continued in a cheerful tone:

- When Mr. Governor told me about you, he was impressed by your astuteness and your bright mind. But ... I had no idea of your cleverness!

Dalya was unable to hold herself back, she asked in a curious voice:

- Did you know Mr. Iskander Balthazar?

Professor Canfield replied proudly:

- Yes. Iskander Balthazar and I were an old acquaintance. We are of the same German origin. Our families have emigrated in this country, on the same boat ...

Dalya jumped:

- Did he tell you why he chose me as his Heiress? Why me and not someone else of his family or friends? Why did he allow me and my family to live in the annex house near the grand Mansion? Why did he insist I study in this school? Why do I have to undergo the challenges to get his fortune? And what are these challenges? And how can i...

Professor Canfield was surprised by the many questions of the little girl; he interrupted her with an innocent laugh:

- Oh, Mademoiselle!... I'm afraid I don't have all the answers to your questions!

Dalya said in a pleading voice:

- It's because ... it's because Mr. Balthazar left me no explanation of his decision.

Professor Canfield sat down near Dalya, and he replied:

- Since the time that we met, Iskander was always a visionary man; all his decisions were very well calculated and extremely well planned. I don't have a slightest idea on why he chose you as a potential Heiress, or what are these challenges that you will have to pass. Nonetheless ... There is no doubt that Iskander Balthazar noticed something in you. Perhaps you don't realize it yet ... but I'm confident and convinced that time will unleash many answers.

Dalya dared to ask one more question that occupied her mind, for a long time:

- Professor ... Mr. Balthazar's Snow Panther ...

- You are wondering why she protected you the other night, against the nephew ... against Mr. Ferdinand Edelman's attack?

Professor Canfield guessed effortlessly the little girl's thought. Everyone in Georgetown city knew about this incident ... but nobody could properly explain why the Snow Panther Séraphine had acted that way. The animal had always been very docile and calm.

- It's just that ... she follows my every move. Whenever I walk through the garden of the grand Mansion, she's always present and staring at me. Explained Dalya.
- Séraphine was very attached to Iskander Balthazar. I guess that after losing her Master, she feels a little lonely. I think it's just her curiosity about her new neighbors, you and your family. And yet ... it is only but a hypothesis. Despite all of our scientific progress, we still don't know much about animal's behavior.

Dalya was a little disappointed to have no clearer answers to her multiple questions. Professor Canfield observed the little girl, for a long moment with a slightly more serious gaze. A strange thought occupied Professor Canfield's mind. He thought aloud:

- For a long time, the entourage of Iskander Balthazar ... his family, his friends, and even his lawyers ... almost everyone was eager to get their hands on his fortune. Iskander was very well aware of their thirst of money, and it made him deeply sad. For many years, he has lost hope in his entourage. However ... however, something happened during his last days. I don't know what it is exactly ... but it seems that ... something has restored his faith in the goodness and the generosity of human beings ...

Dalya sat silent and immobile. She didn't understand what the Professor meant by these strange thoughts. After some seconds, Professor Canfield pulled himself together, and then he continued in an amused tone:

- Anyway ... your case is unique, Mademoiselle! According to your answers in the evaluation, you surpass our brilliant 15 years old level students in some subjects. On the other hand, there are new subjects that you never learned, such as Literature, Arts ... and because of this unbalance, and your unknown period of time you will be attending this school, you have not been admitted to this year's class. You cannot join the other students, I am very sorry for that. Nevertheless ... I then proposed to teach you lessons in some subjects for the next weeks that you will be spending with us, in order to adjust your level and catch up on some knowledge ... is Mademoiselle ready to start?

Professor Canfield displayed his encouraging smile. Dalya replied without hesitation:

- Yes, Professor ... ready!

The next July days were very busy for Dalya. Every morning at 7:15, she walked through the garden of the grand Mansion, under the punctual watch and the presence of Séraphine, the Snow Panther. Dalya met with Professor Canfield in the classroom from 8:00 AM to 5:00

PM, with a little 30 minutes break in between. She quickly devoured her buttered bread and milk, every day in a small quiet place, before continuing her classes.

Every day, she learned so much more than the previous one. Professor Canfield was nice and kind with her. He had fun teaching her and encouraging her to ask any questions. Together, they advanced in their catch-up at a high speed. They roamed all the subjects that were missing to Dalya: Literature, Arts ... and they adjusted her knowledge in Physics, Mathematics...

And at the end of each day, Dalya came home with a little heavier head, walking by the grand Mansion, where the Snow Panther Séraphine was waiting patiently for her. And just like every previous night, Dalya joined her parents and her little sisters around the dining table, to share their last meal of the day. Her father repeated to her every night:

- Keep your ears wide opened and study well! You must work very hard to pass the challenges that will allow me to have this fortune! I'll be rich forever!

And her mother repeated to her every night:

- She's wasting her time! She is a failure and an idiot! She will be nothing other than a veggy seller. She is better in doing the dishes, cleaning the floor and working as a maid for her family ... at least she is better on that, than attending these stupid classes!

And just like every previous night, Dalya never answered back, she was always quiet and she ate her dinner silently. Old or new house, Dalya's mother forced her daughter to do the dishes, not caring much of her daughter's fatigue state, after a long day of intensive classes. Mrs. Augustine never hesitated to pinch her daughter's cheeks if she forgot to take out the garbage or clean the dishes well. The only change for Dalya was her new room! When she stepped in and closed the door of her bedroom, Dalya felt relieved and happy to be finally alone, away from her abusive parents.

Chapter 12

The box is alive

On Saturday, July 12th, 1890.

After helping her mother clean up the annex house and her father clean up the cart, Dalya had the rest of the day free. Since several days now, Dalya tried many times to open the strange small box left to her by Mr. Iskander Balthazar; she inspected it carefully, turned it in all directions, but without having any idea of what it could be or how to open it. This afternoon, Dalya put the little box in her purse, she told her mother that she was away for a while and she left the grand Mansion.

Uncle Giorgi's workshop was filled with tools as bizarre as you can possibly imagine. The small windows light up the place in a barely visible light. Dalya walked in with very careful steps, hoping not to break or drop anything.

- Uncle Giorgi! She called, looking to her right and left among the crowded tools.

A little voice came out of the end of the room:

- I'm here, Biggo! Come on in!
- There is something I would like to show you, uncle Giorgi.

Her uncle's silhouette appeared among the piles of bizarre objects:

- What is it?

Dalya handed him the small box that she was carrying in her purse:

- It has been many days now since I've had it; I've failed to know what it is. I don't know what's inside of it. I couldn't even open it.

Uncle Giorgi took the box in his hands, he looked at it with large magnifying glasses, and he turned it around in all directions. After a long silent moment, he put the box on his workshop table, and he asked his niece:

- Where did you get that box from, Biggo?
- Mr. Iskander Balthazar left it to me.
- I've never seen such a thing. This box is closed. But ... I can feel something inside of it ... except that it has no opening ...
- Exactly ... how do we know what's inside, then? Should we break it? Asked Dalya

Uncle Giorgi took a little clamp; he tried to open the box. The clamp barely touched the box, that it broke in two within a second. Dalya and uncle Giorgi were surprised. Uncle Giorgi took a bigger clamp. As soon as he made a slight movement, the bigger clamp also broke.

- Alright ... I think we must first try to find out what this box is made of, before we open it. He murmured before disappearing into a corner of the room.

He came back seconds later with a liquid jar and a piece of fabric:

- This is dioxin ... with the contact of iron, it produces a chemical effect.

Uncle Giorgi moistened the piece of fabric with a little liquid, and he rubbed the box. There was no reaction.

- Well ... well ... let us move on to something else!

Uncle Giorgi picked up a match from a drawer; he lit it while whispering:

- If there is any reaction with fire ... it means that it is copper...

By keeping the match closer to the box for several minutes, Dalya and her uncle didn't see the slightest reaction. Dalya and her uncle spent quite some time in the workshop, trying liquids and products on the box, but still without any reaction or results. When finally, after their multiples attempts, uncle Giorgi sat down on his chair and he stared at the box silently, caressing his mustache in a spinal way. After a long silent moment, he murmured in a hesitant voice:

- I wonder if ... But this is very rare ... could it be? ... It would be impossible ... yet, we have tried mostly everything ... it is all that remains ...

He took a tiny razor blade, and he rubbed the surface of the box until he could have a pinch of powder on the blade. In a very prudent move, he placed the pinch of powder on a glass surface and he looked through a large tool that hold a dozen enlarging and magnifiers glasses, that he had created. As soon as Uncle Giorgi looked through his magnifying glass tool, he jumped on his chair:

- Holly muffin!! Holly muffin!!

He looked at it again, and then he turned to Dalya, amazed and astonished:

- It's titanium!

Dalya didn't know what her uncle was talking about. He explained:

- Biggo ... this box that was given to you, has been created with a very new metal ... so new it is not yet recognized in our modern chemistry base!! It is very complex and more resistant than steel metal. That's the reason why the clamps I used at first broke easily, and all the products that I have tried, had absolutely no effect on the box. This metal is extremely rare. I don't know how this box was made ... but it's amazing!

- How can we open the box, then? asked Dalya
- Well, in modern chemistry, there is not yet any clear and complete information about this metal, or how to destroy or change it. I don't even know how this box was made! Holly muffin!! This is a first for me! I'm afraid it will never open ... I'm sorry Biggo.
- Thank you for trying, Uncle Giorgi.
- But ... even so, I think you should keep this box carefully! It's a pretty rare thing, Biggo!

When she left uncle Giorgi's workshop, and although she still couldn't open the box, at least Dalya knew what material it was made of. Dalya returned back to the annex house. In her bedroom, Dalya carefully placed the box on the desk. The mystery of the strange box will eventually unfold some other day, Dalya thought.

On Saturday, July 19th, 1890.

A week later. Mrs. Augustine Bouvard asked Dalya to do some grocery shopping. Early in the morning, when Dalya arrived at the market in front of the Toscana restaurant, she was surprised at the scene. The kiosks of vegetables, lettuce and salads, fruits, fish and eggs ... nearly all the kiosks were empty. There were very few goods on the kiosks, that day. And yet, it was only the beginning of the working day. Dalya was confused.

Even the flower kiosk was almost empty. The owner, Lalla Fatim Fadl was picking up some flowers fallen on the floor. Dalya came near the old woman, to help her and pick up the rest. Lalla Fatim Fadl was an old woman of nearly 70 years old. She was wearing a long light pink dress, a gray apron, and a small scarf was holding her long white silver hair. Lalla Fatim Fadl was selling flowers on the Saturday market, in front of the Toscana restaurant. She was also well known to take care of pigeons, feeding them seeds and water. Sometimes, there could be till twenty pigeons in her modest home. All the neighboring merchants had an absolute respect for this old woman. She had a very nice character, sweet, and despite her age, she kept the traits of a unique beauty.

One day, long ago, Dalya heard Lalla Fatim Fadl talk about her country, far away from America. A country with hundred spices, jewels from the sea, and voices rising up in the sky many times a day. And the name Lalla Fatim Fadl was inspired by a great Queen in this country.

- They came today ... didn't they? The crows robbed everything, as usual. Asked Dalya, while picking up petal of roses off the ground.

Lalla Fatim Fadl stood up and she replied in a soft voice:

- Power strips some people off their humanity.
- But why do they do this? Aren't they supposed to protect us instead of robbing and ruining us? Asked Dalya.

The old woman smiled at the little girl. With a confident voice, the old woman said some strange words:

- Oh, my child ... never ever worry ... for injustice is always paid ... sooner or later.

Later at night.

The eventful and hot steaming day was replaced by a calm and fresh night. The moon light dipped Georgetown city in a soft serenity and peacefulness. Lalla Fatim Fadl sat on a small chair outside the door of her modest poor home. From time to time, she threw bits of bread on the ground to the traveling pigeons that stopped at her door. The old woman closed her eyes for a moment to enjoy the gentle breeze of wind that delicately touched her aging skin. The night was beautiful and serene.

When suddenly, Lalla Fatim Fadl was shaken by an abnormal noise. When she opened her eyes, the old woman noticed about twenty pigeons in front of her on the ground, behaving in a very odd way. All the pigeons turned around in a circle, their wings wide open, their heads-up, and they made a strange sound. It seemed that the pigeons were ... suddenly happy and dancing. The old woman knew many things about pigeons; she has raised them for several years now. She observed the pigeons dancing on the ground, wings wide open, head looking up toward the sky, Lalla Fatim Fadl wondered aloud:

- What is it my children? What is happening to you? What is going on?

Suddenly, all the pigeons rose up in a single movement toward the sky, and they turned around forming a large circle. Several other pigeons joined the circle. Pigeons of different colors, types, sizes ... they all flew and joined in the large circle. It was strange and majestic. The old woman stood up from her chair, witnessing the scene with surprised eyes. At this precise moment, Lalla Fatim Fadl had a strange confident feeling:

- A little thing will rise up ... a little thing will unite us ... and the world, this little thing will shape up!

Like all the previous nights, Dalya lay down on her bed and she closed her eyes to get some sleep and rest. Gradually, she heard a strange sound, a repetitive sound. She was so exhausted; she didn't have the strength to open her eyes. She taught that it was only a cricket on her window. But the sound didn't stop and it was getting really annoying. Dalya had to open her eyes, and what she noticed was quite surprising; the sound was coming from the box!! And a little light was shining from the box too!!

Immediately, Dalya jumped out of her bed, she turned on her lamp and she sat down in front of the box that was placed on top of her desk. Dalya couldn't believe her eyes:

- Is this real? ... The box reacts ... alone? ... But ... uncle Giorgi said this box may never open ... how did it ... why ... how is that even possible?

When suddenly, a small rectangular opening appeared on one side of the box, and a little piece of paper came out. Dalya pulled it out with a hesitant move, and she read the content:

Inaugurate your fate
Of the first breath write the date
And unlighted your path will be for life

Seconds later, another little paper came out of the box. Dalya pulled a white and empty paper this time. She didn't understand exactly what was asked and what she had to do. And most importantly ... how is it possible that this box can react all alone by itself?
Dalya read over the message a dozen times, murmuring:

- It seems to be indications ... inaugurate your fate ... of the first breath ... write the date? ... I have to write a date, but which one? ... first breath ... first breath ... our first breath is on the day we are born. The date of the first breath write ... I have to write a date of birth?!

Dalya, a little hesitant, she took a pencil and wrote on the white paper her father's birth date: January 20th, 1848. Dalya waited for a moment, to think about what to do next. And then, for a second, she had a pretty crazy idea; Dalya took the paper on which she wrote her answer, and as soon as she placed half of the paper on the edge of the rectangular opening, the little piece of paper was quickly swallowed inside the box. A few seconds later, a reply came out:

Answer incorrect

And the first message was issued for the second time:

Inaugurate your fate
Of the first breath write the date
And unlighted your path will be for life

Another empty white paper came out of the box. Dalya was confused:

- The day of the first breath ... What first breath? Which date of birth?

Dalya thought for a few minutes, and then she wrote her little sisters Ari and Adi birth date: April 07th, 1888. And as soon as Dalya placed the paper on the opening of the box, she received the same message as before:

Answer incorrect

On the 3rd attempt, Dalya hesitated for a moment, and then she wrote her own birth date:

December 12th, 1878

The paper got swallowed by the box, in an instant. And never Dalya could have imagined what will happen right after that!!
On one side of the box, the small rectangular outlet remained open. The top side of the box unlocked, a transparent and luminous oval-shaped glass cage, straightened up slowly. The cage was bonded by 4 gold cylinders forged in the shape of vine plant.

When the box stopped moving, Dalya approached it slowly. She could see a strange kind of round clock inside the transparent cage. Dalya was surprised; it wasn't hours and minutes clock, but days and months. A small needle was fixed on the date: December 12th, 1890. The largest needle was between 19th and July 20th, 1890. This very night!

Dalya couldn't believe her own eyes:

- The box works ... alone!! By itself!! ... And it's all because of my birth date!! But ... how can it be? What is all that for? Who created that box? What's its use and purpose?

The small rectangular outlet in the box, released another paper. Dalya took it with a hesitant and confused move:

Pleased to assist you
Mademoiselle Dalya Kartal Bouvard.
From the Moon light, I am powered
5 clues when requested will be granted
The challenge will be as followed:
Before midnight of each December 12th, one question will be asked.
I permit you continuity, if I am answered without a fault
When all the 7 lessons will be assimilated
The challenge will be completed
And the Heir will be proclaimed.

Dalya jumped and took a step away from the box:

- But ... how ... how did this box knew my name? ... How can this box produce messages alone? ...What is this? ... How does this box work?

The bright and transparent glass cage became pale; the light of the box went gradually off. But Dalya's curiosity has just lightened on. She thought no more of sleeping, she wasn't even exhausted anymore. She just couldn't let go of the little paper in her hands, and she read it at least a dozen times.

Every day brought new unanswered mysteries to Dalya. What are these challenges and questions? How can she ask for clues? How does the box know her name? How does the box work? Who created this box? Why did Mr. Balthazar pick her and not one of his true Heirs to answer these questions? Why does it have to be many questions and not only one? When does this test end? ...

Monday, July 21st, 1890.

After her discovery, Dalya walked Monday morning toward Mr. Ernest Laszlo's office in order to inform him of what had happened. He allowed her in his office, after the secretary made her wait a few minutes outside. Mr. Ernest Laszlo's office reflected perfectly well his character; a big luxurious room, cold and dark, despite the warm and bright climate outside in the street. Huge velvet curtains blocked the daylight coming through the large windows. A large shiny black wooden desk was placed in the center of the room, with 2 big chairs in front. A long rectangular meeting table in a corner with several chairs around. The parquet was in dark wood floor, a large chandelier was reflecting cold white light in the office. A huge chimney occupied a wall. Several paintings were hung on the wall, covered with dark wallpaper. The place made you shiver.

-   What is it now? Asked Mr. Ernest upset, sitting behind his big desk, without taking his eyes off a file he was reading.

Dalya announced in a shy voice:

-   It is about the challenges that Mr. Iskander Balthazar mentio...
-   What about them? Mr. Ernest grew impatient.

Dalya continued:

-   I think I know what these challenges are, Sir.

For the first time since her arrival in his office, Mr. Ernest Laszlo put down the file off his hands and he looked at Dalya with an arrogant stare:

-   A little beggar girl ... has solved the mystery of this Will ... the mystery that many qualified and distinguished lawyers have not been able to explain?

Dalya had no choice but to answer yes by a nod of her head. She remained standing still in front of the man's big desk. Mr. Ernest Laszlo asked her with a mocking smile:

-   I'm listening.

Dalya swallowed her fear. She never felt comfortable in the presence of Mr. Ernest. She replied in a small voice:

- The box that was given me by Mr. Iskander Balthazar, will ask me questions.

The Lawyer thought he misheard her, he asked again:

- A box ... will ask you questions?
- Yes, Sir ... That's what I've discovered when the box turned on and requested me to wr...

Mr. Ernest was unable to contain his anger, he yelled with a threatening stare:

- DO YOU TAKE ME FOR AN IDIOT??!! YOU COME BOTHER ME IN MY OFFICE, TO TELL ME THAT NONSENSE??!!

And before Dalya could do or say anything, two men entered Mr. Ernest's office, at this precise moment. It was Mr. Wilfrid and Lyor Laszlo. They were both carrying many heavy files that they put down on their employer's desk. Lyor Laszlo was surprised to see Dalya Bouvard in his father's office. Mr. Wilfrid greeted Dalya with a smile, and he spoke in a jovial tone to Mr. Ernest:

- We have just finished the pleading of tomorrow morning's case, Mr. Ernest. All the files are ready; the only missing thing is your checking on some points.

Mr. Ernest opened a file that Mr. Wilfrid handed him, and without even looking at the little girl still standing in front of him, he said in an irritated voice:

- I have no time to lose with a little beggar! Go play somewhere else!

Although very intimidated by the odious behavior of this man, Dalya considered that the information she held was very important to tell, Mr. Ernest should know what the little strange box provided her as information. After all, his Law office was in charge of this Will, and his son Lyor Laszlo was her legal guardian.

While the three men were discussing one of the file in front of them, and instead of heading to the office exit, Dalya stepped forward toward the three men. When Mr. Ernest raised his head, he was surprised to see that the little girl was still in his office, and she was even handing him a little piece of paper. Mr. Ernest took the paper with a quick move and he read it. After a few seconds, he seemed to have read the paper 5 or 6 times. Mr. Wilfrid and the young Lyor standing on each of his sides, and filled with curiosity, they leaned their heads and they were able to read the note. Dalya explained in a slow voice, happy to have finally managed to inform Mr. Ernest, as arrogant and stubborn as he is.

- The box reacted alone Saturday night, Sir. It requested a birth date. And when I wrote my birth date, the box let out this note. A clock came out of the box too, not a regular clock, it was not indicating hours and minutes, but days and months. The small needle is fixed on December 12th, and the biggest needle moves according to the current day.

Mr. Wilfrid was the first to answer, a bit hesitant:

- So then ... the challenges are in the form of questions that will decide your legitimate inheritance ... and each question will be before midnight of every December 12th?
- Yes, Sir...

Lyor asked Dalya, curious and confused:

- How did the box lit up?
- Alone. By itself. I didn't touch it. Said Dalya
- How did the box ask your birth date? Mr. Wilfrid was stunned by this new discovery.
- A small rectangular outlet just appeared on the side of the box and a paper came out asking me to write the date of the first breath. I tried 2 times, to finally figure out that it meant my birth date.

When Dalya was explaining what had happened, only Mr. Wilfrid seemed delighted and fascinated. Lyor Laszlo had a serious look, and Mr. Ernest Laszlo thought aloud:

- The challenges will be questions provided by this box ... 5 clues given to answer every question ... every December 12th ... and how many questions will there be?

Mr. Wilfrid replied:

- It is not clearly stated how many questions there will be, Sir. The message reveals only that when the 7 lessons will be assimilated, the challenge will be over. 7 lessons ... can that be 7 questions? This is not very clear.

Suddenly, Mr. Ernest Laszlo addressed Dalya with an accusatory tone:

- And what proves to me that you are not lying? That you made this ridiculous note? Why should I trust a little beggar like you?

Dalya had no answer to these questions. She had not lied; she reported all the facts to Mr. Ernest. Yet, she went silent and mute. It was Mr. Wilfrid who dared to speak at that moment:

- A box that lit up all alone by itself and provide messages, one must admit that this is not a very common object. But if Mademoiselle was lying, why did she insist to inform you, Mr. Ernest?

It was a good point, Dalya appeared relieved that Mr. Wilfrid answered back on her behalf and Mr. Ernest seemed compelled to accept this argument, but not quite calm for long:

- So ... What does it mean??!!

Mr. Wilfrid was also confused by this new discovery, yet he was more joyful than his employer:

- It seems, Mr. Ernest ... that the right to the fortune of the late Governor is decided by ... this box, left to Mademoiselle Dalya Bouvard.

Mr. Ernest appeared to lose his cold blood increasingly, he asked Wilfrid:

- Did he spoke to you about this box? Were you aware of it? Was it mentioned in your meetings?
- No ... absolutely not!! Neither Lyor and nor myself, were aware of his plans. Wilfrid immediately answered.
- The Governor never shared his decisions with us. He only revised the documents of his fortune and the evaluation of his assets. Lyor confirmed Mr. Wilfrid's words.

Mr. Wilfrid said in a fascinated voice:

- He was a very discreet gentleman. But ... one must admit, it is a remarkably clever thing to do coming from Mr. Balth...

Mr. Ernest gave a furious fist on his desk:

- BUT THAT IS SO NOT REASONABLE!!! IT IS NOT A GUESSING GAME THAT WILL DECIDE THE FUTURE HEIR TO THIS CURSED FORTUNE!!! THIS CHALLENGE IS INACCURATE AND A RIDICULOUS CONDITION!!

Mr. Ernest was enraged to discover that this inheritance case was getting more and more complicated. But his employee, Mr. Wilfrid replied calmly without losing his natural smile:

- It seemed that these are his wishes, Mr. Ernest. At this point, we have no other choice but to believe Mademoiselle and wait until December 12th.

Mr. Wilfrid ignored his employer's rage and he seemed very pleased to arrange some upcoming plans:

- I will personally inform the school Headmaster of Royal Georgetown College, that Mademoiselle Dalya Bouvard's admission will be extended. Her classes will continue until December 12th.

Mr. Ernest became all red. A simple procedure of heritage transition turned into a disaster. And although he accused Mr. Wilfrid to be responsible for this failure, Mr. Ernest Laszlo was well aware that Mr. Balthazar was solely responsible for the appointment of his Heir. Mr. Ernest liked to control everything ... Oh, but it seems that this time around, he couldn't control a bit of a thing!

Mr. Ernest swallowed his rage as well as he could, and he spoke in a menacing tone, to the little girl still standing in front of his desk:

- Let me know about all the messages that come from this cursed box! From now on, I wish to be informed as soon as possible! Is that clear enough?

Mr. Wilfrid escorted Dalya toward the exit of the office. And before he returned back to his work place, he said to her in a more serious and grave tone:

- Mademoiselle Dalya Bouvard ... I can't urge you enough about how much this box is crucially important! It will decide of your right to the fortune of Mr. Iskander Balthazar. You must keep it safe! At all costs!!

Mr. Sloan Wilfrid was very different from his employer. Although he rarely spoke to Dalya directly, Mr. Wilfrid was always nice and courteous toward Dalya. She respectfully replied:

- Yes, Sir. I will.

Dalya was hoping to find any answer to her questions, who did not cease to multiply every day; questions about Mr. Iskander Balthazar, questions about the Will, questions on his decision to name her Heiress, questions about the Snow Panther who keeps following her ... But now, the curiosity of Dalya has shifted a little more toward this strange box.

At the Royal Georgetown College.

Awaiting the arrival of Professor Canfield, Dalya was sitting alone in the usual classroom; she examined the little box for the 10th time. When a voice surprised her, and made her jumped off her chair.

- How did you get that box?

A man in a checked elegant suit and a bow tie, stood just in front of Dalya. Professor Canfield entered into the classroom without Dalya even noticing him. He looked at the box, surprised. Dalya replied:

- Mr. Iskander Balthazar left it for me. I got it from the Bank coffret. Have you ever seen this box somewhere else, Professor?

Professor Canfield put down his large folder on his desk and he approached Dalya:

- In the few last months where I visited him in his office at the grand Mansion, Iskander Balthazar seemed ... lost in thoughts and preoccupied by this box. He spent long hours looking and staring at it. At that time, I found his behavior very odd. And when I asked him what was it and what was inside that box, he quickly changed the subject.
- Why is that? Asked Dalya.
- I have no idea. Iskander was sometimes very mysterious and withdrawn. But it seems that this box was extremely important and valuable to him. He left it to you, you say?
- Yes, Professor. Do you know the origin of this box? How does it work? Did Mr. Balthazar make it?

Professor Canfield took the box in his hands; he looked at it for a moment, then placed it back on Dalya's desk and said:

- Iskander was a visionary, a wise and a highly-educated man ... but an inventor? I've never seen him make or create anything. He was a great collector of art items. But I don't know the origin of this box.
- Professor Canfield ... this box turned on by itself. It wrote me this message.

Professor Canfield looked at Dalya with a confused stare:

- This box ... turned on? ... What do you mean by itself?

Dalya was expecting a surprised reaction. She told him all about the exchange she had with this box, and she gave him the same notes that she had previously shown the lawyer, Mr. Ernest Laszlo. Except that Professor Canfield, after having a brief moment of confusion, he had a completely different reaction than Mr. Ernest Laszlo. When Professor Canfield read the paper coming from the strange box, he laughed full heart in an amused tone:

- That wicked Iskander! Even after his death, he never ceases to fascinate us!

After the end of her classes at school, Dalya ran immediately to her uncle's workshop. And without being able to hold her excitement, she yelled all breathless:

- Uncle Giorgi! Uncle Giorgi! It opened! It let out a piece of paper, and after I wrote my birth date, it then asked me to wr...
- Hold on a minute!! One minute!! Breathe Biggo!! He interrupted her with a lost voice. What opened? Who released a paper? What are you talking about?
- The box that Mr. Balthazar left me!! Said Dalya excited about her discovery.
- How did it open? When? How did you manage to open it? He asked, curious as everyone.
- Nothing at all! I didn't even touch it!

In her uncle Giorgi's workshop, Dalya explained to him what had happened with the box. Dalya had hoped that her uncle would have more answers to her questions, and that now he would know at least how the box works.

- It is ... extraordinary ... simply stunning! He repeated in an amazed voice.
- No one knows how this box works. Not even my teacher at school. He was a great friend of Mr. Balthazar. He noticed the box in his office during his last days alive. And yet, he doesn't know anything more about it, than you and me. The box opened alone. Is it magic, uncle Giorgi?
- I don't think so ... no ... it is much more complex than I thought.

Uncle Giorgi examined the box from all angles. Dalya repeated to him everything that happened at least 3 times. He asked over and over many questions to make sure he understood well. Then finally, uncle Giorgi sat back on his big old worn out chair:

- Extraordinary ... I've never seen such a thing in my entire life ... the person who designed and created this box had to spend a lot of time to make it. And this person must be out of standards intelligence ... never have I ever met someone who can create a box like that. It's as if this box was ... alive and smart!

Dalya watched the little strange box placed on the table of the workshop. She was as much amazed as her uncle Giorgi in front of this particular box. After a long moment of silence, uncle Giorgi muttered aloud:

- Alive and smart ... this box looks like my distant cousin Excel Bouvard. I could never reach her intelligence level and vivacity. It's true that ... it looks like her a lot, alive and smart. It's as if this box was my cousin Excel ... it's an Excelbox!

Uncle Giorgi found no more answers to the many questions of Dalya. Except maybe a name for the mysterious strange object: the Excelbox!

Chapter 13

Meeting the neighbors

Wednesday, July 30th, 1890.

Since one month now, Dalya has been following her private and accelerated classes with Professor Canfield. She spends all her days at the Royal Georgetown College. When she comes home, and since she was no longer working like before with her father, sometimes she would play with her little sisters, and other times she would help her mother with the housework.

This afternoon, having completed earlier her classes at school, Dalya found her little sisters Ari and Adi playing with their two prefabricated toys in the living room of the annex house. Their favorite and only toys were caterpillars, made of round cotton small cushions that Dalya sewed and created for them; Ari had blue and green round cushion caterpillar, and Adi had pink and orange round cushion caterpillar. Her mother had already prepared dinner; she was busy sewing some clothes. Dalya decided in her free time, to take a walk in the surroundings of the grand Mansion.

Dumbarton Oaks Park was a place filled of neat and beautiful gardens, all kinds of flowers were planted in perfect symmetry and trees in all forms were standing tall and strong. A nice smell of freshness invaded the place. Right after the exit of the grand Mansion, a small lake was a home to swans and other birds that were resting before their take off and return on their path. It was a beautiful and peaceful place.

Dalya walked slowly behind a little woman who was few steps ahead of her. The woman was carrying a large bag, and was surely coming from downtown. When suddenly, the woman lost her balance and she stumbled. The large bag got torn apart, all its content got deployed on the ground. Dalya didn't hesitate for a second; she hurried to help the woman to stand up on her feet:

- Is everything alright, Mam? Are you hurt? Do you need assistance?
- Oh … this … damn … bag! This is the second time it rips! Exclaimed the woman, trying heavily to stand up.

Dalya picked up all the purchases from the ground and she put them back in the bag again. She made a stronger knot in the bag to keep it tight for good, at least until the woman arrives to her home. Then, Dalya said:

- I can help you carry this big bag to your home, Mam.
- Oh, thank you dear child!! That's nice of you to help me. I'm already late actually.

The woman looked friendly, she was small and curved under her long beige coat, little bright eyes, and her brown hair with white highlights was under a hat decorated with a pretty satin bow. Despite her advanced age, the woman was in her fifties, her skin tone was clear and white, embellishing her wrinkles. Dalya lifted the bag, and went on her way walking near the woman. Across a little lake, the woman asked Dalya:

- It's the first time I see you in this neighborhood, my child.
- I had some free time this afternoon; I am taking a little walk in the area. It is a pretty place. Said Dalya.
- Oh, yes! It's the most beautiful place in Georgetown city. The most distinguished people live a few blocks from here. It is quiet and calm. But not very convenient for shopping, especially when the drivers are not available ...
- You live in this neighborhood too? asked Dalya
- I have been working here for 12 years now, for the only French family who lives in this corner of the city: the Poirier family. I take care of Mrs. Marianne Poirier.
- It's nice to meet you, Mam.
- Oh, dear child! No need to call me Mam. Forgive my dizziness, I haven't even introduced myself. My name is Glorina. You can call me just Mrs. Glorina, like everyone does. How about you?
- I'm Dalya.

Mrs. Glorina paused and stopped walking for a moment; she examined the little girl, in a doubtful gaze:

- Are you ... the new resident in the annex house of the grand Mansion?

Dalya didn't know how Mrs. Glorina got this information; Dalya bowed her head to confirm.

- Mademoiselle Dalya Bouvard? ... But ... oh Dear!! You are the Heiress!

The woman froze, all astonished, before continuing:

- You are ... the Heiress of Mr. Governor Iskander Balthazar!

Dalya replied in a shy voice, her cheeks blushing:

- I'm not an Heiress ... it is not confirmed ... nothing has been decided yet ...

Mrs. Glorina appeared confused and disturbed; she tried to take back the big heavy bag from Dalya's hands:

- Oh dear!! ... What have I done?! ... Forgive me, Mademoiselle ... I wasn't expecting to meet you this way! I am so ashamed for giving you my big heavy bag to carry!! My apologies Mademoiselle! I'm so sorry!

Dalya insisted to hold the large bag herself:

- It's alright. I am glad to help, Mrs. Glorina. I will be happy to walk you home.

The woman stared at Dalya, all shameful, not knowing what to do or what else to say. When Dalya continued to walk, Mrs. Glorina followed her. To ease the woman's uncomfortable reaction, and also to change the subject, Dalya asked all curious:

- Do you know some of the neighbors living in the area, Mrs. Glorina?

The woman replied proudly, with a delighted smile:

- All of them!! After walking for 12 years on the same road, you learn lots and lots of things about the neighbors. There is the great and retired Admiral Clayton in this house ... He is considered a true legend in the Royal Navy. And on this side, there is the Bowman family ... very nice and polite people, they have made a fortune in the hotel industry. And a little further, we'll go through the Chinese Embassy, they have such beautiful flowers in their garden ...

Before they arrived at the French Poirier family home, Mrs. Glorina had named all of the houses on their road. Dumbarton Oaks Park was surrounded by embassies of several countries: Denmark, Italy, Hungary, Great Britain ... and several Noble families of Politicians, Ministers, Doctors, Scientists, Businessmen ... Many distinguished people lived here. Dalya got a clearer view of her new neighbors.

When Mrs. Glorina paused in front of an iron shaped door, she opened it and she entered a lovely garden filled with blue, red and white flowers, a big 2 floors house stood at the center of the garden. Several windows reflected the clear blue sky; the front door was brown wood, with a small candle on top. The House was not as big as the grand Mansion, but it was elegant and refined.

- Come on in, please.

Mrs. Glorina insisted on Dalya to follow her inside the House. Entering through a 2nd door behind the Mansion, Dalya found herself in the kitchen of the Poirier home. The pans and utensils were well ordered, stored on shelves and hanging on the wall. A big oven and lever were placed under large windows, offering a great view of the garden outside. A large table surrounded by a few wooden chairs, was installed in the middle of the kitchen. Dalya placed the bag of Mrs. Glorina's purchases.

- Take a seat, Mademoiselle. Please make yourself comfortable. I will be with you in just a minute!

Mrs. Glorina took off her coat and she wore a nice kitchen apron decorated with several Butterfly knots in several colors. Then, Mrs. Glorina asked Dalya:

- May I serve you a piece of a cherry pie? I made it myself this morning. It's exquisite!
- I'd better be going; I don't want to disturb you.
- Oh, but it's the least I can offer you, for being nice and helping me!!

The pie was really delicious!! The best pie Dalya has ever tasted. At the first bite, Dalya displayed a delighted smile; Mrs. Glorina laughed:

- I guess that my pie had conquered you, Mademoiselle!! I am very pleased that you like it. I don't mean to brag, but the best pies are made in my kitchen. I've learned some great recipes from my dear grandmother, bless her magical sweet hands!

Mrs. Glorina got busy unpacking the groceries on the same table, while Dalya finished eating her pie.

- Do you work alone in this house? Asked Dalya.
- Oh, yes! There's only me and two drivers. One available to serve Mr. Richard Poirier, Mrs. Marianne's son. And another driver is at the disposal of Miss Francine Poirier.

Dalya was not a curious person, but Mrs. Glorina was a chatty woman, Dalya listened to Mrs. Glorina, while really enjoying the pie:

- Miss Francine is Mrs. Marianne's only daughter; she comes to visit her mother almost every day. Because Mrs. Marianne Poirier does not come out. So, I am the only one in charge of all the grocery shopping, the cleaning and the cooking. Usually, one of the two drivers takes me to the market to get my groceries, but today they were both busy, and I couldn't wait any longer ...

Suddenly, Mrs. Glorina thought aloud:

- Oh, dizzy me!! I forgot to buy onions for Mrs. Marianne's soup! How dizzy I've became! The drivers won't be available until next week. I was planning for a nice onion soup for Mrs. Marianne. Dizzy me!! I'll just have to go back to the market tomorrow, and postpone the laundry for another day, maybe on the weeken...
- I pass near the market every day, I can get you some onions, after finishing my classes tomorrow. Said Dalya with a sympathetic smile.

Mrs. Glorina did not believe what she just heard from Dalya. She replied, with a very confused expression:

- What? ... What did you say?

Dalya repeated her offer:

- I walk near the market every day. Tomorrow after school, I can bring you some onions. That way, you won't have to go back to the market tomorrow.
- You wish to bring me onions?! Mrs. Glorina exclaimed, all amazed.
- Yes. Dalya answered spontaneously.
- But ... you're an Heiress, Mademoiselle. You're not supposed to do the grocery shopping.

Dalya naturally, replied with a smile:

- I'm not an Heiress yet.

Mrs. Glorina appeared stunned by the strange ways and manners of the little girl. She whispered nervously:

- Well, in that case ... you'll really save me time and trouble. The drivers won't be free until next week, and I still have the laundry, the ironing, washing the windows and ... are you sure you don't mind at all, Mademoiselle?
- It will be my pleasure, Mrs. Glorina.

Mrs. Glorina appeared happy and relieved not having to go to the market a 2nd time and wasting hours. She continued to unpack and store her groceries. A detail caught Dalya's attention, she asked timidly:

- You said that Mrs. Marianne Poirier doesn't go out a lot to town?
- Oh no, she doesn't come out of her bedroom, even less of the house. Replied Mrs. Glorina.
- But ... why? Asked Dalya

Mrs. Glorina let out a pity sigh:

- Mrs. Marianne spends all day locked in her bedroom because of her illness. Her misery has been since almost 6 years now. She was a very active, very enthusiastic, and always busy woman in her work. And now ... Poor Mrs. Marianne, she can't even go out to the garden like before to take care of her roses that she loved so much.
- An illness stops her from coming out of her bedroom? Dalya had never heard such a thing.
- Yes, that's right. Sometimes she has excruciating pain in all her bones, and she does not sleep for several nights. She speaks very rarely, she almost lost her voice. She only writes what she wants or makes us a sign. She no longer receives visitors since a long time, besides her children. And the slightest cold wind or too hot sunshine hurt her skin. She remains silent and motionless for days and days ... it is a complicated disease. I heard doctors once say the word: fibromyalgia.
- Isn't there a remedy to relieve her? Dalya was curious.

Mrs. Glorina sighed disappointedly:

- Oh, Mademoiselle! ... I have watched so many doctors come in and out of this house, but no cure has been useful so far. Mrs. Marianne spends all days, hold up in her bedroom.

When Dalya finished her pie, she thanked Mrs. Glorina, who escorted her toward the main door:

- Thank you so much for your kind help, Mademoiselle.
- My pleasure, Mrs. Glorina.
- Oh!! Oh!! Before I forget ... do you like English sweet cream?
- I don't know what it is. I have never tasted it before. My mother doesn't cook much sweet things. Replied Dalya.
- Tomorrow afternoon, I will prepare a good peach and English cream pie, just for you! Answered Mrs. Glorina, all excited and joyful.

Dalya was pleased to have met Mrs. Glorina, and especially to be able to help her. Mrs. Glorina was a little chatty, but very nice and a great baker!!

Dalya crossed the little garden of the French Poirier family, toward the exit. When suddenly, she noticed a shadow that watched her through a large window from the 2nd floor of the house. Being far, Dalya couldn't clearly see who it was. But the shadow followed Dalya until she left the garden. Who could it possibly be? And why was it watching her?

The next day, after she finished her classes, Dalya stopped in front of the grocer to buy onions. She walked toward the house where Mrs. Glorina worked. Right after the big lake, Dalya pushed open the garden's door, and she walked across the lovely garden toward the second door behind the house. When Dalya looked up, a shadow watched her from the exact same window as the day before. Dalya didn't know who was that person looking at her, but she continued on her way to the kitchen door. As soon as she rang the doorbell, Mrs. Glorina appeared:

- Good afternoon, Mademoiselle! I'm so glad to see you again! How nice of you to have got me what I needed!! Thank you very much!! Coming in, please!

Dalya placed the onions bag on the big kitchen's table. Mrs. Glorina was already preparing dinner; the table was full of cutlery, fruits and vegetables. Mrs. Glorina pulled out a plate, she put it in front of Dalya and she served her a large piece of peach and English cream pie:

- Here you go, Mademoiselle! Nothing but goodness. A pie like you never tasted before!
- Thank you. Dalya replied with a big smile.

Mrs. Glorina asked the little girl, while cutting apples into small cubes:

- You told me yesterday that you were taking classes? Are you attending a school?
- Yes. But only until December 12th. I had an admission in the Royal Georgetown College. I'm taking private lessons with Professor Canfield.

Mrs. Glorina placed her cubes of apples in a pan and she added sugar to caramelize it. As soon as the woman heard the College's name, she was astonished:

- Oh!! ... But it is a prestigious school, Mademoiselle! All the children of the nobility and wealthy people, they study there! You are very luck Mademoiselle! You must have been very smart to be admitted there!

Dalya blushed:

- It's Mr. Iskander Balthazar who insisted that I attend classes in this school. He has also granted us, me and my family, to stay in the annex house of the grand Mansion.

Mrs. Glorina continued to move her caramelized apples in the pan, and she murmured in a sad tone:

- Ah ... That Mr. Iskander Balthazar! He was a great man. One of a kind. He did so much for this city and this country.

Dalya straightened up and she asked:

- Did you know him?

Mrs. Glorina turned around toward Dalya, and she replied:

- Yes, a little. I've known him since the first day I worked at the Poirier house. He was a very discreet and courteous man. We met some times when he walks on the road. He greeted a Minister and a Maid, in the same way, with the same words and the same voice tone!

Dalya dared to ask Mrs. Glorina, a question that nobody seemed to find a clear answer to, up until this day. And since Mrs. Glorina knew Mr. Balthazar, Dalya hoped that she could help her understand:

- Mrs. Glorina ... Do you know why Mr. Balthazar nominated me as his Heiress?

Mrs. Glorina emptied the contents of the hot pan in a plate. The smell of the caramelized apple cubes was delicious and mesmerizing. Mrs. Glorina raised her head up toward the little girl, and she replied with a gentle smile:

- I knew Mr. Balthazar only from far. I'm afraid I can't answer for him and help you understand his decision, Mademoiselle. But ... If there is one thing I've learned in life. It is that our kindness always comes back to us. And be sure Mademoiselle Dalya Bouvard, that there is more kindness in your little finger than most people have in their entire body.

While Dalya still didn't have any clear answer to her question, she was very touched by the woman's nice words. After a few minutes, Mrs. Glorina announced:

- All is ready! I finished Mrs. Marianne's dinner platter. I will take it to her bedroom.
- Can I come with you to meet Mrs. Marianne? If it's alright, of course. Asked Dalya

Mrs. Glorina was a little surprised by the little girl's request:

- Well ... Yes ... Certainly ... If you wish so. She didn't sleep well last night. The pain has intensified in these past days ... so you won't meet Mrs. Marianne in a very good shape.

Dalya herself was surprised at her own request. Her spontaneous curiosity made her want to meet this great woman. When Mrs. Glorina took the dinner platter, Dalya followed her upstairs to Mrs. Marianne's bedroom. They left the kitchen; they passed through a living room. Beige chairs and divans were installed everywhere, a bright parquet covered the floor, a large wooden cabinet filled with decorative vases, stretched on both sides of a wall, a big fireplace was installed in a corner of the living room, the large windows let appear a beautiful view of the garden.

But what held Dalya's attention the most; it was an enormous painting covering an entire wall. Around 50 vases painted in blue and white colors. The patterns on the vases were several shades of blue representing gardens, flowers and trees of various shapes and sizes. Dalya had never seen such a beautiful painting. A true Masterpiece!

Going up the stairs, Dalya followed Mrs. Glorina into a long corridor. While walking, Dalya felt a door has just opened behind her. When Dalya turned around, a shadow stared at her. The same silhouette which appeared on the window, whenever Dalya crossed the garden. This time, it was in the long corridor leading to Mrs. Marianne's bedroom. Dalya couldn't figure out who it was. But at least now, she was convinced that the shadow was following her every move.

Mrs. Glorina opened the door with one hand, holding the dinner platter with the other hand and she walked into a dark bedroom. Dalya hesitated for a moment before entering the room. She decided to take off her shoes, and place them in the corridor, outside the bedroom door. Then, Dalya entered the room of the great woman, wearing only socks in her feet. Mrs. Glorina didn't even notice that Dalya had removed her shoes.

When Dalya took a few steps inside the room, she could barely discern the furniture. Big thick and heavy curtains prevented light to enter. Only some lanterns provided soft light to the bedroom. In the center of the room, a large bed was placed. A silhouette was asleep. Mrs. Glorina placed down the platter on an adjacent table, and she said in a soft and whispered voice:

- Mrs. Marianne? Your dinner is ready.

The silhouette turned around in a very slow movement and she gently straightened up on her bed. Mrs. Glorina pulled aside one of the curtains to let the last light of the day come into the room. She then returned near the great woman and she helped her by placing a few cushions on her back. Dalya stood motionless and silent.

After few rays of light came into the room, Dalya was able to see the long white silver hair of the great woman. Dalya never saw such a beautiful hair color. Mrs. Marianne Poirier was an old woman, tall, svelte and slender. Her body seemed tired. And even under the wrinkles covering her face, from the top of her 73 years old, she was a beautiful great woman. She wore a blue night gown in refined satin that illuminated her pale and delicate skin. She was very quiet.

But what surprised Dalya the most, were the eyes of the sick woman. Not only big beautiful emerald green eyes, but eyes filled with tears. The woman seemed to have cried for days. Small tears still ran down her cheeks.

Mrs. Glorina gently dried the great woman's face, and she placed the dinner platter on a small bed table next to Mrs. Marianne. After eating a few bites, Mrs. Marianne became aware of the little girl's presence, who was standing in a corner of her bedroom. Mrs. Marianne stared at Dalya for a while. Mrs. Glorina noticed that, and she informed Mrs. Marianne:

- Oh!! Dizzy me again!! I haven't even presented you our new guest; Mrs. Marianne ... This little girl is Mademoiselle Dalya Bouvard. We have met on the way back from downtown, yesterday afternoon ...

Mrs. Marianne couldn't stop looking at Dalya, the great woman stared at the little girl who wore a boy overall, a yellowed shirt with sleeves lifted up, a big cap on her head, and ... Socks? The woman seemed confused to understand why Dalya was present in her bedroom without her shoes on, and with only socks on her little feet. Mrs. Glorina whispered to Mrs. Marianne, while continuing to serve her dinner:

- She's the little girl who was appointed Heiress of the fortune of late Mr. Iskander Balthazar, the Governor of our State. And ... I can assure you that this young Mademoiselle is very different from the other Heirs of the noble families that I know. She is very polite and kind. Yesterday afternoon, she insisted to carry my grocery bag herself, up until here! And she had offered to buy me the onions that I forgot to bring!

After few minutes, Mrs. Marianne finished her meal. Mrs. Glorina stood up, and she took the platter away. Dalya followed Mrs. Glorina toward the exit. Before closing the bedroom door, Dalya looked one last glance at the great woman. Mrs. Marianne was still staring at her, tears of pain flowing down her cheeks. Dalya smiled at her, and then she gently closed the door.

On the way back home to the grand Mansion, Dalya couldn't help thinking about the great woman who couldn't get out of her bedroom and who was crying out of pain. It must have been very difficult and heavy to be held by an illness. Mrs. Marianne must be a rich and a noble woman, yet without the ability to go out; it was a very a miserable and a hard life.

Chapter 14

What if ...?

Friday, August 1st, 1890.

In the evening, Dalya finished rinsing dishes; she placed down the plates and cutlery near the lever to let them dry for a few minutes, before storing them in the kitchen cupboards. Mrs. Augustine was busy getting her little twins into bed. Mr. Antman disappeared as usual, right after dinner, to an unknown place. Dalya took her bag, she pulled out few papers that Professor Canfield gave her. She sat on the kitchen table chair. Dalya started writing and answering the questions on the work paper, one by one. When suddenly, Dalya felt someone pinch her cheek in a brusque move and it was very very painful. Her mother's voice pierced her ear:

- WHY DIDN'T YOU PUT BACK THE DISHES IN THEIR CUPBOARD?!

Dalya said in a trembling voice:

- I am waiting for ... the dishes to dry a little ... only until I can finish an exercise that Professor Canfield gav...

Mrs. Augustine squeezed so hard Dalya's cheek, that the little girl had tears in her eyes because of the severe pain. Her mother yelled with all her might:

- YOU KNOW PERFECTLY WELL THAT I HATE WAKING UP THE MORNING AND FINDING THE LAST NIGHT DISHES STILL ON THE COUNTER!! HOW MANY TIMES MUST I TELL YOU TO IMMEDIATELY STORE THE DISHES IN THE CLOSETS!! I DON'T CARE ABOUT YOUR STUPID FOOLISH CLASSES!! YOU'RE AN IDIOT AND YOU WILL ALWAYS BE ONE NO MATTER WHAT YOU DO!! STICK THAT VERY WELL IN THAT SMALL IDIOT HEAD OF YOURS!

When she finally dropped Dalya's cheek with a violent move, Mrs. Augustine left the kitchen, slamming the door behind her just like she usually do, with all her strength. Dalya stood up from the kitchen table; she put her books back in the large bag. Then, she took a kitchen towel and began to dry the dishes one by one. Her cheeks were burning red and painful.

When she finished storing the plates, the cutlery and all the dishes into their places, Dalya took her bag and she locked herself up in her bedroom. As soon as she sat on her bed, tears fall down immediately on her painful and red cheeks. Dalya could never understand why her mother was so cruel and aggressive with her. Dalya could never remember the times when her mother was kind and caring. Yet, Dalya always did the best she could to please her mother. She worked hard to do all the housework and she always did all she was asked to do. But regardless of what Dalya did, it was never enough, and her mother was always evil and violent with her.

Despite her long day, Dalya couldn't fall asleep so quickly. She turned around several times in her bed. Dalya thought about her mother who treated her cruelly, about her father who pressured her to get the money from the heritage, about Director Darkfett who reminded her every day that she didn't deserve to be at school, about the Lawyer Mr. Ernest who hates her and despise her, about the nephew Mr. Ferdinand Edelmen who was eager to get rid of her ...

When suddenly, the emerald eyes of the neighbor woman appeared in Dalya's mind. Why and how did they appear to Dalya at this moment? No one can explain it. But Dalya thought about Mrs. Marianne Poirier, held in her bedroom, unable to have a normal life like she used to before. Dalya remembered the last sad and hopeless look of the great woman. Dalya thought that despite her own difficult moments, she was in a better place than the great woman who could never leave her house because of her illness.

Lost in her thoughts, Dalya's eyes met the Excelbox. Since she and her family moved in this annex house, Dalya always placed this strange box on her desk in front of the window. The small rectangular outlet was always opened. The Moon light entered discreetly through the window of the bedroom and it covered the Excelbox of a silver light veil, converting the transparent glass cage, into a gray smoked glass. The strange clock inside the cage, displaying months and days, was no longer visible, hidden by the gray veil.

Something forced Dalya to get up and it drove her toward this mysterious box. She lit her lamp, and she sat down in front of her small desk. She hesitated for a moment, unsure of what to do, and how to request a first clue. Dalya remembered the first message of the Excelbox. She pulled over the paper from a drawer and she read it aloud:

- 5 clues will be granted when requested ... when requested ... but how can I ask them? What should I do?

Dalya observed the Excelbox for some seconds. Then, she approached the box and said aloud:

- I want to know the first clue.

The box didn't move. Dalya repeated the same sentence in different words:

- What is the first clue?

There was no reaction of the Excelbox. Dalya delicately patted three times on the Excelbox cage. But nothing changed. Dalya thought aloud:

- How do you work? ... The first time you lightened up all alone, I didn't touch you. And the pieces of paper came out one after anot... they came out ... they came out!

Dalya had an idea. She was not so sure if it would work, but she had to try every possible trick. Dalya took a little paper and she wrote on it:

What is the 1st clue?

As soon as Dalya put the tip of the paper on the small rectangular outlet, the note got swallowed and it disappeared inside the Excelbox. The smoked glass turned in one second, into a transparent glass. The clock appeared on the inside, indicating the date of the 1st August 1890. The 4-cylinder wrought of gold, holding the glass cage, flashed a bright burst. And a little paper appeared in the rectangular outlet:

First clue
Dig to the Fund
Plant a kernel
Water at the source
Admire the jewel

As she read the note, Dalya was surprised:

- The Excelbox asks me to dig to the Fund ... but which Fund? What exactly should I plant? What source is it talking about? What jewel should I admire? ... But, it seems that ... These are indications for gardening. Why is the Excelbox providing me with gardening instructions?

Dalya hoped for a somewhat clearer clue. She was not expecting gardening advice. Dalya knew nothing about plants and flowers. Although she was a clever and smart little girl, Dalya understood nothing of this 1st clue.

Monday, August 04th, 1890

Outside Mr. Ernest Laszlo's office, Dalya was sitting in front of the secretary, who stared at her in a haughty and contemptuous look, the same gaze just like her employer's. When the secretary finally let her in the big office, Dalya immediately noticed the presence of a familiar person; Mr. Balthazar's niece, Mrs. Honoré Edelmen. She wore a big gilded hat, a long shiny patterned yellow summer dress and a small cape on her shoulders. She was comfortably sitting on one of the chairs in front of Mr. Ernest Laszlo's large desk. The lawyer seemed intimidated by the woman, to the point that Dalya was very surprised by his respectful and embarrassed voice:

- I assure you of my most loyal respect and esteem, Mrs. Honoré. It was just a simple misunderstanding.
- This misunderstanding cost us very much, Ernest. Some things need to be handled in a more diplomatic way.
- I'm aware of that. I will personally make sure that it doesn't happen again.

- It would really be very ... regrettable ... if another misunderstanding happens for the second time, Ernest.
- Certainly, Mrs. Honoré.

Mr. Ernest Laszlo appeared to contain his angry and rude temper in front of the elegant woman, he asked Dalya in a forced polite voice:

- What is it? Why are you here?

Dalya walked timidly toward his desk, she handed him a paper and she explained in a small voice:

- Good afternoon, Sir... You asked me to inform you of everything about this box. This is the first clue that the box has given me.

Mr. Ernest took the piece of paper and he read it aloud. A confused expression drew on his face instantly:

- What is that ... dig and plant? What jewel? What is all this about? This isn't a clue ... it's a silly game!

Dalya remained silent standing in front of the lawyer, Mr. Ernest. But the little girl felt some sharp eyes observing her very closely. When Dalya turned around her head slowly, she realized that Mrs. Honoré was looking at her in a calm gaze, ignoring completely Mr. Ernest's confused attitude. Dalya was surprised to see the woman smiling at her. It is true that Mr. Balthazar's niece was much different and all the opposite of her brother, Mr. Ferdinand. She was always very calm and poised, mostly smiling, and she spoke in a very soft voice.

- Do you have something else to inform me about? Asked Mr. Ernest.
- No, Sir. Replied Dalya.

Dalya greeted them and then she left the office, under the scornful gaze of Mr. Ernest Laszlo and Mrs. Honoré Edelmen's posed smile.

Thursday, August 07th, 1890

At the Royal Georgetown College, the classes with Professor Canfield were a true moment of happiness for Dalya. Always dressed in his checked suit and bow tie, Professor Canfield was very kind and patient with her, encouraging her to answer and do her best. This afternoon, after finishing the Arts lessons, Professor Canfield took out the Literature book.

- Today, we will study more about a particular writing style. If I ask you, Mademoiselle, to explain this sentence for me: the old man is a turtle. What do you understand?

Dalya thought for a moment, but was unable to guess the meaning of the sentence. Professor Canfield went on to explain:

- Now if I tell you: the old man walks like a turtle …

Dalya murmured hesitantly:

- A turtle moves slowly … so then the old man walks slowly too?

Professor Canfield says:

- Yes! Exactly! This writing style is called metaphors. These are sentences used to explain things more clearly, and bring you closer to their description.

Suddenly, Dalya remembered the first clue provided by the Excelbox, a few days ago. She asked him:

- So then … Professor … if for example, I read: dig to the Fund … what could it possibly mean?

Professor Canfield answered her question:

- The fund may point to the earth on which we walk on … or the origin of something. Dig may be another way to say search deeper. Dig to the Fund can be an expression to say that you must listen more ardently, observe, or specifically look for something, search …

Dalya's face lit up. She finally understood what the clue meant! The Excelbox wanted her to look for something. But what was Dalya supposed to be looking for? Why and how?

For the rest of the day, Dalya was lost in her thoughts; she couldn't stop thinking about one and only question:

- What does the Excelbox want her to search for?

Dalya walked toward the annex house, to find Ari and Adi playing in the garden, her father was home early fixing a last step on the stairs, her mother was preparing the dinner table.

Dalya didn't sleep easily that night; all she could think about was the first clue. Sleep was slow to come, so Dalya stood up; she lit her lamp, and she sat down on the desk, in front of the Excelbox. She read the 1st clue several times, thinking aloud:

- Dig to the Fund … search for something … Plant a kernel … What kernel? Then water at the source … the source … the source … you irrigate with only water. So, the source is water. Then admire the jewel … If we dig, we plant, we water … then certainly there is a plant or a flower that grows up. But the first sentence … search for something … what am I supposed to look for exactly?

Finding no answers to her questions, Dalya decided to go back to sleep. She turned off her bedside lamp; she lay down in her bed and closes her eyes, waiting for sleep to come … when suddenly, Dalya straightened up and she jumped out of her bed, she turned on her lamp for the 2nd time. She thought out loud:

- When I asked for the first clue, I was thinking about Mrs. Marianne Poirier … what if…?

Friday, August 08ᵗʰ, 1890.

As usual, Dalya walked all the way to the Royal Georgetown College, to attend her classes. For the entire previous night, Dalya had a question stuck in her mind. As soon as she stepped into the classroom, Dalya sat in her chair, and she waited for her teacher. When the Professor came in, and before he could open his bag and pull out his books, Dalya said:

- May I ask you a question, Professor?
- But of course, Mademoiselle.
- I heard of a disease that prevents the person from coming out of their house. It's called fibromyalgia. I would like to learn a little more about it, if that's possible ...

Professor Canfield seemed a little bit surprised by the little girl's question. He stood up from his chair, and he smiled back at her:

- I know exactly where to find the answer to your question. Follow me, Mademoiselle.

Dalya and Professor Canfield left the classroom; they toured the empty corridors and headed toward the other side of the school. They walked for few minutes, until they arrived in front of a small desk office. Dalya never saw a place as organized as this office. Shelves were well ordered each with a small label pasted below, written in a pretty handwriting. Several pots of pencils were arranged on the desk, and each was for a specific type: black pencils, colors pencils, inks pencils, adhesives, and scissors. Small rectangular boxes were placed on each other, with small tags: mails, forms, letters ... Dalya was amazed by the neatness and meticulousness in this office. In a corner, there was a little green plant that stood straight and a little white, green and red flag of a country. A small sign had a name on it:

Miss Guendolyn Knigaski
Library Assistant
Royal Georgetown College

Sitting in front of her office, Miss Guendolyn was a 35 years old woman; she was focused writing on a large folder. She had silky ruby red hair attached in a bun. She was small high, chubby, had a porcelain skin, lovely hazel eyes embellished her face. She was wearing a pretty light purple dress.

Professor Canfield approached the office and he spoke to the woman. Dalya could not hear what they were whispering. But at some point, the woman looked surprised at Dalya. Then, she said, with a pretty different accent and a sweet voice:

- If you would like to follow me, please.

They all entered into an enormous place. 10 meters long walls were covered with shelves filled with books. Hundreds and hundreds of rows were organized in a symmetrical way. Large windows embellished the place, letting in all the day light. Some windows were colorful. Others were simply transparent. At the center of the great Library, tables and elegant wood chairs were placed. Giant chandeliers hung above, and despite the day light, they were lit on, which made the place look majestic!!

Dalya couldn't believe her own eyes. It was the first time in all her life, that she could see so many books, entire walls filled of books. She remained motionless and amazed. Until the sweet voice of Miss Guendolyn reminded her to follow her:

- This section corresponds to the books, encyclopedias, articles and brochures of medicine. You will find everything you need. The ranking is by alphabetical order.

And addressing Dalya, Miss Guendolyn said:

- You can consult books on the desks, right here. Although you are not an official student in this school, you have Professor Canfield's permission, and so the right to come here any time you want. If you need anything, please let me know.
- Thank you Miss Guendolyn. Replied Professor Canfield, all amused to see Dalya astonished by such a place. He continued:
- There are an endless number of books here, of any kind, topic, type, level, and age. Everything that you are looking for or would like to read. I believe it could be a nice change for you, from the daily newspapers. You can stay here for now. In an hour, we will get back to our lessons. Meet me in the classroom when you are done.
- Thank you, Professor. Dalya smiled back at him.

Immediately, Dalya headed toward the section indicated by Miss Guendolyn. She consulted the titles of the books on the first shelf:

- Anatomy General ... Anesthesia and resuscitation ... Approach of the respiratory system ... All cardiovascular vocabulary ... Analyze of Human biochemistry and physiology...

After a 10 minutes' quest, Dalya searched in the 5th book shelf:

- Diseases of diabetes ... Diseases of hearts ... Disease of respiratory system ... Disease of the human body! That's what I need! Disease of the human body ... it must certainly contain all the informations about the illness I'm looking for!

Dalya stretched her arms with all her strength to take this book, but she could not reach in the 5th book shelf. She jumped 2 times, without being able to get there either.

When suddenly, a young woman of Asian origin, approached Dalya. In the early thirties, the woman was tall and very slim. She had long black straight hair, waving graciously at each of her movements. She had her eyes drawn in Asian way, and skin as soft as a rose petal. She was wearing a long right dress, refining her size, in embroidered silk, and an enhanced collar. Dalya didn't know who was this young woman; a teacher? a visitor to the Library? a supervisor in this school?

The young woman pulled out effortlessly a book from the 5th shelf, and she handed it to Dalya. And before Dalya could thank her, the young woman disappeared into another corridor. Dalya examined the book that was given to her:

- It's ... the book of rare diseases ... but ... this isn't the one I wanted.

Dalya put down the book on the Library desk, among a few other books she had already chose to consult. After many long minutes of reading and searching, Dalya was surprised to find the answer to her question in ... the book that the young woman handed her, by mistake!

Dalya was able to understand a little more about Mrs. Marianne's illness. She noted all the information that she needed on a paper:

"... The disease Fibromyalgia is a pain throughout the body, most often it is a severe pain associated with fatigue and sleep disorders, preventing the person to perform simple daily movements. The nerve being very painful and sensitive, all contact with cold, wind, and heat can intensify the pain. Patients suffer from least movements like walking, talking, chewing food or simply smiling. The treatment of this disease is limited to painkillers ... "

Dalya put back into their places, all the books that she used, and then she headed out toward the exit of the Library.

When Dalya passed through the office of Miss Guendolyn, the woman watched the little girl until she disappeared in the hallway. Miss Guendolyn had seen thousands of students attending this school. But the Library assistant felt something strange about this new student who wore a boy overall, a big bonnet on her head and old shoes. At that moment, Miss Guendolyn had an unusual strange feeling.

Dalya was so happy and thrilled to have access to the Library. She was impatient to discover all the books there. Around the dinner table in the annex house, Dalya described to her father the school Library. He answered while serving himself dinner:

- Yes ... Yes ... it is good! But it's the money that matters the most, way more than the books!! Don't forget that you must succeed the challenges so that I can have the fortune of Mr. Balthazar! It must be your one and only goal!
- How on earth can books be useful for a silly idiot girl like her? Said her mother in a mocking tone, while trying so hard to feed both her twins at the same time. Ari and Adi threw back in the air any food's spoon coming from their mother.

Dalya went silent; she understood that her parents were not interested to hear about the school Library. Dalya finished her plate silently, she cleared the table, and she washed the dishes and put them back in the closet. Then, Dalya walked quickly to her bedroom. She pulled off the paper where she had written all of the informations collected on Mrs. Marianne's illness. Dalya finally understood why Mrs. Marianne didn't come out of her room. It was a very difficult and incurable disease. Now that she understood what the first sentence of the clue meant, the second sentence seemed to be as complicated as the first one. Dalya thought aloud:

- Fibromyalgia ... It's a pain throughout the body ... so she can't get out of her house, walk or move ... and also an intolerance to the wind, the sun, the heat and the cold ... she cannot talk for long, or chew too much. And she cannot leave the room ... Plant a kernel ... a seed, a flower, a plant, a fruit ... water at the source ... to water ... how can gardening tips help Mrs. Marianne? ... There is nothing that Mrs. Marianne can do outside ... she cannot even get out of her bedroom! How can she go gardening and care for the roses she planted? That's not possible ...

After a long moment of reflection, Dalya noticed the shadow of an idea. She kept thinking aloud and digging for ideas in her head:

- Mrs. Marianne can't go gardening ... she cannot move. But ... what if ...?

Dalya was not so sure that her idea would work out. But she was determined to at least try.

Chapter 15

The Gardener of the grand Mansion

Saturday, August 09th, 1890.

The Gardener of the grand Mansion was a big tall man, strong and vigorous. He had gray chalked eyes, blond hair with white highlights, and slightly pink tanned skin because of the summer sun. He was wearing a long gray apron attached to his back, a little blue shawl tied around his neck, and big green boots. Dalya met him several times when she was leaving for school and on her way back too. The Gardener of the grand Mansion always looked serious and severe, Dalya never saw him smile. And although he was sixty years old, he was still working actively and ardently.

It was a beautiful day, a clear sky and fresh air. The Snow Panther, Séraphine, was lying down on the grass, enjoying the rays of sun warming her fur. When she noticed Dalya approaching, the Snow Panther straightened her head up and she followed the little girl in her usual stare.

The Gardener, a few meters away from the Panther, was busy washing a black luxurious car; he didn't realize Dalya's presence behind him. A few buckets of water and towels were on the floor in front of him, a sponge in his hand, and a dry cloth on his shoulder. Dalya approached him, with a little smile:

- Good morning, Sir...

The Gardener turned around, surprised by the presence of the little girl, wearing a boy overall, yellowed shirt with sleeves lifted up, and a large cap on her head. Without a word, he continued his cleaning. Dalya said:

- My name is Dal...
- I know who you are!! He interrupted her, in an authoritarian and harsh voice.

Dalya asked nicely:

- I recognize this car ... it was Mr. Iskander Balthazar's car, wasn't it?

The Gardener ignored Dalya and he kept cleaning with a wet sponge, dipping it in the bucket filled with soaped water.

- Are you Mr. Gardener, the man who takes care of the grand Mansion gard...
- So, what? The Gardener grew impatient.
- I was wondering if you can please, teach me how to plant flowers ...

The expression on the Gardener's face showed that he didn't expect this kind of request. He looked at the little girl standing in front of him, and then he said in a firm, authoritarian voice:

- No! That's not possible!!
- Why not? Asked Dalya curious.
- You are Mademoiselle Dalya Bouvard! He replied, as if his answer should have been obvious for the little girl.
- And ... so? Said Dalya, who couldn't understand the reason of his refusal.
- You are an Heiress! The Gardener appeared to lose his calm.
- I'm still not an Heiress yet. Answered Dalya with a disarming innocence.
- Masters don't do gardening! He said in a severe tone.
- But ... why not? Asked again Dalya, always too curious.
- What do you mean why not? These are the manners of high and distinguished society! Masters never do gardening!! And they don't get dirty either!! Shouted the Gardener in an upset and angry tone.

During a long silent moment, and hearing no more irritating questions, the Gardener thought that the little girl had left the place. He continued to clean the Black car. When he turned around to the other side of the car, the Gardener couldn't believe his own eyes. The little girl had taken a little sponge, she had wet it in one of the buckets and she was cleaning Mr. Balthazar's car, under the shocked eyes of the Gardener:

- But ... What are you doing?
- I am helping you clean the car, Mr. Gardener. Said Dalya with a big smile.
- Who asked you to do so?
- No one. Said Dalya without losing her enthusiasm.
- So ... Why do you do it? The Gardener appeared puzzled; he didn't understand what Dalya was up to.

Dalya replied all innocently, without hesitation:

- I like to clean cars. That's what I was doing with my father at the end of each working day. We used to clean our cart.
- But I'm the employee of the grand Mansion! It is my job to clean it up! The Gardener lost his patience in front of the very unusual questions and strange manners of the little girl.
- Yes, Mr. Gardener, I am aware of that. But I like to do it anyway. Insisted Dalya.

The big man suddenly yelled:

- DROP THIS SPONGE IMMEDIATELY!! DO NOT TOUCH ANYTHING ANYMORE!! IN HOW MANY LANGUAGES MUST I EXPLAIN TO YOU THAT YOU CANNOT DO GARDENING OR WASH A CAR!! AND STOP CALLING ME MR. GARDENER!!

Dalya jumped off her place; she released the sponge in the big bucket in front of her, and she moved a step back. The Panther, still lying down on the grass a few meters away from them, did not move. Séraphine felt that Dalya was in no danger. Her little head was staring at Dalya in a neutral look, its long tail moved in the air, once a while.

The Gardener turned back around and he took over the car cleaning, while ignoring Dalya. The little girl couldn't understand the good manners of high and distinguished society; she saw no harm or shame in gardening or cleaning a car, being rich or poor. And the Gardener couldn't understand the little girl's strange manners, her curious questions and her lack of understanding something that seemed obvious. Dalya waited for a moment, hoping that the Gardener will change his mind. Dalya watched him for a long time. She got tired eventually, so she left and went back home.

But even if she was pushed away and ignored, Dalya wasn't the kind to give up that easily ...

The very next day, Sunday, August 10th, 1890.

Dalya searched for the Gardener in the grand Mansion. She found him in another side of the garden. The Snow Panther was close to the big man; the creature was sometimes stretching her legs, and sometimes running to catch a butterfly. This time, the Gardener was busy doing some gardening work; he was returning the earth soil using a big gardening fork. Near him, there were dozens of little pots, each filled with a red rose, of a splendid color. The Gardener got aware of Dalya's presence, when he turned his head around to take one of the rose pots near him, in order to plant it. And before he could say anything, Dalya greeted him with a nice smile:

- Good morning Mr. Gard...

She paused, remembering that he forbade her yesterday from calling him Mr. Gardener. She remained motionless, in front of him. The Gardener pretended not to see her, hoping that the little girl will get bored and will disappear after a few minutes. But a long time went by, without Dalya leaving the Gardener's side. Until finally, he raised his head toward her, and he looked at her with an angry and a threatening stare, hoping to scare her out of his sight and hopefully she will leave him alone. That's when Dalya dared to ask him politely:

- Can I watch you while you are working, Sir? ... Please ...

Politeness disarms the most difficult and hard characters. In front of the little girl's obstinacy, Mr. Gardener lost his words; he stared at Dalya for a brief moment and he said in an angry voice:

- Rosenwald!

The Gardener continued his work. From that single word, Dalya understood that it was the big man's name. And since he didn't yell at her to go away, she guessed that he allowed her to stay close by, and watch him work. The Gardener remained speechless in front of the politeness and the courage of this strange little girl, despite the fact that he has been hostile and rude with her, the day before.

Dalya approached him to better see the moves that he was doing with his hands, turning the soil and planting the roses. When it was time for the 3rd rose to be planted, the Gardener turned around to find Dalya, handing him over the flower pot. He looked at her in a cold stare, and he took the pot in a quick move. When he had finished planting his 3rd rose, he fixed the plant with a stick. Dalya asked:

- Why should we hang the flowers with sticks?
- Because they need support to grow. They are still fragile and not strong enough. He replied in a serious voice, without looking at Dalya.

When the Gardener turned around to pick up the 4th rose, he was astonished at what his eyes were seeing. Dalya was sitting next to him; she had already made a hole in the ground, in exactly the same way like he did. She took the contents of a pot, a small red rose, with her two hands; she placed it gently and delicately on the hole. Then, she looked at the Gardener and she displayed a little innocent and very proud smile. Mr. Rosenwald couldn't believe what Dalya had just done, without his permission, nor fearing his anger and his bad temper. The Gardener barely hid his surprise, he was disarmed by Dalya's smile. He pulled himself together and yelled:

- Well?! …What are you waiting for? … You need to quickly fill the hole through the earth! Otherwise the flower will die!

Dalya complied rapidly; she took some of the earth soil with her two small hands and gently dispersed it around the flower.

- Faster!!! Faster!!! He exclaimed.

She hurried up.

- Make some holes with your fingers around the rose! And fill the holes with water! Ordered the Gardener, while he pointed at a container full of water.

She stood up and pulled the water container, and then she made holes with her little fingers on the ground around the flower, and she watered the plant. Dalya was dirty, it was her first time gardening, but she was so proud of her achievement and her little planted rose.

At that moment, the Gardener, Mr. Rosenwald observed the little girl in a slightly different look than before. Sometimes, just as you plant roses in the ground, other things can be planted in people's hearts …

The days that followed, Dalya learned many things about gardening; the different names and seasons of flowers and trees, how to preserve them, how to plant, cultivate, water and take good care of the plants. Even if Mr. Rosenwald often spoke to her in a cold and severe voice, he didn't forbid her from staying near him, or doing some work at the garden; Dalya always remained polite and smiling. And Séraphine, the Snow Panther, she kept watching the little girl, in a calm and tranquil stare.

After working with him for a few days, a tiny little detail held Dalya's attention; Mr. Rosenwald was limping. When she watched him for hours, she realized something strange ... it was as if he had a foot shorter than the other ... Never Dalya have seen such a thing. It was clear and obvious that Mr. Rosenwald made a lot of efforts to walk normally and straight in the presence of Dalya. But sometimes, he got tired of such efforts or simply he forgot, he limped. Dalya couldn't dare to ask him questions about his foot shorter than the other. She didn't want to embarrass him or cause him any uncomfortable feeling.

Friday, August 15th, 1890.

In the afternoon, at the end of her classes, Dalya headed toward the Library of the Royal Georgetown College, and she passed through the Library assistant's office, Miss Guendolyn. The woman watched the strange little girl enter, in a curious stare.

Dalya walked toward the medical section, and she knew exactly what she was looking for. She examined many books, to find one entitled:

Malformation of bone-related diseases

She put down the book on the desk and she read one page after another. After minutes, Dalya wrote a few notes on a piece of paper; she returned the book to its place, and walked toward the Library's exit.

Suddenly, something just held her out. Dalya paused for a moment, and she looked at Miss Gwendolyn's office, who was a few steps away. The woman was busy in her usual duties. Dalya stepped back and she returned to the book sections. This time, she surpassed the section of medical books, she took a few steps in a different aisle, and she searched the titles, to finally pull out one book and flipped quickly its pages. Dalya spotted a particular sentence, she repeated it a few times out loud, then she placed the book back to its place, and she headed, this time for good, into the Library's exit.

Miss Guendolyn was sorting envelopes into different folders. When suddenly, she thought she heard a shy little voice saying:

- Priyaten Den.

Miss Guendolyn looked up to find in front of her a little girl wearing overall and a large cap on her head. For a second, Miss Guendolyn thought she was dreaming and that she heard the little girl wish her a good day in her native language, the Bulgarian. Except that Dalya repeated once again her sentence, with a smile and a voice slightly more confident than the first time:

- Priyaten Den.

Miss Gwendolyn's face lit up instantly, her cheeks turned all red. She had not dreamed, she was indeed greeted in her native language!

Since all her long years of service in this Library, never a student or a teacher had ever noticed the little flag on her desk, or got curious of its origin, or even spoke to her in her own language. Dalya had not pronounced it correctly, and Miss Guendolyn knew it wasn't the little girl's native language, but she was all surprised, astonished and moved by the gesture of this strange new little girl. Miss Guendolyn hardly pulled herself together and she said in a voice full of gratitude:

- Thank you, Mademoiselle ... you too.

Chapter 16

A simple Gardenia flower

Sunday, August 17ᵗʰ, 1890.

It was a beautiful summer morning. The Gardener, Mr. Rosenwald was watering the plants in the south wing of the grand Mansion, and he was lost in his thoughts. When suddenly, he believed he heard Mr. Iskander Balthazar's voice behind him. He turned immediately, and noticed Dalya standing and smiling at him. She repeated her question:

- Will you leave me some flowers to water?

Mr. Rosenwald seemed confused; he murmured while staring curiously at Dalya:

- He used to ... ask the exact same request ...

Dalya didn't understand what Mr. Rosenwald meant:

- What? Someone else asked the same question as me?

The Gardener pulled himself together at once, and he coldly replied:

- No one!! Never mind!!

Mr. Rosenwald rapidly regained his upset and serious usual behavior. He continued to water the plants. Dalya was holding an empty pot in her hands, she asked him politely:

- Can I take one flower, please? It's for someone who I...

Mr. Rosenwald interrupted her with a wave of his hand, showing her to serve herself from the carriage filled with pots of flowers of different types and colors. There were several red carnations, pink bodices, white daisies, some lilies ... but what Dalya preferred the most, it was the Gardenia flower. She planted it in her pot, she filled it with a bit of soil and she watered it carefully.

Immediately, Dalya ran toward the exit of the grand Mansion. After few minutes, she arrived at her destination; the home of the French neighbors, les Poirier. When Mrs. Glorina opened the door, she was thrilled to see the little girl, and she invited her to come inside. Dalya asked:

- I hope I am not disturbing you, Mrs. Glorina.
- On the contrary, Mademoiselle! I am very happy that you stopped by! I don't get many visits in this house. I was just about to bring the breakfast platter to Mrs. Marianne... replied Mrs. Glorina while inviting Dalya to follow her into the kitchen.

- Can I get ahead of you, to Mrs. Marianne's bedroom, if you don't mind? I brought her a flower. I hope she likes it. Asked Dalya, who was still holding the pot in her hand.
- How nice of you, Mademoiselle! It's a beautiful flower! She will love it, that's for sure! I'm waiting for the bread to heat up for a few more minutes. But go ahead, please!! I'm coming in a minute. Said Mrs. Glorina, while arranging the rest of Mrs. Marianne breakfast platter.

Dalya passed through the same corridor as before. And as soon as she took a few steps in, the little girl felt a door opening in the corridor, and she was convinced that the same shadow followed her, like the previous times. When she arrived at the bedroom door of the great woman, Dalya took off her shoes; she put them outside in the hallway, and she gently opened the door. The bedroom was dark, the large curtains allowed only little light to enter. Dalya walked slowly toward Mrs. Marianne's bed; the great woman was lying down and awake, she seemed lost in her thoughts, her eyes watching through the darkness. Dalya spoke in a soft and shy voice:

- Good morning to you, Madame.

Mrs. Marianne turned her head around, to find Dalya in front of her. She seemed surprised to receive visitors, and even more surprised that her visitor was a little girl she barely knew. Dalya was still holding the flower pot in her hands. She approached Mrs. Marianne and greeted her in a nice voice:

- I hope you are feeling better today, Madame.

Mrs. Marianne straightened up in her bed with slow movements, and she looked at the little girl, without speaking a word. Dalya guessed that Mrs. Marianne was wondering the reason of her presence. Dalya continued, smiling:

- In the school where I take some classes, there is an enormous Library ... and I've searched about the illness that prevents you to expose yourself to the sun, the wind and the cold. I heard that before your illness, you liked spending time out in your garden, to take care of your flowers. And ... since you can't move now to your roses ... so then ... I thought maybe it's time they move for you!

Dalya presented the white flower to Mrs. Marianne, so that the great woman can take a better look at it. Dalya explained:

- It is not like the roses that you already have in your garden. But ... it is a lovely flower that I like very much, it is called a Gardenia, and delivers a wonderful smell, it is a beautiful white color, the leaves are the greenest of all ... I've planted it and I've watered it especially for you, Madame.

Still without any slight reaction from Mrs. Marianne, Dalya turned around and she walked toward a big window in the middle of the bedroom. She put down her flowerpot on a table in front of the window, and then she opened slightly the large curtains. The light of this beautiful day helped the flower shine bright:

- I will leave it to you, right here. A small glass of water every day and a few hours of sun will make it bloom longer. That's what I've been taught by the Gardener of the grand Mansion, Mr. Rosenwald. I hope, you like it, Madame?

The great woman stared at the little girl for a long moment, to a point when Dalya began to doubt herself, and think that maybe it was a bad idea, maybe she shouldn't have intervened and entered the French family's house, maybe what she had just did was clumsy or offensive. When suddenly, Dalya was interrupted by Mrs. Glorina bringing the breakfast plate to Mrs. Marianne:

- Good morning Mrs. Marianne! It's good that you are awake! It looks like a beautiful day today!

Mrs. Glorina placed down the platter near the bed, and she helped Mrs. Marianne to eat her breakfast. Dalya having had no reaction from Mrs. Marianne, she shyly whispered to Mrs. Glorina:

- I better go and leave you to your work, Mrs. Glorina.

Mrs. Glorina turned around toward Dalya and greeted her:

- Glad of your visit, Mademoiselle. I hope to see you soon!

Dalya took a last glance at Mrs. Marianne. The great woman kept starring at Dalya in a silent and strange air. Dalya smiled timidly at her, and then she left the bedroom. The same silhouette on the window, followed Dalya until she crossed the garden and left the home of the French neighbors, les Poirier.

When Mrs. Glorina finished helping Mrs. Marianne take her breakfast, she took the platter and was about to leave the bedroom. Before closing the door, Mrs. Glorina addressed the great woman:

- If you need anything else, Mrs. Marianne, just ring me. I will be right down stairs to take care of the laundry today; it is a sunny da...

But Mrs. Glorina realized that the great woman wasn't listening to anything she was saying. Usually, Mrs. Marianne lies back on her bed, quite immediately after taking her meal. She used to spend all her days lying down on her bed, sleeping or observing the sky through the little opening in the curtains.

Except that day, and for the first time since a long time, Mrs. Glorina noticed that the great woman didn't lay down back on her bed immediately. Mrs. Marianne remained motionless, sitting on her bed, watching the beautiful flower on the table near the window. Mrs. Glorina thought that this reaction was a little odd.

Dalya didn't clearly understand how the Excelbox clue could help improve the life of the great woman. Mrs. Marianne's illness was incurable. Dalya had perfectly followed the instructions of the clue. She searched about the disease at the school Library, she planted a flower in a pot, and she even watered the Gardenia flower before she offered it.

Is it all what the Excelbox has asked her to do? Was it that simple? How can a flower improve a person's life? But no doctor has been able to heal Mrs. Marianne ... was the Excelbox mistakenly thinking that it could find a cure? Dalya thought about these questions, on her way back to the annex house of the grand Mansion.

For Dalya Bouvard, offering a Gardenia flower to a sick person was a simple gesture of kindness and empathy. The little 12 years old girl didn't realize that she was offering much more than a Gardenia flower. She offered ... much more ...

Chapter 17

A planted seed

Tuesday, August 26th, 1890. In the kitchen of the grand Mansion.

- I saw them both! With my own eyes! Explained Océanie Shell.

The Cook assistant of the grand Mansion pulled out the plates from a closet and she displayed them on the large wooden table, installed in the middle of the kitchen. Océanie Shell was a young girl; her curly dark chestnut hair was nicely arranged in her white work bonnet. She had big curious eyes of a hazelnut color and a sharp nose searching for any smell or any new facts in the grand Mansion. Her very pale skin showed off some redness on her cheeks whenever she made an effort. She was wearing a long dress and a long white apron.

- Ma è Impossibile! You didn't see well! Replied Mr. Ferrero Lutché, with his Italian accent.

He was the Chef Cook of the grand Mansion. He listened to the latest news of his assistant Océanie, while being busy adding some last herbs in the soup for tonight's dinner. Mr. Ferrero Lutché was curious as well, to know what was going on in the grand Mansion. He was small and chubby, but had very light and twirling steps. He was wearing a large white apron, a big hat on his bald head, a checkered red and white scarf around his neck. And he had a small tidy mustache. Very meticulous and cheerful, Mr. Ferrero Lutché was able to cook several dishes simultaneously without mixing any recipe.

- Yes, I am sure of what my eyes have seen!! I am telling you, I saw both of them talking! I couldn't hear exactly what they were saying, but I saw them both! Insisted Océanie.
- Incredibile! You're ... Certain? Asked Mr. Ferrero, in a scandalized voice.

Before Océanie could answer the question, Cristelle, the girl who was in charge of the household in the grand Mansion, entered the kitchen. She was holding a large basket full of beautiful red apples, which she put on the kitchen table. Despite her small size, chubby weight, and her active moves, Cristelle could be easily discerned from other employees of the grand Mansion, thanks to her wavy chocolate color hair. She was barely 20 years old; she had sweet almond color eyes, a big pink smile and white teeth shining through her sugar brown skin.

Cristelle was followed by two men. The first one was Mr. Benjamin Bûchebois, the employees' Manager and the person in charge of the grand Mansion's supervision. And the second one was Igor Richter, his aid server. Mr. Benjamin Bûchebois was a tall man, he had a slow and firm walk, a white net skin, straight salt and pepper hair, immaculately arranged, eyes underscored by some dark circles underneath. All throughout the day, he wore a very elegant black suit, a white ivory shirt, white gloves and a bow tie finely wound on the neck.

Igor, the Aid Server entered in fast steps. He was of the same age as the 2 girls, Océanie shell and Cristelle, the early twenties. His platinum blond hair was all bristling and mixed. He was in charge of serving the meals and helping Mr. Benjamin Bûchebois in his everyday tasks. As soon as they were all inside the kitchen, Océanie announced:

- You'll never guess what I saw! The new Heiress and Mr. Weil Rosenwald were talking in the Garden!

All the present people in the kitchen were surprised of what they had just learned. Océanie continued:

- And I am sure of what I saw! They spoke for several minutes yesterday. And today, the little girl came back and she remained near Mr. Rosenwald for about an hour...
- What were they talking about? Asked Mr. Benjamin Bûchebois, with a nice French accent.
- I couldn't hear their conversation. But I saw with my own eyes Mr. Rosenwald talking to her and the little girl helped him in the garden work! Océanie was outraged but proud of her news.
- She helped ... water and cut the plants? Exclaimed Igor before settling first on the dinner table.
- But ... Perché ... why? Asked the Chef Cook Mr. Ferrero Lutché aloud.
- Many strange things have been going on in the grand Mansion since the passing away of the Governor. Mr. Benjamin Bûchebois said in a surprised voice, and he sat down on a chair in front of the dinner table.
- Perhaps this little girl just enjoys gardening, replied Cristelle in an amused tone.
- It's very clear that she has much to learn to be accepted in noble society. Exclaimed Océanie with a haughty air.
- And then what ... ancora? Domani she will want to cook? She will not put one foot in my cucina in any way! Nobody come vicino mia cucina! She shouldn't dream of it! Yelled Mr. Ferrero Lutché threateningly, while pointing up his wooden spoon.

Mr. Benjamin Bûchebois answered in a sarcastic voice:

- Well ... It may not be such a bad idea after all ... One must admit that it has been a long time since we had good tasty soups ...

When hearing this remark, the Cook Mr. Ferrero was about to explode, he became angry:

- MIO soup?! MIO soup?!
- And it's happening again!! Cristelle raised her eyes up at the sky in a desperate voice, after attending this next scene for the thousand times.

The Cook, Mr. Ferrero put a large pot of soup on the table, in a brusque move, and he exclaimed in an accusatory tone toward Mr. Benjamin Bûchebois:

- I remind you that it is your colpa! Your fault! You tell me no salt, no butter, no pepper, no cheese, no milk, no herbs, no spices, not this, not that ... how am I supposed to cuoco lo soup?

Mr. Benjamin Bûchebois answered in a quiet voice, while cleaning his watch with a white napkin:

- We, in great France, we can make exquisite soups without vegetables, with only onions, chicken broth and wa...
- And here we go again too! Exclaimed Cristelle for the 2nd time.

The Cook Mr. Ferrero lost his cool:

- You say us italiano ... siamo incapaci? Are unable to cook like you?!

Mr. Benjamin let go a proud and a provocative laugh:

- But, Monsieur ... the entire world cannot cook like us. We, in great France, we master perfectly the refined gastronomy. It is an important science ...
- It's ridicolo! We are the Maestro of the pasta and the sauces ...
- Well ... somehow ... It is true that you have one or two good dishes, yes ... but we, in great France, we are the only ones able to create exquisite and refined dishes ...

Igor served himself some soup without waiting for anyone to start. Océanie ignored the brawl that started between the Italian Cook and the French Householder. Océanie was lost in her thoughts:

- I'm curious to know how the little girl managed to make the Gardener be so nice with her ... to the point that he even allowed her to help him in the garden!!

Cristelle served herself some bread that was still warm and she immediately replied in a sarcastic tone:

- Maybe she just asked politely! You should try it too, it works every time!

Océanie made a mocking face toward Cristelle. Igor said, his mouth full between two bites of bread:

- Me ... as long as we get paid ... for our work and we get our salary at the end of the month ... it doesn't matter to me who will be the boss in this house.

The fight between the French householder and the Italian Cook calmed down after a short time. While eating dinner, all the employees of the grand Mansion were amazed by hearing this news. No one thought that one day Mr. Weil Rosenwald could be nice to anyone and more surprisingly toward a little girl. The Gardener was very discreet, always severe, very withdrawn and difficult to talk to.

When suddenly, the Gardener Mr. Weil Rosenwald entered through the door from behind, he settled directly on the dinner table and he served himself diner. A silence invaded the kitchen for a couple of minutes, everyone wanted to ask the same question but no one dared to speak. When finally, Cristelle began:

- The new neighbors are discreet. I see the little girl when she crosses the garden of the grand Mansion to go to school each morning. She looks calm.

Having no reaction of Mr. Rosenwald, the Cook Mr. Ferrero Lutché continued:

- I heard that her mother is ... una donna pazza ... crazy! She is a fanatic about cleanliness. She cleans the floor 5 times per day! And I was also told that from the outside, her mother seems to be an Angelo. But inside, she's ... Diabolical!

Mr. Benjamin Bûchebois continued:

- For me, it's the father who surprises me the most. How could a vegetable merchant easily get a job at the Toscana restaurant? We, in great France, such a thing would have never happened. He must have some real and high qualifications to work for such a prestigious restaurant!! That's a shady affair.
- Perhaps a stroke of luck. Said Cristelle.

Igor said with an amused tone:

- No no no! It's a bit too much for luck, don't you think?! A fortune, a home for the family, a job for the father, and an admission in a school for the little girl ... It's way too easy!

Mr. Benjamin Bûchebois poured himself water, before thinking aloud:

- Anyway ... Séraphine seems bewitched by the little girl ... I will never forget her aggressive reaction toward the nephew Mr. Ferdinand Edelmen! Since the time I have been working in this house, the Snow Panther never had such a behavior. Never!

The Cook Mr. Ferrero added a handful of salt and butter into his bowl of soup, and he said:

- Séraphine allows persona to approach her. But it almost looks like she ...
- ... She likes the little girl? It could be! Cristelle finished the sentence of Mr. Ferrero Lutché.
- I will not have a little 12 years old girl as a Master, it's outrageous! Fortunately, she was forbidden to enter the grand Mansion by Mr. Ernest Laszlo! Mr. Benjamin Bûchebois exclaimed with a defiant air.

And for once, the Cook Mr. Ferrero approved his colleague's remark.

- I admit ... it is quite unusual to have a 12 year's old little girl running the grand Mansion. Igor thought aloud.
- Anyway ... the little girl seems to be nice. Cristelle replied.

Océanie exclaimed in a mocking and scornful tone:

- Nice or not, this little veggy seller does not look like an Heiress. She's always dressed as a boy, always in those merchants overall. She speaks very rarely, probably because she is aware that her manners are too savage. She will never be part of high distinguished society, I'll tell you that! ... You can tell she's an idiot just by the wa...

When suddenly, Océanie was interrupted by the Gardener Mr. Rosenwald, who put down his spoon in a sudden aggressive and brutal move, to the point that the entire cutlery on the dining table bounced at once. The Gardener Mr. Rosenwald gave Océanie a cold and threatening look, and then he said in a firm and strong tone:

- ENOUGH TALKING ABOUT HER!

Silence and shock invaded the kitchen. After some tense seconds, the Gardener took on his spoon and he continued to eat his soup. All the employees continued to eat their meals in a total silence. Mr. Benjamin Bûchebois and Mr. Ferrero Lutché exchanged a confused look. Océanie became all red and she didn't dare to speak again. Igor grimaced and he finished his plate. No one dared to talk about the new neighbors in front of the Gardener, Mr. Weil Rosenwald.

But Cristelle was very curious. Why did Mr. Rosenwald had this reaction when Océanie spoke unkindly of the little girl? Did Cristelle understood and heard correctly? Was the Gardener defending the little girl? ... Well that would be a first!

But what could have changed the behavior of Mr. Rosenwald? Didn't he despise all human contact? Wasn't he cold and severe to everyone? What is it about the new family that moved into the annex house? What has softened the heart of the coldest man of the grand Mansion? What were the conversations about between Dalya and Mr. Rosenwald? And how did this little girl manage to be defended by Mr. Rosenwald?

So many questions without answers appeared in Cristelle's mind. But curious as she was, she soon was about to discover the truth behind it all.

Something new and strange was planted and growing. Cristelle could feel the change coming. But she wasn't the only one.

The French neighbor, Mrs. Marianne Poirier, lying down on her bed; she usually stares at the big window with a distracted and sad expression. Except on that day, the great woman was watching the little Gardenia flower and she was smiling.

The Library assistant at the Royal Georgetown College, Miss Guendolyn Knigaski, sitting on her desk at the entrance of the Library; she was usually busy and plunged in her paperwork. Except on that day, she was observing the little flag on her desk and she was smiling.

After finishing his dinner, the Gardener, Mr. Rosenwald went his bedroom, in the employees' side of the grand Mansion. A large bed was placed at the corner, a wood table desk and a chair were in front of the big window, many tools and craft utensils were put on the desk and on the floor, a little gray brick fireplace was standing along the wall.

The Gardener took off his big work apron. Then, he removed his large green gardening boots and he put on his ordinary shoes. As usual, at the end of each day, the Gardener put on his coat to go out, and to turn on all the lights outside in the garden of the grand Mansion.

When he got up from his chair and took a first step, the Gardener quickly noticed that something strange was happening. He sat back immediately, thinking he must have been dizzy because of too much sun that day. The Gardener pulled himself together, he stood up again and he walked a few steps forward. He stopped, and looked at his feet.

The Gardener walked without ... limping!! He walked normally! For the first time in 50 years, he normally ... walked!

Mr. Rosenwald sat on his chair, trying to contain his feelings, fear and joy mixed altogether. He didn't understand what was going on and how this could have happened. He removed his shoes and he examined it more closely. The Gardener noticed a small piece of black gum stuck on his shoe. He muttered aloud:

- But ... What is that thing? How ... how did it stuck? Who did thi...

The Gardener froze in his chair, while recalling the many times where he turned around to see the little girl cleaning his shoes. He always thought that this Heiress was crazy to clean the shoes of a Gardener, she was too naïve and had no refined manners. But he was far from imagining that Dalya pretended to clean his shoes, and that in fact she was fixing the piece of rubber on the pair of shoes of his short leg.

The Gardener wore back his shoe again; he took a few steps in the bedroom, and for the first time in 50 years, he felt ... comfortable.

Mrs. Marianne Poirier, Miss Guendolyn Knigaski, Mr. Weil Rosenwald, Cristelle ... everyone felt a little seed that got planted in their hearts and it was growing up. None of them understood what it was exactly. But they were all smiling.

And as the Excelbox fairly predicted. Something has just dug itself a small place, it gently and discreetly planted itself, watering the cold hearts with nice polite smiles, and it was flourishing graciously. That something left everyone astonished and amazed, as if they were watching a jewel, never before displayed.

Chapter 18

Meeting Miss Francine Poirier

Friday, August 29th, 1890.

On her way back from school, Dalya met Mrs. Glorina, the employee at the French family house; les Poirier. Mrs. Glorina was walking back from downtown. When Dalya caught her up on the road, Mrs. Glorina welcomed her with a bright smile and her usual enthusiastic voice:

- Well, what a nice surprise to meet you, Mademoiselle Dalya Bouvard!
- Good afternoon, Mrs. Glorina. How are you today?
- Very well, Mademoiselle. Thank you very much for asking. Are you coming back from school?
- Yes, I had a busy day of lessons. My head is a bit dizzy. How about you?
- I was at the grocery store to get some herbal tea and spices. And you must come home with me, to enjoy a delicious pear pie!! You deserve it very well, after a busy day at school!!

Mrs. Glorina insisted on Dalya to follow her. After pushing the garden's door of the Poirier house, Dalya noticed a black car at the entrance. Mrs. Glorina explained to Dalya:

- It looks like we have visitors … It must be Miss Francine who came to visit her mother. She's finally back from her vacation.

When they stepped inside the kitchen, Mrs. Glorina put her bags on the table, and she asked Dalya to take a seat. She cut a large piece of a pear pie and served the little girl. Dalya didn't wait for an invite to eat, the pie was so delicious! While Mrs. Glorina arranged the dinner platter of Mrs. Marianne, she added a cup of tea and a teapot on the set. When Dalya finished her pie, she followed Mrs. Glorina upstairs, toward the bedroom of Mrs. Marianne. Mrs. Glorina entered first and she greeted politely:

- Good afternoon, Mrs. Marianne. Good afternoon, Miss Francine.

When Dalya took a few steps into the bedroom, she noticed the presence of another woman, other than Mrs. Marianne. Miss Francine Poirier was in the end of her thirties, very very fat and a small size, a pale white skin, long coal black hair, black eyes, a cold look, a very thin pink mouth. Miss Francine was unfortunately ugly, compared to the beauty of her mother, Mrs. Marianne. One would have trouble believing that she was her daughter. Miss Francine was sitting on a divan in the other side of the bedroom, while Mrs. Marianne was lying down on her bed as usual. Miss Francine asked with an arrogant and bored tone:

- Do we have to wait forever to be served tea in this house?

Mrs. Glorina replied only with a forced smile. Miss Francine continued:

- Who is this?

After putting the dinner platter next to Mrs. Marianne, Mrs. Glorina put a cup of tea and a teapot on a table, in front of Miss Francine. Mrs. Glorina answered:

- It's Mademoiselle Dalya Bouvard, our new neighbor. She comes to visit Mrs. Marianne sometimes.

Dalya smiled at Miss Francine and greeted her politely:

- It is nice to meet you.

Except that Miss Francine stared at the little girl, from head to toe, in a disapproving gaze, and she didn't say a word or return the greeting.

Mrs. Glorina helped Mrs. Marianne eat her dinner, while Dalya walked toward the flower pot that was still in the same place. Mrs. Marianne followed Dalya's every move, just like all her previous visits. Miss Francine was also curious of this little girl's behavior. Dalya opened the window just a little bit, she removed the curtains a little, and she sprinkled the flower with a bit of water from a container.

- Who brought this horror here? My mother doesn't like flowers! Said Miss Francine in a mocking tone.

Mrs. Glorina turned her head around, and she answered immediately instead of Dalya:

- It's called a Gardenia flower. Mademoiselle Dalya planted it herself in this pot. She offered it to your mother. This flower smells so good; your mother had no objection to keep it in her bedroom.

It was very clear enough that Miss Francine didn't like Dalya's presence, and also the fact that a person gives her mother a gift.

- So then ... you are the little peasant who has been bothering my mother lately?
- Mademoiselle Dalya Bouvard is the Heiress to late Mr. Governor! Replied Mrs. Glorina all proud.
- Not yet an Heiress, as I know. Miss Francine interrupted her in a mocking tone.

Mrs. Glorina continued to assist the great woman in eating her dinner, while Dalya remained silent and took care of the Gardenia flower by cutting out few leaves. When Mrs. Marianne finished her meal, Mrs. Glorina stood up and she asked Miss Francine:

- Would you like to be served your dinner now, Miss Francine?
- No. I will wait for my brother.

Mrs. Glorina took the platter, and made an eye sign toward Dalya to follow her instantly. Dalya smiled and said goodbye to Miss Francine, who didn't answer her back. Instead, Francine Poirier stared at the little girl in a cold arrogant air.

Then, Dalya turned toward Mrs. Marianne and she greeted the great woman, as well. Usually, Mrs. Marianne would look at the little girl in a neutral and motionless gaze. But tonight, and for the first time, Mrs Marianne smiled back at Dalya. And she had a very lovely smile. Her emerald green eyes were bright and alive, for once. Even Miss Francine sitting at the other side of the room, have noticed her mother smiling at the little girl. Dalya left the bedroom, and she followed Mrs. Glorina, back to the kitchen.

- May the Lord help me stand that woman! Exclaimed Mrs. Glorina as soon as she arrived in the kitchen. That Francine is unbearable! At each of her stays in this house, she gives me hard time. She criticizes everything that moves!
- Does she also live here in this house, with her mother? Asked Dalya.
- Oh no! Fortunately not! Francine has her own apartment in downtown. She is not married, she never had children, she has no job or occupation other than her bridge parties with her superficial friends!! Her brother, Mr. Richard Poirier is paying for all her expenses and he watches over her from afar...
- But ... Why doesn't she take care of her sick mother? Asked Dalya.

It seemed a little strange that the great woman needed assistance, and poor Mrs. Glorina had alone all the house to take care for, while Miss Francine without any major occupation or a family of her own or a job, she took no time to help and take care of her own mother. Dalya couldn't help but wonder about that.

Mrs. Glorina was embarrassed by the little girl's question; she didn't think Dalya was that smart to notice. Mrs. Glorina replied in a hesitant tone:

- Well ... Miss Francine is ... she is unable to take care of her mother. She is not ordinary ... like us.

Dalya realized that Mrs. Glorina was avoiding looking at her. How isn't she not ordinary like us? Miss Francine seemed a little snob and arrogant, but normal. Not daring to bother Mrs. Glorina more than that, Dalya greeted her, she thanked her for the delicious pie and she left the house. On her way back to the grand Mansion, Dalya couldn't stop thinking that the French neighbors, les Poirier were ... somehow odd people.

Chapter 19

When you are forced

Monday, September 1st, 1890.

The back to school in the Royal Georgetown College has officially begun. During the last 2 months of Dalya's accelerated private lessons, the school was empty, there were only few teachers and employees who occupied the corridors or the Library.

Now, Dalya had the opportunity to see the school gradually being filled with students. And on their first day, hundreds of students were talking, running, laughing, walking through the endless corridors of the school. All the girls wore long black skirts, white blouses and black jackets, silk knots on their ponytails, white socks and black shoes. The boys were also dressed in white shirts, black jackets and long pants. Nearly all the students were tall and strong.

Before starting her usual lessons with Professor Canfield, Dalya was requested at Director Darkfett office. Dalya waited on a seat in front of the Executive Secretary's office; Miss Uplerine Amana. A girl of the same age as Dalya, was sitting next to her. Dalya could not clearly see her face; the girl was looking down at her shoes. She was a small size, and chubby; her light brown hair was divided into two long braids tied with a pretty pink ribbon at the end. She was wearing the same school uniform as the other students.

Some students, girls and boys, walked by the corridor sometimes. They whispered and laughed with each other. Dalya was convinced that their stares and whispers were on her:

- Is it really her?
- Are you sure? She doesn't look like an Heiress!
- Look at what she's wearing! A boy overall!
- But, what is she doing here?
- She worked at the market before? You're sure?
- Look at her shoes!
- How did she manage to get accelerated lessons?
- I wonder if she will finish the school year in our school ...

The Secretary, Miss Uplerine Amana, looked at Dalya with discreet and curious glances, while sprinkling some water on a little green plant, near her office. When the Director rang, Miss Uplerine Amana said in a sweet voice:

- Miss Amira Mounier. You may enter now.

The girl sitting next to Dalya, stood up and opened the door of the Director's office. After 15 minutes inside, the girl came out in hurried steps, her head always down, and she disappeared in the Corridor. But Dalya could clearly notice that the girl's eyes were all puffy red and wet. Then, Miss Uplerine Amana spoke to Dalya:

- Mademoiselle Dalya Bouvard. It's your turn, now.

Despite the soft weather of September's month, the office of Director Darkfett was freezing cold, just like his character. He welcomed Dalya with a vicious smile:

- Rejoice!! You have only 3 months and couple of days left with us!!

Dalya wasn't happy at the idea of leaving school. She enjoyed her lessons with Professor Canfield, and spending all her free time at the Library, with Miss Guendolyn. Behind his desk, Director Darkfett examined Dalya for a little while, before he continued:

- I guess you noticed that the back to school started today. All the students will join their classes this week. And as expected, you are not allowed to take any course with our distinguished students. So then, you will continue your private lessons, all alone, with Professor Canfield.

The Director stood up from his chair and he approached Dalya; he spoke in a quiet but menacing voice:

- Open your ears carefully, you little vermin! You are not, by any way, allowed to get close to any student. Take off your mind the idea of making friends in this school. You are not of the same level as these noble students, and you will never be! I have agreed that a veggy seller follow lessons in this school ... only temporarily!! But I will not allow in any case, my students being disturbed by your kind! Is that clear enough for you?

Dalya didn't dare to look at Director Darkfett in front of her. He continued:

- At the slightest contact with any student ... I will be very pleased to throw you out of this school! Do you understand my words?

Dalya was relieved to exit Director Darkfett office. She was well aware that the Headmaster did not appreciate her presence in his prestigious school.

Later that night, at the annex house of the grand Mansion.

When dinner finished, Dalya took care of the dishes. Her mother put the twins in bed. Dalya's father wore his jacket and he walked toward the exit, just like all previous days, since a long time now. Dalya was still confused where her father went almost every night. But this time, before going out, Dalya's father approached her and he asked in a whispered voice, fearing that his wife might hear him:

- Did you talk to Mr. Ernest Laszlo? About what I asked you for?

Since several days now, Dalya's father was harassing her to ask the lawyer, Mr. Ernest Laszlo, for an advance of the inheritance money. Her father repeated his request almost every day. And Dalya tried to explain to her father, that they have not yet the right to this fortune. But, Antman Bouvard stubbornly insisted:

- Ask him for money! We need it! The salary they give me at the Toscana restaurant is only 13 dollars, it is not enough to feed th ...
- But ... the Lawyer Mr. Ernest Laszlo said that your pay would be 26 dollars? Dalya interrupted him spontaneously.

Antman Bouvard was not expecting this question. He looked at his daughter with threatening eyes, and he yelled:

- I'M NOT ASKING YOU TO DO THE POLICEMAN WITH ME! DO WHAT I TELL YOU TO DO! ASK HIM MORE MONEY! PERIOD!

Antman Bouvard left the house furious, slamming the door with all his strength.

As the days passed, Dalya had more unanswered questions in her mind:

- Where did her father disappear every night?
- How much exactly was her father's salary at the Toscana restaurant?
- Is it Dalya who had mistakenly heard Mr. Ernest say 26 dollars or was her father hiding half his salary?
- Why would her father lie about it?
- Why does her father absolutely and eagerly want to get money from Mr. Balthazar's fortune?

The very next night, when Dalya's mother and her twin sisters were just about to sit around the dinner table, Dalya's father came in, just in time to share this meal with his family:

- Good evening family! He said in a cheerful voice.
- Did you get the money to buy groceries for tomorrow? I have nothing left to cook! Said Mrs. Augustine, in an angry and authoritarian tone, before her husband could even sit on the dining table.

Dalya's mother rarely greeted you or said good evening, and she never cared to know how your day went on. It didn't matter that they changed houses, neighborhoods, a new job and a new life; Dalya's mother evilness didn't change a bit. It was as if the happiness of other people seriously bothered her. She never waited for her husband to have some rest after a long day at work; she would always and immediately ask him questions about money. Of all her mother's mean behavior, this was the one that Dalya hated the most. When you are in a good mood, you can be sure that Dalya's mother will do everything to demean you, humiliate you and make you feel incapable. Dalya could clearly see that her mother rejoiced to stick the knife in the wound.

Instantly, Dalya's father changed his attitude, his face darkened. He hesitated a few seconds, to answer in a much less joyful voice than before:

- Tomorrow I'll bring ... money for the groceries ...

Mrs. Augustine raised her voice tone. She stared at her husband with a disgusted and contemptuous look:

- I need the money today! Not tomorrow! I said we have nothing to eat! How many times do I have to tell you that? Should we die of hunger so that you realize it?

Dalya's father couldn't contain his anger and cold blood, he replied upset:

- How do you expect me to find money in the middle of the night? I said tomorrow, I'll bring you some!
- YOU AND YOUR DAUGHTER, YOU ARE GOOD FOR NOTHING! INCAPABLES! IDIOTS! Mrs. Augustine yelled, while she put the plates on the dining table, with brusque and violent moves, the plates almost broke.

The dinner took place in a complete silence. Dalya's father didn't say another word, Dalya didn't dare to speak; Mrs. Augustine helped her little twins to eat, and she muttered frequently:

- Incapables! Idiots! Good for nothing!

At the end of dinner, when she was cleaning the dishes, Dalya observed her father put his coat on and he was about to go out. Antman Bouvard approached his daughter and he ordered her with an aggressive tone:

- As soon as possible, you will talk to Mr. Ernest Laszlo to give you more money from that fortune! Is this clear enough?

Dalya answered yes by bowing her head.

Chapter 20

Cristelle guessed right

Monday, September 08th, 1890.

A week later, in the annex house of the grand Mansion, Dalya came back home a little earlier than usual; she had finished sooner her lessons with Professor Canfield that day. Her little sisters Ari and Adi were still in naptime. Her mother was ironing shirts and pants. Dalya helped her mother fold some clothes and she went up to her bedroom after that. Dalya placed her only two shirts and two pants in her big empty closet. Having some free time this afternoon, Dalya pulled out her shoes, the only ones she had, and she polished them with an old little brush and a dark powder; she was lost in her thoughts. During the last few days, many questions occupied Dalya's head:

- How will I manage to ask money from Mr. Ernest Laszlo? Would he accept? And if he refuses, how will my father react? How will my family survive? What should I do to help my family?

Dalya was done polishing her shoes, but her questions were not done yet. She placed her shoes on the edge of the bed, and she put down the brush on top of her little desk, near the Excelbox. It is at this precise moment, that Dalya remembered the presence of the strange box. The small rectangular outlet was still open. The transparent glass cage waited patiently for the Moon light, in order to get its power recharged. The golden clock inside the glass cage was clearly visible. The small needle was always fixed on December 12th. The big needle indicated the date of nearly 3 months before.

For a moment, a strange idea came to Dalya's mind. Before joining her mother in the kitchen to help prepare dinner, Dalya stood for a minute in front of her desk and she thought:

- I wonder ... if ... if this strange box could be useful for the second time, to help me out of this situation?

Dalya sat down in front of her desk. After a few minutes of hesitation, Dalya took a piece of paper and she wrote on it:

What is the 2nd clue?

As soon as Dalya placed the note on the rectangular outlet, the paper was absorbed inside the box. And seconds after, the Excelbox let out a little piece of paper:

Second clue
Quiet and reticence
Silence will answer
Let the noise be
Life will take over
Pressure everything cleans
And what paths it will open!

Dalya was expecting a more enterprising message, just like the first one. She was hoping for a clue to deal with pressure from her father who is forcing her to ask for money, and to deal with the rude temperament of the lawyer, Mr. Ernest Laszlo, who would surely refuse to give any money.

- Quiet and reticence ... This is what it suggests me to do? ... Silence will answer. But ... it's not logical as a sentence?! ... Let the noise be? ... Life will take over. This clue is way unclear ... what does the Excelbox means by life? How can pressure open paths? ... And what paths are to be opened anyway?

Dalya was confused. She didn't understand the Excelbox's second clue. She was hoping to find a hint that will help her to overcome all the pressure at home and to handle the upcoming situation. But Dalya was a little disappointed that the Excelbox didn't help her this time...

Saturday, September 13th, 1890.

The Toscana restaurant was full at lunch time. The servers displayed the most delicious dishes and meals in front of the customers. Beautiful candlesticks light up the entire place. A delicious sweet and salty smell hung in the air. Visitors came in and out of the restaurant without a pause. The headwaiter greeted customers and walked throughout the tables to ensure a perfect service.

- Everything is so delicious here! Mr. Wilfrid was carefully reading the menu of the Toscana restaurant.
- The 1st year Law exams are in 3 weeks! Lyor, who was reading a different paper, he seemed a little worried.

Focused in both their readings, the two men were sitting on the same usual table as Mr. Balthazar did before, in front of the large windows of the Toscana restaurant.

150

- I hesitate to order timbales of eggplant or ... fish Carpaccio Mariné. Mr. Wilfrid was focused on the menu card; he straightened his glasses to better read and choose.
- I have to finish all my legal cases before the exams. I can't delay them for later. Continued young Lyor, letting go of a sigh.
- The new pasta with béchamel sauce and fresh mushrooms seems delicious! This dish deserves to be picked up today ... even if the lasagna looks tempting too...
- But I have many legal cases. I will probably be short of time to complete all the work at the office, if I want to devote myself to study for the exams. I should only deal with the most urgent legal cases this week.
- Oh! Green salad with soft goat cheese and pâté de foie gras! It must be tasty! Exclaimed happily Mr. Wilfrid.
- And I can't even attend the hearing of the Dorian case. This exam's date will also force me into missing the Elizabeth Jane Cochrane conference!
- Chocolate tiramisu ... caramel flan ... Pannacotta ... lemon meringue ...
- Between my exams and my work at the office, my schedule has become overloaded! Lyor exclaimed while lying back on his chair.
- You forgot an important meeting in the headquarters of BalthEnterprise next week. Mr. Wilfrid said with calm and an amused voice, without removing his eyes from the menu of the restaurant.
- What are you talking about? What meeting? Asked Lyor.
- You are responsible for all the late Mr. Governor's affairs. Next week, there will be the acquisition of a new land for the expansion of a factory. Your father requires your presence to sign the papers for this transaction ... As the legal guardian of Mademoiselle Dalya Bouvard.

Lyor Laszlo had completely forgotten this important meeting. He had some hard time accepting this new imposed role on him:

- That is the last thing I needed right now! Being the baby sitter of a little 12 years old girl!

Mr. Wilfrid continued, without losing his cheerful smile:

- She came to the office today, to inform us of the 2nd clue that she had received lately. And given the not so happy mood of your father this morning, I took the message of Mademoiselle Dalya, and brought it to your father, myself.

The young Lyor replied in an annoyed tone:

- This girl has turned upside down, not only my father's and Mr. Edelmen's plans, but also mines! No one saw that coming!

Mr. Wilfrid smiled, all amused:

- You will be surprised to know the 2nd clue of this admirable box. It can be helpful to all of us.

- It must be a guessing game, again. This situation is driving me insane. I have other more important things to deal with than playing nurses of a little girl! Lyor groaned, in an upset and tense attitude.
- Quiet and reticence ... Quiet and reticence. Mr. Wilfrid repeated in a dreamy voice.

Confused, Lyor looked at Mr. Wilfrid:

- What? ... Why should I be quiet and reticent of my opinion about this girl?

Mr. Sloan Wilfrid seemed to have fun teasing his young apprentice:

- This is what the 2nd clue indicates to do ... quiet and reticence ... I find it a much valuable advice! Sometimes the best thing to do is ... to do nothing at all!

Exasperated by the excess of joy and the incomprehensible words of his mentor, Lyor raised and rolled his eyes up, and then he continued to read his papers, trying to organize his hectic schedule for the upcoming days. Mr. Wilfrid continued to read the menu of the Toscana restaurant, in a focused and serious air too, before calling the server:

- Finally, I will order ... salads numbers 4, 6 and why not the 8 ... the Pasta dishes numbers 9, 10, 12, and ... the number 14 lasagna, as well. For the dessert, I would take the numbers 16, 17, and ... since it has been a long busy week, also the 18 and 19. That will be all, I think. Thank you.

Lyor and the server stared at Mr. Wilfrid, they were astonished and surprised. The server dared to ask with a hesitant and respectful voice:

- You have ordered ... all the dishes on the menu, Sir. Are you sure of your choice ... Sir?

Mr. Wilfrid took off his little glasses, he put them on the dining table, and he replied with a large and amused smile on his lips:

- Quiet and reticence ... silence will answer!

Tuesday, September 16th, 1890.

Dalya waited patiently in the living room of the grand Mansion. While she was observing the paintings hanging on the wall, the living room door opened. It was Cristelle, the maid in charge of the cleaning of the grand Mansion; she stepped inside holding a big pot, a broom and few towels on her shoulders. As soon as she realized Dalya's presence, Cristelle took a step back:

- Oh! Sorry, Mademoiselle. I thought no one was here. I will come back later to clean ...
- No, please. Do what you came to do. I am waiting for Mr. Ernest Laszlo. He should arrive soon.

Cristelle walked in hesitant steps toward the fireplace of the living room. Dalya displayed a smile and she introduced herself:

- I'm Dalya Bouvard. It's nice to meet you.

The maid appeared surprised and stunned by the politeness and spontaneous behavior of the little girl:

- I'm ... Cristelle. The cleaning maid of the grand Mansion.
- Cristelle ... it's a very lovely name. Where does it come from, if I may ask? Dalya questioned.

Cristelle blushed and murmured:

- Thank you, Mademoiselle. It is South American.

Cristelle put her cleaning tools near the fireplace, she kneeled down and she started cleaning up the edges of the chimney. Dalya came close to her and asked:

- Would you like me to help you?

Cristelle didn't believe what she has just heard. She doubted her own ears. She turned back toward the little girl and she was much shocked by the question, especially coming from an Heiress:

- Euh ... No ... thank you ... Mademoiselle.

When the door on the side of the Garden opened behind Dalya, it was her father this time. Antman Bouvard walked toward his daughter and he asked her in a whispered voice:

- Have you told Mr. Ernest Laszlo?
- He has not come here yet. He is talking now with the head manager of the Grand Mansion. Replied Dalya.
- Don't forget!! He has to give you the money today. We need it urgently!

For many weeks, Dalya has been under pressure from her father; she tried by all means to avoid and not to ask for money that doesn't belong to them. Dalya was sure that the lawyer, Mr. Ernest Laszlo will refuse her request. More so, Dalya still couldn't understand how her father manages the money. Dalya tried one last time, reasoning her father:

- But ... I don't understand ... the money you receive from the restaurant should be enough for all our expens....

Antman Bouvard seized Dalya's arm and he pressed it very hard, to the point that she could not move anymore. He yelled in an aggressive voice:

- LISTEN TO ME, YOU SILLY TWIT! REQUEST THAT MONEY WITHOUT ASKING ME MORE QUESTIONS! I AM THE MAN HERE! I AM THE ONLY ONE IN CHARGE AND CAPABLE OF HANDLING THIS FAMILY'S MONEY, AND

CERTAINLY NOT YOU! IT WILL BE MY WAY TO MANAGE AND NO ONE ELSE'S WAY!

When Dalya's father realized the presence of Cristelle in the living room, hidden by the armchairs near the fireplace, Antman abruptly dropped off his daughter's arm and he left through the back door of the garden, staring with threatening looks at Dalya. Cristelle remained motionless and confused, not understanding what was going on.

The door opened for the third time, it was the lawyer, Mr. Ernest Laszlo, followed by Mr. Sloan Wilfrid and his son Lyor Laszlo. The three men settled on the chairs. Mr. Ernest Laszlo lit a big cigar and he spoke to Dalya:

- You asked to see me. So, what do you want?

It was not the first time that Antman Bouvard forced his daughter's hand to do something wrong. When Dalya was working with him selling on the cart, her father forced her to cheat on the quality of the goods by polishing it with the spark plug, and to lie about the origin of their fruits and vegetables by telling clients that it came from the best farms. He would even sell merchandise too ripened or much less ready to eat. On several occasions, Dalya was forced to borrow money from people she knew, and to beg to unknown passersby. She did so to help feed her little sisters. Dalya and her father worked hard, but Antman Bouvard always lost away all the money they earned. And whenever Dalya tried to advise him to keep reserves, her father always became angry and aggressive. Whether right or wrong, Antman Bouvard's money management was the only managing way that mattered to him.

Deep inside, Dalya knew very well that cheating and lying was not the honest and right thing to do. She was ashamed to beg for money and having the need to borrow. But with her father's bad management, Dalya had no choice; to survive and feed her little sisters, Dalya had to accept everything. Except that whenever her father forced her hand, Dalya was growing increasingly distant from him.

- Well then? ... What did you want to ask me for? Mr. Ernest Laszlo insisted. The Lawyer was impatient in front of Dalya's hesitancy.

After a silent moment, during which the three men looked at her curiously, Dalya answered the lawyer Mr. Ernest, in a polite voice:

- I wanted to ask you ... to tell you ... thank you for allowing me a chance in this school. I am learning new things every day. Professor Canfield is an excellent mentor. I am aware that it wasn't your decision, Mr. Ernest Laszlo. But I wanted to thank you for arranging my admission at this school.

The Lawyer Mr. Ernest waited a moment, and then he asked:

- And ...?
- And ... that's all, Sir. Dalya whispered shyly.
- You made me come all this way, just to tell me that?! Mr. Ernest exclaimed, furious, before getting up and moving toward Dalya, with a menacing stare:
- Listen very well, you little vermin! No need to feel comfortable in this new house or that school. In a few months, everything will end up, and you will return with your family in your previous rat hole! My time is precious; I have better things to do than to be the legal guardian of a veggy sel...

Despite Mr. Ernest's threats, Dalya spontaneously interrupted him and she said with a natural and calm voice:

- But ... I thought Lyor Laszlo was my legal guardian?

Mr. Ernest Laszlo became all red in a second, he gasped in rage. He was not expecting such audacity. Mr. Wilfrid could barely hold his laugh. Meanwhile, the young Lyor Laszlo was surprised to see someone so small and so tiny stand up to his father, when he himself couldn't.

Having lost his temper, Mr. Ernest Laszlo yelled, with all his strength, toward Dalya:

- LITTLE VERMIN! YOU WILL GO BACK TO LIVE IN THE STREET!! IN YOUR RAT HOLE! I WILL MAKE SURE OF THAT!! BECAUSE THAT'S WHERE YOU TRULY BELONG! YOU LITTLE BEGGAR! THAT'S WHAT YOU WILL ALWAYS BE!! A BEGGAR FOREVER!!

Mr. Ernest Laszlo left the living room, exploding with rage and anger, he opened the door with such a brusque move, that the large windows trembled. His son, Lyor Laszlo immediately stood up and he joined his father. As for Mr. Wilfrid, he observed for a little while, the little girl still standing. And before joining his employer outside, Sloan Wilfrid murmured with an amused tone:

- To see him being put into his place ... it doesn't happen very often in a lifetime!

Dalya remained motionless in her place without daring to move. She didn't understand why Mr. Ernest Laszlo hated her so much. It is true that her nomination in this Will confused the plans of the Lawyer Mr. Ernest Laszlo and the nephew Mr. Ferdinand Edelmen. But it was Mr. Iskander Balthazar who's responsible for it. Dalya had never asked any of this to happen.

Some only seconds later, Dalya's father came into the living room by the garden's door, and he asked his daughter, with an excited air:

- Well then? How much Mr. Ernest will give us? When is he giving us an advance of this fortune's money?

Dalya gathered all her courage and she replied with a calm voice:

- Mr. Ernest Laszlo ... refused. I asked him for money, but he told me it is only at the end of all the challenges that we will have access to the fortune of Mr. Iskander Balthazar. Only after I succeed, and not a day before. He didn't want to hear anything else.

Her father became pale and surprised. He didn't expect this bad news. He looked at his daughter in a disappointed and disgusted air:

- YOU LITTLE INCAPABLE! YOU HAD ONE SINGLE TASK TO DO, AND YOU'VE FAILED TO CONVINCE THIS LAWYER! YOU NEVER HAD A STRONG CHARACTER, AND YOU NEVER WILL! YOU'RE REALLY A GOOD FOR NOTHING!

Antman Bouvard left quickly the living room of the grand Mansion; he slammed the back door so brutally. And Dalya was left standing, without daring to move.

Cristelle, who was still on her knees in front of the fireplace, she observed the little girl, with a compassionate stare. Cristelle has been present at this scene since its beginning, and she seemed to finally understand the situation. The maid of the grand Mansion was surprised of what took place before her eyes; the little girl endured the insolent character and insults of the Lawyer Mr. Ernest Laszlo, and she chose to lie, to not obey her father, and to not ask advanced money of the fortune.

And as strange as it sounds, Dalya was relieved she had lied. A weird idea appeared in her little head. When she was about to pronounce her father's request to the Lawyer, Dalya remembered the 2nd Excelbox clue. Dalya heard a little voice whispering in her ears:

- Calm and reticence ... Calm and reticence ... Silence will answer ... Let the noise be ... Life will take over ...

And having no other better way out of this difficult situation, Dalya chose to remain silent and refrained herself from asking money from Mr. Ernest Laszlo. Even though Dalya had to endure the lawyer's insults and her father's pressure.

After a few minutes of a tense silence, Dalya turned around and she came near the fireplace in the living room; she knelt down, she took a small broom and she started cleaning the ashes, under Cristelle's shocked and scandalized eyes, who exclaimed instantly:

- But ... Mademoiselle! ... you are an Heiress!... you can't ...clean the fireplace ... you ...

Dalya replied politely:

- I don't have much to do right now anyway. I would like to get busy ...
- But ... Mademoiselle ... you'll get dirty!

Dalya looked Cristelle in the eyes and she said:

- Please.

Cristelle was overwhelmed; she had no other choice but to let the little girl clean the chimney with her. Dalya was silent and calm, but she looked beaten down and crushed by the pressure and the insults. Getting busy with housework seemed to calm Dalya. For some silent minutes, Cristelle rubbed the edges of the fireplace with a wet cloth, while Dalya picked up the ashes in a small pot.

After some time, they both finished cleaning the fireplace. Dalya stood up and she smiled with difficulty, at the maid of the grand Mansion:

- Have a good day, Cristelle.

Before Dalya would leave the living room through the garden door, Cristelle held back the little girl with a hesitant voice:

- Mademoiselle ... I ... would you please follow me?
- Where? asked Dalya
- There is a place I think you should see. Replied Cristelle, wiping her hands and dropping her cloth on the pots.

Dalya followed her; she was curious to see what the maid Cristelle wanted to show her. They went outside the living room. But before crossing the big hall, Dalya froze in her place and she said with an unsure voice:

- Mr. Ernest Laszlo forbade me from walking inside the grand Mansion. If he knows that I came here inside with you, you might have proble...

Cristelle turned around toward Dalya and she interrupted her in a whispered voice:

- That is if he knows ... If he knows!

Dalya and Cristelle crossed the big hall, and they headed toward the opposite side of the grand Mansion. Arriving in front of a big door, Cristelle made sure that nobody was following them, and then she opened the door and entered.

Dalya's sadness evaporated in a second. She found herself in a huge oval room of 3 floors. All the walls were filled with shelves up to the ceiling. Small stairs stood tall to reach all the shelves. There must have been a million books at least; all types, shapes, and colors. A large golden fireplace stood majestically in one corner. Luxurious divans and comfortable chairs were placed everywhere. The light in this room didn't come from the rectangular windows giving a view to the garden. The light in this room came from the ceiling! ... The huge oval ceiling of the room was a transparent painted glass in multiple colors and geometric forms, with drawings of sun, moons, clouds, planets, and stars. Sun rays passed through the glass ceiling and reproduced its drawings on the glistening white marble floor. Little Golden sculptures stood in every corner, adding a sumptuous glow to the room. The school Library was huge, but not as luxurious as this place. Dalya remained speechless. She has never seen such a magnificent place!

Cristelle said all proud and smiling:

- I have often seen you holding books in your hands, on your way to school. I thought that you liked to read. This was the Governor's private Library, and it was also his favorite place. He spent days and nights here.
- It's ... Gorgeous! That's all what Dalya could pronounce.

The Snow Panther was lying down on one of the divans. As soon as she noticed Dalya, Séraphine straightened her little head, and wagged her tail up. Dalya watched Séraphine moving from the divan, walking slowly and royally toward the large fireplace of the Library. The Snow Panther sat in front of the fireplace and stared at a portrait that was hang up above the chimney.

Dalya came close the grand painting; there was Mr. Iskander Balthazar sitting next to a woman of unmatched beauty, and a little animal on the woman's lap. On the portrait, Mr. Balthazar looked much younger. He has always been very handsome; brown hair, sparkling light purple eyes, a proud and imposing look, a smile lighting up his face. He was wearing a very elegant gray suit. The woman in the portrait had long gold wavy hair, white and delicate fresh skin, pinkish cheeks, big clear hazel eyes, a slim allure, a beautiful kind and caring smile. She was wearing a blue embroidered dress, and wonderful bright white pearls embellished her long neck. Dalya had never met someone like her before; the woman radiated a grace and a warm sweetness.

Realizing that Dalya was observing the portrait, Cristelle explained to her:

- It is Mrs. Irea Senderlson Balthazar. The Governor's wife. She was a beautiful woman, a unique kindness, sweet and gentle with everyone. When she died because of a sudden illness 7 years ago, Mr. Balthazar never recovered from this loss. He loved her very much. She was the light of his life.
- Have you known them for a long time?
- Oh, yes Mademoiselle ... long enough to respect and admire them. Mr. Balthazar and his wife have always treated their employees with dignity and empathy.

Dalya recognized the little animal on the portrait, thanks to the sapphire eyes she already knew:

- It's ... it's Séraphine when she was a baby, isn't it?
- Yes. This little hair ball has grown up a lot!
- How did Mr. Balthazar found her? Dalya was always curious to know.
- I heard that on a trip in a faraway country, called Asia ... Séraphine was chosen for Mrs. Irea.
- Chosen for her? Asked again Dalya.
- Yes ... Séraphine was offered to Mrs. Irea. Since the time she has been brought to the grand Mansion; Séraphine has always been kind and protective of Mrs. Irea and Mr. Balthazar.
- Does she ... does she always do that? Stares at people, and follow their every move? Asked Dalya, she was curious of the Panther's behavior.

- Oh, no Mademoiselle! Cristelle laughed all amused. Séraphine ignores everyone!! She never showed any interest in anyone other than Mr. Balthazar, his wife, and the Gardener. She follows the Gardener because he is responsible to feed and clean her. She doesn't even notice me! It takes me an hour to chase her from a room, so I can clean it correctly. I've never seen an animal so capricious and stubborn. She always gives me a hard time when she lays on the divan ...

Dalya was surprised of that answer; she thought the snow Panther followed everyone, just like she does with her. To be the only one followed by this creature, it seemed strange ...

Other than that, Dalya had a specific question in her head since several months now; her first contact with the snow Panther in the Toscana restaurant. Dalya remembered the surprise and astonishment of all the present people that day, including Mr. Balthazar, Mr. Wilfrid, and Lyor; when Séraphine bowed in front of her. Dalya asked, a bit hesitant:

- Cristelle ... have you ever seen ... did this Snow Panther ever bowed to her Masters, Mr. Balthazar and his wife Mrs. Irea?

Cristelle froze for a moment, and she looked at Dalya with a big amazed smile:

- So then ... the rumor is true!! Séraphine did bow in front of you?!

When Dalya confirmed with a head sign, Cristelle's big eyes rolled around in all directions:

- Oh!! So, the Cook of the Toscana restaurant didn't lie to me then? And all this time, I thought he was being funny! It's amazing! I have been told that it happened ... but I couldn't believe it! It's incredible!!
- Do you have any idea why the Snow Panther made this gesture toward me?
- Oh ... well Mademoiselle Dalya, I have known Séraphine for a long time, and I have never seen her bow to anyone, not even her Masters. Her attitude toward you is a bit strange and weird ... except that I can assure you, Mademoiselle ... Séraphine is much smarter than what people think!

Dalya observed for a while the portrait of Mr. Iskander Balthazar, Mrs. Irea Senderlson and baby Séraphine. The man and the woman were quite different from the rest of the Edelmen's family, which Dalya had met during the Will reading. The nephew of Mr. Balthazar, Mr. Ferdinand Edelmen was very arrogant, snob and eager to have this fortune. And his sister, Mrs. Honoré Edelmen, although she seemed calm, she always looks at Dalya with a strange gaze. Mr. Balthazar and Mrs. Irea appeared to be humble, honest and caring people. New questions overwhelmed Dalya's little head, but this time not about the Excelbox or the events of the inheritance or the decision of Mr. Balthazar's fortune ... this time, it was about the strange behavior of the Snow Panther, Séraphine.

The grand Mansion hid very well its secrets.

Meanwhile, Cristelle examined Dalya a bit closer. Before their meeting today, Cristelle felt that this little girl was different from everyone else. Now, she was convinced that

Mademoiselle Dalya Bouvard was unique of its kind. Something about this little girl, reminded Cristelle, of the same characters of her former employers, Mr. Balthazar and Mrs. Irea.

Cristelle stared at Mademoiselle Dalya Bouvard who was observing the portrait at the top of the fireplace. Cristelle hesitated a few moments, and then she finally decided to say:

- Mademoiselle Dalya Bouvard ... If the pressure becomes too much in the annex house ... You can come to this place to breath. No one will ever know.

Dalya turned around toward Cristelle. She was touched of Cristelle's empathy and kind offer. Cristelle understood the pressure that the little girl was going through, and she tried to help ease her stress, by offering her a place to evade the heaviness, even for some minutes.

Dalya approached Cristelle and she gave her a spontaneous hug, with tears in her eyes:

- Thank you so very much!! Thank you so very much!!
- You are welcomed ... Mademoiselle. Replied Cristelle.

Cristelle was happy that Mademoiselle Dalya Bouvard had her smile back again. And she was especially happy to discover that the little poor girl wearing a boy overall and a big cap, was spontaneous, had natural and polite manners. Dalya Bouvard was not what the other employees of the grand Mansion thought she was. Cristelle was happy to have guessed right. And Dalya was happy to discover a splendid place.

The Excelbox was perhaps right, again this time ... Pressure cleans everything ... and oh what paths it will open!

Chapter 21

The triumph of silence

Thursday, September 18th, 1890.

Leaves were gradually losing their green color, trees magnificently displayed their brown yellow and red new coats, birds were leaving the big lake and they continued their migration toward another city, air was slightly cold and sweet. The weather was often rainy and grey. September fall has settled in Georgetown city.

Dalya walked in hurried steps, in order to avoid the upcoming rain that was forming above. Except that she barely stepped on the road to Dumbarton Oaks Park, that Dalya felt a few drops falling from the gray sky. Dalya didn't want to arrive at the grand Mansion all wet, so she ran the best as she could. When she paused to take shelter under a large tree, Dalya noticed Mrs. Glorina, the housemaid of the French neighbors, struggling against the wind and the first drops of rain, the woman was trying to pick up the laundry, before it gets soaking wet. Having no chance to reach the grand Mansion without getting wet too, Dalya decided to enter the house of the French neighbors, les Poirier, and help Mrs. Glorina by quickly picking up her laundry. When finally, they both entered the kitchen of the Poirier house, Mrs. Glorina said, all breathless:

- Thank you ... Mademoiselle! ... Fortunately, you were here to help me today ... Otherwise, I would have been forced ... to rewash everything again!!

Dalya greeted her:

- You're welcome. I was taken by surprise by the rain too, and I forgot my umbrella. Do you mind if I stay here for a minute, just until the rain stops a bit?
- But of course, Mademoiselle! It's the least I can do. I believe that a good apple and cinnamon tea, will do both of us some good. I will make one, right away!

Dalya thanked her with a smile, before asking:

- How is Madame doing today?

Mrs. Glorina replied while putting on the table two cups, two plates and some cookies:

- Mrs. Marianne is doing alright; it's nice of you to ask about her. It has been long time since I've seen you in the neighborhood?
- Yes. Between my intensive lessons at school and helping my mother in the house, I don't have much free time lately.

Dalya and Mrs. Glorina enjoyed their good hot tea. The butter and raisins cookies were exquisite. The rain didn't seem ready to stop any sooner, Dalya helped Mrs. Glorina to prepare the dinner platter of Mrs. Marianne, and then she followed her to the upper floor to the bedroom of the great woman. As soon as they opened the bedroom's door, Miss Francine sitting in her usual chair, sighed aloud:

- Is this little one going to disturb us often?

Mrs. Marianne was sitting on a chair in front of a round table. She was wearing a long robe. Mrs. Glorina put the platter on the table in front of the great woman, and she replied in a proud voice:

- Mrs. Marianne has never refused to receive Mademoiselle Dalya Bouvard!

Miss Francine stared at Dalya with her usual cold and arrogant look. Dalya felt that her presence bothered Miss Francine, but she couldn't know the reason why. Dalya walked toward the plant to water it and take care of it. Mrs. Glorina sat on a 2nd chair in front of Mrs. Marianne and she helped her eat dinner. When suddenly, Mrs. Glorina exclaimed:

- How dizzy I have become! I forgot to bring bread! Forgive me Mrs. Marianne; I will be back in a minute!

Mrs. Glorina left the bedroom, leaving Dalya alone with Mrs. Marianne and her daughter. The great woman continued to eat her dinner in slow moves with her hands. As for Miss Francine, she was staring at every move made by Dalya, who was watering the plant. When Dalya finished, she looked around to occupy herself while waiting for the return of Mrs. Glorina. Dalya walked toward Mrs. Marianne's bed; the cover and pillows were disordered, Dalya adjusted them and folded them neatly. When suddenly, Dalya heard a question:

- But ... What exactly are you doing?

Dalya didn't know to whom this question was addressed, she raised her head to find Miss Francine and Mrs. Marianne, both were looking at her with confused and surprised face expressions. Mrs. Marianne has stopped eating. Miss Francine repeated her question a 2nd time and Dalya understood that the question was addressed to her. Dalya replied spontaneously:

- I ... I am arranging Madame's ... bed covers.
- And why is that? Asked Miss Francine, looking confused.

After a hesitant moment, Dalya answered:

- Forgive me ... I don't understand your question, Miss Francine.
- Why are you arranging the bed covers? She repeated, with an impatient voice.

Dalya really didn't know what to answer. It seemed a very strange question to her. Mrs. Marianne and Miss Francine were staring at her with a surprised look; they were both curious to know the reason for the little girl's behavior. After some tense seconds of silence, Dalya said the only answer she felt appropriate for this question:

- Why not?

Mrs. Marianne and Miss Francine didn't expect at all to hear this reply. Dalya continued all naturally and naively:

- Every day, I arrange the bed in my room. It is normal to arrange our blankets and pillows. My little sisters, Ari and Adi have also learned to make their own beds, since a while now. They organize their blankets and pillows themselves.

Miss Francine said in a shocked and mocking voice:

- But it is the maid who is in charge of all the house work! Including arranging the beds and adjusting the covers!

Dalya replied without hesitation, in a calm and polite voice:

- I didn't know that. Forgive me. I thought the maid was employed to help us only in household tasks that are difficult for us, or when we are sick or being too busy. But I don't think that the house employees must do everything for us, including making the beds and adjusting the covers. It seems to me that it's the least thing we can do.

Miss Francine was as lazy as someone can be; she has never cooked, washed laundry, cleaned her own house, or took care of anyone, not even her own mother. Miss Francine could barely hold her anger. She was out of words and didn't know what to answer to Dalya. On the other side of the bedroom, Mrs. Marianne noticed her daughter Francine's fury and embarrassment, and the great woman didn't hold her giggle. And it was the first time that Dalya heard the great woman laugh. Mrs. Marianne continued to eat her dinner, while softly giggling and looking amused. When Mrs. Glorina returned back with warm bread, she had no idea of what happened during her absence.

During all Dalya's following visits to Mrs. Marianne, Miss Francine always made harsh and mocking criticisms toward Dalya, even more hurtful and aggressive than before:

- You would make such an excellent house employee instead of an Heiress ...
- I wonder what Mr. Balthazar could see in you ...
- Your peasant manners and behavior are very funny ...
- Don't you have any other clothes than this boy outfit and those old shirts ...
- I hope that you're not dreaming to belong to high noble society ...
- I'm sure you know how to clean the horses better than the employees ...

Mrs. Glorina got used to Miss Francine's arrogant and rude character; she preferred to ignore her words. Mrs. Marianne always remained silent and quiet, paying little attention to what her daughter was saying. Dalya wanted to answer Miss Francine's criticism. But each time, Dalya was retained by a little voice, whispering in her ear:

- Silence will answer ... let the noise be ... life will take over ...

Dalya was afraid to offend Mrs. Marianne, by daring to answer her daughter. So then, everyone was always silent, while Miss Francine never ceased to criticize, mock, and belittle Dalya Bouvard, until she leaves Mrs. Marianne's bedroom. This scene was repeated every time Dalya visited Mrs. Marianne.

Thursday, September 25th, 1890.

On that day, something strange happened. While Dalya, Mrs. Glorina, and Mrs. Marianne were all silent, and each occupied in their usual tasks, Miss Francine was talking as mockingly and rude as usual:

- Why did you bring a flower to my mother? It is clear that we should not expect you to know the manners of high noble society. Couldn't you find anything more refined to offer? A flower is ridiculous and stupi...
- It's a pretty flower, I think. Said a man's voice, interrupting Miss Francine.

Mrs. Glorina, Dalya and Miss Francine bounced at once. When everyone turned around, a young man was standing next to the bedroom's door. He was tall, thin, of white skin tone, clear green eyes of a neutral look, a perfect nose, a thin mouth, neat blond hair; he must have been about 20 years old. He was wearing a black suit with a white shirt and an impeccably arranged bow tie, which made him look very elegant, he was holding a coat in one hand, a hat and white gloves in the other hand. He was a very attractive young man. Miss Francine blushed and she didn't say a single more word. Mrs. Glorina continued to assist Mrs. Marianne to finish her meal. Dalya continued to clean the dead leaves of the Gardenia flower, and she couldn't hold herself from taking discreet and curious glances at the handsome young man. He spoke to Miss Francine, in a calm but authoritative voice:

- Isn't it time for you to go rest in your apartment? ... The driver is waiting for you outside.

Miss Francine didn't wait to be asked again, she stood up immediately and without greeting Dalya or even her own mother, she passed next to the young man and she left the bedroom, in an upset but obedient attitude. The young man spoke to his mother in a much softer and nicer tone:

- Good night to you, mother.

Mrs. Marianne smiled back at him. Before closing the door, the young man looked at Dalya. He stared at her with a curious look, from head to toe, and he seemed a bit confused to see the little girl wearing only socks. He greeted her with a little head nod. And then, he disappeared.

Later, in the kitchen, Mrs. Glorina laughed while putting down the empty platter on the table:

- We have been saved by Mr. Richard Poirier today! One more word of this Francine and I would have thrown the dinner platter on her face!

164

Dalya couldn't contain her laugh either. Mrs. Glorina continued in the same amused tone:

- It's because Miss Francine fears her brother so much, although Mr. Richard is younger than her.

Dalya thought it was quite strange, she asked all curious:

- But ... why does she fear him?

Mrs. Glorina continued whispering, afraid to be heard by someone:

- It's because ... Miss Francine has a mental illness, a kind of psychosis, since many years ago. She had spent 2 years in a psychiatric hospital. She was imagining people and things that do not exist. She begged her family to get her out of the psychiatric hospital. But only her brother Richard had agreed to help her, provided that she will stay calm, make no problems, take her medication on time and attend her medical checks every month.
- And so ... If she upsets him, Mr. Richard can take her back to the psychiatric hospital? Asked Dalya.
- Yes! Fortunately, Mr. Richard Poirier exists! He is the only one who can handle his difficult sister!

Dalya dared to ask Mrs. Glorina:

- Mr. Richard ... is he the only son who lives with Madame?
- Yes, he is the only one who lives in this house with her. He works day and night. He is very discreet, almost like a ghost, you won't be meeting him so often. He is so talented and competent, that despite his young age, the Ministry offered him an important and prestigious job in the Government. And at the same time, Mr. Richard takes care of his late father's heritage ... I don't know how he succeeds in everything! A deceased father, a mother with an incurable disease, a sister very capricious and with a mental illness ... and he is still sane, succeeding in his career, and handling his father's heritage ...

On her way back home, Dalya couldn't forget her brief moment with Mr. Richard Poirier. Was he the person watching her through the large windows, every time she passes through the garden? Was he the person who stares at her behind a door, whenever she passes in the corridor toward Mrs. Marianne's bedroom? Why was he following her every move? Why did he stop his sister in her usual criticisms? Why did he intervene that day?

It was the first time that Dalya met Mr. Richard Poirier. And many questions bounced in her little head. While walking toward the grand Mansion, Dalya remembered some words that her mind was whispering many times lately:

- Silence will answer ... Let the noise be ... Life will take over ...

The 2nd clue of the Excelbox was much more useful than what Dalya thought. Often, when we don't dare to defend ourselves, when we struggle to evade people's criticism and attacks, it is at this precise moment when the silence rises and answers people who provoke us. And we don't need to say any word ... life takes over to protect and defend us.

Chapter 22

A game

Sunday, September 28th, 1890.

Dalya dried the dishes and she rapidly placed them back in the closet. When her father put his coat on and went outside, Dalya wore her shoes and she also left the house. Her mother was busy putting her little twin sisters into sleep, she probably won't notice her daughter's absence. On that day, Dalya was determined to discover where her father disappeared every night since several months now.

Antman Bouvard walked quickly toward downtown. Dalya had to run, in order to not lose sight of her father. When he arrived at the old port of Georgetown, Dalya hid in a corner from her father. She didn't want him to discover her presence. When Antman entered a pub, Dalya came close to a small window that gave a view of the inside of the pub. The place was a mess; several little round tables were placed everywhere, surrounded by many chairs occupied by men. Servers sneaked between the tables to serve food and drinks. Chatter, screams and men's laughs made a clear noise; Dalya could hear everything said from the outside. Her father sat down at one of the tables surrounded by 4 men. Dalya had never seen these men before, and she didn't know who they were. They all joyfully greeted her father:

- Antman! We are glad to see you among us.
- Luckily you joined us tonight; we were getting bored without you!
- Antman was the only one missing to our gathering tonight!
- We gladly offer you the best chair of our table!

Dalya's father pulled out of his pockets a stack of money and he put it at the center of the round table, near some coins. Immediately, the 4 men around the table yelled joyfully:

- Oh, oh, oh! It's a nice amount of money you got there!
- Our night is about to be great, guys!
- Are you ready to lose like before, Antman?
- Antman is the best player! Never short of money, and never short of hope to win!

One of the men held little white cards in his hands; he mixed them and handled them with clever quick moves. Then, he distributed the cards to all the men, including Dalya's father. Antman Bouvard took his cards and he seemed very pleased and proud of the attention he received from his 5 friends …That night, Dalya understood.

The next day, when she finished her classes, Dalya walked back home. On her way, Dalya didn't care about the landscape on the road, or the people walking close by her; Dalya's mind was lost and occupied by many questions. What Dalya had seen the day before, kept her up all night. She was not pleased and happy to discover her father's secret.

When Dalya arrived at the annex house of the grand Mansion, her mother had already cooked and served the dinner table. Mrs. Augustine was in a good mood, she was smiling. The table was well garnished; there was a big stuffed chicken, a large plate of cooked vegetables with spices, a delicious apple pie, a big bowl of fresh green salad, hot buttered bread ... Dalya didn't understand where all this food came from. And above all, it was rare to see her own mother in a good mood. Mrs. Augustine didn't even care about her daughter's confused face, she said with a happy tone:

- Your father has brought back a large sum of money today! 26 dollars for this month! We can buy the groceries for the entire month, and buy blankets for the winter and get new clothes and we can g...

Dalya wasn't paying attention to what her mother was saying. Dalya finally got an answer to all the questions that tormented her since a while now: 26 dollars! That's the exact salary that Mr. Ernest Laszlo said her father would receive, for his work in the Toscana restaurant. So then, Dalya was not mistaking or misheard the Lawyer. Her father was indeed being paid 26 dollars in salary per month! Except that Antman Bouvard declared only half of this sum to his family.

And even when Dalya was working with him in the market, Antman Bouvard always declared only half of their earnings. For a long time, Dalya thought that she miscalculated their daily earnings. And she couldn't understand her father's low sales figures. But it wasn't Dalya's mistake at all ... her calculations were all correct!

Her father always hid half of the money they had worked so hard to get. Antman Bouvard spent half of his earnings on the cards' game with his 4 new friends. Dalya finally understood!

That night, her father came home, just in time for dinner, and he exclaimed in his usual cheerful tone:

- Good evening family!
- Ant Ant Ant! The little twins yelled all excited.
- Oh oh oh ... it's a beautiful feast we have here tonight! Exclaimed Antman, his eyes amazed in front of the well garnished dinner table.

Dalya didn't dare to say a word of what she had discovered the day before; she preferred to stay quiet and take dinner with her family. She watched her mother happy and laughing for once, she looked at her father relaxed and proud for once, and she observed her little sisters Ari and Adi amused by the funny faces that their father was performing. And although diner was delicious and the table was filled and everyone was joyful, Dalya ate silently and sadly.

Silence doesn't ease all the tensions; it doesn't solve all the problems. But often, silence makes us discover new things, and people you thought you knew. Silence encloses our voice sometimes ... but it surely opens our eyes.

Chapter 23

When all is lost...

Saturday, October 04th, 1890.

Although she had a free day, Dalya woke up early. She cleaned her bedroom, and then she went downstairs to the kitchen. Her father had already left for his work. Her little sisters Ari and Adi were still asleep. Dalya couldn't help but notice that the living room and the kitchen were plunged into total darkness. All the windows and curtains were closed. Her mother had lit some candles. While the sun was bright shining outside, and it was a beautiful sunny clear day; the inside of the annex house was dark. Dalya wondered aloud:

- What is going on? Why are all the windows closed?

Her mother, Mrs. Augustine who was preparing the bread dough on the kitchen counter, naturally replied:

- I cleaned up all the windows of the house yesterday. I don't want them to get dirty again!

Dalya thought for a long minute; she tried really hard to understand her mother's thinking, which seemed often illogical and bizarre. After a moment of reflection, Dalya was still confused:

- So then ... we will live in darkness ... in order to keep the windows clean?

Dalya's mother, Mrs. Augustine Bouvard rarely noticed the futility of her own ideas and behaviors. She took care of her home, but not always in the smartest way. Not knowing what to answer, Mrs. Augustine pretended not to have heard her daughter. Dalya also gave up trying to understand why in a sunny day, they were forced to use candles. Dalya sat at the kitchen table to eat her breakfast. When suddenly, her mother asked in a furious tone:

- Where is the milk that I asked you to bring yesterday afternoon?

Dalya hesitated for a moment; she completely forgot to buy it on her way back from school. Her mother raised the tone of her voice:

- Why did you forget?

Dalya replied spontaneously:

- Because I had a very busy day with Professor Canfield.

Mrs. Augustine looked at Dalya with an angry face expression:

- So, what?? Why did you forget?

Dalya answered naively:

- Because ... it happens to everyone to forget things ...

Dalya's mother was surprised by her daughter's reply. Mrs. Augustine didn't like to be confronted. Mrs. Augustine preferred that you stay silent, standing still and your eyes looking down, while she screams at you, insults you, harasses you and abuses you. On the other side, Dalya could never understand her mother. Mrs. Augustine always asked this same illogical question: why did you forget? And Dalya could never find a correct answer to this question. Apparently, Mrs. Augustine didn't know that forgetting is a human trait, it happens to all of us occasionally when we are too busy or hurried or tired.

Mrs. Augustine got aware of her limited aptitude and mind, so she did what she had always mastered the best in her life; she screamed with all her might:

- **EVERY YEAR YOU BECOME MORE IDIOT THAN BEFORE!** WHEN ARE YOU EVER GONNA LEARN? WHY DO I HAVE AN IDIOT GIRL WHO ALWAYS FORGETS?

Dalya interrupted her mother, in a calm tone:

- But ... don't you ever forget anything? Doesn't it ever happen to you?

Mrs. Augustine was so paralyzed by her daughter's answer; she looked at Dalya with her usual evil and mean stare. When Mrs. Augustine ran out of insults, she walked out of kitchen and she slammed the door, as strong as she could, the walls trembled. Dalya finished eating her breakfast in silence. Then, she left the house to buy some milk, before her mother makes another angry scene.

Dalya crossed the passage to the grand Mansion, under the Snow Panther's stare, observing her from inside a living room, through a large window. The Snow Panther's tail and tattooed light gray fur could never go unnoticed.

A tall silhouette stepped out of the kitchen door of the grand Mansion, and he also walked toward the exit. Dalya could perfectly recognize the Gardener Mr. Rosenwald, because of his blue shawl. He was wearing a large coat and a black hat, he didn't limp over anymore. He walked in front of Dalya, not realizing that she was walking right behind him, a couple of steps away.

Dalya continued on her way to downtown. When she passed by the Holy Rood Cemetery, the Gardener Mr. Rosenwald had already entered the place and he seemed to know his way among the graves. October was a gray and cold month. All the trees had lost their coats, and the leaves were covering the ground with a beautiful red yellow and brown carpet. A cold and delicate wind caressed your face once a while. The sky was printed with gray clouds. That day, a serene calm invaded the Holy Rood Cemetery.

After a short walk, Mr. Rosenwald sat down near a little grave. Even though Dalya was a bit far away, she was able to see that the Gardener was sad while he watched the grave in front of him. The Gardener was a big tall man, very strong and tough, always serious and intimidating. Never Dalya would have thought to see him so miserable and sad. Dalya thought that the deceased person had to be very dear to Mr. Gardener.

Dalya continued her way to downtown. She bought milk at the grocery store, and then she returned back home, on the same road. Mr. Gardener had left the cemetery. Curious as she was, Dalya decided to follow the pathway the Gardener had taken earlier, to learn about the person he visited this morning. When she arrived at the Tomb where Mr. Rosenwald was sitting, Dalya read:

In the beloved memory of
Gabrielle Attias Rosenwald
(1878-1889)

Dalya wondered:

- Gabrielle? It was a girl, then! ... 1889 ... she passed away almost a year ago. She was nearly my age! ... and she has the same family name as the Gardener ... Rosenwald ... Could she be his daughter? ... Or maybe a relative?

And it wasn't the only strange thing that Dalya happened to see, that day!

Walking back to the grand Mansion, Dalya passed by the French neighbor's home, les Poirier. She noticed 5 gentlemen standing at the front door of the house. The men were about to enter inside their cars parked in the driveway. They were all wearing long black coats and big hats. Dalya also noticed that all the men were carrying a large embroidered leather brown bag, which she recognized immediately. It was the Doctors' usual bag.

Dalya wondered why so many doctors were present at the Poirier's house? Were they checking on Mrs. Marianne or someone else? Did Mrs. Marianne's condition worsened? Is she alright?

On that day, Dalya came back home with the milk needed ... but also with many questions in her little curious head.

Sunday, October 05th, 1890.

The next day, Dalya's father brought back home a carriage full of peaches. For many days, Antman has helped a friend in renovating and painting his house, and the friend repaid Antman back with tons of peaches.

- These are really good peaches! He exclaimed all joyfully.
- What should I do with all this quantity? Where can I store them? It will rot very quickly! Dalya's mother was furious.
- You can make peach sauce ... jam ... or pies! Dalya's father was already unloading the peaches from the carriage into large cases.
- Peass sauce! Zam! Pies! Peass sauce! Zam! Pies!! The little twins Ari and Adi screamed merrily. They eagerly helped their father unload the carriage and put the peaches in the cases.
- And I suppose you're the one who's going to cook all that? Dalya's mother reprimanded her husband in a severe tone.
- We don't have to keep everything for us ... Give some to families and friends! Dalya's father turned his back on his wife, to avoid her angry look.
- Peass sauce! Zam! Pies! Peass sauce! Zam! Pies!! The twins were happy.
- How will I give away these peaches? It's heavy and a lot!! Why do you always have to bring me extra chores and worries?
- Can I take 4? Dalya asked her father.
- Yes ... Yes ... Take as many as you want!! Antman said, ignoring his wife's criticism, and continuing to unload the carriage.

Dalya put thirty big juicy peaches in a bag apart. After helping her father carry all the fruits from the carriage, and store them in a corner of the kitchen, Dalya left the annex house.

On her way out of the grand Mansion, Dalya found a white silhouette lying down on a huge tree branch near the exit door. The Snow Panther was staring at the little girl with a quiet and serene look, sitting on top of the big tree.

Dalya never again came close to the animal, since the incident with the nephew Mr. Ferdinand Edelmen, in the living room of the grand Mansion. And even though Dalya was curious about the weird behavior and persistent stares of the Snow Panther, Dalya never felt threatened by this creature. On the contrary, Séraphine's presence reassured Dalya. And it was a strange feeling.

On that day, Dalya dared something she had never done before. She pulled out of her bag 2 big juicy peaches; she slowly came near the tree, and she put the peaches down on the ground, always under Séraphine's calm stare. Then, Dalya continued her way out of the grand Mansion. After few seconds and steps away, Dalya turned her head around; the Snow Panther has quickly stepped down from the tree and was munching the fruits. Dalya smiled gladly. Because she protected her once, Séraphine deserved to enjoy some good juicy peaches.

Dalya stopped at the French neighbor's House, les Poirier. When she opened the small door of the garden, the shadow on the window appeared. Dalya continued toward the kitchen's door. When Mrs. Glorina opened the door, dressed in her usual colorful butterfly knots apron, the little woman exclaimed:

- What a pleasure to see you, Mademoiselle!
- Good morning to you, Mrs. Glorina. I hope I am not disturbing you.

- Don't ever say that! It always makes me happy to see you!
- I brought you some good peaches today. My father received an entire full carriage, and we had way too much. So, I thought that you and Madame would like some delicious peaches.
- Oh! That's kind of you, Mademoiselle! They will be very good in a pie with an English cream. I will make one, just for you, Mademoiselle!

Dalya sat down on one of the kitchen chairs and she watched Mrs. Glorina pouring some vegetables' soup in a large bowl. Dalya hesitated for a moment, and then she dared to say:

- I was walking close by here yesterday, because I had some grocery shopping to do downtown. I've noticed that you had visitors ...

Mrs. Glorina buttered two pieces of bread, and she sighed:

- Oh, yes!! Mrs. Marianne had some very difficult days, this week. Her pain intensified throughout her body. Poor Mrs. Marianne! She screamed out of pain.
- So the gentlemen outside yesterday were doctors? ... They came to check on her? Dalya asked.
- Yes. Mr. Richard brought in emergency, almost all the doctors of Georgetown city. Her illness is incurable, they prescribed for her only painkillers and sleeping pills.
- And how is Madame doing today?
- Much better than yesterday. Her pain decreased, this morning. She didn't sleep well for days. But, last night she was finally able to sleep a couple of hours.

Minutes later. When Dalya and Mrs. Glorina reached the second floor, and before entering Mrs. Marianne's bedroom, Dalya took off her shoes despite Mrs. Glorina's insistence. The Maid could never understand the little girl's weird attitude in leaving her shoes outside the bedroom. When Mrs. Glorina entered the room, she announced in a cheerful voice:

- Mrs. Marianne ... Mademoiselle Dalya Bouvard came to visit you today!

The great woman was lying down on her bed; she looked at the little girl. Dalya was glad that her daughter Miss Francine was absent, that day. Mrs. Glorina put the lunch platter on a little table near Mrs. Marianne, and she sat on a chair close to the bed. Dalya came near Mrs. Marianne; she pulled out of her bag one big juicy peach, and she showed it to Mrs. Marianne, displaying a big smile:

- Today, I brought you peaches, Madame. They are very good on this October month. They will be delicious in a pie or in jam.
- But what a great idea it is! Jam! Exclaimed Mrs. Glorina. It has been a long time since I've prepared any! I will start making it, this afternoon!
- It will be good for you to have some, Madame. My uncle Giorgi says that there is nothing better than fruits to get your strength back.

Although tired and exhausted by her previous awake nights, Mrs. Marianne smiled at Dalya. Mrs. Glorina peeled the peach, while Mrs. Marianne drank her vegetable soup, with a slow movement. Dalya turned around toward the Gardenia flower pot that was still placed on the table. The flower had grown graciously, and it became more beautiful than ever; a multitude of green leaves appeared, other white flowers with snow petals awoke, and the fresh and sweet smell was even more present in the bedroom.

During all her previous visits to Mrs. Marianne Poirier's bedroom, Dalya usually opened the window curtains just a little bit, enough to let in some day light and some fresh air for the Gardenia flower.

Except on that day, Dalya remembered her mother's strange idea. Mrs. Augustine closed all the curtains of the house, on a bright sunny day, and she chose to live in darkness, so as not to tarnish the cleaned windows.

In all houses, we have the choice to live in the darkness or in the light. We have the choice to close the curtains or to open the windows.

And even if someone closes all curtains and windows of our house, nobody can lock you up in the darkness, except yourself. Nobody can prevent you from seeing the light, except yourself. Because no matter the house where we live in, no matter the situation where we are, whether we decide to close or open the curtains, whether we decide to live in darkness or in a bright light ... whatever we decide, it is always always always our own choice!

Dalya suffocated in the dark. The big curtains of Mrs. Marianne's bedroom have always dipped the place in a dark and depressed air. And for the first time since her visits to Mrs. Marianne, Dalya dared to open the curtains all widely. And in a second, Mrs. Marianne's bedroom was illuminated by the magnificent light of the sunny day. Mrs. Glorina exclaimed:

- What a beautiful day it is!

Dalya turned around to see if the great woman was upset because the curtains were wide open. Mrs. Marianne observed Dalya, in a curious but quiet gaze, without any objection.

Dalya had never really seen Mrs. Marianne's Bedroom during this much daylight. All the room's furniture seemed to be alive suddenly, becoming more visible and brighter. The wallpaper displayed some beautiful lilies. The armchairs, divans, drawers, bed tables ... All the furniture was luxurious and refined.

And for the very first time since she came into this bedroom, Dalya discovered the clear silhouettes on the large painting that was hanging on one of the bedroom walls. Dalya came closer to better see the silhouettes on the painting. A man and a woman were sitting on two chairs. A girl and a boy, almost of the same age and of the same size, they stood behind the man and the woman. A little boy was standing next to the woman; and she had her hand on the little boy's shoulder.

Dalya recognized Mrs. Marianne and her daughter, Miss Francine. Mrs. Marianne's facial features have hardly changed, despite her illness. Mrs. Marianne had long light brown hair down on her shoulders, white and smooth skin, and her beautiful green eyes lightened her face. She was wearing a beautiful purple velvet dress. Miss Francine was standing behind the man, wearing a white girl's dress, she had black hair in a ponytail, and she was much thinner and less ugly than now. And on the portrait, Miss Francine had the same arrogant and cold look since her childhood.

Mrs. Glorina had just finished helping Mrs. Marianne eating her meal; she realized that Dalya was staring at the big painting. She came near the little girl, and explained to her:

- Here … it's Mr. Rodolph Poirier, the eldest son of Mrs. Marianne and late Mr. Poirier. He chose to live his life far away from here and not care about anyone but himself. He visits us very rarely. And there … it's Miss Francine, her only daughter. And the man is the late husband of Mrs. Marianne.
- He passed away a long time ago? Asked Dalya.
- Yes … 6 years ago.

Dalya remembered something:

- The first time we have met, Mrs. Glorina, you told me that Madame fell ill, about 6 years ago. It's the same period when her husband Mr. Poirier has passed away …
- Yes, that's right. Mrs. Marianne had a very hard time at the loss of her husband. She was so sad. And despite all the efforts of her son Mr. Richard, Mrs. Marianne lived a heavy depression … She has been through some very dark days. Mr. Poirier was the mainstay of the family. A few months after his disappearance, signs of the illness appeared on Mrs. Marianne.
- Mr. Richard Poirier … is he the little boy on the portrait? asked Dalya

Mrs. Glorina said with a caring smile:

- Yes, it's him. Richard Poirier is brave; although young, he took his father's place instantly. He took good care of his mother. There is not a single day he spends away from her. He does all his best to help and comfort her.

Dalya noticed the resemblance between the little boy and his mother. They had the same shaped faces, sparkling green eyes; they were both wearing the same cloths' color and they had the same smile. As a child, Mr. Richard Poirier was a chubby little boy; his cheeks were full and pink. His hair was a pale blond. He was wearing a purple suit, custom-made on him, with a small bow tie, which made him look very cute.

An object on the painting caught Dalya's attention. Mrs. Marianne was wearing an emerald green ring on her left hand that was resting on Mr. Richard's shoulder. It was such a beautiful jewel; a sparkling green stone, surrounded by shining white diamonds. The ring was of the same color as the eyes of Mrs. Marianne and her son, Mr. Richard. Mrs. Glorina guessed that Dalya was attracted by the famous ring, she explained to the little girl:

- It was an expensive ring that belonged to Mrs. Marianne. It was offered by her husband on their wedding day. Unfortunately, Mrs. Marianne has lost that ring on the same day of her husband's death. We searched for months, without being able to find it. I peeled the garden myself, for several weeks. Mrs. Marianne was very sad to lose a memory of her husband. She has never worn any other jewelry since then!

Mrs. Glorina returned near Mrs. Marianne; she took the lunch platter, and left the bedroom. Dalya looked at the big painting one last time; she turned toward Mrs. Marianne, who was smiling at her. Dalya greeted her back with a kind smile:

- Good day to you, Madame.

In her bedroom at the annex house of the grand Mansion. Dalya was sitting in front of her little desk, trying to complete homework that was given to her by Professor Canfield. And despite all her efforts to focus on her study, Dalya couldn't stop thinking about the French neighbor, Mrs. Marianne Poirier and the Gardener, Mr. Weil Rosenwald. These two people had lost loved ones, and this loss appeared to have affected them very hardly. Mrs. Marianne suffered a crippling disease, and the Gardener shut himself up in his cold and tough character. Dalya hoped to help them and bring some ease of their losses. Or, at least make them truly smile again. But nothing can replace human beings that we have lost forever.

Dalya read over the Mathematics' exercise, several times without being able to focus on its content. Tired of her long day, Dalya closed her homework book. When she had a concern in her mind, it was very difficult for her to focus on anything else.

For some long minutes, Dalya sat in front of her little desk, with her arms folded, staring at the Excelbox. The large glass cage was covered in a thing mist, attracting the entire moon's light. The 4 cylinders in shaped gold were shining in all their glory. The small rectangular outlet was open and empty. In a spontaneous movement, Dalya took a piece of paper, and she wrote on it, without really thinking:

What is the 3ʳᵈ clue?

Right away, the Excelbox took inside the paper, and a few seconds after, it issued another:

Third clue
When all is lost
To up raise your gaze
His last word
Has not yet been sealed
When everything is seized

Everything is back granted
And it's from up gracious
A true generosity indeed
A possibility to remake
In your own way and will

The Excelbox always came up with unexpected and enigmatic answers. Dalya raised her head up and she looked at the night sky from her window, wondering:

- When all is lost ... to up raise your gaze. Up? That means the sky ... but why would I look up to the sky when I lose something? How can it be useful?

Dalya read over the clue a 2nd time:

- When everything is seized ... everything is back granted? How can something removed be granted back? These are two contradictory words in the same sentence?! ... A possibility to remake, in your own way and will. But ... what possibility is it talking about? Remake in my own way ... but what should be done in my own way? I don't understand.

Dalya put the 3rd clue paper on her little desk, and she laughed at herself:

- I thought I would have a clue to relieve the French neighbor, Mrs. Marianne Poirier and the Gardener, Mr. Rosenwald, from the heavy loss of their loved ones. How silly am I! It's impossible! The people we have lost are gone forever. Their loss can never be replaced ...

For once, the Excelbox was mistaken. That's what Dalya thought...

176

Chapter 24

A perfect incident

Tuesday, October 07th, 1890.

This afternoon, in Georgetown city, a cold weather was predicted. Although the sun rays were more present than the gray clouds, the air was dry and the wind reigned as Master. October was an indecisive and unpredictable month.

Lyor Laszlo's little office was the complete opposite of his father's workplace. The large windows without curtains, invited all the day light in this place. The office was not just brightened, but warmer as well. Nearby the windows, there was a large pot of beautiful little flowers called crocus; purple blue petals, orange in the inside, and fresh green leaves. Lyor Laszlo was not a Gardener or a plants' expert, but he particularly liked this rare and precious flower, he took good care of it himself. And the flower paid him back very well, his little office was flooded with a warm sweet mesmerizing scent.

In the middle of the office, there was a small desk jam-packed with several registers, books, pencils, and papers. A big couch was installed in one side of the room, clearly indicating that the owner of this office spends many nights here at work. A small Library was set in a corner of the office, it was filled with books, files, records of all shapes and forms and colors ... and because of the lack of space, some books and records were piled on the floor.

Mr. Ernest Laszlo abruptly entered his son's office, without knocking on the door or even greeting him:

- Here is the file of the Adjutor case. I would have given it to someone more competent than you, but everyone is busy. The hearing is advanced for tomorrow afternoon. I encircled all the important elements and left my remarks on this case inside the file. Our defense should be ready by tomorrow morning, first hour! It's urgent!!
- Yes Sir, I will get to it immediately. Lyor Laszlo answered his father while taking the file from his hands.

When his father stepped out of his office, Lyor closed the books and files that he already had on his desk, and he opened the new folder given to him. While turning the 3rd page of the new file, Lyor noticed a little piece of paper with his father's handwriting:

To remake ... In your own way and will

While Lyor was reading the paper for the 10th time, Mr. Sloan Wilfrid stepped into his office, holding his coat and hat in hands:

- Are you coming to the evening in honor of Governor Stephen Grover Cleveland? It should be quite interesting!
- I ... have the Adjutor defense ... to prepare for tomorrow. Replied Lyor, looking confused.
- They advanced the hearing date? I didn't know that. Why? Asked Mr. Wilfrid.

Lyor didn't answer him, but he kept staring at the little piece of paper in his hands. Noticing the confusion of the young Lyor, Mr. Wilfrid realized that something was bothering his young apprentice:

- Is everything alright Lyor? What is going on?

The young Lyor handed him the paper:

- I found this note ... inside the Adjutor file ... that my father gave me.

When Sloan Wilfrid read the content of this note, a strange smile displayed on his lips, and a witty sparkle lit up in his eyes. Sloan Wilfrid pulled himself together at once, and he ordered Lyor with an enthusiastic voice:

- Well then, what are you waiting for? Get to work, young man!!
- Is this really my father's handwriting? Did I understand well his instructions? Lyor asked in a hesitant voice.
- Yes, yes!! This is the handwriting of Mr. Ernest Laszlo ... and his message is very clear! So roll up your sleeves, because this is your chance to win your first Law case!
- So ... I can prepare this case, in my own way? I seriously have my father's approval to prepare the defense ... in my way? Lyor was struggling to believe his father's note.

Mr. Wilfrid let out a little amused giggle:

- I will ask my secretary to prepare a strong coffee for you. Tomorrow morning, I'll be at the office earlier. If you need me, let me know.

Before stepping outside and closing the office door, Mr. Wilfrid turned toward Lyor and smiled:

- Do your best, Lyor!

Immediately, Lyor Laszlo pulled himself together. He sided all the documents and files in a corner, he emptied his office right away, he searched for specific books in his small piled up Library, he was given a cup of coffee from Mr. Wilfrid's secretary, and then he rolled up his sleeves and started to prepare the defense of that case. The night promised to be long and busy. But it was a chance that Lyor Laszlo was not willing to miss!

6:30 AM the next day. The first sun rays were invading the empty offices of Mr. Ernest Laszlo Law firm. Mr. Wilfrid was the first to arrive; he hung up his coat and his hat in his office, and then he walked toward the coffee machine to prepare two cups of coffee.

Then, Sloan Wilfrid entered Lyor's office. The young man was awake and active despite his sleepless night at the workplace.

- Here's a good cup of coffee ... and warm croissants for you, to help you win your first Law case! Exclaimed Mr. Wilfrid in a joyful tone.
- I've finished writing my defense. I would like your opinion on it. Said Lyor while he handed a few papers to his mentor.

Mr. Wilfrid sat down on a chair, he put on his glasses and read carefully, while Lyor drank quickly his coffee and ate the croissants. After a long silent moment, Mr. Wilfrid thought aloud, in a serious tone:

- The defense is solid from all sides. All the arguments you have put forward are important. The idea of the secondary arguments is ... I must say ... original and useful. You used a new technique ... and it is well organized.

Mr. Wilfrid looked toward the young Lyor and he said with an honest voice:

- I have nothing to add ... really nothing to add to your defense. It's a very good job, Lyor!

Lyor Laszlo was happy and relieved of his mentor remark. Mr. Wilfrid continued:

- It proves that not only you are good at this job, but you also have the ability to add new, simpler and more productive ways to our work!
- It also proves that I have a great mentor, and that I've learned his lessons. Replied Lyor, between two croissant bites.

Mr. Wilfrid who has always considered Lyor Laszlo more than just his employer's son, he smiled, grateful for this compliment and proud of his student.

Minutes later, Mr. Ernest Laszlo was carefully reading the defense that his son Lyor had prepared throughout the previous night. Lyor stood before his father's office, he seemed anxious, waiting for his verdict. Mr. Wilfrid was quiet, sitting on the chair in front of his employer's desk. After a long moment of silence, Mr. Ernest put down the papers on his desk and he said in a calm but cold voice:

- This is not what I have asked for.

Lyor was shocked of his father's reaction:

- You ... you asked me yesterday afternoon, Sir ... to prepare the Adjutor's defen...
- Yes. It's true. But I don't see in these notes, the usual defense structure we ordinarily use in my Law firm! Mr. Ernest interrupted him.

Lyor replied spontaneously:

- That's because ... I prepared a defense in my way, Sir...

- And why did you do it your way? Who authorized you to do so? His father asked with an upset look.

Lyor murmured in a confused tone:

- You, Sir...
- Don't be ridiculous!! Why would I allow an incompetent apprentice to prepare an important defense file in his own way?! You don't have the qualifications to be a lawyer! You're far from being one, by the way!! So then, why did you dare to work this defense as you pleased?

Lyor was struggling to understand his father's anger:

- I followed ... your instructions, Sir.

Mr. Ernest seemed to lose his patience and calm:

- What instructions?! What are you talking about??!

Mr. Wilfrid didn't want to miss this long-awaited moment, for all the money of the world. He replied at Mr. Ernest Laszlo, with a mischievous grin:

- You left an instruction note to Mr. Lyor, yesterday.

Lyor handed the piece of paper to his father:

- Isn't it your handwriting? ... It was in the folder when you gave it to me, Sir.

Mr. Ernest froze in his chair, holding the little note in front of him and murmuring:

- But ... This isn't ... She came to inform me ... it's the 3rd clue, a possibility to remake, in your own way and will ... I just quickly wrote it on a piece of paper...

Mr. Wilfrid exclaimed, pretending to be horrified by this incident:

- Oh! But it's a very unpleasant misunderstanding!

Although the situation in Mr. Ernest's office was serious, Mr. Wilfrid didn't hold himself from sticking the knife in the wound. Sloan Wilfrid explained in a falsely sorry voice:

- What an unfortunate incident!! You forgot this little note in the Adjutor file, Mr. Ernest. And we thought that it was your instructions to prepare this case!!

Mr. Ernest lost his words. But Sloan Wilfrid was not short of them. Sloan Wilfrid displayed his most joyful and amused smile, and he continued in a cheerful voice:

- But still, it was a good opportunity for us to discover the capabilities of Mr. Lyor Laszlo! His work was well done; his defense is very well organized. I even admit being pleasantly surprised at his new idea to add the secondary arguments ...

Mr. Ernest became red; he was forced to swallow his anger. He was shocked that Dalya's interruption in his work session, made him do a mistake. Mr. Ernest listened without daring to interrupt Mr. Wilfrid explanations; he threw angry and furious looks toward his son Lyor, who was still standing motionless and silent in front of this incident. On the other hand, Mr. Wilfrid was proud of his student's work:

- It's a new way of work much more simple and effective than ours ... it will give us an advantage to win the case. Don't you think Mr. Ernest, that Mr. Lyor has a new way of doing things, a more productive and efficient way?
- Alright ... alright! ... Anyway, we have no time to prepare this defense again. We have no choice but to work on Lyor's notes.

Mr. Ernest replied in a furious and angry tone, forced to admit, for the first time ever, that his son has done a good job ... in his own way.

After leaving his father's office, Lyor Laszlo held Mr. Wilfrid's arm, with a quick move:

- You knew that the note my father wrote, was not addressed to me!! You were aware that it was the 3rd clue of this little girl and not instructions from my father to handle this case!!

Mr. Wilfrid turned around and he answered the young Lyor, with an innocent giggle:

- Of course, I did!! ... I knew it the second you gave me this note to read. It's been 10 years that I work in this firm, and never Mr. Ernest Laszlo would allow any of us to change the coffee machine, even less give us the freedom to prepare a file in our own way!
- But ... why did you do that for? Asked Lyor, confused and surprised.

Mr. Wilfrid smiled:

- I admit I was curious to know your father's reaction about your skills and competence.

Sloan Wilfrid patted young Lyor's shoulder and he continued in a more serious tone:

- Someone is not that far from being an excellent lawyer, someday. And today, your father admitted ... well, he was forced to admit that you are worth more than what he believes. Congratulations dear Lyor, you have just stunned him! Bravo!

Lyor was left standing in shock, words failed him, and he was confused and speechless. Mr. Wilfrid went to his office, while singing with a joyous air:

- A possibility to remake ... in your own way and will ...

Chapter 25

An aventurine

Friday, October 17th, 1890. Late in the afternoon.

Dalya was in charge to clean the leaves all over the garden, while her two little twin sisters played with a ball near her. Ari and Adi wore their little gardening boots, pink turtleneck sweaters and black pants, waterproof jackets a bit too large for them, and big hats. Mrs. Augustine was sewing some clothes, sitting on the balcony of the annex house and Mr. Antman was busy cleaning the cart in the garage.

When Dalya finished gathering the leaves in a second corner of the garden, she turned around and was shocked to see her little sisters having fun spreading the leaves that she gathered earlier in another side of the garden. Ari and Adi were throwing themselves at the mass of leaves, and they ran throughout the garden while dropping leaves from their hands. Dalya exhaled in an exasperated tone:

- I don't pick up leaves for you, so you can have fun spreading them around! Let me work!
- Ari and Adi play with Dindin! The little girls shouted simultaneously while dispersing the remaining leaves in their hands.
- No no! I don't have time to play with you. I still have half the garden to clean. Go play with dad and leave me alone!

The little twins Ari and Adi ran immediately to the garage where their father was working. After a few minutes, Dalya could hear their screams of joy and fun from far.

After some while, when Dalya was still working, the little twins Ari and Adi came running toward her, showing off small iron cylinders in each of their arms. When the twins were moving their hands, pretty sounds were heard. Having no money enough to buy toys, her little twin sisters have always managed to have fun with ordinary objects.

- Dindin! Dindin! Looky! Looky! They screamed at the same time, showing Dalya their new bracelets making sounds.
- Yes, yes, it's nice! Said Dalya, while continuing to pick up the dead leaves.

After a brief moment, Dalya finished gathering the leaves in a corner of the garden. But when she turned, Dalya discovered her little sisters Ari and Adi using leaves for the 2nd time, and putting them above their heads. The little twins sprinkled the leaves everywhere around them screaming:

- Pincess Cown leaf! Pincess Cown leaf!

This time, Dalya lost her cold blood. Her little twin sisters always gave her a hard time. Dalya asked them in a pleading tone:

- Go play somewhere else! Please!! Why do you always get me trouble? I'm tired of your fooleries!

The little twins Ari and Adi understood that Dalya won't play with them that day. So, Ari and Adi decided to leave their big sister alone and they ran to the annex house. Dalya restarted her work from the beginning for the 3rd time.

Many minutes later, when Dalya finished cleaning the garden and picking up all of the leaves, her mother called her to come home for dinner. And at the end of their meal, Dalya cleaned and dried the dishes, and she went to her bedroom to get a deserved rest, after a hard long day.

Nothing prepared Dalya for the scene that she was about to find in front of her, after opening the door of her bedroom. Her bed was filled with ribbons, pens and pencils. Her school bag was opened on the ground; all of its content was dispersed everywhere. Books and papers were spread in the entire room. Professor Canfield's homework papers were all colored in red and green stars. Ribbons and tissue pieces were all over the bedroom. Dalya's desk was messy. Only the Excelbox that Dalya had placed on a shelf above the desktop was intact in its place.

In front of the horrible and chaotic state of her bedroom, Dalya let out a shocked scream:

- But ... what happened?! ... who did this? ...why are my books thrown everywhere?... why are my homework papers colored?? ... but ... how ... who ...!??

Suddenly, two tiny happy voices were heard, simultaneously, at the bedroom's door:

- Ari and Adi made ... zolies bracelets! Looky Looky!

Dalya turned around to discover her little twin sisters showing off their little tiny hands, wearing bracelets encircled by ribbons, which they painted on colorful hearts, suns, flowers, and other scribbling. Dalya understood that her sisters have used everything in her bedroom to decorate their iron bracelets, which their father gave them earlier. Dalya was in shock:

- And ... and you had to put my bedroom upside down to make your bracelets?! You had to do all this mess to have fun?!

The little twins Ari and Adi exchanged a confused look, for a brief moment. And then, they smiled to their big sister and asked:

- Dindin wants zolies bracelet?

Furious and upset, Dalya pulled herself together, she took her little sisters to their bedroom and she put them in their beds. When she returned to her messy room, Dalya closed the door and sighed. Although she was exhausted; Dalya had to clean up the mess on her bed and on the floor, to be able to sleep. It took her an hour to get things back in order. Dalya placed the pencils, ribbons, scissors and adhesives in their box. She adjusted her bed, her cover and pillows. She sat on the floor to pick up her school bag. Dalya gathered white papers all wrinkled and scribbled with colors, muttering aloud:

- But what am I going to tell the Professor? What is he going to think of me when he sees my homework paper ... colorful? But why did they do that? Why do they always create me trouble?

While she cleaned the last things dispersed on the ground, Dalya noticed one of the bracelets on the floor, hidden by the edge of the bed. Dalya took it and she examined it. Ari and Adi were extremely clever for fooleries, but they were also clever for making toys. Her little sisters took colorful ribbons, and they have drawn all sorts of patterns on the ribbons: Sun, hearts, leaves, stars, clouds ... then they have surrounded the cylinder with the ribbon until the iron disappeared. And they made a knot at the end to hold the tape tight. The final result looked like a nice bracelet anyway.

When she was finally lying down on her bed for some rest, Dalya observed the bracelet she was holding in her hand. Despite her anger and her fatigue, Dalya could still smile, and she thought:

- My sisters are little pests ... but they always manage to remake things in their own way.

All of a sudden, something strange happened, right at that moment. Dalya repeated loudly in a confused tone:

- To remake in your own way ... in your own way and will ...

Dalya, lying down on her bed, she observed the bracelet in her hands; she turn it over and over, a dozen times. When suddenly, Dalya's eyes froze on the green painted ceiling of her bedroom. A few months ago, when they have just moved in the annex house, and when the renovations were going on, her father didn't have anymore white paint for the ceiling which was damaged by humidity. Mr. Antman used the only remaining paint he had left, for Dalya's bedroom. And it was a beautiful green that Dalya loved to watch.

- When all is lost ... to up raise your gaze ... a green ceiling ... a possibility to remake ... a green ceiling ... at your own way and will ...

Dalya looked at the green ceiling for one second, and at her little twin sister's bracelet the other second. When suddenly, Dalya jumped out of her bed in one swift move:

- I found it!!

The next day, Saturday, October 18th, 1890.

At the front door of the workshop, Dalya called:

- Uncle Giorgi? Are you there?

A big noise and a voice were heard simultaneously coming from inside the workshop:

- Yes! Come in Biggo!

Dalya found her uncle Giorgi inside, all covered in black powder, he was trying to fix a little item in a strange machine that he built. Dalya was curious to know what the machine was about, but she will ask him about it another time. That day, Dalya came for something else:

- Uncle Giorgi, can you help me make this, please?
- But of course, Biggo! Anything you want! He exclaimed immediately, before even knowing what she was asking him for.

Dalya gave her uncle a paper with her notes. Uncle Giorgi wiped his hands with a cloth, and then he read the paper. The expression on his face changed in an instant. He seemed surprised of what Dalya wanted to create:

- I must admit ... I have never tried it before ... and it will not look like the original one.
- I know. My friend Maurice Gus knows things about gemstones. This morning, when I visited him, he was able to provide me with some. He told me that at first, it will probably not be perfect, but with a few precise moves, I can make a pretty object out of it.

Dalya showed Uncle Giorgi a little stone in her hand:

- Maurice called it an aventurine stone. It comes from the South. Do you think it's possible to make this item?

A long moment of reflection followed, where Uncle Giorgi was thinking aloud, and building a plan in his mind, while caressing his mustache. When gradually, his face lightened up with a big smile, and he finally said all proud and determined:

- It can be done!... Yes we can, Biggo!

Instantly, Dalya and her uncle Giorgi started their work.

During 5 days, after the end of her classes at school, Dalya would spend several hours, in the workshop of her uncle Giorgi. He helped her to solder and fix this little object. He showed her the exact movements that she had to do in order to polish and tighten it. After several attempts and many days of hard work, Dalya showed the little object to her uncle, who finally exclaimed:

- It's great work, Biggo! It's perfect!!

Wednesday, October 22nd, 1890. At the end of the afternoon.

Mrs. Glorina was cleaning up the living room of the French family house, les Poirier, when she heard someone knocking at the door. Once she opened, Mrs. Glorina greeted the visitor with her usual smile:

- Good afternoon, Mademoiselle Dalya Bouvard!! Please come in.
- Hello Mrs. Glorina. I see you are busy today.
- Yes! Mr. Richard will be receiving some friends in a few days. I was cleaning the living room.
- Would you like any help? Asked Dalya.
- You are always kind and nice offering your help, Mademoiselle! But no thank you dear, I still have only the windows to clean ... I have almost finished.
- Can I see Madame for a moment, if she is free? asked Dalya
- Of course!! You know very well that Mrs. Marianne likes your presence!

Dalya followed Mrs. Glorina toward Mrs. Marianne's bedroom. The great woman was sitting on a big chair, in front of a table and facing the large windows. She was wearing a long blue velvet robe, and she had a warm fur cover on her legs. Mrs. Glorina came close to her and she announced:

- Mrs. Marianne ... Mademoiselle Dalya Bouvard would like to see you, for a moment.

Mrs. Marianne smiled at Dalya, without saying a word. Mrs. Glorina placed a little chair near the great woman, before leaving the bedroom, leaving them alone. Dalya sat down and she addressed the great woman:

- I hope you are feeling better today, Madame.

Mrs. Marianne inclined her head to confirm. Dalya hesitated for few seconds, she didn't know how to present the item that she had spent hours and days to create, she was unsure if it was a good idea or not, she didn't know whether Mrs. Marianne would be pleased or offended. After seconds of hesitation, Dalya gathered her courage, she took out a little box from her pocket, and she placed it on the table in front of the great woman:

- This is for you, Madame.

Mrs. Marianne was curious to know what the little girl would offer her this time; she took the little box, and then opened it with a slow movement.

And for many long silent minutes, Mrs. Marianne observed the content of the little box. Dalya remained silent, patient, while watching the great woman. And one could clearly notice that Mrs. Marianne Poirier never expected to receive such an object!

Some surprises make you happy, other surprises may touch you ... But sometimes, there are some surprises that revive you for the 2nd time.

Thursday, October 23rd, 1890.

Richard Poirier knocked at the door before entering his mother's bedroom. She was sitting alone in her usual chair in front of the large windows. The end of the day announced a cold and lonely night. Richard greeted his mother, before he sat on the empty chair, near her:

- Good evening, mother. How are you feeling today?

Mrs. Marianne didn't answer her son; she was observing her hand. Richard realized that his mother was lost in her thoughts, and he noticed a strange thing on his mother's finger: a ring of silver metal surrounding a well-cut shiny stone of emerald green color.

When Mrs. Marianne finally realized her son's presence in the chair near her, she presumed that he would be curious about the ring. And struggling to speak since a long time, Mrs. Marianne took a little paper, she wrote on it, and handed it to her son Richard:

She offered it to me

Richard didn't immediately guess who offered this ring to his mother. She received no other visitors, besides him and his sister Francine. But when Mrs. Marianne pointed to the Gardenia flower placed on the table in front of them, Richard understood right away what his mother meant. Mrs. Marianne continued to write:

She made it herself for me

Richard smiled:

- Made by her? … This is an unusual idea.

He asked his mother, always in a respectful and sweet voice:

- But, why did she offer you a ring? … did you desire one, mother? … It looks very much like the ring that you have lost; many years ago … did you talk to her about it?

Mrs. Marianne answered no with a head sign. Richard was confused:

- So then … why did she offer you the same lost ring? … and how did she guess you wanted one?

Mrs. Marianne also wondered about these questions. She never spoke to the little girl.

Rich as she was, Mrs. Marianne could have bought a more valuable ring than the lost one, but she didn't wore any other jewelry after her loss. She was very sad to have lost her husband, and she felt careless to have lost a dear memory of him.

Many years passed by, Mrs. Marianne Poirier almost forgot about this ring … until today … when she received the same ring, from a strange 12 years old little girl.

And since some time now, Richard Poirier was amazed and curious about the strange little girl who frequently visited their house. Nobody ever thought to offer his mother a ring, not even Richard himself.

For some silent minutes, Richard observed the aventurine ring on his mother's hands, and he thought loud:

-   This ring has not the same value, nor the same brightness than the lost emerald ring, but ...
    I guess that she spent many hours of work, in order to offer it to you ...

Mrs. Marianne smiled at her son. She agreed with him. Although this ring was imperfectly created by a little girl, Mrs. Marianne was glad to feel it in her fingers. A bright spark appeared in the woman's emerald green eyes, and a smile drew itself on her lips. It was a happy and sincere smile that Richard had not seen on her face since a very long time.

Another question was also in Richard Poirier's mind since a while now; he asked his mother, in a confused tone:

-   And why does she call you Madame? Why doesn't she call you like everyone else does, Mrs. Marianne?

His mother let out a little amused laugh, and she wrote:

She seems to have chosen to call me Madame

No one appeared to understand the behavior of this strange little girl. Richard and his mother remained seated for a long silent moment, observing the sunset through the big windows of the bedroom.

Dalya Bouvard couldn't bring back Mrs. Marianne Poirier's husband, and no one can. It is obvious that we cannot replace lost people, but ... what about lost things?

A strange little box found the right words for that matter. At first, Dalya Bouvard understood nothing of the 3rd clue. But after some thinking and working, the Excelbox proved to be somehow right ... when all is lost, to up raise your gaze ... when all is lost, always lift your head up ... and you will surely find something to do!

Mrs. Marianne thought that her life was over, that her role was over. But the Excelbox disagreed ... Oh but, Madame ... the last word of fate has not yet been sealed!

Chapter 26

The most beautiful flowers of the city

Friday, October 24th, 1890.

Every Friday afternoon, Mr. Weil Rosenwald, the grand Mansion's Gardener, entered the cemetery for his regular visit. But this day, he arrived much earlier than his usual time.

During his last previous visits, the Gardener was surprised and confused of what he found on the grave that he visited. A big beautiful flower bouquet was placed on the grave. These flowers, Mr. Weil Rosenwald knew them very well. In the entire Georgetown city, these flowers were found in one and only place. The Gardener was shocked:

- But ... These are the flowers of the grand Mansion's Garden!! ... these are the flowers that I planted and watered, myself!! ... who steals them?!... how and when does this thief steals them?!

Mr. Rosenwald couldn't understand why the grand Mansion's flowers were placed on the grave. Nobody knew that the Gardener visited this cemetery every Friday; none of the employees of the grand Mansion ever knew his secret. Mr. Rosenwald couldn't afford to buy beautiful flowers for this grave. And honest as he was, the Gardener had never dared to take a single flower of the grand Mansion's garden.

But this time, Mr. Rosenwald was determined to find out who was stealing these flowers. He was ready to unmask the thief and give him a good lesson to remember!!

The Gardener hid behind a tree near the grave. After a few minutes, Mr. Rosenwald noticed someone little approaching and entering the cemetery. The big bouquet of flowers that the little person held in his hands, was hiding all his face, he walked in hurried steps. When he arrived at the grave, the little person slowly put down the new flowers on the ground; he cleaned the grave off dead leaves and he put aside the old wilted flowers. Then, he decorated the grave with fresh flowers that he had just brought. The Gardener, still hiding behind the tree, could clearly hear the little person talking aloud and laughing:

- These are the most beautiful flowers of Georgetown city. If Mr. Gardener knew that I stole them ... He'll be angry and furious!

When the little person finished decorating the grave, he stood up and addressed the grave in a more serious tone:

- I don't know who you are ... but I'm sure you were someone very dear to Mr. Gardener. That's why you deserve the most beautiful flowers of the city ... even if I have to steal them!

Still hiding behind the big tree, the Gardener's anger evaporated in a second. The last thing Mr. Weil Rosenwald expected to see was Mademoiselle Dalya Bouvard, stealing the flowers of the grand Mansion's garden, cleaning this grave, and decorating it carefully. He watched the scene without daring to intervene or make any noise.

It is true that we cannot replace people that we have lost. But we can take care of people who are still alive and who are dear to us.

The only thing Dalya thought to do in order to help Mrs. Marianne, was to replace a lost precious Emerald ring, with an aventurine ring. And to help Mr. Gardener, Dalya replaced old wilted flowers, by placing on the grave, the most beautiful flower bouquet of the city.

The Emerald ring and the splendid bouquet generated new things. The French neighbor, Mrs. Marianne Poirier couldn't take her eyes of this imperfect Emerald ring. The Gardener froze in his hidden place, while observing the magnificent flowers on the grave.

A feeling of hope steadily replaced despair ... a feeling of confidence steadily replaced doubts and fears ... a tiny sparkle of power was growing strong in the face of sadness.

On that day, many things were steadily being replaced. Because when everything is seized, everything is granted back to you ... and for the second time, everything is much better and well done ... as difficult as it may seem, as strange as it may sound, it is for sure a true generosity indeed. But, hold on a minute ... isn't it what the Excelbox had already revealed?

Chapter 27

A distinguished birthday party

Monday, November 03rd, 1890. Late in the afternoon.

When Dalya came back from school, as soon as she crossed the grand Mansion's door, she was called by a familiar voice. The housemaid of the French neighbors, Mrs. Glorina was right behind her:

- Good afternoon, Mademoiselle Dalya ... I am glad I caught you on time, before you go home.
- Good afternoon to you, Mrs. Glorina. Did you come for me, all the way up here?
- Actually, yes ... I'm here to invite you to Miss Francine's birthday party, which will take place this Saturday. Mrs. Marianne insisted that I inform you, in person!

Dalya was surprised:

- Are you sure? Miss Francine doesn't seem to like my presence in the hou...

Mrs. Glorina objected sharply:

- It doesn't matter what Miss Francine thinks! It's a direct request of Mrs. Marianne Poirier herself!! She and I are expecting your presence! The party starts at 3 PM. But you are welcomed anytime!

Dalya had no time to answer or confirm, Mrs. Glorina walked away:

- Goodbye, Mademoiselle! Saturday then! We'll be expecting you!

Dalya went back home, happy and surprised to attend a party of wealthy people, for the first time in her life. She was always curious to know what was going on in the events of the rich and distinguished people.

The following days, Dalya's mind was busy by two things: Miss Francine's gift and the dress Dalya would wear to this party. Dalya had no money to buy a gift for a distinguished person, and she didn't have any dress. The only clothes Dalya ever had, were yellowed shirts, stitched pants, a faded overall, a large cap, and black shoes ... boy's clothes. Dalya never wore a girl's dress before, ever in her life.

Dalya couldn't study at home, without her mother yelling at her to wash the dishes or clean up the kitchen, and without her father pressuring her about the inheritance money. That's why, the school's Library was a safe heaven for Dalya, she enjoyed sitting on a little desk in a quiet corner of the school's Library, in front of a large transparent window, and far away from the scrutinizing stares of the other students. The large windows of the school Library offered a splendid view over Georgetown city.

In order to improve her knowledge in the Arts, Professor Canfield gave Dalya a list of oil-paintings to describe in 150 words each. The Arts were a subject completely unknown to her a few months ago; so Dalya had a lot to catch up on, and a little trouble to understand the lessons. For some minutes, Dalya observed a painting printed on a book in front of her, and she was thinking aloud:

- Johan Laurentz Jensen ... artist from Denmark. It's a painting of flowers, a large bouquet of white and pale pink roses, with green leaves, a black vase, a dark background that illuminates the bouquet of flowers... and some closed roses... and ... and ... and I think that's it ... what else should I say to complete 150 words about this painting?

After a while of silence and focus, Dalya laid back on her chair, unable to find an extra word for this painting's description. When she raised her eyes from her homework paper, Dalya noticed the presence of a person sitting at a Library desk, few rows in front of her.

A young woman with Asian features was staring at Dalya, in a strange way. It was the same woman who helped Dalya reach a book at the 5th shelf of the Library, 4 months ago, when Dalya was seeking information about Mrs. Marianne Poirier's illness.

Since her first days in this school, Dalya had the feeling that this young Asian woman was observing her, in a different way than all the other people at the College. Whenever Dalya walks in the school corridors, whenever she comes and leaves the classrooms, whenever she sits for hours in the Library, whenever she walks in the school garden ... Dalya always felt the strange stares of this young Asian woman on her.

The Library assistant, Miss Guendolyn had informed Dalya, that this young Asian woman was the music teacher in this school, and her name was: Miss Haîyang. Dalya couldn't understand why this woman followed her every move and why she stared at her so often. It was a strange behavior...

A few long seconds later, the young Asian woman, Miss Haîyang stood up; she picked up the books on her desk, and she left the Library, taking one last quick look at Dalya. And while heading toward the exit, a little book fell from the stack that the teacher Miss Haîyang was carrying. Nobody noticed the book falling, not even the teacher herself. Only Dalya did. She stood up and picked up the book from the floor. And before she put it back on a bookshelf, Dalya read the book cover:

- A magical tale ... by Charles Perrault.

Back to her little desk, Dalya read the first pages of the book, curious to know the subject of its content. Except that by reading the first words of the first chapter, Dalya was unable to put the book down. For almost an hour, Dalya completely forgot her homework in the Arts, and she remained motionless sitting on her desk near the window; her eyes focused on the book, devouring it one page after another, without a pause. A pumpkin, mousses, a pink dress ... The story was so captivating that Dalya didn't notice time flying by.

A moment later, a young woman with ruby red hair, stopped in front of Dalya. She was pushing a cart filled with books about to be put back on the shelves. Miss Guendolyn asked Dalya in a happy tone:

- Good afternoon, Mademoiselle Dalya Bouvard. How are you doing today?

Dalya was so charmed by the book; she didn't hear Miss Guendolyn greeting her. The young woman had to repeat her sentence:

- Hello ... is anyone there?

When Dalya finally noticed Miss Guendolyn's presence near her; she smiled:

- Yes ... sorry I didn't see you, Miss Guendolyn ... good afternoon ...

Miss Guendolyn let out a little giggle:

- You were so lost in this book. What are you reading?
- The music teacher, Miss Haîyang dropped it on her way out of the Library. It's a story written by an author ... Mr. Charles Perrault. It's called ... a magical tale.
- Ah!! ... Now I understand ... I've read this book before ... It's a beautiful story. I am sure you will love it! Exclaimed Miss Guendolyn.
- I love it already ... it's magical!

And before Miss Guendolyn would leave Dalya and continue her work pushing the book cart and putting back the books on the shelves, Dalya asked:

- Miss Guendolyn ... I was wondering if I can have your opinion on something ... I am invited to a distinguished birthday party of a neighbor. They are wealthy people. I don't know what gift should I bring. Do you have any ideas?

Miss Guendolyn replied without hesitating a second:

- A manuscript book! ... a book by your handwriting. You can copy poems, stories or quotes ... a book is always the best gift you can give. All wealthy people are educated and cultured. And with a book as a gift, you are always sure to please!

Dalya thought it was a great idea too. With no money to buy a manuscript, Miss Guendolyn was nice to offer her a little empty book note, beautifully decorated on the edge. Dalya didn't search very long for what she wanted to write. She decided to copy the beautiful story that the teacher Miss Haîyang dropped: the magical story by Charles Perrault.

Wednesday, November 05th, 1890.

Now that her gift was ready, Dalya had only a dress to get. Since her childhood, Dalya wore boys' pants and shirts; it was more convenient to work and to help her father in the market.

Dalya didn't dare to ask her father for money to buy a dress, and she knew no one who could lend her one. The only person she knew, who can find a solution to almost every problem, it was her uncle Giorgi!

- A girl's dress? I built machines, I made tools ... but I've never created a dress before. What a great challenge! We need ... material, fabrics, little and big needles ... and sewing threads. Uncle Giorgi murmured before disappearing inside his workshop.

Dalya helped her uncle Giorgi, as best as she could. She brought from home, all the ribbons and colorful fabrics she could find. She emptied her bag on the big table, at the same time where her uncle Giorgi put down fabrics and a large pair of scissors.

For a long thinking minute, Uncle Giorgi observed his niece from head to toe, and he asked her to raise her arms and turn around several times. Then, he took a long pink fabric, he wrapped it on her quickly from her feet to her neck, he wrapped the fabric on her arms, then he made two butterflies' knots on her shoulders to fix the long fabric. A few minutes later, uncle Giorgi took a step back, and he exclaimed joyfully:

- We're done!

When Dalya moved, and she took a single step forward, she fell to the ground like a brick. That's when Uncle Giorgi whispered in a less confident voice:

- And I think we're going to start again ...

He then had a 2nd creative idea. Uncle Giorgi and Dalya gathered together all little fabrics. He took a belt, and made many holes, one centimeter apart. Then, he fastened this belt on Dalya's waist, and he tied the little fabrics in each of the belt's holes. A few minutes later, Dalya was wearing a skirt made up of a hundred little multicolored fabrics; she looked like a ... hot air balloon. Uncle Giorgi sat down on his chair, caressing his mustache:

- It's a bit more complicated than I have thought! ... Let's try something else!

Uncle Giorgi never loses his enthusiasm. He stared at Dalya for some silent minutes, and then he jumped off his chair:

- Goose feathers! That's what we need!
- Goose ... feathers? Dalya was worried of her uncle's crazy ideas sometimes.
- Yes! I'll make you a dress with feathers! I remember seeing a woman's dress with feathers. It will be like a kind of fur. He replied all excitedly of his new idea, before disappearing outside his workshop.

Dalya was confused:

- A dress in feathers? But ... how will I manage the smell? I will smell exactly like a goose!!

A few moments later, Dalya heard a thunderous noise outside the workshop. Suddenly, her uncle Giorgi ran inside his workshop, holding only 2 feathers in his hand, he screamed:

- AAAAAIE! AIE AIE AIE! AIE AIE!!

Uncle Giorgi was followed by an army of angry 12 geese; they were pinching his feet and chasing him all around in the workshop. Noises of angry geese, screams of pain, feathers in the air, dust off everywhere, items and tools crashing to the ground ... the workshop turned into an arena. Dalya froze in a corner, laughing and watching the scene.

While her uncle Giorgi was fighting against his 12 geese, Dalya sat in front of the large table of the workshop; she took a paper and she drew a sketch. After a few minutes, uncle Giorgi, all red and breathless because of his escape, he was able to calm his geese and keep them outside by closing the door of his workshop. He turned around toward his niece and he said in a spontaneous tone:

- Well, thinking about it ... goose feathers are not that very fashionable these days ...

Dalya laughed at her uncle's misfortune. He noticed the drawings that his niece made; he took the paper in his hands and he examined it:

- Alright ... now I understand your idea and what we should do ... we can start with the skirt, then the corset, the neck ... and finally the shoulders ... It's possible ... Yes ... Yes... it can be done! Here is our plan of work, then!!

Hours passed away, several fabrics and pieces sewed, sewing threads cut, models redesigned, and ribbons changed several times ... after a while and lots of hard work, a pink and white dress began to emerge. When Dalya finally wore her dress, her uncle exclaimed proudly:

- Challenge completed!!

The dress collar was round, surrounded by a pretty pink ribbon. The sleeves were sewn up to elbows with a pretty pink bow. The white corset refined perfectly well Dalya's thin size. The dress skirt was in pale pink fabric, extended up to a few centimeters above the ground, giving Dalya the allure of a Princess. Dalya gratefully and happily thanked her uncle; she promised him more of his favorite fruits in his usual basket delivery.

Saturday, November 08th, 1890.

At 3:00 PM, Dalya wore her new made dress. Having no money to buy girls' shoes that will match her dress; Dalya waxed firmly the only black shoes she had. And for her hair, Dalya arranged it in a chignon. Then, she took the gift in her hands and she came downstairs to the kitchen.

The little twins Ari and Adi were sitting in their usual chairs, in front of the dining table. Dalya's mother was trying to calm them down and make them eat the fruit compote, but the little twins threw in every direction, full tablespoons of food, while screaming:

- Zitotaaaa! Zitotaaaa! We want Zitotaaaa!
- It's the fruit compote ... it is very good ... it's raspberry and peach and honey and ban...

- Zitotaaaa! Zitotaaaa!
- What is Zitota, anyway? ... this is the fruit compote, it's delicious ... just try a bit of it!

Dalya's mother turned around to take a napkin, when she realized Dalya's presence in the kitchen. Immediately, Mrs. Augustine let out a mocking laugh:

- What is that!! ... What are you wearing?! ... You look even more stupid!! ... What is this rag!!? ... You're ugly and ridiculous in it!

Dalya was not expecting this answer from her mother. In fact, Dalya never heard her mother encourage her, advise her, or even just tell her a compliment. All what Dalya has ever received from her mother were criticisms, reprimands, thunderous screams, mean laughs, pinching cheeks, slamming doors and breaking plates.

In front of her mother's diminishing laughs, Dalya remained speechless. It was not an elegant and lavish dress, for sure, but Dalya was happy and satisfied with her uncle's work. They have spent hours and days to create it. Mrs. Augustine didn't refrain her mean and diminishing laugh:

- You think that by wearing this piece of rag, you will belong among distinguished people? You're dreaming, you little idiot! You'll never be somebody! You're a nobody!

When Ari and Adi turned around, and noticed their big sister Dalya wearing a dress for the first time ever in her life, the little twins exclaimed joyfully and in admiration:

- Oh! Dindin zolie!!! Dindin very zolie!!!

The little twins' reaction calmed Dalya's disappointment from the wicked and evil laughs of her mother. Without saying a word, Dalya walked in the kitchen, she pulled out a small jar out of a cupboard, and she put it in front of her mother. Instantly, the little twins Ari and Adi screamed joyfully, while extending their little hands toward the jar filled with green olives mixed with herbs and oil:

- Zitotaaaa! Zitotaaaa! Zitotaaaa!

The green olives with herbs, that's what the little twins meant by the word Zitota. And only Dalya knew what their little twin sister wanted. Mrs. Augustine stared arrogantly at Dalya, and she said with a cruel tone:

- You really look ridiculous in this rag! Even more idiot than before!

Without answering or even trying to understand this free cruelty, Dalya stepped out of the annex house, under the scornful stares of her mother and the joyful screams of her little sisters. Dalya held firmly in her hand Miss Francine's gift, wrapped in a pretty paper. And she walked toward the exit of the grand Mansion.

Minutes later, Dalya arrived at the door of the French neighbors, les Poirier. She noticed a dozen of luxurious black cars parked at the entrance. Dalya walked toward the kitchen's door.

Usually, the kitchen of the French neighbors was quiet and empty. Except on this day, Dalya met many men inside the kitchen; the ones dressed in white outfits were cooking, and other men in black suits carried platters and drinks outside the kitchen.

When Dalya met Mrs. Glorina, the woman exclaimed in an excited tone:

- I'm so glad to see you here, Mademoiselle Dalya!

Mrs. Glorina was wearing an elegant clear blue dress that made her look sweeter and different from her usual housemaid outfit. She hugged Dalya, and then she observed the little girl:

- How pretty you are, Mademoiselle Dalya!! And you look so lovely and pretty in this dress! ... Mrs. Marianne is in the living room with all the other guests! She is waiting for you!

The idea of facing strangers all alone, gave goosebumps to Dalya. She asked Mrs. Glorina, begging:

- Can I stay here and help you serve?

Mrs. Glorina protested in a rigid tone:

- No no no! Of course not! ...You are going to have fun and meet distinguished people from high society! Your place is not in the kitchen, it's in the living room! Go! Now!

Mrs. Glorina gently pushed Dalya toward the kitchen exit, and she returned to continue her orders to the cooks and servers. Dalya walked in slow hesitant steps toward the living room.

There were about thirty men and women, all dressed alike. Men were in black suits, black ties and white shirts. Women wore long dresses in dark colors; dark blue, dark brown, dark green, all in lavish fabric lace, silk and satin, with shining and expensive jewelry around their neck, on their hair and hands. Some were sitting on divans, others standing near the fireplace. The men and women were chatting, laughing, and drinking.

Suddenly, Dalya noticed a familiar silhouette: Mrs. Marianne Poirier. Dalya approached the great woman, who was sitting on a big chair near a large window. It was the first time that Dalya met Mrs. Marianne without her sleeping robe. The great woman was wearing a long green algae dress, embroidered with shiny gemstones and elegant lace fabric. A warm fur cover was placed on her legs. Mrs. Marianne's long white hair was arranged in a chignon; a few locks of hair fell on her shoulders.

Dalya noticed that the only jewel Mrs. Marianne wore, was the green aventurine ring Dalya gave her a few days before. And although she was afflicted by illness and age, Mrs. Marianne Poirier had lost nothing of her majestic beauty.

- Good evening to you, Madame. Thank you for inviting me, today. Said Dalya

Mrs. Marianne replied with a nice smile. She was very pleased to see the little girl attend this party. Mrs. Marianne made a sign toward Dalya to sit on the chair near her.

While sitting next to the great woman, Dalya observed the guests; beautiful women in their refined dresses, elegant and courteous men, servers offering drinks to the guests, smooth music was played. Dalya was amazed by all these distinguished people and this refined luxurious party.

At a moment, Dalya noticed Mr. Richard Poirier among the crowd. He was wearing a dark suit, a silk black bow tie, a white shirt, his hair was neat, and he looked very elegant. He greeted the guests, talking to ones, smiling at others. Dalya noticed that Mr. Richard Poirier was sociable in public. When he got close to Mrs. Marianne, Mr. Richard bowed to his mother, he kissed her hand, and then he spoke to her in a gentle and caring voice:

- Good evening to you, mother. You look beautiful and elegant tonight.

Mrs. Marianne replied with a smile. Then, Mr. Richard greeted Dalya in a more formal tone:

- Mademoiselle.
- Monsieur. Said Dalya, while blushing.

Richard observed Dalya for a brief moment, with a curious quick look, before he was requested by someone behind him; Richard turned around and disappeared into the crowd of guests. A few minutes after, Mrs. Glorina appeared holding a platter of different juices. She asked Dalya, all excited:

- So then, are you having fun? Do you like the party? You will be amazed at the big birthday cake that I've prepared! It took me days to complete it!

Mrs. Glorina served Mrs. Marianne and Dalya, 2 glasses of juice before leaving in hurried steps and disappearing into the crowd. All the guests greeted Mrs. Marianne Poirier in a respectful way. Men kissed her hand, women made a reverence. Dalya thought that the French family, les Poirier must be important and distinguished people.

Suddenly, the crowd went all silent, a person entered the living room, and all the guests applauded. It was Miss Francine Poirier. She was wearing a long black dress, a big shining necklace hid all her fat neck, a huge white fur around her arms, her hair was arranged in a high hairstyle, and large feathers were attached to a tiara on her hair. She was followed by seven women dressed in the same extravagant fashion. Miss Francine greeted all the guests, laughing with some, and thanking others. Then, she sat on an empty chair, in the other side of the living room, always surrounded by her seven friends.

The party continued for several minutes. At a moment, a carriage entered, carrying a gigantic cake, pushed by 4 servers, and followed by Mrs. Glorina. The carriage entered slowly, under the applause of the crowd and it headed toward Miss Francine. She let out a few screams of joy and surprise. Five floors of nougat cream cake, caramelized apples and pears cut into shape of roses, ornaments of sweets and candies around the cake in each floor. Dalya had never seen such a magnificent cake!

When the carriage stopped, the crowd gathered around and sang happy birthday to Miss Francine. At the end of the song, Miss Francine blew out all the candles under applauses. Then, one by one, the guests presented their gifts to Miss Francine. She opened them immediately, letting out every time screams of joy and surprise, while thanking the guest.

Mrs. Marianne made a sign toward Dalya to go and meet Miss Francine. Dalya obeyed and stood up right away. When she noticed Dalya Bouvard among the crowd, Miss Francine screamed in a cheerful and loud voice:

- And here is the veggy seller who claims the fortune of Mr. Governor Iskander Balthazar!

The crowd went all silent and they all turned around to stare at the little girl. Dalya was not expecting this introduction and even less the attention of all the guests. Under the haughty gaze of Miss Francine, the giggles of the seven women around her, the glances and whispers of the guests, Dalya dared to address Miss Francine, in a polite voice:

- Happy birthday, Miss Francine. Dalya said, before handing her a little gift.
- Is it something else that you have created, because you have no money? Asked Miss Francine in a mocking tone, while examining the wrapped gift in her hands. Miss Francine continued aloud:
- Ladies and gentlemen ... If any of you would be interested in jewelry made of iron and street stones, Dalya Bouvard is an expert!
- So then, she is the one who gave Mrs. Marianne that ridiculous metal ring? Asked a woman next to Francine, while observing Dalya from head to toe.
- Does she make any wood jewelry too? Asked a man in a curious voice, which triggered a wave of laughs among the guests.
- Even straw jewelry, if you wish, my dear! Replied Miss Francine in a laugh.
- I am curious to know the designer of this ... this dress. A woman approached Dalya, while scrutinizing her in a surprised stare.
- Look no further my dear, it can only be the fruit of her creations. Replied an elegant man.
- I always have pity on people who dream to be like us. They often forget that we are born noble and rich. Said a woman, with a mocking and pity tone.
- Your dress will go perfectly well on my little dog. How much is it for a miniature copy of your dress? a woman asked Dalya, in a serious and interested tone.
- Why do you want to make your dog wear such an atrocity? Questioned Miss Francine in a shocked tone. This little girl already looks like an ugly ducky!
- Well said!! An ugly ducky! Exclaimed another woman with an amused tone.
- Ugly ducky! That's right! A man laughed.
- Ugly ducky! Very clever Francine Poirier! Marveled a woman.

Dalya stood still in the middle of people who laughed at her and said offensive critics. Dalya didn't know what she had to do to get out of this situation. She searched with her eyes for someone who could save her and help her. Dalya noticed Mrs. Glorina displaying a compassionate look few steps away from her; Mrs. Glorina seemed unable and powerless to intervene in front of the guests. Mr. Richard Poirier seated on a chair; he followed the scene with a cold and neutral serious stare, he wasn't laughing like all the other guests. His mother, Mrs. Marianne Poirier was a couple of steps away from Dalya. And even if the great woman couldn't speak; Dalya could clearly see her shocked and sad eyes. At that moment, Dalya felt lonely and weak.

When Miss Francine opened Dalya's gift, she didn't scream joyfully like with the other gifts. Instead, Miss Francine let out a horrible crushing and loud laugh:

- The ugly ducky is offering me ... a manuscript!

A wave of laughs filled the entire living room, instantly. Dalya didn't understand why everyone was laughing. The Library assistant, Miss Guendolyn assured her that a book was the perfect gift to offer to rich and cultured people, and Dalya thought it was a great idea too. Miss Francine continued in a cold serious voice:

- It's the dumbest gift I have ever received! How dare you offer me such a thing?! I guess we cannot expect that an ugly ducky like you, knows good manners of high society!

Dalya couldn't understand Miss Francine's reaction. Dalya didn't know much about the good manners of rich people; she knew only the good manners of poor people. And Dalya has always thought that a gift should be accepted and thanked for, no matter we like it or not; the most important thing was the kind gesture and attention behind the gift.

Miss Francine examined the book in her hands:

- What a stupid and grotesque idea! ... a book ?! is that the best you can offer? ... and you offered a cheap iron ring to my mother? What were you thinking? ...Seriously, you offer only stupid gifts ... and besides, I don't like to read ... this book is useless for me!

Suddenly, with a brusque move, Miss Francine threw the book on the floor, under the scornful laughs of all the guests. Dalya's throat tightened. She never thought that her gift would be thrown on the floor. The story that Dalya chose to rewrite, was beautiful and inspiring. Dalya spent hours copying it in the manuscript, in order to offer it as a gift. The same goes for Mrs. Marianne Poirier's aventurine ring. Dalya spent entire days trying to shape it and produce it in the workshop of her uncle Giorgi. Never Dalya thought that her gifts will be mocked and diminished.

For the first time in her life, Dalya felt humiliated. Under the mean and arrogant laughs of the guests, the pity looks of Mrs. Glorina, the neutral and cold face of Richard, the sad eyes of Mrs. Marianne; Dalya understood that no one could help her, protect her or defend her, at that moment. She had to act alone. With her cheeks red, her lips pale, and her throat tight, Dalya held her tears as best as she could. As soon as Dalya took a step toward Miss Francine, all the laughs evaporated and a heavy silence invaded the living room. Everyone was curious to see what the little girl was about to do.

Dalya Bouvard slowly picked up the manuscript thrown on the floor. And then, with her most beautiful brave smile that she had, Dalya left the place, under a heavy and tense silence.

On her way back home, Dalya walked in hurried steps. When she arrived at the grand Mansion, she walked toward the annex house, but suddenly, she stopped. Dalya hesitated for a second. After the difficult moment she has been through in the French neighbor's house, Dalya didn't need to hear her mother's criticism and cruel remarks. So then, Dalya turned around and she walked toward the grand Mansion. When she opened Mr. Balthazar's Library door, the fireplace was already burning. The flames light up and warmed the entire place. Dalya sat on the cushions on the floor, in front of the fireplace.

And right at that moment, Dalya let go of something that she was holding for a very long time: her tears. They flowed without stopping. Her pink and white dress got wet in seconds. Dalya cried her heart out, alone, in front of the fireplace of the grand Mansion's Library.

After long minutes of silence, a calm and gentle voice appeared out of nowhere. It was a familiar voice that Dalya knew very well: Mr. Sloan Wilfrid!

- I don't know the reason why Mr. Governor chose you to become his Heiress, or why he imposed the challenges. However ... I don't think he would be delighted and reassured to know that his 12 years old Heiress cries at the slightest difficulty that she faces.

A silhouette stood up from a chair. Mr. Wilfrid had a book in his hand, he put it back on the Library shelf and he took another one. And this time, Mr. Wilfrid sat on a chair near Dalya. He continued to speak in the same calm and gentle voice, while flipping the book pages:

- Respect has to be earned, and it is not given without effort. Don't expect everyone to instantly respect you and like you. If you are lucky by any miracle, you might inherit the second biggest fortune of this country. And you don't even have a prestigious education or a noble lineage. So then ... don't be surprised and disappointed if people don't miss any opportunity to humiliate you and destroy you.

  If you can't handle the pressure and the free cruelty, it would be wiser to give up now. Because if you think that things will get better, if you think that these people will make it easier for you ... think again Mademoiselle Dalya Bouvard. It is only but the beginning!

Dalya looked at the man, without daring to speak. Mr. Sloan Wilfrid was right in every word he said. And Dalya agreed.

A shadow sneaked between the chairs and walked slowly toward Dalya. The Snow Panther lay down on a carpet on the floor, near the little girl.

Silence settled in. Mr. Sloan Wilfrid continued reading his book. Dalya and the Snow Panther remained motionless and quiet, observing the dancing flames in the fireplace of the grand Mansion's Library.

Chapter 28

Two little pests

Friday, November 14ᵗʰ, 1890. Late in the afternoon.

Dalya couldn't stop thinking about what happened in the birthday party; she thought about Miss Francine and the guests' laughs, the pity looks of Mrs. Glorina, the sad eyes of Mrs. Marianne, and Mr. Wilfrid's words in the grand Mansion's Library, later that night ...

The little girl was less interested in what was going on around her. Dalya couldn't focus much on her private lessons with Professor Canfield. She was unusually lost in her thoughts, less dynamic and more silent than before; Dalya was even making mistakes on some simple questions. And at the annex home, Dalya was discreet and quiet. When she took care of the house chores, Dalya often ignored her mother's criticism and her father's pressure. Dalya shut herself up in her head, thinking about one and only question:

- *Should I quit now?*

During her free time, Dalya would gladly help the Gardener to water plants, to remove pots, and to pick up the dead leaves. In the immense garden of the grand Mansion, Dalya actively assisted the big man, she gladly occupied herself. It allowed her to lighten up her mind and breath. The Gardener, Mr. Rosenwald didn't complain of the little girl's presence. He even teached her flowers and plants names, their different origins and uses. Gardening was doing so much good to Dalya.

The little twins Ari and Adi followed their big sister everywhere. In the annex house, whenever they noticed their big sister wearing her gardening boots, Ari and Adi would scream and beg and escape and follow their big sister outside. Dalya allowed her little sisters to play in the garden of the grand Mansion, while she was helping Mr. Rosenwald, but on very strict conditions: never cut flowers or plants, never touch the gardening equipment, and never disturb or upset Mr. Gardener. Ari and Adi were always behaving good ... almost always.

- Why is this plant placed on all the surroundings of the grand Mansion? Asked Dalya, watering long purple flowers.
- Lemongrass has a repulsive smell for mosquitoes. This is why it's best to plant it near the windows, to keep them away from getting inside. Replied the Gardener, busy planting some little flowers.
- This plant has a really good smell ...
- Yes, indeed. And its leaves can be used in some meals too. Continued the Gardener.
- The leaves can be eaten? Marveled Dalya. I wonder what it tastes like?

- I often cut some leaves for the Cook of the grand Mansion, Mr. Ferrero. He adds it in soups or salads. He even used it once to garnish a p...

Suddenly, the Gardener who was sitting down on his knees, planting a flower, he dropped his gardening fork and gloves, and he ordered Dalya in a serious tone:

- Don't move!

Dalya didn't understand the Gardener's reaction:

- Why? What's going on?

When Dalya turned her head around, she was shocked. Her little sisters Ari and Adi were playing only few steps away from the Snow Panther.

- ... Can she hurt them? Dalya's voice trembled.

The Gardener stood up in a very slow movement, his eyes staring at the little twins and the snow Panther:

- If she can hurt? Yes. If she will hurt? I don't know. I can't predict her behavior. Séraphine doesn't allow anyone to touch her, apart from her late Masters and me.
- What should we do? Dalya asked with an anxious voice.
- I will move to the left to get Séraphine's attention. You go right and try to attract your sisters toward you. But calmly and without making any sudden moves!

The only problem was, as soon as Dalya and the Gardener did one step in opposite directions, Ari and Adi spontaneously turned their head around and they noticed the Snow Panther lying down on the grass near them. Immediately, Ari and Adi exclaimed simultaneously in a cheerful voice:

- Oh! Zolie kitten! Zolie kitten!

Séraphine also realized the presence of a little pair of twins, she straightened up her head and ears, her long tail rose up, she let out a little grunt, she showed off her sharp teeth and her claws came out of its paws. But Ari and Adi were not intimidated by the allure of the Snow Panther and even less by her growl or its sharp teeth, the small twins ran straight toward the Snow Panther. Dalya's heart stopped beating:

- But ... Do something!! Please ... She will hurt them!

The Gardener looked lost and confused; he didn't know what to do to intervene. Séraphine was a good docile and quiet animal, but if the little girls touch her, he didn't know how the animal will react:

- Hold on a minute!! If we do a brusque move, Séraphine may get angry ...

Dalya couldn't wait and do nothing, while her little sisters were running toward their loss. Dalya was about to run to stop her sisters, but the Gardener retained her by the arm tightly, she couldn't move:

- Hold on one minute!! we cannot intervene, we might provoke the Panther!! Just wait!!

Dalya tried to escape the Gardener's hands:

- But ... let me at least distract the Panther! She doesn't know them! She may think they are a threat ... she may hurt them!

Mr. Rosenwald replied in a serious grave voice:

- We don't know what she is capable of doing. Séraphine is not sociable. If we all run toward her, she may have a reac...

When suddenly, the Gardener stopped and he let go of Dalya's arm. Both the Gardener and Dalya were astonished and shocked of what was happening in front of their eyes.

The little twins Ari and Adi were having fun in discovering the big face of the animal. Ari was trying to grab the long agitated tail of the Snow Panther, while Adi was curious to see the large teeth and she was trying to force the animal to open its mouth. And the strange thing in this scene was ... the Snow Panther was calm and quiet, still lying down on the grass, she let the little twins marvel and caress her head and tail. Ari and Adi laughed innocently:

- Zolie kitten! Zolie kitten!

The Gardener murmured, amazed and confused:

- I don't understand what's happening ... Since they brought her as a baby, Séraphine has never allowed anyone to touch her! ... and even less play with her! It's a strange behavior!
- So then, she won't hurt them? Asked Dalya terrified while watching her little sisters.

The little twins Ari and Adi caressed the Panther's fur, exclaiming in marveled voices:

- Soft kitten! Zolie kitten! ... oh very soft kitten !!

Ari and Adi didn't seem afraid or terrified at all by the Snow Panther. When suddenly, the twins had the crazy idea to both sit on the back of the Panther. And still calm and serene, Séraphine watched for a moment the two tiny creatures settling on her back. And then with a slow movement, the animal stood up. The twins Ari and Adi were thrilled, seated one behind the other, holding on the long hair of the Panther, in order to not fall. Séraphine walked gently and slowly, toward the Gardener and Dalya. When she came near the man and the little girl, the Snow Panther bowed her two front legs, which allowed the little twins to get off her back exclaiming, all happy:

- Thank you little kitten! Thank you zolie kitten!

And under the shocked stares of the Gardener and Dalya, the little twins Ari and Adi gave a hug to the Panther, they surrounded with their little arms, the big neck of the Snow Panther:

- Next time little kitten! Zolie kitten! Thank you! Thank you!

The Snow Panther, always quiet and poised, she walked inside of the grand Mansion. Dalya grabbed her little twin sisters by the hands, relieved to see them alive and in one piece. Nor the Gardener nor Dalya understood what had just happened in front of them. The Gardener murmured in a shocked voice:

- Nobody has ever dared to do that … ever!

As soon as they entered the kitchen door in the annex house, the little twins Ari and Adi ran to their mother all excited:

- We played with little kitten! Zolie kitten in big garden! Very soft and zolie! We on the back of kitten and then … a tour in garden! Can we bring kitten home? Please … please!
- What kitten? What are you talking about? Said Mrs. Augustine while preparing a soup.

Dalya's face was pale, still healing from the shocking scene that happened in the immense garden; she sneaked quietly toward her bedroom, when her mother called her:

- There is a kitten in the grand Mansion?
- Yes.

Dalya couldn't say another word, because her voice was trembling and her mother would realize she was hiding something.

- Can we bring kitten home? It is a zolie kitten! Very sweet and soft! The twins jumped, while holding on to their mother's apron.
- Yes … Yes … alright! … Dalya, next time bring that kitten home. We can use a little company here.

Dalya replied only by a nervous smile. She didn't dare to tell her mother that the zolie little kitten with who her little twins played this afternoon, was actually … Mr. Iskander Balthazar's Snow Panther! … A real Panther!

Dalya doubted that her mother would find the company of the Panther, lovely and reassuring. Since the time that they have moved in the annex house of the grand Mansion, Dalya and her father didn't reveal to Mrs. Augustine Bouvard the existence of this animal, living just steps away from them. They already had difficulties to convince Mrs. Augustine to move into this house!

After dinner, Dalya took care of the dishes. Her mother took upstairs the little twins to give them their baths and put them to bed. Her father went out, as usual, to join his friends and their cards game.

While drying the dishes, Dalya thought about the scene of her little sisters playing with the Snow Panther, Séraphine. And despite the fright that this incident has caused, Dalya couldn't help but notice that her little sisters were happy and thrilled playing with this Snow Panther. The little twins lived real moments of happiness in this annex house, they had their own bedroom, and an immense garden to play in, every day. Dalya's heart was heavy:

- What if I don't succeed in these challenges? Should I give up now before my family get used to this annex house? Wouldn't it be wiser to leave this home now?

Dalya couldn't stop thousands of doubt questions invade her little head. She finished storing the dishes in the kitchen's cupboards and she walked upstairs to her room.

When she opened her bedroom's door; Dalya was thunderstruck by what she found; two little chubby creatures, laughing full heart, wearing clear pink onesies in cotton and beanies on their heads, both were holding ... the Excelbox!

Dalya's heart stopped beating. She couldn't breathe no more and she froze. The little twins noticed their older sister, and their giggles instantly stopped. Ari and Adi exclaimed in a guilty air:

- Oh ... oh!

Dalya, breathless, managed to say in a calm voice:

- One ... more ... move ... and I will ... strangle you.

The twins remained motionless in their place, without moving a muscle, Ari and Adi were well aware that their older sister was very angry because of their foolery. A brief moment of silence and absolute stillness, followed up.

When suddenly, a little sound was heard and a tiny paper came out of the Excelbox, which was still held by the little twins. Slowly and gently, Dalya took the Excelbox from her sisters' hands, and she put it on her desk with very careful movements. The little twins were still immobile and silent, watching their big sister, with innocent and angelic stares.

When Dalya turned around toward her little twin sisters, she exploded with anger and chased them to their bedroom:

- YOU ARE A THREAT TO THE HUMAN SPECIES!! IF I TAKE YOU ... ONE MORE TIME ... TOUCHING THAT BOX!

In a flash of light, the twins ran in hurried steps, toward their beds. And despite the threats and screams of their big sister, Ari and Adi couldn't hold back their laughs and giggles:

- Sorry Dindin! Sorry Dindin! Sorry Dindin!

Dalya firmly closed the little twins' bedroom door, to make sure they won't come out until morning. They have done enough fooleries for one day.

Dalya returned to her bedroom, her heart exhausted by so many shocks in one day. When she came near her desk, Dalya pulled a little paper that was still on the edge of the Excelbox:

- It's the 4th clue! ... but how did it come out ?... how did Ari and Adi managed to ask for it?

Dalya was unable to explain how this clue was requested. And when she read the paper, surprise and confusion appeared on Dalya's face:

The fourth clue
Never pepper without salt
Never dark without dawn
Never fall without arise
Never mockery without recast
If surrender is before the fight
So why two hands
And why two legs?

Dalya thought for a long moment:

- Salt and pepper ... dark and dawn ... fall and arise? ... They are opposite words. But why are they put in the same sentence? What is that supposed to mean? Mockery and recast? ... The recast ... is it like the transformation of metal? But why the recast is the opposite of the mockery? It doesn't make any sense. If surrender is before the fight ... then ... so this time, I have a question as a clue? ... really?

And it was a very strange question. Why do we have two hands and why two legs? Dalya thought about it for a long moment, without being able to find an appropriate answer.

Saturday, November 15th, 1890. In the morning.

The Lawyer Mr. Ernest Laszlo came out of his office building in hurried steps. He was followed by Mr. Sloan Wilfrid and his son, Lyor Laszlo. The younger men haven't worn their coats and hats yet. Mr. Ernest Laszlo was furious to find that his parked car was unusable:

- What is that?!! The car's wheel is ruined?!!

The driver stood up in a quick move, holding in his hand a cloth and a large hammer, he replied to his employer, in a panicked voice:

- We can repair the wheel ... Sir ... If you can just wait for some min...

- I can't wait one more minute!! My car had to be ready on time!! I'm tired of your incompetence!! Interrupted Mr. Ernest Laszlo, on the verge of an anger crisis.
- Yes, Sir ... My apologies Si....
- I don't care about your excuses!! Find us another car, immediately! I can't miss my appointment with the Minister!!

While wearing his coat, the young Lyor Laszlo, had a strange feeling of seeing a familiar silhouette under the car. But he pulled himself together, thinking it was just a figment of his imagination. Mr. Sloan Wilfrid was holding a file in his hands, and checking some papers one last time, before their important meeting. While Mr. Ernest Laszlo was reprimanding his driver:

- You should have checked the wheels this morning!! What were you doing during that time? Should I teach you how to do your work too?!
- I'm sorry ... Sir ... all the wheels were fine this morning ... and suddenly this wheel has f...
- If I miss this appointment because of you, you won't have any job with me anymore!! I can't stand your incompetence and your lazin...

All of a sudden, a little proud voice interrupted Mr. Ernest Laszlo:

- It's alright now!! It's all settled!

Mr. Wilfrid's sunglasses fell on the file he was holding in his hands. Lyor Laszlo turned left and right, seeking the source of that voice among the passersby in the street. Mr. Ernest Laszlo froze in his place, and he seemed confused. Only the driver didn't look surprised to hear that little voice. The driver turned around and he helped a little silhouette to come out from under the car. She was wearing a small worn overall, a white shirt, a large cap, and small black shoes. She was holding a hammer and a screwdriver tool, her hands were black dirty and she had a few dark spots on her nose and cheeks. She spoke to the driver in a confident tone:

- The wheel is firmly fixed, now. It was just a small car nail that came out. And I checked all the other 3 wheels too. They're all well fixed. You can drive safe now!

Mr. Ernest Laszlo, Mr. Sloan Wilfrid and Lyor Laszlo were speechless and shocked to meet Dalya Bouvard, in this state, coming out from under their car. Mr. Ernest Laszlo asked in a confused tone:

- What are you ... how do ... why are you here?

Dalya replied spontaneously:

- I came here to inform you of the 4th clue, Sir. And I noticed that your driver struggled to repair the car wheel. It was easy to restore anyway. I helped him.
- You ... you know about mechanics? Mr. Wilfrid asked, letting out a surprised giggle.
- In wheels, yes ... Thanks to my uncle Giorgi, I learned to change the wheels of my father's cart, all by myself. Replied the little girl, proudly.

Lyor wasn't the only one to be surprised to meet a little girl skilled at repairing the wheels of a car. Mr. Ernest lost his voice too. While Mr. Wilfrid observed Dalya with a fascinated look.

- Here is the 4th clue, Sir.

Dalya handed a paper to Mr. Ernest Laszlo. And when the lawyer read it, he exclaimed:

- What's this nonsense? ... why do we have 2 hands and why 2 legs? ... it's a ridiculous question!

Mr. Wilfrid replied immediately, while observing the tiny dirty hands of Dalya Bouvard:

- Well, we may not know why we have 2 legs ... but we know why we have 2 hands! They can be useful to repair the car wheel and attend an important meeting on time.

Mr. Sloan Wilfrid smiled at Dalya. And she smiled back at him, too.

The 4th Excelbox clue settled in the little girl's head, for a while. And curious as she was, Dalya tried her best to find an answer for it. The next day, she asked her mentor, Professor Canfield. He put his checked jacket on his office chair as usual, and he explained:

- Well ... Mademoiselle Dalya ... This is an interesting question! ... This subject is part of the existential enigmas. For example; why are we created? why is there one habitable planet? Why are there so many species, instead of one?... there are only some theories, but no exact answers for these subjects ... and for the question that you asked, you should consult Science and Philosophers books ... and also maybe Medical books. There is a little section in the school's Library ... you may not find an exact clear answer ... and I am sorry that my humble knowledge can't help you, this time, Mademoiselle.

At Professor Canfield's advice, Dalya consulted the school's Library at the end of her classes. She searched in the Science, Philosophy and Medical sections. She even looked in the sections of Chemistry, History, Natural Sciences ... for many hours. Dalya didn't find exact informations to the question asked by the Excelbox.

With no answer to this unusual question, Dalya decided as a last resort, to consult the smartest person she knew: her uncle Giorgi. But he had no reply, too. Dalya had no choice but to wait; some answers need a little more time to reach us...

Chapter 29

Thanksgiving Day

Saturday, November 22nd, 1890.

The Thanksgiving holiday was the time of the year that Dalya preferred the most. Each year, the merchants of the market in front of the Toscana restaurant; the neighbors, friends and families, they all gathered over a great meal. This year, Dalya dared to ask the Lawyer, Mr. Ernest Laszlo if her parents could organize a party in their annex house. The garden was big enough to host many guests.

- Really?! ... you celebrate Thanksgiving? Mr. Ernest Laszlo seemed surprised.
- Yes, Sir ... It's a holiday that everyone enjo... Dalya answered, in a shy voice.

The lawyer interrupted her, with an arrogant and mocking voice:

- I never thought that people of your kind have parties. Aren't you all poor merchants? And you still find money to organize and have a party?

Dalya couldn't understand Mr. Ernest Laszlo's words. She wondered why the poor people shouldn't have the right to celebrate like everyone else. Isn't it a holiday for everyone to enjoy?

- The annex house is yours until December 12th, do whatever you want in it. After all, only a few weeks, and you will return to your rat hole! Mr. Ernest Laszlo replied in a mean voice.

Besides his rude and degrading remark, Dalya was relieved and happy that Mr. Ernest allowed the Bouvard family to organize a party in the annex house. On the same day, another Thanksgiving feast was planned in the grand Mansion, in honor of late Mr. Governor Iskander Balthazar. The Lawyer, Mr. Ernest Laszlo was the host of this prestigious party.

Thursday, November 27th, 1890.

That day, Mr. Ernest Laszlo was accompanied by Sloan Wilfrid and his son Lyor Laszlo; they waited for the guests in the living room of the grand Mansion. While smoking a big cigar, Mr. Ernest Laszlo gave his instructions to Mr. Benjamin Bûchebois, the head of the Mansion:

- It's important that this party goes on just like the previous ones organized by Mr. Governor. We are receiving distinguished and high society people. Everything must be impeccable Benjamin ... is that clear?
- We will make sure of it, Mr. Ernest. The household employee replied.

210

After a while, the guests arrived at the grand Mansion, one after the other. A long tail of luxurious black cars was formed in front of the grand Mansion's entrance. Men in black suits, elegant capes, silk gloves and hats, were welcomed by Mr. Ernest Laszlo. When the nephew Mr. Ferdinand Edelmen, accompanied by his sister Mrs. Honoré entered the living room, Mr. Ernest Laszlo hurried to greet Mr. Ferdinand Edelmen. The lawyer whispered to his friend:

- Only a few days left ...

Mr. Ferdinand Edelmen smiled for the first time, since many months. The Governor's nephew settled on a big divan, as legitimate Master of the grand Mansion. His sister, Mrs. Honoré was wearing a yellow gold necklace even more sparkling than her long blond hair, and a very elegant silk black dress. She was surrounded by many distinguished women, complimenting her refined taste and beauty.

All the women wore long dresses of only dark colors and in luxurious fabrics, they wore big lavish furs, shining and expensive jewelries, diamonds and tiaras attached to their hairs. Most of the men were fat, with large mustaches and bold hair, holding cigars and drinks. The handsome young men were standing and laughing, in an arrogant tone. The women were sitting on the big divans, talking with such protocol and restrained manners. An orchestra was installed in the great hall of the Mansion. The musicians played violin, flute and other instruments, a gentle and pleasant music. In the grand Mansion, the Thanksgiving party was surely very luxurious and refined!

On the same day, the party that took place across the garden in the annex house, was a different kind. Dalya's parents had invited almost all their friends, and they had plenty. Thirty people; men, women, children, old, young ... they were all dressed in a multitude of scarlet colors; pink dresses, orange skirts, blue jackets, brown pants, green blouses, purple shawls, red hats ... They were all dressed modestly, but they all chose their best clothes for this thanksgiving party.

Dalya's father was helped by some friends to set up a huge tent in the annex garden. A long buffet table, covered by many white tablecloths, was placed in a corner.

Laughs and talks became loud with the arrival of guests. Every one of them carried dishes, plates and containers, covered by white kitchen towels. As soon as they entered the annex garden, all the guests put their dishes and plates on the long buffet table, before greeting the Bouvard family and the other visitors. They all were amazed by the annex house and the enormous garden of the grand Mansion.

Everyone was joyful and active. Dalya's father, Mr. Antman greeted the guests one after the other, while guiding some men to install tables and chairs in the garden. A few old men were busy making fall crowns out of leaves, for the little children.

Dalya's mother, Mrs. Augustine, was happy for once. And on that day, Mrs. Augustine proudly and arrogantly took her friends on a tour inside the annex house:

- Here is the living room, I decorated it myself. We spend here all our nights, as a happy family.
- It's a pretty kitchen you've got there, Augustine! Exclaimed a friend.
- Thank you my dear. Although I find it a bit too small. Replied Mrs. Augustine.
- It's a clean and organized house. Said a woman.
- Yes, indeed! I am pleased with the renovations that my dear husband did. Before we arrived, the house was dull and uninhabitable. My husband refused to stay here, but I insisted! Fortunately, I managed to convince him not to miss this opportunity! If it wasn't me who insisted, my family wouldn't be in this house!!
- And are you going to live here for a long time? Asked a friend.
- But of course, my dear! Can you imagine me going back to our old 2 rooms' house? Mrs. Augustine laughed.
- Can we visit the bedrooms above? A woman asked.
- Certainly my dear!! I invited you all today specifically to give you a tour of my modest house. Upstairs, you'll find the two bedrooms of my adorable three girls. My bedroom is the largest room, of course...

In public, Mrs. Augustine was a loving, welcoming and calm person. She never hesitated to lie and show off an angelic side of her. But in private, Mrs. Augustine was ... something else.

Dalya's little sisters, Ari and Adi were running constantly in all directions, laughing and giggling. They wore little pink identical dresses, with a big ribbon around the waist and a large bow on the back. Uncle Giorgi made these dresses for his nieces, to their big delight. And Dalya wore the dress that her uncle made her too.

When the annex garden was filled with almost 30 people, Dalya's father stepped above a long ban, to be seen and heard by everyone:

- Hello Hello everyone!! ... welcome all of you ... I'm happy to see all of our dearest friends among us today. Now, and as it is a tradition, our Dean of Merchants, Mr. Kenan Einsenberg will deliver the speech on this special day.

Mr. Antman came down to make way for another gentleman. This man had a strong and authoritarian voice; he didn't need to make an effort to be heard:

- On this blessed day... we thank God we survived until now. And we pray that courage and strength never give up on us. We thank God for all of his gifts and mercies on us. We thank God for the blessings of the soil and the sky, for life and all its colors, for hope and happiness in our hearts.
  And although I have never met him during his lifetime, it seems important today and in this place, to pay tribute to a great man ... the Late Mr. Governor Iskander Balthazar. We thank him for what he has done for us all, the people of this blessed country. May God be generous to Mr. Balthazar, as he was generous to us all.

When the man finished, everyone applauded. The tradition of Thanksgiving was that after the gratitude speech, everyone would listen to a song of grace. Dalya's father invited a woman to stand at the center of the party; she was known to everyone as Lalla Fatim Fadl. The flowers' saleswoman and the pigeons' guardian. The great woman slowly made her way toward the center of the garden. She was wearing a long light pink dress, a shawl in clear gray wool hook on her shoulders, a small scarf covering half of her bright silver hair.

When she reached the center of the tent, Lalla Fatim Fadl sang a glorious song, in a beautiful emotional and strong voice. Everyone was still and quiet, even the children were silent, listening to Lalla Fatim Fadl singing:

I am grateful for things of the past

They brought me here where I am

All the lessons I've learned

And the upcoming task

All helped me better become

I am grateful for the people met

For those who remained

Becoming allies

And for those who left

Of their own free drive

I am grateful for all the kindness

For life, hope, strength and health,

And on this holly joyful day

I thank God

To have filled our table of meals and plates

I thank God

Of blessing me with these shared smiles,

I thank God

For this fertile land, this fertile sea and this wealthy sky

When Lalla Fatim Fadl stopped singing, everyone cheered loudly. It was touching and magnificent. Right away, Dalya's father invited the crowd to serve themselves from the buffet. Immediately, a long line got organized around the long buffet table. Each guest used plates and cutlery first, and they waited their turn.

The rich people's feast was very different from the poor people's feast.

On the other side of the garden, in the grand Mansion, the servers walked between the guests, offering food on large silver shiny platters. Tiny bites were placed by dozen on each platter. Mini savory appetizers of liver fat and mushrooms, fresh mini Artichoke and cream corn appetizers, mini quiches of parsley salmon and lemon herbs, mini duck pâté, mini snail bites, mini white bread sandwiches with fish egg, mini lemon pies, mini dark chocolate tarts ... very refined and luxurious food. But mostly ... all in very mini quantities!

In the grand Mansion, all the wealthy women were very thin and skeletal. And as strange as it may seem, they all politely refused everything the servers offered, food and juices. The women pretended not to be hungry at all, while most of them were very pale and seemed about to faint in any second. Men, on the other hand, were very fat in their elegant costumes; they swallowed the mini food, gathering 3 pieces in one swoop.

The poor people's politeness was quite different from the rich people's politeness. Dalya's parents could not feed all their guests; the crowd was about 30 people. Therefore, all the guests had brought each a dish prepared according to their own resources, their tastes, and even their origins. The dishes of all the guests were placed and put on the long buffet table.

There were dishes of all kinds, types, forms and quantities. The long buffet table was so filled with dishes piled up one next to the other, that the white tablecloth no longer appeared. And when poor people came together and helped each other, their buffet looked like this:

- A big pot of Hungarian goulash Soup; made of meat, potatoes, onions, and peppers
- 16 Italian pasta dishes of spaghetti, ravioli and lasagna, dipped in herb tomato sauce
- 11 dishes of cabbages stuffed with vegetables and rice
- 9 large pots of mashed potatoes,
- 28 pans of vegetables sauté in garlic and olive oil; peas, carrots, sweet potatoes, potatoes and Zucchini
- 4 large chicken tagines, with lemon and olives
- 22 plates of red meat roasted, served with a sweet cranberry sauce
- 16 huge turkeys stuffed in cornbread
- 7 big moussaka gratins made of eggplant, caramelized onions, meat and herbs
- 18 large dishes of strudel with apples, cinnamon, red fruits, peaches and jam
- 10 exquisite pumpkin pies with cream

Alfie jaq filled one time his plate and one time his mouth. The 11 years old boy was careful to not smear his red tie that he was so proud of. When suddenly, a voice called him:

- Alfie jaq?! I thought you were sick and unable to work today?!

Alfie turned around toward a boy of the same age as him, with a large green cap on the head. It was his business partner, Maurice Gus. Alfie replied, with a full mouth, and a nervous smile:

- I ... healed quickly!

Before Maurice could reprimand his partner Alfie, because he avoided him all day to come to the party and to eat too much ... and before Alfie could promise his friend Maurice that he will be careful about his weight but only after the thanksgiving party ... the two boys were both interrupted by Dalya who placed down with difficulty on the buffet table, a large plate full of hundreds little caramelized squares. Dalya signed:

- It's ... incredibly ... heavy! Have you ever tasted this pastry? They are small squares of thin dough soaked in honey and orange flower water, with a mixture of dried fruits, finely crushed and placed between the dough. It's called a ... Baklava. The new Turkish immigrants made it. It is a delicious pastry! ... who wants some?
- 2 pieces please! Alfie and Maurice simultaneously answered without hesitation, offering their plates, already full.

One thing is for sure, meals unite appetites and souls.

The Thanksgiving feast in the annex house was not exclusive to some people only. Everyone was gladly invited. Dalya insisted on the Library assistant to come, and although Miss Guendolyn was hesitant at first to attend the party, she finally accepted Dalya's invitation. And to join the tradition, Miss Guendolyn prepared a big plate of Orehovki cookies, a coconut pecans recipe very well known in her country, Bulgaria. Miss Guendolyn was delighted and thrilled to attend this party, instead of spending Thanksgiving alone, as in all her previous years. She wore her ruby red hair in a lovely chignon and she wore a pretty lavender dress.

Dalya served a plate of Turkish pastry to her little sisters Ari and Adi. When a familiar voice near her, exclaimed:

- Always very thoughtful and kind ... Demoiselle!

Dalya turned her head around to be in front of Mr. Kenan Einsenberg, the Dean of Merchants. She knew the big man, very well. When Dalya worked with her father in the market in front of the Toscana restaurant, Mr. Kenan Einsenberg often made a tour among the sellers, to solve their worries and problems. In his sixty years old, Mr. Kenan Einsenberg was a tall man, strong and robust, very clear brown eyes, white hair, always wearing a long big green coat, and he had a big copper beard that made him look intimidating. He was respected by everyone.

Mr. Kenan Einsenberg always relied on his crutch to walk. He had lost his left leg. A wooden leg replaced it and it allowed him to keep his balance even without the crutch. He was a great character; very strict, fair, truthful and authoritarian. He always addressed grownups with a strong voice, and he always spoke to children in a soft tone. However, Mr. Kenan Einsenberg devoted a special kindness toward Dalya Bouvard; he has always been curiously nice and protective toward her.

- May I serve you some Turkish pastry, Mr. Einsenberg? Dalya asked him nicely.

The Dean of Merchants answered back with a smile, and he offered his plate.

- Enjoy it, Sir. It's very delicious. Said Dalya, while giving him back the plate all full.

For a long minute, Mr. Einsenberg observed Dalya, and he said in a calm but serious voice:

- I remember when you came into this world. It was the coldest night of all winter ... you were born very sick, tiny and fragile. Everyone, even your own parents, were convinced that you won't survive one more night. However ... when I watched this tiny baby's sapphire blue eyes ... there was something strange in them. And even after 12 years, I still see the same strange thing in these sapphire blue eyes ...

There might be an impossible challenge ahead of you. But life has blessed us with 2 legs to stand up strong in the face of all storms of our destiny. And even when life takes back a leg ... even when it seems impossible for us to get back up and walk again ... life replaces your loss with a crutch and a 2nd wooden leg, much strong and solid!

I believe that this sick and fragile baby, survived for a specific and greater reason than we all think!

Dalya remained still and immobile, listening to the strange words of the great Dean of Merchants. It was the first time that the big man spoke to her that way. Mr. Kenan Einsenberg smiled at Dalya, and he continued in a more joyful and relaxed voice:

- Thank you for the Turkish pastry, Demoiselle!

Speechless and motionless, Dalya observed Mr. Kenan Einsenberg walk away. Dalya repeated in her mind every word he had said, trying to understand what the big man meant. When Dalya was interrupted by her father, who asked for some Turkish pastry, she pulled herself together and filled the plates.

All the guests ate with big appetite and until being full, yet the food was still plentiful. Once everyone has emptied their plates, some merchants settled with musical instruments in a corner of the garden. They composed cheerful and joyful northern music. The little twin sisters, Ari and Adi began dancing in a circle with the other children, holding hands and dancing around. The music became increasingly loud, and so the laughs and applauses.

Young boys and girls joined the little children's dance, forming a larger circle around them. The young people were much more accurate and they danced in synchronized steps. Everybody was dancing the same circled dance. The circles were moving slowly but joyfully. People cheered and gathered around the young dancers. When suddenly, an older man invited a woman to join the dance, and other mature men and women followed them instantly.

On that day, Uncle Giorgi was wearing his best clothes; a pink shirt, green pants, beige jacket and a brown bow tie. He looked funny, colorful, but surely handsome in his suit.

Uncle Giorgi came near a woman, in hesitant steps, and he said in a cheerful voice:

- It's a joyful dance, isn't it?

The Library assistant, Miss Guendolyn replied all amazed in front of the show:

- Yes ... it's nice to look at them ...
- It's even better when we participate! Whispered Uncle Giorgi, with a brave voice.

All of a sudden, Uncle Giorgi took Miss Guendolyn's hand, and before she could even realize it or refuse it, she found herself in the middle of the dance with the other people. The older men and women formed a larger circle around the young people. Everyone was laughing and dancing. Dalya happily applauded. It was the best time of the year that she preferred the most!

This is what the poor and the rich people's party looks like. Surely, there are some things that money cannot buy; like a successful party, an abundant buffet of all origins and types, a fun and cheerful dance, an endless and real laughs. Surely, the Bouvard family and their friends were much poorer ... but, they were much happier.

You would think that the two parties in the grand Mansion and in the annex house, are separated by only a little garden and some big trees. But really, as you can see, they are two very different worlds!

Later that night. Dalya put her little twin sisters Ari and Adi into bed. They slept as soon as their heads touched the pillows. Dalya returned to her bedroom, she was tired, but she had the best day ever since a very long time. When she was lying down on her bed, Dalya thought of what Mr. Kenan Einsenberg, the Dean of Merchants said during the party:

- Life has blessed us with 2 legs to stand up strong in the face of all storms of our destiny. And even when life takes back a leg ... life replaces your loss with a crutch and a 2nd wooden leg, much strong and solid ... the sick and fragile baby, survived for a specific and greater reason than we all think ...

Dalya thought for a moment:

- 2 legs to stand up strong in the face of storms...Could it be that the Dean of Merchants answered the Excelbox's question?...and if he is right, does it mean that the Excelbox encourages me to continue?...but why? ...what does the Excelbox want from me?...and why did I survive when I was a fragile sick baby?... Mr. Kenan Einsenberg said that I survived for a specific and greater reason ... what is it then?... how will I know it?

Caught by the fatigue of the busy day, the little 12 years old girl fall asleep right away... leaving many questions unanswered until another day.

Chapter 30

Madame is busy

Saturday, November 29th, 1890. In the morning.

- When you are done cleaning the dishes, check if your sisters have finished their milk bottles. Dalya's mother ordered her, while finishing her embroidery.

Dalya placed the last clean plate of breakfast in the cupboard, and then she walked upstairs to Ari and Adi's bedroom. When she opened the door, Dalya found Adi alone, standing on the edge of her little wood bed. The second bed was unoccupied, with only an empty bottle in it.

- Where is Ari? Dalya panicked.
- Mimibottle! Mimibottle! Adi repeated laughing.
- What is it?! What bottle?! Where is Ari?! Dalya asked her little sister Adi, hoping she would tell her where her twin sister was.

Dalya made a quick tour in her sisters' bedroom; she searched everywhere, under the beds, near the closet, behind the chair, in the toy box, under the covers ... There was no trace of Ari. Her little sister Adi wouldn't stop jumping and repeating joyfully:

- Mimibottle! Mimibottle!
- Where is Ari?! Where's your twin pest sister?! Dalya stared at Adi for a few seconds.
- Mimibottle! Mimibottle!

Eager to find her little sister Ari, Dalya stepped out of her sisters' bedroom, she searched in her own room, and then in her parent's room ... still no trace of Ari. Dalya returned to her little sisters' bedroom, with Adi always alone in her bed. Dalya thought aloud:

- What should I do? ... But where did that pest go? ... I must warn mother ... but she will have an anxiety attack and it won't help to find Ari ... I must warn father first ... but he is already at wor...

When all of a sudden, a little burp was heard in the twins' bedroom. Adi froze and went silent. Dalya clearly heard a burp in the bedroom, but it wasn't from Adi. Where did that sound come from?!

Suddenly, a 2nd burp was heard. This time, Dalya guessed the source of the sound. Dalya heard the rot right behind her ... but was it really coming from behind the door of the twin's bedroom?

When Dalya closed the bedroom's door, she discovered Ari standing in the corner, on the tips of her toes, trying to finish the last sip... of her sister Adi's milk bottle!

- What are you doing here? ... Why do you have your sister's bottle? ... How did you get out of bed?... why did you disappear and steel your sister's bottle?

The only answer that Dalya could have, was a 3rd burp from Ari and a spontaneous laugh of the twins Adi and Ari. Not only little Ari had completed her own milk bottle, but she also stole her sister Adi's bottle, and she drank it quietly while Dalya was going crazy to find her.

Dalya swallowed her anxiety; she cleaned her two little sisters, she dressed them up and then brought them down in the living room near their mother. Mrs. Augustine ordered Dalya to take the little twins outside in the garden, while she finishes the last part of her embroidery. Dalya tried to avoid taking care of her sisters, but Ari and Adi started yelling and jumping:

- Little kitten today! Zolie kitten today!
- Yes ... Yes ... go look for the little kitten in the garden ... said Dalya's mother, in a careless voice.

When Dalya stepped outside the annex house, she knelt down in front of Ari and Adi, she looked them in the eyes, and then she ordered in a serious voice:

- Now you listen to me, you two! Séraphine is not a kitten! It's a big big animal. It's not a toy. You need to stay away from the big Snow Panther. Do not disturb her. If she's upset, she can bite ... and it will hurt a lot.
- Very a lot? Or a bit a lot? The little twins asked.
- Very very a lot ...
- Oooohhh! Ari and Adi exclaimed with a serious voice.
- So ... if you see the big animal, do not get near her ... agreed?
- Oki! Oki! Ari and Adi answered simultaneously and seriously.
- And you should leave her alone. Is that clear enough?
- Yes! Yes!

Dalya was reassured that her little sisters have finally understood to stay away from the Snow Panther. Dalya was not afraid of Séraphine's reaction. In fact, the most dangerous creature was not the Snow Panther ... the most dangerous creatures were Dalya's little sisters. These tiny chubby two pests were able to cause real disasters!

As soon as they arrived in the immense garden of the grand Mansion, Ari and Adi released their big sister hands and they ran toward the grand Mansion screaming joyfully:

- Zolie kitten! Soft kitten! Zolie kitten! Soft kitten!
- Yup ... It's very clear!! Sighed Dalya.

The grand Mansion's Gardener, Mr. Rosenwald was cutting leaves using a small scissor. He was a true craftsman. He was so focused in his task; he barely noticed the little twins running near him. Fortunately, this time, the Snow Panther Séraphine was sitting on a large tree branch. Ari and Adi observed her from the ground, screaming and jumping:

- Little kitten! Zolie kitten!

Séraphine let down her long tail, in an amused move. Ari and Adi jumped and laughed, raising their arms up and trying to catch the great Panther's tail. When the Gardener noticed that Dalya was watching her little sisters with a slightly worried look, he said:

- She will not hurt them, now ... She actually seems to enjoy and like their presence.
- Oh ... but I am not worried about Séraphine's behavior, Mr. Gardener. It's my two little pests' sisters that concern me. They are really very talented for all imaginable fooleries. Ari and Adi are able to provoke the most quiet and cold human ... and animal characters.

The Gardener pointed out to Dalya to water some plants, near the large windows of the grand Mansion's Library. She gladly took the big water hose and pulled it to the place where he showed her. Dalya came close to Mr. Rosenwald's bag, and to avoid getting it wet, she moved the bag to a drier place. Except that a small notebook fell from the bag. The Gardener, Mr. Rosenwald being far away, Dalya was curious to know what it was. She dropped the water hose and she opened the little book. Dalya noticed a pretty handwriting, drawings of plants, explanations of the origin of flowers and how to take care of them, explaining how and when they grow ... It was a gardening manuscript! Dalya has never seen one like that before, more precise, simpler and easier to understand. There were details and many drawings explaining very clearly how to plant, turn the soil, cut ... When suddenly, Mr. Rosenwald's voice startled Dalya.

- What are you reading? He asked as he came near her.

Dalya answered in a hesitant voice:

- This ... this manuscript fell out of your bag, when I removed it, to avoid getting it wet ... forgive me, Sir... I didn't mean to be indiscreet ...

When Mr. Rosenwald noticed the manuscript in Dalya's hands, he was surprised that she discovered it. Dalya dared to ask him, in a polite tone:

- Are these your notes, Mr. Gardener? Is it your manuscript?

The Gardener murmured some strange words, in a sad voice:

- She ... she wanted to learn gardening ... she loved staying in the garden all day ...
- Who is she? Asked Dalya

Having trouble talking about his painful memories, the Gardener sat on the grass, he seemed crushed and miserable. Instantly, Dalya sat near him. When the Gardener took the manuscript in his hands and he slowly turned its pages, he repeated heartbroken:

- She went too early, way too soon ... she wanted to learn my job ... I wrote this manuscript for her ... but went too early ...

Gradually, Dalya understood what the Gardener was talking about. The grave he visited at the cemetery ... the little girl of Dalya's same age ... she was very dear to the Gardener.

The Gardener looked so devastated. And although curious to know if this little girl was his daughter and how she passed away, Dalya didn't dare to ask him questions about his private life. All she could say was:

- I'm sorry for your loss, Mr. Rosenwald.

After a brief moment of silence, Dalya displayed a compassionate smile, and she asked in a kind encouraging voice:

- You can teach your gardening skills, to me! I learn fast and quick. And I love gardening work, it's fun and appeasing.

The Gardener stared at Dalya with a surprised and confused look; he could never understand this little girl's behavior and her insistence on doing gardening work and house chores. The Gardener always considered her as an Heiress, and not an inch less. Dalya continued, barely holding her amused laugh:

- ... and Ari and Adi will gladly learn gardening. They will be happy to get dirty in the slightest occasion. You can be sure of tha... wait a second ... I don't hear them anym...

When Dalya realized that she no longer heard the voices and laughs of her little sisters, she panicked. Instantly, Dalya turned around calling:

- Ari!! Adi!!

Dalya turned around right and left searching for them. The Snow Panther was alone, always sitting on the tree branch. And a couple of steps away, Dalya noticed her little sisters. And these tiny two pests were never in lack of ideas to have fun! Ari and Adi took the water hose that Dalya had previously released a few minutes ago, and they were watering themselves in turns. The little twins were all wet from head to toe. Their hair, their clothes, their little boots, their hats ... They were soaking wet!!

- WHAT THE HELL ... WHAT ARE YOU DOING?!

Dalya screamed. She quickly stood up and ran to take away the garden hose off their hands. The little twins answered innocently and joyfully:

- Ari and Adi are zolies flowers! We water zolie flowers! Ari and Adi are zolies flowers!
- No!! No!! You are not flowers! You are two pests that I have to watch every single minute of the day! Can't you pause fooleries for one day?! Mother is going to be very upset!
- Ari and Adi are zolies flowers! Ari and Adi are zolies flowers!

The little twins yelled happily, while holding tightly the hose, and they stubbornly refused to let it go. Dalya tried to pull the hose with all her strength, but although little, the twin sisters were unbeatable at two. By pulling hard, Dalya's hand slipped from the garden hose, and she fell in a pool of mud. When Dalya stood up, she was all covered with mud from head to foot. The little twin sisters laughed full hearts in front of their sister all dirty. Dalya screamed:

- I'LL MAKE YOU REGRET THAT!!

The little twins Ari and Adi escaped, screaming and laughing so hard, while Dalya hunted them through the immense garden trying to catch them and cover them with mud, too. And while still sitting on the grass, The Gardener observed this scene of the three little girls screaming, running, and laughing.

Life is strange sometimes, isn't it? ... It removes a dear thing and replaces it with three. How? When? And why? Nobody knows the reasons. But sometimes, life unfolds in a way that keeps us speechless.

Despite the tears in his sad eyes, despite his heart broken by a painful past, The Gardener Mr. Rosenwald watched the three little girls. And for the first time, since many many years ... he smiled!

The Excelbox seems to teach us some quite interesting things ... Because no matter how much our dark night is long, it is never without a dawn.

Later in the evening. Dalya sat in front of her desk in her bedroom. After giving a bath to her little twin sisters, she put them in their beds and she cleaned herself too. Dalya opened the gardening manuscript that the Gardener lent her to read. She promised to return it back in perfect condition. The more Dalya read through this small notebook, the more she was impressed by the details, the easy explanations, the perfect drawings of this precious manuscript. Dalya thought aloud:

- It helps to learn gardening so easily and clearly!

Except that an idea caressed Dalya's mind, at this moment:

- If Mr. Rosenwald had not lived a painful loss; he wouldn't have wrote a gardening manual, as useful and practical as this one! ... Gardening kept Mr. Rosenwald busy from his sadness ... this fall has helped him better recover and arise ... this fall has helped him better recover and arise ... fall and arise ... fall and ... ar...

All of a sudden, Dalya straightened up in front of her small desk. She flipped the manuscript a 2nd time, and then a 3rd time. Dalya took out of her drawer the 4th clue paper, and she wondered:

- Opposite words! ... Never pepper without salt ... spicy and salty. Never dark without dawn ... after every dark night, there is day light. Never fall without arise ... after each fall ... the person can recover!

Dalya stared at the Excelbox placed on her desk, right in front of her. The oval glass was in smoked clear gray color, the clock inside showed the date of the last Saturday of the November month. Only the cylinders surrounding the oval glass cage sparkled from the light of the full moon. Dalya spoke to the Excelbox, in a hesitant voice:

- But ... is it possible then? There is hope for her? ... But how? Everyone said that it was not possible ... so then how? They are not alike. Mr. Rosenwald recovered well from his fall; he focused all of his sadness into gardening. But then again, the situation is very different for her...

The Excelbox didn't react. Dalya continued to read the 4th clue and think aloud:

- If surrender is before the fight, then ... If we give up before even fighting ... but she can't do anything, she cannot even get out of her bedroom, even less gardening or writ...

Dalya froze. Her little brain was starting to see a little more clearly. An idea brusquely settled in her mind, Dalya jumped off her seat:

- If surrender is before the fight, so why two legs and why two hands! ... It sounds really crazy and insane ... but ... she still has two hands!

The next morning, Sunday, November 30th, 1890.

It was the last day of November, and also maybe the last chance for Dalya to help the French neighbor, Mrs. Marianne Poirier.

Dalya knocked at the door of the French neighbor's house, les Poirier. When Mrs. Glorina opened the door, she didn't expect to find the little girl at all. Mrs. Glorina was very shocked. Dalya didn't visit Mrs. Marianne and Mrs. Glorina, since Miss Francine's birthday incident. For sure, Dalya hesitated to visit again the French neighbors, but Dalya never hesitated to help others. Mrs. Glorina hugged Dalya tightly, and she exclaimed:

- Mademoiselle Dalya! I'm sincerely sorry for what happened the other day! I never thought that Francine would be capable of such cruelty! I'm sincerely so so sorry for not being able to help you when you needed me and I didn't ev...

Dalya interrupted the woman with a reassuring smile:

- You don't have to apologize Mrs. Glorina. It's not your fault, at all. I understand that Miss Francine has a mental illness, I don't blame her, and I am not upset at her either.

Mrs. Glorina objected in a firm and furious tone:

- But no Mademoiselle! Having a mental illness is not an excuse to be rude and humiliate people! You are way too nice and polite to think so!... I wish I could take off Francine's ridiculous wig in front of everybody, and yell on her face all the things that she d...

Dalya had to stop the woman:

- Mrs. Glorina, forgive me to interrupt you, but is Madame available? May I see her for a minute?

Mrs. Glorina instantly answered Dalya's request:

- But of course, Mademoiselle! If only you knew how much sad Mrs. Marianne was about you! She refused to receive Miss Francine for days! She was so upset that her daughter humiliated you, in front of everyone. We couldn't dare to bother you, Mrs. Marianne and me thought that you will never return to visit us again!

Dalya followed Mrs. Glorina until Mrs. Marianne's bedroom. In the corridor, a door opened slowly, Dalya felt the same shadow staring at her and following her to the great woman's bedroom. But on that day, Dalya wasn't concerned about who was watching her. This time, Dalya was focused on the purpose of her visit. When Mrs. Glorina opened the door and entered, she announced to the great woman, in a happy voice:

- Mrs. Marianne ... you have a visitor today!

When Dalya walked in, Mrs. Marianne turned toward her. The great woman was sitting near the table in front of the large window; the curtains were wide open, a beautiful view stretched across the horizon. Mrs. Marianne's face changed instantly. She couldn't contain her joy and surprise. Dalya approached her, and she asked her with a lovely smile:

- How is Madame feeling today?

Mrs. Marianne smiled happily. She took Dalya's hand and squeezed it tightly. Dalya understood that Mrs. Marianne was happy to see her again. Dalya noticed that the great woman was still wearing the aventurine ring she offered to her, couple of weeks ago. Dalya felt proud, even if Miss Francine laughed about it, at least the great woman was well pleased of her gift. Dalya sat down on the chair in front of Mrs. Marianne, and she spoke to her, in a serious tone:

- I came today, Madame, to talk to you about something.

Mrs. Marianne observed her with a curious stare. Dalya continued:

- I heard Mrs. Glorina say that you were a nurse before. And it was a job that you loved.

Mrs. Marianne confirmed with a head sign. Dalya took out of her pocket a little paper, where she wrote her idea:

- Madame ... I understand that your illness prevents you from going out, interacting with people, moving, and talking for a long time. But I was wondering if ... if it would be possible to bypass the disease?

Mrs. Marianne didn't understand what the little girl meant by bypassing the disease. When Dalya handed her the little paper with her idea written on, Mrs. Marianne took it in a slow move, and she read it. The great woman's face showed off a surprised and shocked look. Seconds later, Mrs. Marianne took a small empty paper; she scribbled a note and handed it to Dalya, who read:

Impossible

Dalya expected this refusal. Everybody would disagree about it. It was insane! Except that somehow, the little girl was convinced that it would work! She preferred to try and fail, rather than never try at all. The little girl had already prepared solid convincing arguments in her head, the night before. Dalya explained in a dynamic voice:

- The disease has weakened your body, I understand that. But there are several other organs that are still very well functional! You are still active with your 2 hands, I'm sure you have an excellent memory, and your eyes' view is intact. That's all you need...

Mrs. Marianne gave a head sign refusal. But this move didn't stop Dalya from defending her idea:

- Madame ... Think of all the people who will benefit from your knowledge! It would be an amazing contribution! I am sure you have a great amount of informations to share. And to not use any of it, it would be such a waste!

Mrs. Marianne observed the enthusiastic little girl with a sympathetic stare. The great woman scribbled on a paper and gave it to Dalya, who read for the 2nd time:

Impossible

Dalya was not ready to give up yet. She pulled out from her pocket a small paper and she handed it to Mrs. Marianne, who read carefully:

Never pepper without salt
Never dark without dawn
Never fall without arise
Never mockery without recast
If surrender is before the fight
So why two hands
And why two legs?

Dalya explained to the great woman:

- It is a clue that I got from the Excelbox. A strange box given to me by the late Mr. Governor. It gives me answers whenever I ask for them. The clues are interesting ... If surrender is before the fight, why do we have two legs and two hands? ... Madame, I am well aware that you are sick and ill with an incurable disease. But I understand from the

Excelbox clue that we are much stronger than what we believe we are ... and there is always a rise after a fall ... there is always dawn after dark ...

Mrs. Marianne watched Dalya for a brief moment, and then she wrote on a paper:

I cannot

Dalya took the pen from the hand of the great woman, and she changed the written sentence, scratching 3 alphabets and muttering aloud:

- Well ... Madame ... I think there are way too many words in this sentence!

I cannot

Mrs. Marianne remained motionless for a few minutes. Dalya offered the great woman, a moment of silence, to allow her to think. Dalya was well aware that her idea was completely ... insane! But as odd as it may seem, Dalya was convinced that it will work. In front of Mrs. Marianne reluctance, Dalya had almost exhausted all the arguments she had prepared the day before, except one. Dalya interrupted Mrs. Marianne in her thoughts, and she said her last argument:

- Madame ... Do it for him ... for Richard Poirier, your son.

Mrs. Marianne was surprised at what Dalya dared to say. The great woman was about to write another no on a paper, but she paused. Slowly and gradually, a strange feeling of strength invaded the great woman. After a long minute, Mrs. Marianne Poirier smiled. And at this precise moment, Dalya Bouvard knew, that she had finally ... succeeded.

Monday 1st December 1890.

Late in the evening. The driver parked the luxurious black car in front of the main door of the French neighbor's house. Richard Poirier was going out for his work. He took his coat and white gloves. In the hall, Richard met Mrs. Glorina who was carrying his mother's dinner platter. He informed Mrs. Glorina:

- I might come back very late tonight. There is no need for you to prepare my dinner.

Richard noticed that his mother's dinner platter was still filled, the food was intact. And Mrs. Glorina, holding the dinner platter, looked confused. Richard asked:

- What is happening? Mother didn't eat her dinner?

Mrs. Glorina hesitated for a moment, and then she finally said:

- Your mother doesn't wish to eat now, Mr. Richard. She asked me to come back later.

Richard became worried. He insisted:

- Why is that? Is she alright? Is something wrong? ... is the pain coming back?

Mrs. Glorina looked at Richard Poirier, and she replied with a confused smile:

- Well ... actually, your mother is busy, Mr. Richard.

Richard Poirier never thought to hear that his mother would be busy, especially after her incurable illness, and the long depression she suffered after the death of his father. His mother spent all her days, lying down on her bed or sitting on a chair starring at the sky. That night, Richard decided to turn back around, and check on his mother, himself.

He gently opened the door of Mrs. Marianne's bedroom. She was sitting on her big chair in front of the table. Richard came close to her, without making a noise, he was curious to know what his mother was busy doing. Interested and confused, Richard observed his mother, while she was writing slowly but actively. The table was full of papers, books, notes, pencils. Richard came a little more closer to the table, and he noticed that all the papers had his mother's handwriting. Surprised to see this scene, Richard asked:

- Mother ... what is happening? What are you doing?

When Mrs. Marianne realized her son's presence, she instantly handed him a little note that she had prepared for him, earlier. Richard read aloud:

List of things I need:
White paper and black ink
Book approach of medical surgery
Anatomy human body book
Book of infantile diseases
Book of natural therapy...

Richard stared at his mother for a while; he still didn't understand what was going on. It was the first time in years that his mother asked him to provide her with books and writing supplies ... her request was unusual. Richard dared to ask nicely:

- Mother ... Can I at least know what you are doing and what are you up to?

This time, Mrs. Marianne gave her son a different little paper note. Richard realized that it wasn't his mother's handwriting, but someone else's. He read the note 5 times just so to be sure he understood it correctly. He stared at his mother, who continued to write in slow but determined movements. Richard put back the note on the table, and he interrupted his mother:

- Mother ... are you sure you want to do this? who told you this idea? isn't it exhausting for you to do it? won't you feel pain after tiring yourself?

Mrs. Marianne took a little paper and she wrote on it:

I'm busy now, come back later

Never Richard Poirier thought to be put out by his mother. He read the note at least 5 times.

Richard left the room in silence. And before he closed the bedroom's door, he looked at his mother one last time. Sitting in front of the table, her beautiful white silver hair fell on her shoulders; she was writing slowly, and occasionally consulted a book in front of her.

Richard couldn't believe, that after all these years, one day, his mother would be motivated and occupied by something other than her disease. Aware that he couldn't do anything against an incurable illness, Richard Poirier had tried everything in his power, to support his mother.

Every evening, Richard left to his work with a heavy heart, feeling helpless toward his mother. And as strange as it was, for the first time in very long and many years, Richard Poirier left to his work, with a happy and a light heart. He was glad that his mother kicked him out of her bedroom, because he was bothering her.

Richard Poirier smiled. A smile full of love and tenderness toward his mother that he loved more than anything in the world.

Chapter 31

An unexpected visit

Friday, December 05th, 1890. In front of the Toscana restaurant.

Alfie jaq was sitting on a bench; he was busy writing notes on a small notebook, and thinking aloud. Maurice Gus, his business partner, was cleaning his shoe polish box with a cloth.

- It should be ... about 336 dollars per year. Multiplied by 6 years, it's going to be ... 2 016 dollars! So then, we need ... 28 dollars each month, in order to open our grocery store in 6 years!
- With your newspaper's sale and my shoe polish work, we win 5 dollars per month. We need to find another way to increase our profits. Replied Maurice.

The enormous goal couldn't slow down the perseverance of the two boys. Alfie froze for a couple of minutes. His brain was focused on searching for new ideas. When suddenly, he exclaimed:

- What if we chose our sale's places?
- What do you mean? Asked Maurice

Alfie explained to his partner:

- We walk through random streets all day, to sell my newspapers and polish shoes. What if we choose 5 or 6 specific crowded places to visit, every day?
- Interesting idea ... we can go to the Starluck Café! Men gather there almost every afternoon. Maurice understood and approved of Alfie's idea.
- Or the new pastry Goodness Factory! They created chocolate éclair and English cream ... exclaimed Alfie, in a dreamy air.

Maurice shook his friend Alfie:

- Our goal is to fill our pockets ... not our bellies! Focus on the goal! Focus on the goal!
- Yes ... Yes ... right ... right!! Replied Alfie.

Dalya interrupted her two friends:

- Hello, Alfie. Hello Maurice. How is business doing today?
- Hi Dalya! Alfie stood up to arrange his newspapers in his backpack.
- We found an idea to increase our profits. Maurice explained. We'll visit the Starluck Caf...
- Pastry Goodness Factory, first! Then the Starluck café. Alfie interrupted him.

Maurice rolled his eyes up, before turning toward Dalya:

-   How about you? Is everything alright? December 12th is close. How do you feel?
-   I don't know ... it doesn't look good. Dalya sighed

Alfie carried his bag full of newspapers; he adjusted his red tie and said:

-   Don't worry, Dalya. If you can't have this fortune, Maurice and I, we'll be millionaires before our 18 years old, and we will name you associate with us!

Maurice closed his shoe polish box; he wore his green cap and he said in a serious voice:

-   Yes! I approve! ... and anyway, you are better off with us than with these rich people! They have money, but they lack a lot of good manners!

Dalya smiled and watched her two friends leave to their sale's point, while quarreling:

-   Starluck Café!
-   No. Pastry Goodness Factory, first!
-   But how are we supposed to stop passersby in front of a bakery?
-   I just want to take a glance at the new chocolate éclair!
-   Alfie!! You'll gain 3 more pounds, just by looking at these chocolate éclairs!!
-   Maurice!! It won't hurt you either to gain 3 pounds. You look like a skeleton.
-   The only pounds I need ... are pounds of dollars!
-   Nonsense!? There are no pounds of dollars ... There are only pounds of gold.

A few days away from her birthday, Dalya was stressed and anxious, her heart beats fast and her throat tightened. Her father reminded her every day; morning and night:

-   You have to succeed in answering this question! I need this money! It's once in a lifetime opportunity! If you don't succeed, you go back to sleep on the kitchen floor and to sell your potatoes bags!

Dalya's mother too, didn't miss a day to demean her. Dalya was forced to listen to the crushing words of her mother every day; morning and night:

-   It's not even worth waiting for your birthday, you won't succeed!! Do you think the question would be simple for a stupid girl like you? You're dreaming silly twit. You're an idiot and you will always be one! You'll forever be a veggy seller and a servant for your family!

With all the pressure that her parents were putting on her, ahead of her birthday, Dalya was choking. She couldn't sleep, eat, laugh or breathe properly. Dalya often escaped to the grand Mansion, where she spent almost all of her time assisting the Gardener Mr. Rosenwald, in his gardening work.

While she was planting beautiful roses in the garden of the grand Mansion, Dalya heard a strange voice behind her saying hello. Dalya turned around to see an unexpected visitor: Richard Poirier, the son of Mrs. Marianne, standing right in front of her!! He repeated his sentence in a formal and serious tone:

- Good morning.
- Good ... morning. Said Dalya, lost and confused.

Several questions appeared in Dalya's head, at that moment: why was Mr. Richard Poirier present in the grand Mansion? What did he want from her? What could have possibly made him come all the way here?

Richard Poirier spoke in a calm voice, while observing Dalya in a curious stare:

- She lived many years of depression and with an incurable disease. The best doctors in the country couldn't help her. And a little 12 years old girl only... was able to revive her.

Dalya remained motionless in front of Richard, she didn't understand if his sentences were compliments or reprimands. Intimidated by the handsome young French neighbor, Dalya didn't dare to speak. Richard asked with a curious and amused tone:

- Someone whispered to my mother the idea of writing a simplified guide about the nursing profession, for schools and hospitals ... I supposed this idea came from you?

Dalya confirmed by a head sign. Richard replied:

- She didn't stop writing, since many days now. She is quite busy creating this guide. She complains much less about her pain.

Richard hesitated for a second, before asking a question:

- There is something ... that you do, and no one seems to understand it. Why do you always take off your shoes before entering my mother's bedroom?

Dalya replied naturally:

- Shouldn't we do it? Madame was kind to receive me in her bedroom ... it seemed a polite thing to do when you visit someone ... to take off your dirty shoes, before entering their rooms ...

Richard Poirier was curious to know the answer to his question, but of all the possibilities that he have thought about, none matched Dalya's reply. Richard observed Dalya for a long minute, and then he turned toward the exit of the grand Mansion. A question was on Dalya's mind for a while; she dared to ask Richard before he disappeared away:

- The shadow ... that always follows me from the window and in the corridor ... it's you?

Surprised by this smart and direct question, Richard smiled at Dalya:

- I'm curious to know how the ugly ducky will become a swan.

With a quick move, Richard turned around and left Dalya before she could say one more word. It was the first time ever that Dalya and Richard had a conversation. She looked as his silhouette walking away of the grand Mansion. Dalya was very proud to have succeeded in helping Mrs. Marianne, and she was delighted to hear that her new occupation kept the great woman busy from her illness.

Despite that Miss Francine humiliated and called Dalya ugly ducky in front of all the guests, despite all the very rude manners, indecent remarks, provoking and mocking criticisms that were supposed to destroy her ... Dalya felt strangely changed ... She felt a bit more resistant and stronger than before. The mockery may break, or reshape you in a stronger metal. Sometimes ... mockery is the best thing that happens to you. When mockery is never without a recast...

Chapter 32

A little mosquito

Thursday, December 11th, 1890.

In the afternoon, when Dalya entered the annex house, many packages and boxes were placed at the entrance of the house. All the furniture was covered in big white sheets. The kitchen cutlery was huddled in a corner. Dalya asked:

- What is happening?

Dalya's mother, Mrs. Augustine answered in a cold tone:

- Well … we no longer live here! We're moving out!

Dalya stared at her mother. Mrs. Augustine realized her daughter's confusion, and she answered with a mean laugh:

- Because you seriously think you will succeed tomorrow?!

Dalya dared to answer:

- How can you be so sure of what will happen tomorrow?

Dalya's mother screamed in a cruel voice tone:

- YOU'RE A NOBODY AND YOU WILL STAY A NOBODY FOREVER! PEOPLE LIKE YOU ARE DESTINED TO WORK IN THE MARKET! THAT'S ALL YOU WILL EVER DO IN YOUR MISERABLE LIFE, YOU LITTLE STUPID TWIT! WORK AT THE MARKET AND SERVE YOUR FAMILY UNTIL YOU DIE! WHEN WILL YOU EVER LEARN WHO YOU REALLY ARE?! **EVERY YEAR YOU BECOME MORE IDIOT THAN BEFORE!!**

Dalya didn't expect any encouragements from her mother. In fact, since long ago, Dalya expected nothing from her own mother. Dalya stared at her for a long moment. Her mother opened the large boxes, with brutal moves and she threw in the cutlery, the pans, and all the kitchen tools. It made a deafening and crushing noise. Dalya's mother never missed an opportunity to slam doors, break the dishes, to scream and yell, to act in a violent and aggressive way. While filling the boxes, Mrs. Augustine laughed cruelly:

- You're an idiot and you will always be! When will you ever learn who you are?!

Since always, Dalya never answered her mother's criticisms and insults. Except this time, Dalya replied to her mother, in a calm but confident voice:

- I hope that I will never stop learning who I really am. Because if one day, I stopped learning ... that means that I stopped growing and improving.

Dalya's mother, Mrs. Augustine was short of words. It was the first time ever that her daughter dared to reply to her abuses and insults. And before Mrs. Augustine could say anything else, Dalya left the kitchen, and she locked herself in her bedroom. Sitting on her bed, Dalya thought for a minute:

- What if my mother is right? What if I am just an idiot girl, who will never succeed in anything in her life? What if I can't answer the challenge of the Will? What will happen to my family if I don't succeed? What will become of us?

Many questions of doubts and fears invaded Dalya's mind. When her eyes met unintentionally the small box placed on her desk, Dalya observed the Excelbox for a long moment. The oval cage was made of transparent glass. The small rectangular outlet was open. The strange clock inside was clearly visible. The large and the small needle, were only one day apart. And given the slim chances that she will succeed tomorrow, Dalya thought she could at least know what the 5th clue is about.

Dalya stood up from her bed and she came near the Excelbox. In a spontaneous move, Dalya wrote on a small paper, her last request of a clue. And the Excelbox issued its last little note:

The fifth clue
To the unknown and the end
Proceed confident and certain
Guided by the écrin
Until become an essence
Powerful and human
At the last hour
The sky will state up
A thunderstorm will line up
And we'll see about that

Dalya sat in front of her small desk. The Excelbox was still emitting incoherent clues:

- To the unknown and the end ... proceed confident and certain? How can I trust what will happen tomorrow?

Dalya's mother, Mrs. Augustine Bouvard was already moving out a day in advance, so sure of her daughter's failure. Her father, Mr. Antman Bouvard was threatening his daughter if she failed to succeed this challenge. The Lawyer Mr. Ernest Laszlo and the nephew Mr. Ferdinand Edelmen were impatient to see her fail and proclaim the rightful Heir. So the 5th clue of the Excelbox was strange and weird. With a heavy heart and sad tears in her eyes, Dalya laughed at herself:

- Confident and certain?! Really?!

Later that night. In a dark and narrow street on the South side of Georgetown city, Miss Haîyang, the music Professor at the royal College, walked with hurried steps. She turned her head around frequently to make sure that no one followed her. At the end of the street, there was a small barely visible door. The young woman checked one last time the empty street, and then, she opened the door and she entered.

Nothing could have predicted that such a place existed inside Georgetown city. At the entrance, a large open square garden was installed at the heart of the house. Hundreds of candles were lit in each corner, illuminating the different planted trees and flowers. A fresh smell flew everywhere in the air.

Miss Haîyang continued down a hallway of the house, and she stopped in front of a door. Miss Haîyang knocked twice, and she stepped inside. There was an old man and a young girl, both sitting on a thick carpet on the floor. Silent and quiet, the old man and the young girl seemed to be waiting for her. Instantly, Miss Haîyang took place near the young girl.

Both the old man and the young girl were of the same Asian origin as Miss Haîyang, and they were all wearing traditional high collar shirts and neat clothes. The old man was called Master Fong Ka-Ho. In his mid-sixties, Master Fong Ka-Ho was a small svelte man, but with a strange intimidating allure, and a serene calm look. And the young girl was Tudi; she was the young waitress at the Toscana restaurant. She was easily recognizable by the cherry blossom pin in her hair.

Miss Haîyang greeted the old man, in front of her, bowing her head. The old man asked Miss Haîyang, in a serene voice:

- Míngtiān cèshì?
- Yes, Master. The event will take place tomorrow, in the grand Mansion. It's the first Challenge of the Will.

Addressing the young Tudi, Master Fong Ka-Ho was curious:

- Nǐ quèdìng nǐ kàn dàole shénme?

Tudi answered with a confident voice:

- Yes, Master, I am very sure of what I have seen at the Toscana restaurant, I was there. The creature bowed in front of this little girl.
- Zhè shì dì yī cì?
- It is the first time ever that the creature bowed to anyone, Master.

After a few minutes of silence, Master Fong Ka-Ho asked:

- Yǔ zhī zǐ fāshēngle shénme?

Miss Haîyang replied:

- I've searched about this incident, Master. It seems that the nephew of Late Mr. Governor, Mr. Ferdinand Edelmen was about to attack and hurt the little girl. And that's when the creature intervened to protect her.
- Qíguài … Qíguài

Miss Haîyang and Tudi exchanged a confused look. Both women wondered what was going on in their Master's mind. It was true that the happening events were strange and unexpected. The young Tudi was puzzled, and Miss Haîyang seemed worried. Master Fong Ka-Ho noticed that:

- Nǐ rènwéi?

Miss Haîyang hesitated for some long seconds:

- She … she is just a little girl, Master. She's only 12 years old. It has never happened before. Usually, she chooses grown up people.

To answer Miss Haîyang's doubts, Master Fong Ka-Ho smiled:

- A little mosquito can hold up awake all night, the strongest and toughest man … one must never underestimate the size of a person.

Miss Haîyang wasn't totally reassured, but she agreed with this answer:

- It's true, Master … we always learn from your wisdom.

And although no one had an exact explanation for the strange events, Master Fong Ka-Ho thought aloud in a calm voice:

- If she bowed to this little girl … she then has made her choice. And her instincts are never wrong … Keep an eye on the little girl … follow her every move …

Miss Haîyang and Tudi bowed simultaneously in front of Master Fong Ka-Ho:

- At your command, Master.

Chapter 33

December 12th, 1890

Friday, December 12th, 1890.

Early morning. Dalya felt the sunlight on her cheeks, coming through the large windows of her bedroom. The sun was up, and it promised to be a very long day. Dalya cleaned herself and changed her clothes, then she walked downstairs into the kitchen. Mrs. Augustine didn't answer her daughter's greetings, and even less wished her a happy birthday. As soon as Dalya sat in front of the breakfast table, her mother let out a mean laugh:

- I hope that you have enjoyed your last night in this house! Our hard kitchen floor is waiting impatiently for you, tonight!

Dalya remained silent. She ate her bread and drank her milk. Minutes later, her father, Mr. Antman entered the kitchen, in a happy mood. When sitting at the table, Mr. Antman said in a cheerful tone:

- Great day today, isn't it?! I'm one step closer to this fortune! This money is important for all of us! I'll be rich forever!

When Dalya didn't answer, nor raise her head, her father squeezed her arm very hard and he repeated in a threatening tone:

- You must succeed today! Is that clear, enough?

Dalya answered by bowing her head. And without finishing neither her bread nor her cup of milk, Dalya stoop up and she left the annex house, without pronouncing a word. At the exit door of the house, Dalya could hear the rest of her parents' conversation:

- But when are you ever going to realize that she is only an idiot and a failure?
- She doesn't have a choice! I will have this fortune, by will or by force!
- Don't be such a fool, Antman! She is only capable of selling vegetables, washing dishes, and serving us as a maid for the rest of her life ...
- Capable or not, I don't care! This fortune, I will have it! She must succeed today!

Dalya no longer had the strength, nor the energy to hear the crushing criticisms of her mother, or the pressure of her father. Dalya headed toward the Royal Georgetown College, for her last day of classes.

On the stairs of the Georgetown school entrance, Director Darkfett was standing. In his usual arrogant tone, the Headmaster was giving orders to a new school employee:

- The flower vases must be watered every day! I don't want to see you forget that, Dadès!
- Yes Missio ... it will be made, Missio. Replied the man with a strange accent.

The new school employee was tall, strong, tanned skin, black hair; he wore a long gardening apron, gloves and big boots. He wore on his head a weird multicolor crochet hat. And he seemed determined to satisfy his new employer, the Headmaster.

Dalya tried to sneak into the school entrance, while avoiding to meet Director Darkfett. But as soon as he noticed her, the Headmaster blocked her way and he exclaimed in a happy tone:

- Mademoiselle Dalya Bouvard! How lucky am I to meet you, today ... on your last day in this school! I hope you had a pleasant experience with us, here!

Dalya remained motionless in front of the Headmaster, avoiding his arrogant eyes. In a sudden move, Director Darkfett raised Dalya's chin and he forced her to look at him in the eyes:

- You must not dream too much, little one! You have tried to be part of a social level in which you don't belong! Never forget who you truly are ... a veggy seller ... nothing more! And that's what you will always be!

When Director Darkfett released her chin, Dalya continued her way toward inside the school. The Headmaster yelled at the new school employee:

- Dadès! Why are the stairs covered with dead leaves? How many times should I tell you to clean them?

The new employee, quickly replied with his strange accent:

- Yes, Missio ... right away, Missio!

Just like in all the previous classes, Professor Canfield was joyfully arranging his papers and books, while waiting in the classroom. When Dalya entered and sat in front of him, Professor Canfield began his class normally, just like all the previous times. Except on that day, after some minutes, Professor Canfield realized that Dalya didn't follow any of his explanations at all. He noticed that the little girl was stressed and very anxious. Never Professor Canfield has seen her in this state before. He stopped his teachings, he put down his book on the desk and he sat down on a chair near Dalya. He asked her in a sympathetic tone:

- Is everything alright, Mademoiselle Dalya Bouvard?

Dalya looked at him for a moment, and then she finally answered in a trembling voice:

- I ... I can't. I'm going to fail this challenge. I will not answer the question tonight.

Professor Canfield replied in a calm and caring voice:

- First of all, you don't know what this question will be about. Secondly, you should always try your best, before declaring your failure. And thirdly, if you do not at least try one time, how will you ever know if you can succeed or fail?

Dalya stayed silent. Although Professor Canfield's arguments were right, Dalya's fears and anxiety didn't easily disappear. Professor Canfield continued:

- Listen to me very well, Mademoiselle Dalya Bouvard. I understand that there is an enormous pressure on you. But, you have been very brave up until today. You have learned so many things in our classes, and you have acquired a lot of knowledge. Everything will be fine.
- How? ... And if I don't succeed ... what will become of me and my family? She asked in a trembling voice.
- No one knows what this question is about. Therefore, it is unnecessary to stress without a good reason. Do your best and everything will be fine.
- Why did Mr. Balthazar made me go through this challenge? Why me and not his nephew or niece or anyone else?
- The only two people who can answer this question are Iskander Balthazar and ... You, Mademoiselle Dalya Bouvard. In the right time, you will understand why the Governor selected you and not someone else.
- Everyone says I'm going to fail ... Everyone tells me I'm an idiot and I will never succeed ... Everyone says that I am good for nothing ... Everyone says th...

Professor Canfield interrupted Dalya:

- Everyone must not have your attention, and certainly not a place in your mind!! The opinion of other people should not worry you. The only opinion that matters is yours, Mademoiselle Dalya Bouvard.

Dalya looked at him with a confused stare. Professor Canfield continued with an encouraging tone:

- Mademoiselle Dalya Bouvard ... no matter what the challenges you are facing, you should always be confident of your abilities and skills. And be sure that many people support you.
- What people? Who? My mother? My father? Mr. Ferdinand Edelmen? Mr. Ernest Laszlo? The school Director Mr. Darkfett? ... What people?

All of a sudden, Dalya had trouble to breath normally. Her heart tightened, she trembled and turned very pale; she was choking. Professor Canfield rapidly understood that Dalya was having an anxiety attack. He stood up and ran to open a window of the classroom. And he helped Dalya to walk and stand up near the opened window, in order to breathe some fresh air. Then, Professor Canfield returned to his desk, he poured water in a glass and he handed it to Dalya. She drank all the water in one gulp. After a long moment of silence, Dalya gained back her normal breathing and she felt much better.

And unexpectedly, at that moment, Professor Canfield had a brilliant idea. He exclaimed:

- Mademoiselle Dalya Bouvard ... I think I can help you to answer this question!

Dalya looked at him, all curious and confused. Professor Canfield smiled:

- We don't have much time! As soon as you feel ready, we will start the training!
- The ... training?

Despite his funny look with his checked suit and his bow tie, Professor Canfield appeared to have a plan in his mind and he was determined to make it work:

- Mademoiselle Dalya Bouvard ... It will be the only preparation that I can give you, in order to help you answer the question! I will make sure that your anxiety attack doesn't happen again!

Dalya appreciated all the encouragements and kind words of Professor Canfield. Since their first meeting, 6 months ago, Professor Canfield has always been nice and caring toward her.

In the following hours, Professor Canfield made Dalya do different odd exercises and workouts, as he called them. And it was a very different class from the previous ones. At the beginning of this course, Dalya didn't understand the moves that Professor Canfield asked her to do. But strangely, bit by bit, Dalya's anxiety calmed down. And at the end of this class, she felt much better than when she arrived.

When class ended, Professor Canfield greeted her:

- Mademoiselle Dalya Bouvard ... This challenge will not change who you really are. And for me, it will always remain a great honor and a great pleasure to have been the teacher of a smart and nice little girl like you.

Dalya was very touched by the kind words of Professor Canfield. And before leaving the classroom, Dalya turned around:

- Professor Canfield ... Will you be present tonight, at the grand Mansion?
- Certainly! He answered with a sweet smile.

Dalya hoped to see Professor Canfield, one last time tonight, before leaving the grand Mansion, leaving the Royal Georgetown College and leaving this life forever. Dalya decided to do one last walk in the school. When she passed in the hallways, students were pointing at her with their fingers and whispering jokingly. Dalya could clearly hear them say:

- Is it really tonight?!
- She is finally going to get out of our school!
- She really thought she will succeed?
- She will never be like us!

Before entering the Library, Dalya paused in front of Miss Guendolyn's office. As soon as she noticed her, Miss Guendolyn hugged Dalya tightly. And with tears in the eyes and pinky cheeks, Miss Guendolyn said in a trembling voice:

- Mademoiselle, no matter what happens tonight ... be sure that the Library will always welcome you! Anytime! You can borrow all the books you wish, and no one will ever know!
- Thank you, Miss Guendolyn. Dalya replied with a heavy heart.
- It was such a great pleasure to have known you, Mademoiselle Dalya Bouvard.
- You too as well, Miss Guendolyn.

Of all the things that she was going to miss the most, the Library was the biggest regret of Dalya. The poor little girl wearing faded overall, a yellowed shirt and a large cap, loved to spend hours and days in the Library, reading all kinds of books and volumes. The Library was the only place where Dalya felt truly happy.

Dalya greeted Miss Guendolyn one last time and she left toward the school's exit, with a heavy heart. She was sad to lose everything, but happy to attend school even if for a short time, and she was especially happy to have met Professor Canfield and Miss Guendolyn.

Lost in her thoughts, Dalya didn't realize that she was walking in the hallway near Director Darkfett's office, close to the school exit. When a woman's voice declared in a confident and amused tone:

- If they think they can stop an essence to spread ... oh we'll see about that ... we'll see about that ...

When Dalya turned around, Miss Uplerine Amana, the Executive Secretary was busy organizing papers in a large folder. There was no one else in the hallway, and Dalya wasn't sure if the words she just heard, came from Miss Uplerine Amana. Dalya asked anyway:

- Excuse-me, Miss Uplerine Amana ... have you been talking to me?

At that moment, Miss Uplerine Amana looked at the little girl, and she smiled ... a confident mischievous strange smile. Needless to say that the words Dalya heard were strange too. Dalya didn't dare to ask for answers, she smiled back at Miss Uplerine Amana, and she left the Royal Georgetown College.

Dalya Bouvard was sad to leave school. However, meeting the lawyer, Mr. Ernest Laszlo for the last time, was a relief. Dalya was well aware that the lawyer didn't like her, and she was always uncomfortable in his presence, she was forced to endure his rude and mean attitude.

When Dalya stepped inside the lawyer's office, Mr. Ernest Laszlo was standing and observing the street through the windows of his office. Mr. Sloan Wilfrid and Lyor Laszlo were busy working and sitting at the meetings' table, a stack of papers and documents were placed on the long table. Mr. Ernest Laszlo turned toward Dalya and he said with a cheerful tone:

- Ah! There you are, finally! I was waiting for your visit today!

Dalya was surprised by this welcome. Even Sloan Wilfrid and Lyor Laszlo, raised their heads from the files, they were curious by the new attitude of the lawyer toward the little girl. Dalya walked inside in hesitant steps, expecting an anger blow any time.

- Do sit down.

It was the first time that Mr. Ernest Laszlo spoke to Dalya in a polite tone, even offering her to sit down. Dalya wasn't comfortable in front of the sudden kindness of Mr. Ernest Laszlo:

- I guess you're here to inform me about the last 5th clue?

Dalya handed him a little paper. Mr. Wilfrid, who had learned to anticipate his employer's temperament, he watched the scene with a curious stare. The young Lyor was surprised to see his father being polite toward the little girl. The two men seated nearby, silently observed the scene, while Mr. Ernest Laszlo continued in a calm voice:

- I suppose it's the last time we will meet ... Mademoiselle Dalya Bouvard.

Dalya didn't say a word. Mr. Ernest Laszlo read aloud the 5th clue:

- ... at the last hour, the sky will state up, a thunderstorm will line up, and ... we'll see about that.

Mr. Ernest Laszlo observed Dalya for some long tense minutes. Then suddenly, he let go a loud and mean laugh. He could hardly contain and stop his laugh. Sloan Wilfrid and Lyor Laszlo exchanged a confused look. Dalya also didn't understand what made the lawyer laugh that much. When Mr. Ernest Laszlo pulled himself together, he said in a mocking tone:

- But it's really nonsense ... you have a sense of humor!

Dalya dared to answer in a small voice:

- I'm not the one who writes the clues, Sir. It's the box given to me by Mr. Balthaz...
- The box of that old fool who almost ruined us all?! Seriously, he thought that with a guessing game, he will be able to prevent the true Heirs to get this fortune?!

Mr. Ernest Laszlo threw the piece of paper on Dalya's face. At that moment, sitting nearby, Mr. Wilfrid recognized the insolent character of his employer, and young Lyor Laszlo recognized his father's crushing nature. Mr. Ernest Laszlo came near Dalya and said:

- Listen to me, you filthy vermin! the only place where you belong is in this hole with gutter rats! you do not belong in our high and noble society ... each social category must accept its real place. If this crazy old Balthazar made a mistake by making you believe that you could become one of us ... Oh, you're just a poor little beggar, and I'm here to rectify this error! You will forever be nothing than a miserable girl selling vegetables at the market!

Dalya had never thought to face so much cruelty and meanness. She was never ashamed of working and selling vegetables at the market, she was never ashamed of being poor. And yet, Dalya couldn't answer these harsh words. She stayed motionless, with her head down.

For a slight moment, Dalya noticed the compassionate smile of Mr. Sloan Wilfrid, sitting a few steps away from her. Except that this time, Mr. Wilfrid couldn't intervene.

As for Lyor Laszlo, who didn't enjoy his legal guardian position, during all these months, he avoided as best as he could a confrontation with his father. Lyor Laszlo blamed Dalya for forcing him into this mess. The young Lyor returned to his work, while completely ignoring the scene between his father and the little girl.

Mr. Ernest Laszlo pulled out of his pocket 2 cents, he threw them on the table in front of Dalya, and he said in a cold voice:

- Here's to feed your miserable beggars family for the next few days. I expect you to leave the annex house tonight!

Dalya didn't move, but her throat tightened, she felt tears in her eyes, and her heart strangled. Mr. Ernest Laszlo enjoyed humiliating and crushing Dalya. In front of the little girl's silence and stillness, the lawyer took the 2 cents on the table, he put them in Dalya's hand in a brusque move, and he screamed:

- NOW GET OUT OF MY OFFICE!! OUT OF MY SIGHT!! I DON'T EVER WANT TO SEE YOU OR HEAR ABOUT YOU AGAIN!! OUT OF MY OFFICE!! NOW!!

Dalya didn't hesitate for a second; she immediately stood up and she left the office of Mr. Ernest Laszlo, under the compassionate stare of Mr. Sloan Wilfrid and the carelessness of the young Lyor Laszlo.

The way back home was long and silent, but walking did so much good to the little Dalya Bouvard. After her scene with the Lawyer Mr. Ernest Laszlo in his office, Dalya needed some fresh air and calm. She walked slowly, observing the beautiful landscape of Dumbarton Oaks Park, for the last time.

When Dalya arrived at the grand Mansion, she met the Gardener Mr. Rosenwald at the entrance door. The Gardener was standing still near the gate, and he seemed to be waiting for someone. As soon as he noticed Dalya, the Gardener came close to her, and he said in a serious voice:

- Good evening.

Dalya was a bit surprised that the Gardener greeted her first. Usually, and since their first meeting, Dalya was always the first one to speak and reach out to him. But on that day, it was the first time ever that the big man was reaching out to her. Dalya didn't know what was going on, but she greeted him back, with her nicest smile:

- Good evening, Mr. Gardener.

After a few seconds of hesitation, the Gardener spoke in his usual cold voice:

- The ... the plants in the South side of the grand Mansion ... they should be watered next week. You will have a long way to walk from your old home, up till here. You need to plan about 30 minutes walking. So don't be late as usual! We'll have a lot of work!

Dalya was surprised and mostly touched by the Gardener's words. The big man was not skilled with words; he was often cold, tough and distant, showing no emotion or kindness. But from his words, Dalya understood that the Gardener hoped to see her again, even though she wouldn't live anymore in the annex house near the grand Mansion. Dalya displayed her bravest smile:

- I will do my best, to not be late, next week ... Mr. Gardener.

For some tense silent seconds, the Gardener observed the little girl with a caring stare. And then, the Gardener murmured in a small voice:

- Goodbye ... Lady Dalya Bouvard.

The Gardener immediately turned around quickly and he walked away. Dalya remained motionless in her place; she seemed struck by a lightning. Did she hear correctly? Were her ears playing a trick on her? ... The Gardener had just called her ... Lady!! In all her life, Dalya has been called all kinds of insults and mean names; but never someone has ever called her ... Lady!!

While still confused and puzzled, Dalya continued on her way toward the annex House. But as soon as she walked a few steps, a familiar voice stopped her from behind. Dalya turned around to see the housemaid of the French neighbors, Mrs. Glorina all breathless coming her way, she was dressed in her usual apron of butterflies knots in multiple colors.

- Thank ... God ... I ... met you on time! ... I have an urgent message ... from Mrs. Marianne Poirier. Here is the letter ... that she asked me ... to give you.

While Mrs. Glorina recovered her normal breathing, Dalya opened the letter and she read the content:

Dear Mademoiselle Dalya Bouvard,

If there is a character that I have not met since a long time, it's empathy. It is a unique quality that cannot be learned. We're born with or without it. And that makes you a golden heart.

Thank you for opening the curtains of my bedroom and bringing light into my days. I am delighted to have met you. You are always welcomed to my house.

Mrs. Marianne Poirier. (Or Madame, as you prefer).

At that moment, Dalya couldn't hold back her tears anymore. The great woman's words were sincere and kind. Dalya was so touched. Mrs. Glorina hugged Dalya tightly and said:

- I will miss you so so much, Mademoiselle Dalya Bouvard! You have always been lovely and polite with all of us! I will always leave you the best piece of my pie! Please do visit us whenever you can! You are always welcomed!

Dalya thanked Mrs. Glorina for her kindness, and she watched the woman leave the grand Mansion.

Everything has a beginning and an end. Dalya Bouvard was a smart and sweet little girl. But even though she wanted to help her family and save them from poverty, some things in life don't always go as we wish for. The Governor, Mr. Iskander Balthazar was nice to give her a chance. Dalya had done all her best. She consoled herself by all the people she had the pleasure to know and meet.

While putting her few belongings in a small bag, Dalya took the letter that the Governor, Mr. Iskander Balthazar left her in the Bank coffret, 6 months ago. Dalya opened it and she read it for the last time, trying to understand the true meaning of his words:

The Sun brightens and softens everything it touches.
And while it offers its light abundantly, it will never cease to shine.

Dalya didn't know what Mr. Balthazar meant by this sentence. Dalya put the letter in her bag; she observed her bedroom one last time, and she smiled. Smiling in the face of defeat, smiling in the face of a battle lost in advance and still moving forward, if that's not an enough proof of real strength indeed!

Her parents and her little sisters were already in the grand Mansion. When she walked few steps in the little garden, Dalya Bouvard observed one last time the annex house where she lived for the past 6 months with her family.

And then ... Dalya turned around, and she walked alone toward the grand Mansion. Walking slowly and surely, Dalya was invaded by a serene and a strange calm. Sometimes, the most opposing feelings appear in the most unlikely moments.

Chapter 34

Very interesting...

Dalya had never celebrated her birthday, in all her life. Her mother always thought it was a stupid party. Her father said it was a waste of time and useless. Dalya didn't hope for a party like the one Miss Francine Poirier had. And she certainly never hoped to have the attention of everyone, on the day of her birthday.

The living room of the grand Mansion was full; almost all the people present were sitting on different divans and chairs arranged in a parallel way, all facing a large desk. Even before entering, you could hear laughs and conversations.

A little poor girl stood outside the door of the living room, for a few moments. She was wearing a faded overall, a yellowed shirt with sleeves lifted up, a large cap covering all her hair, and old black shoes. When finally, Dalya Bouvard stepped inside the living room, whispers and laughs instantly stopped. Dalya walked in slow steps, she placed the Excelbox on the large desk, and she remained standing, motionless.

As soon as Dalya placed the box on the table, the Excelbox turned on all by itself, in front of the astonished and amazed eyes of all the present people, who were discovering the strange box for the first time. In one side, a small rectangular outlet appeared. The top of the box opened, the transparent oval glass straightened up slowly and majestically. Four gold cylinders forged in the shape of a vine plant, held the transparent glass cage. The strange clock inside the cage was clearly visible to everyone. The small and big needles were a few centimeters apart, but both were heading for the same date, December 12th, 1890. The Excelbox imposed silence, admiration and astonishment, on all the present people in the living room!

When the box stopped displaying, the Lawyer Mr. Ernest Laszlo stood up from his chair, and he spoke to the guests:

- Ladies and gentlemen. As it has been agreed upon, 6 months ago, in the Will of late Mr. Iskander Balthazar, the designated Heiress must pass the challenges emitted by this ... box. The indisputable condition to access the fortune of the Governor, is to correctly answer all the challenges that this box will provide. We are witnessing tonight, the First Challenge ... and also the last one!

A wave of laughs filled the living room. Standing in front of the crowd, Dalya silently observed the people present for the event. Dalya recognized the Governor's family, the Edelmen. Mrs. Honoré and Mr. Ferdinand Edelmen were surrounded by several young men and women. Mr. Ferdinand Edelmen was joyful and in a good mood, sitting as Master of the grand Mansion, and smoking a big cigar. Mrs. Honoré, sitting next to her brother, was calm and relaxed.

The Lawyers Mr. Sloan Wilfrid and young Lyor Laszlo were both sitting a couple of chairs away. Lyor Laszlo looked neutral and passive, while Mr. Sloan Wilfrid was strangely quiet; he seemed anxious and more serious than his usual mood.

Because of his checked suit and his bow tie, Professor Canfield was clearly visible in the living room. Dalya was delighted and so happy to see him, one last time. Professor Canfield gave a friendly smile to his student.

Among the crowd, Dalya was also pleasantly surprised to see Uncle Giorgi Bouvard! He insisted to be present on that day, he was curious to know about the challenge that everyone was waiting impatiently for.

Dalya noticed the unexpected presence of a familiar face, because of his copper beard and his wooden crutch; the Dean of Merchants Mr. Kenan Einsenberg himself! This man had always been kind and caring toward Dalya. However, she was surprised to see him among the crowd. Why was the Dean of Merchants present for this event? Dalya couldn't guess, but the big man's presence was reassuring and encouraging. The Dean of Merchants smiled at Dalya.

Outside the door of the living room, Dalya recognized two silhouettes. They were silent, curious, and watching what was happening in the living room. It was the Gardener Mr. Weil Rosenwald and the housemaid Cristelle, the two employees of the grand Mansion!

Dalya's parents and her little twin sisters, sat in the front rows. Her father, Antman Bouvard seemed very worried and anxious. Her mother, Mrs. Augustine Bouvard displayed a mean smile.

Everyone stared at Dalya Bouvard, which easily increased her stress and anxiety. Dalya did not expect all these people to be present for this event.

The lawyer, Mr. Ernest Laszlo ordered Dalya to start. She approached the Excelbox in slow steps. Long before this moment, Dalya was sure that the challenge won't be that easy, and there were high chances that she would fail. However, Dalya decided to finish her role and ask for the question anyway. The requirements of the Will forced her to do it. Dalya took one long breath, and she gathered the rest of her strength and energy. Dalya took a paper, and she wrote on it, with a trembling hand:

What is the 1ˢᵗ question?

As soon as Dalya placed the paper on the small rectangular opening of the Excelbox, the paper was swallowed inside, in a blink of an eye. Seconds later, that seemed hours to Dalya, a little note came out of the Excelbox. Dalya didn't dare to come close and take it, it was the Lawyer Mr. Ernest Laszlo who took the little paper issued by the strange box and he read the content aloud:

Since fate inaugurated
Many things have been unveiled
My first question is
In one word write
The heart of what is finally assimilated

Dalya's heart stopped beating. Whispers and exclamations arouse in the entire living room. Everyone was confused and surprised of the spoken words. Uncle Giorgi appeared puzzled, for the first time ever. Dalya's father was more nervous than before. Professor Canfield's smile disappeared; he folded his arms and stared at Dalya with a serious look. The Dean of Merchants straightened up on his chair, and he observed Dalya while caressing his coppery beard and firmly holding his wood crutch. Mr. Sloan Wilfrid took off his glasses, and he cleaned them with a fabric, in a nervous hand movement.

Dalya's mother, Mrs. Augustine was delighted and satisfied. Since the beginning, Mrs. Augustine repeated day and night, that her daughter was an idiot, who will never succeed. Dalya met her mother's eyes, happy to have been right all this time. Mr. Balthazar's nephew, Mr. Ferdinand Edelmen laughed out loud. The men and women surrounding him, observed Dalya with arrogant and victorious stares, reminding her that she had clearly underestimated Mr. Iskander Balthazar and his conditions.

The lawyer, Mr. Ernest Laszlo announced in a joyful voice:

- Mademoiselle Dalya Bouvard will have until midnight to answer. So, about 35 minutes.

Then, Mr. Ernest turned toward Dalya and he said in an amused and provoking tone:

- Would you like to sit down to think about it?

Dalya didn't refuse this offer, her legs were shaking so much, and she could hardly stand up. She sat on the chair in front of the desk, at the center of the living room. Mr. Ernest Laszlo put in front of Dalya, some blank papers and a pen.

The living room was noisy. Dalya expected a difficult challenge. She could clearly hear the whispers and laughs of some people, and see the shocked and nervous looks of others.

When Dalya's eyes met Professor Canfield, he smiled encouragingly at her. At that precise moment, a distant memory appeared in Dalya's mind. On her first meeting with her teacher, 6 months ago, when Dalya didn't know the answers of the admission tests, in Literature and Arts, Professor Canfield told her:

248

- Whatever the questions in front of you, never return an exam paper without writing a word on it. You may be off topic. But always remember that the most important thing is to try and do your best.

Dalya closed her eyes and she took a deep breath to empty her mind. And just like Professor Canfield had teach her in their last class, Dalya reduced in her head the volume of the sounds, the whispers, the laughs, and the voices of all the people in the living room. Then and gradually, Dalya erased the silhouettes of the present people one by one. The silhouettes of the Edelmen family evaporated in seconds. Her parents' silhouettes vanished. Mr. Ernest Laszlo and all the other gentlemen's silhouettes vanished. The living room of the grand Mansion became empty, in Dalya's mind.

At this moment, Dalya listened to her own voice:

- Alright. Let's start now. The first question is an enigma. Since fate inaugurated ... that sounds like ... inaugurate your fate ... It was the first message of the Excelbox ... when I activated it by writing my date of birth. So, since the fate inaugurated means ... Since the activation of the Excelbox, which would be 6 months ago. Alright. Many things have been unveiled ... the first question is ... in one word write. Write a single word? ... The heart of what is finally assimilated ... assimilated ... learned.

Dalya lay back on her chair:

- The first question is ... I have to write in one word ... all what has been learned, since the last 6 months?

Dalya wrote the question at the top of the blank page, and then she thought in a little voice:

- But ... I learned so many things with Professor Canfield. What is the question about? ... Perhaps the hardest class, Literature ... or the most interesting course, Mathematics.

Dalya wrote down all the classes she had studied with Professor Canfield. Literature, Arts, History, Mathematics, and Physics ... She paused for a moment, and then she said:

- I need to sum up everything I've learned in one word ... but ... I've learned so many things, which class is it talking about?

After a long moment of reflection, Dalya thought aloud:

- The heart of what is finally assimilated ... finally assimilated... does that mean the last lesson that I've studied with Professor Canfield? ... Our last class was History ... but still, how can I sum up everything I've learned in this course, in one word? That's impossible!!

Dalya read over her notes several times. She stared at her paper a little while, thinking aloud:

- The heart of what is finally assimilated ... in one word ... the heart means the most important thing I've learned... But how can I know? Which class? I need more information to answer this question ... it's not clear, at all! I need help ... at least a clue or something to know what cla...

Suddenly, Dalya jumped off her chair:

- The clues! I got 5 clues out of the Excelbox!

Dalya straightened up on her chair; she took a new blank paper, and she wrote down all the clues:

- The Excelbox gave me 5 clues, whenever I asked for them. All these clues are supposed to help me answer this first question. So then ... what is assimilated ... is perhaps not about the classes I learned with Professor Canfield at school!

Dalya was focused reading all the clues for the 4th time, when the Lawyer Mr. Ernest Laszlo interrupted her and he announced in a loud joyful voice:

- You still have 20 minutes.

In a second, Dalya was invaded by fear and doubt:

- I won't succeed ... I have no idea what it's all about. Even with 5 clues ... it is not clear at all. What am I supposed to have learned since 6 months? How ... and what exactly? What is going to happen to my family? Will we go back to our old 2 rooms? Will I go back to sleep on the kitchen floor? My father will be furious when I fail ... How will we survive? My mother was right from the beginning, I should have believed her. My sisters will be so sad to leave the big garden.

Thousands of dark ideas attacked Dalya, without mercy. Her throat tightened, her heart raced, her cheeks burned, her mouth was pale, Dalya was choking and she had trouble breathing.

When all of a sudden ... a strange thing happened. Dalya raised her head up and she noticed an unexpected silhouette ... Mr. Iskander Balthazar himself! He was standing in front of her, smiling and holding the coffee pot spoon in his hand!

Why and how this silhouette appeared to her at this moment? Dalya couldn't guess. However, the great man's smile somehow calmed her anxiety.

Dalya remembered their meetings, his politeness and kindness toward her. Whether she succeeds or not, Dalya was glad to have known Mr. Iskander Balthazar and she was eternally grateful to him for giving her a chance. At this instant, Dalya decided to finish what she had started, not for her, but in honor of Mr. Iskander Balthazar, because he gave her the opportunity to save her family from poverty.

Dalya gathered her strength and energy for one last attempt. She took on her pen and she focused on the pages in front of her. For several minutes, Dalya scribbled on the papers, she thought very hard, she held her head, she took a deep breath, she encircled some words, she crisscrossed other words, she folded her arms, she looked at the papers again and again ...

Then finally, she put down the pen on the desk for the last time. Dalya raised her head up toward the Lawyer Mr. Ernest Laszlo, and she declared in a calm voice:

- I think I have an answer to the question, Sir.

A sudden silence imposed itself on the living room of the grand Mansion. Everyone straightened up; they couldn't believe their ears. The Lawyer Mr. Ernest Laszlo thought he had misheard. He came close to Dalya and he asked her in an arrogant tone:

- You ... you think you found the answer to the question, asked by this box?

For the 2nd time, Dalya replied in the same calm voice:

- Yes, Sir.

The nephew, Mr. Ferdinand Edelmen let out a mean laugh:

- You should search for the question first, to be able to find the answer ... little girl!

A wave of laughs filled the place. Nevertheless, Dalya said in a small voice:

- The first question is: from the moment when this box has been activated, that is 6 months ago ... from that time on, what has been learned, in one word?

The haughty laughs in the living room vanished, immediately. Dalya announced:

- My answer is: Courage.

Mr. Ernest Laszlo and all the people present in the living room were shocked. Nobody thought that Dalya would understand the enigma and provide an answer for it. Deep inside herself, Dalya wasn't totally certain about the answer, but she was totally certain that she did all her best. Dalya realized that whether she succeeds or not, her life will not stop.

Mr. Ernest Laszlo was eager to finish up with this case. He looked at his pocket watch, indicating 10 minutes before midnight. The lawyer asked Dalya in a sarcastic tone:

- Can Mademoiselle enlighten us about her answer?

Usually, Dalya was unable to speak without her parents or people interrupting her, demeaning her, or ignoring her. That night, it was the first time ever that Dalya was about to speak, and people were forced to listen to her. Dalya stood up from her chair, she gathered her strength and cleared her throat, and then she explained in a calm confident voice:

- This box gave me 5 clues, to help me answer the question: for the past 6 months, what has been learned, in one word? ... Each clue is supposed to have taught me something ... and that is the answer to this question.

Thinking of the Gardener of the grand Mansion, and the French Neighbor Mrs. Marianne Poirier, Dalya said:

251

- *The first clue: dig into the Fund. Plant a kernel. Water at the source. Admire the jewel.*

Following the instructions of the first clue, I learned to look way further, not just on the surface, I learned to try and find answers and solutions, and apply them despite the reluctance and rejections. It takes courage to take risks and try. It takes courage to help and support someone in the worst moments of their life. It takes courage to give your time and attention, to not be cold and careless. Because the day where we stop helping each other, is the day where we lose our humanity.

Thinking about the French neighbors, Miss Francine and Mr. Richard Poirier, about the lawyer Mr. Ernest Laszlo and the nephew Mr. Ferdinand Edelmen, Dalya continued:

- *The second clue: quiet and reticence. Silence will answer. Let the noise be. Life will take over. Pressure everything cleans. And what paths it will open!*

I had many opportunities to answer free cruelty and insults. But in staying silent, I learned much more than if I had spoken. It takes courage to speak out and defend ourselves, but it takes even more courage to remain silent and hang on one more second, facing repression, criticism and people's free cruelty. This clue taught me that silence is the best defense. As big and strong as the fire of evil may be, it will always be turned off by small drops of courage and politeness.

Thinking about the aventurine ring of Mrs. Marianne Poirier and the tomb that the Gardener visited, Dalya explained:

- *The third clue: when all is lost. To up raise your gaze. His last word. Has not yet been sealed. When everything is seized. Everything is back granted. And it's from up gracious. A true generosity indeed. A possibility to remake. In your own way and will.*

In this clue, I learned that we cannot replace the missing people, but we can only take care of the people still alive and dear to us. I also learned that nothing can replace the people we have lost, but we can replace lost things.

I learned that when everything is seized from us; health, money, work, family... when we lose something dear to us, we must be courageous and assured that something better will be given back to us... and often better than before. It takes courage to stay strong and solid when we lose everything. And it takes as much courage to believe in better days.

Then, Dalya met the eyes of the Dean of Merchants, Mr. Kenan Einsenberg. She continued:

- *The fourth clue: never pepper without salt. Never dark without dawn. Never fall without arise. Never mockery without recast. If surrender is before the fight. So why two hands. And why two legs?*

To answer this question, a great man taught me that life has offered us 2 legs to stand strong and face our challenges. And when we lose a leg, when it seems impossible to recover ... life replaces it with a crutch and a wood leg, much more solid and resistant. Whether with 2 legs or a crutch, life forces us to be courageous and get up anyway.

Dalya thought about the people she was happy to meet, during the past 6 months; the housemaid Cristelle, the French neighbors' housekeeper Mrs. Glorina, the Library assistant Miss Guendolyn, the Gardener Mr. Weil Rosenwald, Professor Canfield, the Dean of Merchants. Dalya explained:

- *The fifth clue: to the unknown and the end. Proceed confident and certain. Guided by the écrin. Until become an essence. Powerful and human. At the last hour. The sky will state up. A thunderstorm will line up. And we'll see about that.*

This clue, I didn't understand much of it. Only the first 2 sentences. Into the unknown step forward, confident and sure. I've learned that it takes courage to accept the challenges no matter how impossible they might seem, to walk toward the unknown with confidence. It takes courage to accept losing, and be satisfied to have done your best. It takes courage to believe in your abilities.

Speaking to her dad, Dalya looked at him and she continued in a sad voice:

- And even if I am just a little girl, even if the card game seems fun and entertaining. I've learned that when you play with money that your family needs ... when you risk money that should pay for your daughters' school ... when you repress your daughter and you take away from her the potato bags' sales ... when you are forced to lie, cheat, steal and beg for money, in order to survive ... at this moment, the card game stops being fun.

It took me courage to understand and accept that I am responsible for only my own mistakes; I shouldn't pay for other people's mistakes. And it took me courage to not give in to pressure, when I was forced to do something wrong.

Turning toward her mother, Dalya affirmed:

- I learned that it takes courage to believe in yourself, be proud of yourself and love yourself, no matter what people tell you. I learned that it takes courage to endure a violent abusive person who slams doors, breaks objects, and screams insults ... every day of your life.

I learned that it takes courage to confront these cruel people ... they will continue to say that I am an idiot, morning noon and night. I will continue to believe that I am smart, morning noon and night.

Dalya sighed for a second, and then she announced in a serene voice:

- I don't know if my answer is totally correct. But the only thing I learned from all these clues, for the past 6 months ... it's one word: Courage.

When Dalya finished, a tense intimidating silence reigned in the living room, all the present people were immobile and speechless. The arrogant glances turned into confused looks, the haughty smiles disappeared, the relaxed attitudes straightened up. Dalya's parents, Antman and Augustine Bouvard became pale and uncomfortable. No one ever expected to hear these audacious words from a 12 years old poor little girl.

Without even waiting one more second, Dalya took a piece of paper, and she wrote one word:

Courage

It was 11:56 PM. As soon as Dalya placed the paper on the rectangular opening of the box, the note was swallowed inside. The golden cylinders around the oval glass cage, shined with all their strength. The Excelbox lit up.

Seconds later, a little paper came out of the rectangular opening. Dalya didn't dare to approach the Excelbox and take it. It was the Lawyer, Mr. Ernest Laszlo who stepped forward; he took the note from the Excelbox. Everyone in the living room was silent and eager to know the verdict. Mr. Ernest Laszlo stood still, immobile and motionless, holding and observing the paper in his hands. No one in the living room dared to move or speak or breathe.

And then ... something beyond your understanding, just happened...

At this precise moment, the Snow Panther entered the living room. Dalya hoped to see Séraphine one last time before leaving the grand Mansion. The little girl got used to the punctual stares of the creature, every morning and evening, on her way to school. Séraphine walked slowly and majestically toward one person, Dalya Bouvard. The Snow Panther sat close to Dalya for the first time ever, and she looked up at the little girl. Dalya smiled at Séraphine, and one could clearly see that the magnificent creature smiled back at her.

And this was not the only strange thing that happened...

The Dean of Merchants, Mr. Kenan Einsenberg was anxiously holding his wood crutch. When suddenly, the big man felt a little breeze caressing his copper beard. At this precise moment, Mr. Kenan Einsenberg had a strange feeling ... that something was about to begin.

Professor Canfield, just like everyone else in the crowd, he was eager to know the verdict of this challenge. When suddenly, Professor Canfield was invaded by a strange feeling. He relaxed on his chair, he uncrossed his hands, he gained back his calm and serene attitude, and he ... just smiled. A strange uncontrollable smile.

The Gardener, Mr. Weil Rosenwald stood behind the door of the living room, with the housemaid, Cristelle. He couldn't stand the pressure of waiting for the verdict, so the Gardener turned around to leave the grand Mansion, before even knowing the results. When he was walking toward the exit and just before the last step to outside, the Gardener froze suddenly ... and he felt a strange invisible force holding him back from leaving the event.

Focused and curious, Uncle Giorgi was eager to know the fate of his niece, Biggo. Whether her answer was right or wrong, Giorgi Bouvard was already very proud of his niece. He always believed that Dalya was unique and gifted. And while he was waiting to hear the verdict ... in an instant, his eyes lit up, he caressed his mustache, his messy hair straightened up, and a strange feeling overwhelmed him, just like every time he made a new insane discovery.

Since several months now, a strange idea occupied Mr. Sloan Wilfrid's mind. An insane and impossible idea. He just couldn't shake it off his head. But on that night, when Mr. Wilfrid was watching the event, the same strange idea came back visiting his mind. And insane as it was, the idea seemed less impossible than before. Sloan Wilfrid wore back his glasses, and he smiled ... a witty smile, while thinking aloud:

-   Interesting ... very interesting ...

The young Lyor Laszlo was quiet and careless, since the beginning of the challenge. He was eager to finish this case and get back to his work. And while he waited patiently for his father's announcement, all of a sudden, Lyor Laszlo straightened up on his chair, in a swift. Lyor had just remembered something. 6 months ago, in the Bank coffret number: 7047-73 ... a strange letter was addressed to him:

Mr. Lyor Kartal Laszlo,

Between the spines, a rose will be born. And because you were the first to see beyond what she really is, she will be your best fight.

Iskander Balthazar

At this moment, Lyor Laszlo seemed shocked by what he had just understood.

A little silhouette was perched outside the large windows of the grand Mansion; she watched the event happening inside the living room, since its beginning. Tudi, the waitress in the Toscana restaurant, could clearly see people's faces and reactions.

Without hearing a word from inside, and before knowing the verdict, Tudi silently came down the wall, she slowly crossed plants and flowers near the large windows, and then ... Tudi left the grand Mansion, running straight to the South side of Georgetown city.

Inside the living room, Dalya was still standing, and calmly waiting for the announcement of Mr. Ernest Laszlo, just like everyone else. So far, the little poor girl wearing a worn overall, an old shirt, a large cap, and old shoes, didn't know why Mr. Iskander Balthazar chose her, she didn't know if her answer was correct or not, and she didn't know what will happen the next day ... But one thing the little girl was sure of, it's that she had done all her best.

While the Lawyer, Mr. Ernest Laszlo was still standing immobile, holding and observing the verdict paper in his hands, the little girl and the Snow Panther watched the flames in the fireplace of the living room, with defying sapphire blue eyes. The flames were little and fragile, but they grew stronger and refused to be turned off.

Through the windows of the living room, one could see tiny snowflakes sprinkled down from the sky, graciously covering the ground of the grand Mansion. A splendid unexpected snow. Winter began with no one's permission, and no one being prepared for what will follow.

In an ordinary time.

In an ordinary town.

Among ordinary people.

An extraordinary story …. will begin !

Dépôt légal - 2020MO4918
Cover design & print by ALPHA PRINT
www.alphaprintmaroc.com